WHITE HORSE

~Tanya Buck

White Horse

For those who are gone; my brother, my sister, my mom, and both my horses--Andy and Etoile who together helped create Frisco.

Mom will never see this book, but she inspired me and gave me courage throughout its creation.

Special Thanks:

To Etoile, who taught me trust, and Little Andy, for rearing and conking my head hard enough so I could see how to exist in two worlds while having my feet rooted in only one.

To Roger, for supporting me wholly, as only you can do, so I am able take the time to write.

To my writer's groups over the years, without whom I could never have seen the trees for the forest.

To my friends and family; Randy and Dave, you were there from the start of this project and here it is, finally finished.

You've all shown me patience when I likely didn't deserve it and kicked me in the butt when I needed it, and I'll never be able to thank you enough.

Thank you!

~Prologue

At times, I am as the mo'ehno'ha, *the horse. Wild. Free. Afraid.*

Shadows grow long in waiting for me to make the words of the Ve'ho'e, *white man.*

But when I speak this story in the language of Tsitsistas, *The People, the words dance like water over rocks and the sound of each drop joining others makes the music of the river.*

So I begin once more.

The most important part of me is more horse than Tsitsistas. *I share the spirit of the horse, and his feelings are my own.*

I know his love of running free across the tall grass meadows.

I know the panic and the fear at being roped and tethered.

Because of the horse, I know the shelter of the herd, and the trust of a friend.

Because of the Ve'ho'e, *the white man, I know the fear of being alone.*

My people have taken the journey up The Hanging Road. All are gone to the place beyond. Killed by the Ve'ho'e. *My father-White Antelope. And my husband. My brothers and my sisters.*

My new family is El, a woman of the white clan, but she is not like the pale-skinned men. She and the bay horse are all that I care for, all that remain for me to love.

The spirit of the white horse shows me my visions. He tells me the Ve'ho'e *will someday take both El and the bay.*

He does not tell me when.

----Tahcitan, November 27, 1871

~1

"Paizely?" It's my sister's voice, but that's impossible.

Holly is dead.

I remind myself she is gone by chanting this piece of information over and over, "Holly's dead, Holly's dead, Holly's dead," while at the same time, I remember watching the fisted knife plummeting in an arc and gaining momentum, gaining speed, falling faster, harder, plunging blade glinting, down, down faster, down harder...into her.

I hear my own sobs and clench my eyes tighter, and her voice, so soft, so caring, so *real*, asks, "Paizely, are you okay? You're soaked."

This isn't happening, it's not true, it's my mind playing tricks on me, so I ignore her and stare at the floor, but it shimmers vaguely brown, a thousand miles away.

She's dead. Doesn't she know that? I try to stand, but my muscles don't do what I want. I open my mouth and scream, but no sound leaves my throat. *Everything turns red and hot, and I am drowning in blood. Her blood. It's everywhere. On her clothes, on my clothes, in her hair and in my own. I try to run to him, to save her, to stop this, and I can't. I can't. I can't.*

The world stops. I don't breathe. I have no right to breathe. I have nothing. I am nothing. Without her.

"Paize, look at me." And her words sound real...as if my sister is here, beside me. I focus on the memory of her and the intense pain as though it's me who's been stabbed by a knife, just as she'd been and I know, I know, I know this is wrong.

I gaze into a grey mist of heavy nothingness, until finally the kitchen floor begins to shimmer in an undulating wave. Through a haze, a hand reaches for me and I wonder if it's friendly or if it will kill me as he killed her.

And I realize, I don't care.

I hug myself and my blood-soaked tee-shirt clings to me as if it's plastic wrap. Cold. I pull away from the hand that looks so much like hers, I'm certain it is hers. But I know better. Yet, I have no pain, no feeling of loss. I have no feeling of anything because I can't feel, I can't breathe, I can't.

"Paize? Please, honey, look at me." Her words drift to me, surreal and far away.

I am afraid to look. I won't. Enough blood and death to last the rest of my life. I can't stand the thought of seeing her stabbed and bleeding and dead, and this false voice and hand, her voice, her hand...no, I won't look.

My stupid eyes begin to rotate toward the sound of her voice and I don't want to see and I can't shut them and I want to see, and so finally I look.

She is sitting next to me. I whisper, "Holly?"

Her blonde hair floats around her head, backlit by the sun--a halo. She smiles that golden, happy little sister grin, and I feel hope rising. But hope is not a good thing and I know this, so I squash it down. I narrow my gaze on the apparition of my sister. "Holly?"

Even to myself I sound like an idiot.

She smiles again and leans in, but she doesn't touch me. "That was a bad one, Paize. When you're ready, you can tell me about it, but let's get you out of those sopping clothes first."

I'm soaking wet, and I know without looking that I'm not covered in blood. My teeth begin to clack against each other and I know what has happened, but I don't want to think about it now or ever.

The back of my head balloons a throbbing pain, but I nod. She's right, it was a bad one. She hands me a dish towel and I mop my forehead and neck. I let her help me to my feet and I stand, wobbly as a newborn foal. I hold onto the counter and wait for my breathing to settle and my teeth to stop clattering. Across the room, Steve leans against the stove, arms crossed over his chest.

Protectively, I step in front of Holly so I am between her and him.

Holly's killer. Steve, the love of my little sister's life. Even at five-thirty in the morning, he looks like a movie star ready to greet his fans. He's tall and good-looking; from the cleft in his chin, his squared jaw, to his sea-blue eyes framed with rogue blond curls. His mere looks are enough to get him by in life so even on the days when he goes into his paranoid commando mode, he somehow holds onto the boyish charm that endears him to everyone else.

Some people think he's charming.

I glare at him. "Why would you kill Holly?"

My sister gasps. Steve and I lock eyes and ignore her.

He stares at me and frowns. "What?"

I will my muscles to stop shivering, and my voice to stay strong. "I saw you stab her to death."

He laughs. The jerk laughs! With his head back and his shoulders shaking, he guffaws until he snorts. He wipes his eyes. "You're not serious?"

Holly says, "Stop it, both of you, right now. Paizely, let's go."

As if she can tell me what to do. I don't even glance in her direction. "I saw you, Steve. And you know I'm right about this, I'm always right. Why would you kill her?"

He grits his teeth until his jaw muscles bulge. His eyes stay on Holly, and he says to me, "You're crazy. I know you believe your visions and you say they always come true, but this time, you've gone off your rocker. I would never lay a hand on Holly."

I've never liked the guy, and right now, the emotion I feel is best described as one closer to hatred. My premonitions are never wrong and I'll do whatever I must to save my sister. I squint and peel my lips back over my teeth. I keep my voice steady. "I won't let you do it.

Right now, right here, break off your engagement and walk out of her life forever."

Holly makes a sound that very much resembles a cat trying to meow with its mouth closed.

He puffs out his chest and appears both bigger and taller. "Why would I do such a thing? You're nuts. I'm not going to kill her and I'm not leaving her either."

But I hear a slight wavering in his voice.

Holly rushes to his side and takes his hand. Her expression is both exasperated and demanding."Paizely, stop it!"

I pay no attention to her, and glare at him. "You're not going to kill my sister, now promise me you'll leave her alone forever."

He tips his head so his right ear almost touches his shoulder, and squints until his eyes glisten. When he speaks, his voice is shaky. "You saw me stab Holly? And it was a real vision, the same as when you told me about Henry, and how he'd chase a squirrel into the road and get hit by a blue Honda?"

Finally, progress. I whisper, "Yes, Steve."

His jaw twitches. "Why would I kill her? I'd never."

I stare into his eyes. "Then leave her."

Holly clears her throat. "What is wrong with you two? Steve, you're not going to hurt me, I know that. And Paizely, you need to stop trying to break us up."

I don't look away from Steve. "Holly, you can't marry him."

Steve lunges toward me, pointing his finger at my chest. His breathing is loud. "Wait. You're making this up to scare her so you can keep her to yourself. Is that it, Paize? Are you so incredibly afraid of being alone you'd keep Holly from having a life? Really?"

That's not it at all. "Don't turn this back on me, I know what you're planning."

"Paizely, stop it!" Holly says.

Again, he laughs, though with less gusto as earlier. "I'm planning on living with your sister for the rest of my life. I--"

I don't let him finish. "Oh, get off it, Steve! Stop lying and for once, be honest."

Holly tries to say something, but before she is able, Steve shouts, "I can't believe you're willing to make up such trash so you won't be alone. I'll see you later, Holly, I'm not going to stand around listening to this crap." He spins on his heel and stomps out, slamming the door so hard the windows rattle.

"Good riddance, asshole," I say to his back.

Holly's head snaps toward me and I see tears pooled in her eyes. "How could you? You'd pretend this vision so I'll stay here? So you won't be alone? You are out of your mind, and I, I--" She doesn't finish her sentence, instead, she steps past me and out the door, slamming it as hard as Steve had.

I can't believe she'd think I made any of this up for any reason. I couldn't fake having a premonition if I tried. I'm not even sure what happens to me during an episode. All I know is I wake up or come to, or come back to myself a soaking wet driveling wreck.

I go to the window and see the two of them clinging to each other like refugees of some disaster. My eyes blur with hot tears and I stand there watching them, crying. I won't let him kill her.

I want my sister to be happy and have a good life. It's okay if she moves out, if I'm alone. It is.

I'll be fine. She knows I don't allow myself to love anyone, only her, and my horse Frisco. I think I love each of them bigger than normal because each of them is one half of my heart. Having her gone from my everyday world would be hard, but okay, long as she's happy. And alive, let's not forget that important piece of the equation.

Losing those I love hurts too much. Losing them first in visions and then again in real life. I can't handle it anymore and wish it would just go away forever. The idea of losing her is beyond my ability to grasp. That particular bit of hell just can't happen and I will do whatever I need to save her life. I'd die for her in a second. I'd kill for her in a minute.

That idea worms around in my brain for a moment before I squash it away. Could I kill to save her? I know I would. I know this fact deep down in my soul and I stand still, watching them out the window before I step away and shake my head to clear the notion from my mind.

It's a fascinating realization that killing a person to save her life is perfectly acceptable to me, but lying or making up a vision is not. And I wouldn't just kill to kill. No, I am not a murderer.

But I would never try to control her life or lie about something to get what I want, either. Sure, I'd choose a better, more balanced guy for Holly if she asked me, but I'm not making this up so I won't be alone.

He's wrong.

He is.

~2

Love means death. My love for someone, anyway. I love someone…Boom! They die.

I've finally accepted my curse, though Granddad told me it was my talent. I've been plagued with the ability to foretell the future, but only for those I love, and only their deaths. I've never been wrong. My cat, when I was six, was my first correct vision, and the never-ending, ongoing list is long; especially for someone only twenty-seven-years-old.

Following our parent's deaths, I decided I'd never love again. If I don't love anyone, I can't be hurt by their dying. But there is no turning away from Holly. She's the last of my family, and the only person I care about. There is no cliché I could use to describe my feelings for her. She's everything good and kind and is an embodiment of joy and love. We are close in the way twins are, even though three years separate us. We can complete each other's sentences and know the other's mood instantaneously.

We don't look alike at all. I'm taller, and I have darker skin and hair. I easily tan, while she burns. I have green eyes, hers are most times glacier-blue, but when she's angry they turn deep-sea purple. She's petite with perfectly sculpted and symmetrical features, she could be a famous model if she chose. Me, not so much. No, my nose is too big and my eyes are not the same size. In every single picture of me smiling, my left one looks smaller. No, the model-seeking agents would skim right past me, and zero in on Holly.

When Frisco came along, I had no choice in the loving of him. He was mine from the moment I helped his dam deliver him, a big wet colt struggling to stand before he should have. I loved him instantly and totally, as though he was an old friend returning after a long absence. He is still my best friend, other than Holly.

Now, I see Holly in the premonitions, and I won't stand by and say, "Gee, Holly's going to be dead by the end of tomorrow when her asshole fiancé stabs her to death."

I'll do whatever it takes to save her. Her hiding or running away can't stop the premonitions from coming true once they begin. And they have begun. Holly knows, she *knows* how it works. She only has to remember Granddad, Mom, and Dad. Each of them died within twenty-four hours of the damn visions showing themselves to me. Yet, now, suddenly when she's in the premonition, she says she's never believed in my visions. I think she just hides her head in the sand and refuses to believe something so outrageous is possible. Not only is it possible, it's real.

Steve denies he's planning on taking my sister's life. Well, of course he does! What fool would admit he's going to stab someone to death? Even if he isn't aware of what's coming, if he isn't planning to kill her, why can't he accept that if I see him stabbing her, he will? But he won't consider the possibility that it's him who finally goes crackers, not me. Maybe he twists off into some sort of PTSD tantrum and suddenly goes into a rage. I don't care why he goes crazy. I only want to stop him. I need help, but who can I turn to? The cops? Oh, please. You try to get them to step in before a crime is committed. Ain't gonna happen.

The saddest part is even if they packed him into a jail cell, it would only delay the inevitable. I'd kidnap her, but as soon I release her, she'll run straight into his awaiting knife. They must both agree to be apart. It's the only way, and that may not even work. I don't know for sure, since the only time I came close to stopping the premonition was with Henry, our beagle. I'd kept him away from the road for a week, but the first time he was able, he ran in front of the predicted blue car.

The only answer is for me to convince both Holly and Steve to walk away from one another forever. I think if they agree to never be near each other, it could work. I don't believe I have a chance of breaking them up. It's true, the saying, "love is blind". Holly sees Steve as some halo-toting angel with a limp. Neither of them want to accept reality and will stay on a predetermined course ending with Holly's death.

I've already failed with Steve. He blew out of here promising I'd never get him to leave her. She's my last hope and if I fail with Holly, I'll lose her forever. I won't imagine life without her.

From the window, I watch Steve and Holly talking. Finally, Steve gets into the driver's seat, and I hear the ancient El Camino roar to life. Grey smoke billows across the front yard and the irregular rhythm of misfiring pistons fills the morning air. Holly leans into the vehicle and kisses him, squeezes his shoulder, and turns to come back into the cabin. Steve guns the motor, spinning loose gravel into the air behind him, as he peels triumphantly out of the drive. Holly's no longer crying, which is good.

She comes into the kitchen, but doesn't say anything. I steal a glance at her and pour myself a cup of coffee so I have something to do. I cradle it in my left palm, hoping the warmth will seep into my ice-cold skin and make everything all right. Maybe the caffeine will kick-start my brain and I'll think of a way out of this mess.

Holly sits down at the island across from me, her teeth clenched and her eyes narrowed. *Calm down,* I think to myself, and will her to do the same. I take a shallow breath and meter out my words one at a time. They fall hard onto the cobalt-blue counter tiles, and sound empty, like hollow beads bouncing from a string. "Holly, you know I'm right. Steve is going to kill. You."

She doesn't say a word, she just stares at me. I try to read her thoughts and can't. I grip the coffee cup hard enough to turn my bony knuckles skeletal white. She glares at me, leans forward and snarls, "Listen Paizely, and listen closely. You are not psychic, you are not right, and you won't keep Steve and I from getting married, so accept that fact."

Her wedding isn't the issue. I keep my voice steady and I ignore the adrenaline surging into my muscles. "No, Holly, it's not you marrying him I have trouble with. It's him stabbing you to death that's the problem."

She taps her finger on the kitchen tile and the sound matches the pulsating throb in my brain and the steady cadence infuriates me. I grit my teeth and slam my fist down, right next to her *tap-tap-tapping* finger. A smarting twinge snakes up my arm, and I focus on this little bit of pain because it feels good and real--present and *now* rather than some hazy future where the world without Holly would be unbearable.

She sinks back into her chair and simultaneously smiles and rolls her eyes in an irritating way so she looks twelve years old instead of twenty-two. "You're jealous! You resent me having him to love and you're afraid to be alone. Admit it, Paizely, and stop telling me how to run my life. I'm not going to leave Steve."

I don't leap over the breakfast counter and throttle her right then and there, which says something about my incredible self control in the moment."You know how this works, Holly. Please, send him away forever. Maybe you can save yourself by breaking up with him. It's the only thing I can think of that might work."

"Pffft." She huffs, frowning. "Stop with the dramatics, Paize. Find a man to spend your life with and have some kids. I'm not your baby, I'm all grown up now and I'll make my own decisions. I'm getting married, and you need to deal with it."

Words shouldn't be able to hurt this badly, but they plunge into my soul--quick and searing hot. Lose her, I lose the only person who matters to me, and there isn't a damn thing I can do about it. I try not to talk to her as though she's a child even though she is currently acting like one. Forcing my shoulders to relax and lowering my voice, I look straight into her eyes. "Holly. Have I ever been wrong? Granddad explained this to both of us. Remember? You know I'm right. If I see Steve killing you, he will kill you. Period."

Holly's eyes disappear in a scowl of furrowed brows, and she looks through me, not at me; an expression of fury, then fear, cascading across her features. She stands and spins away from me, and stomps through the living room. At odds with her anger, her long blond hair floats behind her calmly, serenely, like a horse's tail as he canters away. "I am not going to listen to this garbage anymore. Steve loves me. You're afraid to be on your own, you're afraid to love anyone in case they die, you're afraid of everything. You need to get help so you can be normal and stop believing that you're some sort of psychic fortune teller. You don't *know* anything."

I watch her leave and remember when she was seven, running through the yard with her hands curled at her chest while she tossed her yellow mane and whinnied, pretending to be a horse. I would chase her, a rope held high above my head, as if I were a cowboy ready to lasso a wild stallion. If I did actually manage to throw the noose around her neck, she'd look at me with the same horrified expression she shot me a minute ago. Scared. Betrayed.

What else can I do to save her?

Holly goes into the other room to stand staring out the window. I know she's calming herself, and I should do the same. I look for something else to dwell on, hoping an answer I'm not currently seeing will surface.

I glance at the video monitor on the counter since it's the end of foaling season and the last three of my mares are due any day. Fuzzy black-and-white images fill the screen and in one stall, there is a dark blob in the corner. I squint my eyes trying to come to a decision whether the blob is just a pile of manure or the amniotic sac that once held a baby horse. I look to the side of the screen and let my peripheral vision decide because, for some reason, it clears the picture--similar to seeing things on a dark night with no moon.

Manure.

Which is pretty much how I view Steve-the-psycho. I will stop him because any other outcome is not acceptable. How to accomplish this is the question I must answer.

I follow Holly's lingering scent of clean fresh citrus--some perfume she wears that I love but can never remember the name of--into the small living room. She appears calmer as she gazes out the window at the curved dirt drive outside the cabin. She sighs. "Look at all the flowers, Paizely." She darts a glance at me, and continues, "They are so fragile still, so small and perfectly set against the green grass. I love spring in Colorado, don't you?"

Yeah, sure. "Holly, look, you have to pay attention here, you know-"

"Paizely, stop it! I'm marrying him whether you approve or not. Steve wouldn't hurt anyone."

"Tell that to the people he shot!"

She sneers. "You're going to be all alone. Grow up and get *over it*!"

I feel my heart flop once in my chest as if it wants to leave before it gets broken. I press on. "Steve-"

"No! Steve nothing. You need to get some help, Sis. I mean it. I've never believed in your talent, and I'm not about to start now. Granddad just went along with the coincidences so you'd feel less…different. You are not psychic. You need to see somebody, I'm serious. "

My hands flutter like wounded birds to my sides--little helpless things unsure where to go or what to do. I clench my jutting hip bones beneath my fingers hard enough to hurt, then straighten my back until I stand my full height of five feet-nine. I tower over Holly by five inches. Stretching my rib cage up and open, I ignore the annoying strand of hair hanging in front of my right eye. Willing myself to remain calm, I say, "You're going to stand there and tell me I was wrong about Mom and Dad? About Granddad? About Henry?"

"Henry? You think you could foretell the death of our dog? Jesus, Paize, you really are messed up."

I seriously consider smacking her upside the head. Instead, I clench my fists tighter.

Holly says, "Get some help today and either accept the reality I'm marrying the most wonderful man on the planet or accept you'll no longer be a part of my life."

She crosses the living room on the way to her bedroom. Once inside, she slams the door harder than ever before, leaving me standing there, shaking, alone.

Since she can't see me, I flip her off, and yell at the door, "You've chosen Steve over me?"

~3

When our parents died in a plane crash six years ago, Holly had been only sixteen years-old. I'd felt responsible for their deaths because I'd known the accident would happen, but they were already in the air by the time I'd seen the fire ball fall from the sky, and I couldn't stop the inevitable. I had promised myself to make up for them being gone by watching over her, so I became her mother, father, sister and guardian combined. Luckily, I was twenty-one and the courts appointed me as Holly's legal guardian since we have no other relatives. I promised I'd do anything to keep her safe and happy.

When Steve came along, I tried to like him as much as she did, and even now, as I pace around the small kitchen, I entertain the idea that I'm wrong about this vision and about him. The fact is, the only thing I have on him is his talking to himself along with the whole snipers hiding in the trees thing. He doesn't look like a victim of war, but he 'd been shot in Iraq and still limps with a shuffling gait dragging his left leg, *slide--thump-step, slide--thump-step.*

He admits to hearing things in the night that prompt him to look for enemies hiding in the pine trees, and seeing him slip into paranoid commando mode is downright disturbing. Last summer we had a picnic down by the creek, enjoying the warmth of the sunny day. We were eating our sandwiches and laughing, when all of a sudden, Steve lunged to his feet and crouched, swiveling his head frantically with his eyes wild and crazy. He muttered to himself and scared both Holly and I so badly we both jumped up and involuntarily tried to help him find whatever he thought was hiding in the woods.

Proof enough for me he's not all there. Holly is more compassionate towards him, saying how he suffers from post traumatic stress and how sad it is he's so afflicted. I felt sorry for him, originally, I did. But in reality, I think it's just one more chink in his armor proving he's not good enough for my sister. She, however, just wants to help him through his rough days.

I can see through him though, and when he freaks out and his eyes go wild while he mutters to himself, it proves he can't be all good, or all there. But maybe he is as decent as Holly believes, and maybe she'll be happy with him for a very long time, and maybe there's nothing for me to worry about.

I can't believe she thinks either I made up the vision, or it appeared because she's getting married. That her leaving me all alone in the cabin would prompt this. She and Steve planned on living in the house Steve had built for the two of them in Evergreen; a mere thirty-minute drive. I would be fine by myself on the ranch, with the horses and dogs. Just fine.

Steve's an ex-military man, and the Army left him with expertise in two areas--hand to hand combat being the first and marksmanship being the second. I can shoot a gun just fine, myself, because when I was just a little girl, Granddad taught me how to load, clean, fire and care for both pistols and rifles. I'm a decent shot.

Holly hates guns and wants nothing to do with shooting any weapon.

I know that he will jump at the chance to show me what a great shot he is, since he loves to thump his macho chest and prove his manhood. As if shooting a gun could prove any such thing. He and I have practiced together at the top of the landslide where the ground has fallen away leaving a rounded backdrop perfect for shooting--

The simple and undisputable truth was that my visions had never been wrong. Tomorrow Holly will die, killed by Steve. Unless I stop him.

I dial Steve's number and chew my thumbnail as I wait for him to answer. Holly can't hear me, but I remind myself to speak quietly when he answers, just to be sure. I have to get him to do what I want.

He answers on the third ring. I say, "Hey Steve, it's Paizely."

"Yeah?"

"I'm sorry about earlier."

His breath is heavy in my ear. "Well, you should be. You sounded crazy, thinking I'd kill Holly. What the hell?"

I bite my lip to keep from screaming at him, and instead, say, "We need to talk, Steve, it's important."

"Are you still hell-bent on the idea that Holly and I split up? 'Cause it's not going to happen and I see no point in arguing with you."

"Listen to me, you need to stay away from her. You know this will happen, remember Rebel? Maybe it's not your intention. Maybe your PTSD makes you lose your mind."

I hear him sigh followed by the distinct sound of cracking knuckles. He breathes deeply into the receiver and says, "You might be able to push Holly around, but you cannot, and will not, tell me what to do, Paizely. Don't even try."

I don't yell at him. I don't say anything for long enough he asks if I'm still there. I answer, "Yeah, I'm here. Actually, I called you because before this morning, before the…vision…I wanted to ask you for some advice.

A long pause, then, "What?"

"Well, remember I told you I bought a new Walther PPK .380? I got it yesterday and I'm, uh, wondering if you would help me with some target practice?"

He only hesitates a moment before replying, "Sure, Paizely, I'd be happy to go shooting with you. When?"

Figures he'd believe I need his help. I roll my eyes. "I think I'll ride Frisco, so can you meet me at the top of the landslide in a couple of hours?"

"If I can borrow Holly's Jeep. You know my Ranchero will never get up there and I don't feel like walking that far."

Steve likes driving the Jeep. I think it makes him feel all masculine and full of testosterone and I wonder what he thinks it does for Holly. My neck hairs stand up and wave in a breeze that isn't present. "Great!" I keep my voice light, so that even to myself, I sound as if I've been inhaling helium. "Thanks Steve, see you there." I hang up and gnaw some more at my nail.

My whole body shivers and I squeeze my eyes shut. I say to myself, "Get it together, Paize."

The irony of Steve's mutterings and mine being done in solitude doesn't escape my notice, but that's not the point.

I ask myself again, *can I shoot him?*

Absolutely. He is virtually a murderer and his victim will be Holly so it comes down to Steve or Holly. No contest.

I can't fathom why Steve would even *want* to stab Holly. And for the tenth time, I wonder if the visions could be wrong. I ignore the screaming in my skull that now commands me to stop thinking this way right now. I have to protect my little sister.

I feel as though I'm losing my mind and riding Frisco is about the only remedy I can think of to try Chewing my ragged thumbnail, I march around the perimeter of the kitchen twice, stopping only to snatch some carrots from the fridge. I grab my flannel shirt and slam the mudroom door on my way to the barn.

I clump across the yard like a lumberjack on a Saturday night looking for a fight, my hands clenching and my thoughts roiling. Yes, killing him right now is a far better solution than waiting for him to stab her to death sometime in the next twenty-four hours. I wish I could do it, I really do. But I'm not a killer. Still, it comes down to my saving her, who knows what I'm capable of doing. Bastard. Why won't he just leave the country? He knows I'm always right when it comes to the premonitions, he experienced the truth of the last one a month ago, when I warned him about his dog, Rebel. I loved that dog, a black and white mutt blessed with a sense of dog-humor that made me laugh every time he came over to visit. Steve loved him too, and watching him grapple with the loss made me empathetic toward him in a way his war injuries never could.

He doesn't have a reason to kill Holly, and yet, he isn't willing to do anything to insure her safety, either.

The sun lights up the world as if trying to make everything look cheerful and happy. I kick a pinecone, and it stops next to a wild purple iris that looks equally thrilled with life. Me, I'm not quite as giddy as either of them. I squint, wishing I'd remembered my sunglasses, but no way I'm going back to the cabin for them.

I flick the metal latch on the barn door and reach for the light switch. From the shadows, my horse nickers low and soft. "Hey Frisco. Wanna go for a ride, buddy?" My voice sounds flat and dead with a hollowness that echoes in my head.

I have to come up with a solution. Getting Steve up the mountain is the first step to keeping him away from her. But then what?

Frisco points his nose up into the air and flaps his lips as if he's trying to talk. On a normal day, I'd laugh, and I try to, but even though the tension in my neck relaxes a little, I'm too angry to smile. I smooth my palm over his left eye and put his leather halter on him. He lowers his head and pushes the door open wider and we walk into the concrete aisle way. He keeps nuzzling my pockets looking for the carrots he knows are there. When he finds one, he takes it between his teeth and eats the entire thing in one bite. He knows better, but does it matter?

I tell myself to concentrate on the mundane, everyday things that Frisco and I do together. I start to groom him in a methodical manner, but end up pulling the comb through his short black mane in quick, jerking motions. Giving up, and cussing at Steve under my breath, I toss the comb into the plastic brush caddy. I take a step back and gaze at my horse. He's a bay with the customary cinnamon body and black legs, mane and tail. Only one hind pastern is white and a small star graces his face. He stands 16.3 hands and I'd left him a stallion hoping to pass on his best attributes and his gentle disposition.

I know some people think it's strange to have a horse as a best friend but I trust him with my life and I honestly do believe he feels something for me. Maybe not love, but something akin to friendship. I am fairly certain Frisco can either read my mind or he understands an awful lot of the English language. I know he picks up on my moods and responds accordingly which can be a good thing or an inconvenient one, depending on the circumstances. Most times though, he takes care of me and I take care of him. We trust each other. Maybe cops with their canine partners can relate, but on average, I'd guess our relationship is both rare and unique.

Saddled and bridled, Frisco is ready. I normally carry a gun when I ride, ever since the pack of coyotes tracked us and wouldn't go away, no matter what I did. The dogs chased them, the coyotes fought back and after that, I left dogs at home and carried a gun. I put my Walther PPK .380 in the saddle holster hanging from the pommel. Ignoring the niggling thought of what I might shoot today, I pat my back pocket, feeling for my cell phone. Got it.

Frisco paws at the cement floor and nods his head up and down as if to say, "C'mon, let's get going." His lips clap until he finally holds his head sideways and sticks his tongue out the side of his mouth. This time, I do laugh--how could I not?-- and lead the way out the door to a stump I use as a mounting block.

Frisco walks along, easy-free, so his back swings in a comfortable rhythm making me wish I was on a boat moored on a tranquil sea. Riding him, I begin to feel a little composed. I ask him, "You think I can stop this from happening?"

He doesn't pay me any attention except to flick an ear toward the foals in the pasture as we pass. I say, "Want to go to the landslide?" As though I expect he'll answer me, which he does not.

At the end of the pasture's fence line, I turn left, toward the Purple Meadow, a huge field where thistle grows bright pink and changes to deep purple by the end of summer. The open field is surrounded by steep rocky hillsides covered in pine trees and huge boulders and looks like a giant bowl of happiness filled with sun and birds. Peaceful at any time of the year, it's one of my favorite places on the 1200 acre ranch. It's Frisco's favorite place too, not because of the panoramic views but because he loves to gallop up the hill from the Purple Meadow toward the old landslide.

The slide was caused five years ago when flooding rains followed the fires that took out most of the vegetation, leaving a level cut-out where the mountain slid so it forms a cirque at the top. And even though a few pine trees survived, it's mostly huge boulders sticking out from soft decomposed granite on the slide side. A deer and elk path winds amongst the rocks and serves as our galloping track.

A soft breeze lifts Frisco's mane and sends my own hair blowing into my eyes. Frisco, however, lets the excuse of a potentially windy day, along with the knowledge of where we are going raise his spirits and he jigs a few steps in anticipation. The gun in its holster bounces against Frisco's withers where it hangs from the D-ring on the front of my English saddle and I hold it steady with my right hand.

My mind won't let go of the worry over Holly and I grit my teeth. I'd always hated this ability, this so-called talent to foretell the future, and Granddad was absolutely wrong when he declared it a gift. I think maybe it would be better to be surprised when people you love die. Aloud, I mumble, "Gift, my ass," and nudge the stallion into a canter. He obliges by digging his hind feet into the soft ground and lunging up, toward the top of the mountain a little faster than we usually go. I sit deeply into the saddle and pull back lightly on the reins, guiding him to slow down. But he doesn't slow, he clamps the snaffle bit in his teeth and shakes his head, letting me know he isn't ready yet, so I let him canter a few more strides. Besides, it feels good to move.

"You'll help me with this, won't you boy?" I ask.

He responds by snaking his head toward the ground and bucking, his muscles contracting with each stride. His crow-hopping is how he expresses himself and most days, I don't mind, but today it's different. As though he's trying to warn me, he begins to buck harder and then launches into a full gallop, gaining speed and ignoring my commands to stop.

This isn't where we typically run. It's not safe for any kind of speed because there are loose rocks and gravel over larger, sharper boulders and branches and who knows what. At the top of this steep trail is the old landslide and if we don't stop, we'll plunge a couple of hundred feet to our deaths.

Frisco must be picking up on how scared I am about Holly--not that he understands what I'm feeling--but he knows I am not my usual calm self. To him, I feel jittery and inconsistent and this puts him on edge and makes him fearful.

He charges up the hill, and it's clear he wants to go even faster. I pull back on the reins harder than I ever have and tell him to walk. Instead, he only drops to a prancing trot like a racking Saddlebred, complete with big, high-stepping strides. I lower my voice and growl, "Knock, it off, Frisco."

His response is to buck again, harder this time and I'm thrown so far off balance, I have to grab at his mane. He jumps up the rocky incline, his haunches bunching and propelling us up, up, up.

We are just about to the top and the edge. I wonder if, when the time comes--now?--will I have a premonition showing me my own end?

If I can steady my mind and settle my own frantic energy, he'll also calm. I know this and so I concentrate on the brilliant green of the springtime grass and the tiny new leaves on the aspen trees.

Just a few yards away, the lip of the old landslide looms like a cavernous mouth. Frisco isn't responding to my cues which isn't like him at all. We are too close to the edge. I haul back harder, pulling at one side of his mouth with all my strength, hoping to bend his neck back to my knee so he'll stop or at lease slow down. "Shit, Frisco!"

He ignores my words and the bit.

From nowhere, a cold wind, sharp and stinging throws gravel into our eyes.

Finally, he stops. His shoulders raise and I know his front legs are curling under him.

I lean forward and his front hooves tap the ground. He doesn't rear up all the way, but threatens to stand on his hind legs, over and over. Like Holly's finger on the kitchen tile. *Tap-tap-tap.*

He tucks his head down to his chest, rolling his neck, then up and back.

And this time, he does rear. I feel his front legs lift and the world tilts back and even more so, until all I see is bright blue sky. I lean forward, hanging on with my legs, scratching for a hold on his neck.

His massive head pitches up and back toward me, backlit by the sun before smashing hard into my temple.

~4

Consciousness swept over me like a wave kissing a shore. Slow and caressing. Silent. And for a moment, adrift in the gauzy foam separating sleep and awake, I felt warm and safe.

I opened my eyes to a jumble of hazy brown impressions and shadowy images of wintry stillness and frost. Above me, the sky hung, heavy and pewter, like a tangible and weighted ceiling that reminded me of the concave dome of a casket. I figured I'd died.

Warmth turned to chill, then to numbing cold. My teeth clattered against themselves, rattling my skull. Lying in the frozen grass, my legs burning with fatigue and my heart pounding, I knew two things: I wasn't dead, and *I had to get away before they saw me.*

Before who saw me?

No one was chasing me. And why was the grass frozen?

I sat up, ignoring the stab of pain that corkscrewed across my temple. I blinked and focused on a wavering frozen field and phantom buildings scattered amongst willow trees. As though seeing two different photographs at the same time, this bleak meadow-image was superimposed over a cliff bordered by sun-drenched pines and wildflowers. A picture of fuzzy rocks and blurry pine trees stood in stark contrast of a gray field. And there, stood a bay horse.

Frisco!

I could see him clearly. He was fading, disintegrating like the people on *Star Trek.* He stood shimmering as if in a double exposed print, his copper-brown body flickered amongst the cliff-rocks, his black legs, mane and tail stark against the bleak field of bleached grass and he was gone.

I opened my mouth to call him, and the cliff disappeared. The world settled into a clear and solid image without the rocks and pines. Without my horse.

My teeth stopped chattering. My mind cleared and I knew this was no vision, just as well as I knew my name was Paizely Marie Dunn, that I was twenty-seven years old, and that I lived on a ranch in Colorado. I bred and trained Thoroughbred horses and my younger sister, Holly, would be murdered the following day. I remembered Holly and I arguing and my inability to convince her that Steve would kill her and now, I've lost my horse. Where was he? Oh God, if he was hurt--

To lose Holly would be hell; the most horrible thing imaginable, but without Frisco, it would be unbearable. Frisco would carry my sorrow and bolster my spirits and help me make it through losing the only person I loved. I had to find him and I had to get home.

I pulled my feet under myself and tried to stand, but my legs refused to cooperate and I slumped to the ground. Five-nine and strong from working horses and bucking hay, I'd only ever felt this helpless when sick with the Flu. Easier to call the horse to me. I couldn't whistle, had never gotten the knack of it, and instead, had taught Frisco to answer to a loud warble I made by tightening the back of my throat and screaming, "Ear-wit." I opened my mouth and called for the stallion, but the shrill sound didn't leave me, instead, it fell heavily on the dull iron-gray morning.

I inhaled deeply and shivered. The freezing air cut through my thin flannel shirt. It was early morning all right, and this most definitely was not a vision. I lifted my wrist to my face. Mickey Mouse smiled back at me, his once-red shorts faded to pink. His white gloved hands pointed to two-oh-seven. But the sun was barely up, although just a minute ago it had been afternoon on the tenth of May.

I reached back and dug around in my back pocket for my cell phone. Gone. It must have fallen out when I fell off of Frisco. Damn horse. What was he thinking anyway, he was supposed to take care of us, not get us killed.

I tried to figure out where I was so I could know where to find Frisco and get us both home. We'd ridden past wildflowers blooming and foals playing in the pasture and yet I saw neither the springtime greenery nor the landslide. Here, it was cold and wintry and not where I'd been at all. This was all wrong. I blinked twice and shook my head hard to clear my vision, but the same frozen grass was beneath me and the sky stayed pewter-heavy and gray.

From inside my own head and yet not, a staccato voice. The choppy, guttural shout was some other language, not English, but I clearly understood the meaning. The command was both strange and familiar, low yet feminine. Translated, it meant, *Run! The men, they come!"*

So authoritative were the words, I curled my legs beneath me, and snapped my head left, then right, trying to decide which way to run. My heart hammered against my ribs. I had to get away. Had to…

The still morning was shattered by a woman's sharp agonizing scream."No!" I looked in the direction of the cry, but couldn't see anyone in the pale light.

Again, the woman shrieked. The sound filled the morning with the terror and agony of a rabbit being torn apart.

~5

For Tahcitan, the dark before the new day had been long. Again, the spirits had visited. This night they had shown her an Iron Horse. Like a long and winding black snake, it made the noise of the *Ve'ho'e*, the white man. After it passed, the smell of meat rotting hung in the smoke around the black head of the iron serpent.

Even in her sleep, she had felt ill.

Awake, she remembered the dream-colors the spirits had shown her. She thought of the black snake's head, and knew it meant death.

The spirits were afraid.

By the light of a small moon, she had left her house of sod. In darkness, she had ridden the stallion across the great prairie, before the rising of the sun.

* * *

Icy-hot needles of perspiration pricked my back and drenched my palms. The woman screamed again.

I dove for the ground. On my stomach, I raised my head an inch and peered through the dead grass. Just far enough away to give the impression of mist floating before my blurred vision, a man held a woman in an embrace. They were about a hundred feet away, beyond the corner of a building. Something about the man reminded me of

Steve and that scared me as much as anything else that was happening. I laid flat and hugged the ground so he wouldn't see me.

The man was tall, maybe six-one, and his hair was the shiny blue-black of a raven's wings with feathers of gray at the temples. Even at this distance, I could feel an evil hatred emanating from him. I tucked my head into the crook in my elbow, and watched from that secure position.

The woman, wearing a caramel-colored Victorian style dress, pushed away from the man, then fell to the ground in a heap.

The man lunged forward and raised his arm. His long, black coat floated around him like the wings of a vampire's cape. He leaned over and with one hand, grabbed the woman by the neck. He shook her. A wolf, killing its prey.

He dropped her and she fell, rag-doll limp, to the ground. He leaned forward and swung a shiny fist in a downward arc.

Shiny fist?

His arm rose again. A stark metal blade rose again then plunged down, down into her body.

Oh God, the woman, the woman in the dress, in the vision. This scene *was* the vision, Holly's death.

A loud buzzing noise, like a thousand flying crickets, swam toward me. The sound increased until it smothered the morning, but I ignored the irritating racket to focus on the man.

I had to stop him from killing her. But my legs wouldn't move--nothing moved except for my eyes and my heart slamming against my ribs. I had to stop him. Save her.

Seconds ticked by in slow motion and still, I stayed locked in the same position. This wasn't like when I had a vision, it was as if I'd been given some paralytic drug. I couldn't make my muscles respond. Maybe someone heard the awful screams and would come to help. I stole a glance at the back of the house, hoping, wishing, praying someone would burst out and help her. The place looked like a morgue, dark, quiet and empty. No one came outside.

The buzzing sound in my ears grew louder. My stomach clenched and my skin felt clammy. I had to do something. I couldn't just watch a woman being murdered. I automatically reached behind my back, groping the waistband of my jeans for my pistol. Damn! I'd left it on Frisco's saddle. I searched around me for a limb or a large rock—anything I could use as a weapon. I found nothing that would stand up to a man wielding a knife.

I glanced back to the couple. The man raised his arm and again, the blade plunged down into the woman's body.

To hell with a weapon, I had to stop him. I bent my knees and rocked forward. The momentum of my upper body should have launched me into a standing position--hell, I was already running, my knees pumping like pistons--but instead of rising, I was tossed to the ground. The field undulated like rolling sea waves as if the core of the earth turned liquid. I clawed at the moving earth and pushed myself onto all fours. What the hell?

Dazed, with spots floating before my eyes, I clung to the tall dry grass. An illogical fear of being flung into space kept my fists wrapped around the brittle grass around me.

The ground heaved beneath me, tossing me like a floating cork. Left. Right. Left. Forward and back. Forcing me down.

The man in the bat-winged black duster turned in my direction, the mist that had hung between us, magically gone. He stood confidently on solid ground, staring straight at me.

* * *

Ella Mitchell looked at the man who had stabbed her and instead of the fear and hatred she should have felt, she recognized him for what he was; a broken man, beaten down until he'd felt this was his only choice. Her eyes dimmed, and her life ran onto the frozen ground. She hoped he'd look into her eyes, but he stared off into the distance.

She reached for him and whispered, "I'm sorry."

* * *

Silence filled a long moment. Then another. Any second now, he'd race to where I clung to the pitching earth, raise his fisted knife and plunge it deep into my heart. I kept my eyes on his.

The man looked away from me. He took a step, then, dragging the other foot, he lurched forward and limped around the side of the house, out of my view. I heard him call, "Saul! Time to get the sheriff."

He wasn't Steve, and the woman couldn't be Holly. Some sick coincidence that he'd killed someone in the same way as my vision. Although he wore the same long, flapping coat as Steve did in the nightmare, this man was taller and his hair was black, not blond, straight, not curly. But he had the same limp as Steve. "Oh my God," I whimpered, and tried to focus my mind on something real. Something that made sense. Holly, home, Frisco.

The thundering beat of retreating hooves brought me back to myself. Real hoof-beats, real horses. Two shadowy figures on horseback rounded the far side of the barn. In the lead was a small hatless man with a shock of orange hair, and following him, the man in the black duster. They spurred their horses to a gallop, and came straight toward me.

I threw myself flat, and tried to become invisible. I held myself still as the frozen dirt. Maybe they wouldn't see me and maybe I'd live. The vibrating rumble of pounding hooves echoed through my skull, and I kept my ear to the ground until the sound turned away from me, fading.

Finally, the earth stilled.

I strained to hear any sound from the men, but the only noise was my own frantic heartbeat and wheezing gasps.

I lurched to my feet and raced toward where the woman lay. I chanted in time with each footfall, "Oh God, Oh God, Oh God." I stumbled and groped my way, slogging ahead in slow motion, my limbs weighing me down rather than plunging me forward. I ran harder, but went slower. The distance to the woman seemed to stay the same, and part of me wished I'd never get there. If she was dead, I didn't want to know.

Two feet from the body, I stopped.

The woman lay sprawled in the grass, her right arm extended over her head as though clawing for something just out of reach. Dark hair curtained her features and hung loosely about her shoulders. Her long dress was hiked up around her hips, one leg was absurdly bent and she was completely motionless.

My brain ticked off a checklist: Brown hair, not blonde. Olive complexion, not pale skin that would burn, and she was smaller than Holly. *Thank God.*

I held my breath to stifle the whining whistle of my own shallow breathing. Maybe if death didn't know I was there, it would disappear, not be real.

Finally, I took a cautious step forward. My riding boots crushed the dry grass with a loud crackle that seemed disrespectful. A bird twittered somewhere far away. An insanely happy sound.

I stood over the woman, staring. Bright red splotches seeped through the calico fabric of the woman's tan-colored dress.

The humming-buzzing sound returned, filling my ears with a steady droning monotone.

I dropped to my knees beside the corpse. Tentatively, I reached out, and using one finger, pushed a few strands of damp, dark hair from the woman's face.

A low groan.

I jumped back, my hand over my mouth to stop from screaming. My pulse thrummed through my veins. I gasped shallow breaths, sucking the cold air in small wheezing sips.

The buzzing grew louder until it sounded like live electrical wires thrumming.

I leaned forward, and holding my breath, I looked closer at the woman's face.

Chiseled, almost perfect features gazed back at me, and to my relief, I saw it wasn't Holly.

Pink light from the rising sun shone in the woman's brown eyes. In the early morning light, the woman's face seemed to be melting in a shimmering wave-like pattern. Shadows drifted across her features like clouds, subtly changing her appearance.

The pulsating waves stopped. The buzzing stopped.
I blinked.
And found myself looking into the face of my sister.

* * *

Just after daybreak, Sheriff Thomas Taylor sluggishly sipped at a mug of bitter black coffee. A candle burned on the table next to him and hazy shadows danced in the corners of the room. Half-asleep, he leaned against the rail-back chair and smiled at the memory of his dream-woman; her black hair, green eyes, and legs as long as a colt's. In his view, she was the prettiest filly for miles around. He didn't generally squander his time looking at women, but this one was different. He wasn't sure if her being a half-breed is what made her so attractive to him or if it was something else. Finally in this dream, unlike real life, she'd spoken to him in a voice that rivaled the melody of a mountain waterfall in springtime.

He closed his eyes, savoring the way her hair had slipped across his hand. How his callused fingers felt the velvety softness of her rather than the tin coffee mug he held. He closed his eyes and his chin fell to his chest and his breathing slowed. A knock startled him awake and he jostled the liquid in the mug but managed not to spill any. Who could be here at this hour? He padded across the plank floor in bare feet and opened the door.

For an instant, he was convinced he was still asleep and dreaming because there, on the wooden porch stood his childhood friend, Frank Mitchell. Frank leaned against the rough lodge pole railing as if it was the most natural thing in the world.

Behind Frank, a red-haired boy who couldn't have been more than fifteen or sixteen-years-old nervously curled his freckled white hands as if wringing a dishtowel. His eyes darted from the back of Frank's head to the ground, then to the horses tied at the hitching post before repeating the entire sequence again.

Sheriff Taylor blinked.

Frank Mitchell couldn't be here. He was dead. Had been dead for eleven years. Died in the Civil War, fighting the Union soldiers. Back all those years ago, the Confederate Army had come to Russellville, Kentucky looking for volunteers, and Frank Mitchell had joined up before the ink on the notices had time to dry. When the war ended and Frank never came home, everyone assumed he'd been killed.

Yet, here he stood.

Franklin Theodore Mitchell had aged well. At thirty-five years old, he was five years older than Sheriff Thomas Taylor. Frank's features deeply contrasted those of his young companion. His chiseled face was a deep coppery-tan, his hair just beginning to gray at the temples. A graduate of West Point and Harvard Law School, he carried himself with the confidence innate to a man of both wealth and training.

A full minute passed before Taylor was able to react, and then his reaction was quick and smooth. He reached across the front of his undergarment for his pistol, and grasped at nothing but flimsy white fabric. Of course the gun wasn't there, it was hanging in its holster, over the post of his bed.

He would die this cold November day, in his underwear, without his boots on.

Briefly, he wondered how bad the pain would be when Frank Mitchell's bullet tore through his chest. And although his heart raced beneath the thin cotton of his undershirt, Sheriff Thomas Taylor was happy to note that he was not afraid.

~6

"Holly?" I whispered. *No, God, please, No! Don't let it be Holly.* But I knew it was my sister.

This couldn't be real. Holly couldn't be here, this was a stranger. Period.

I shuffled backwards. My chest cinched tight around my lungs. Cold sweat tickled my spine and ran down my sides. I shivered. There was no denying it was Holly. Her head was turned to one side, her brown eyes staring blankly. A long silence filled the space between me and my sister. "Hol?"

Holly's response was a frail whimper and sounded like a kitten mewing for its mother.

At the pathetic call, my chest loosened. Again, I slumped to my knees and reached for my sister. I'd gather her into my arms, hold her, and make her well. "Holly, Holly?"

Holly smiled weakly. "Tah-ci-tan--"

What? "Holly, it's me."

Pale blue lids fluttered. "Tat. Run--"

I folded my own large hand over my sister's frail blue-cold fingers. "It's all right. You'll be okay." Yet, even as the words escaped my lips, I knew they were untrue. Holly was not okay. she'd never be okay again and neither would I.

I rubbed her frigid hand. The nail beds were the blue of freshly laundered denim jeans. "Hol? Where are we? I've got to call 911."

Holly's brows furrowed, questioning. She gasped, "Run, Tat. Go." Her eyes closed and her chest sank. She didn't move.

"Don't you die, don't you dare die! Oh God, why didn't you believe me?" Through hot stinging eyes, I stared at Holly's blood-drenched body. She was so still and quiet. I laid my head against my sister's soggy chest and listened.

Silence. I reached for Holly's wrist to feel for a pulse.

Nothing.

Holly was dead, lying in the dirt bleeding like a gutted deer.

Tears streamed down my face and my lower lip bled where I'd bitten it, and I was barely aware of either condition. So much blood. I had to stop the bleeding. I had to save her, she wasn't dead, I wouldn't allow her to be dead. If I took off my shirt, I could make a tourniquet and tie it around her. I began unbuttoning the front, but she wasn't breathing. She needed to breathe, she needed air, then I could bandage her wounds.

I held Holly's head in my right hand, and pinched her nostrils closed so I could push air into her mouth, to her lungs. Over and over, until I was woozy and disoriented from lack of oxygen, I kept on. I only paused to check for the slightest unaided rise in my sister's chest.

But Holly didn't move. I listened to her chest and heard no sound of it beating and no sound of her breathing.

No heartbeat was worse than her not breathing. I yelled, "I won't give up, and neither will you, now breathe, damn it!" Teeth set, I began CPR. *Breathe, breathe, breathe, and compress. Breathe, breathe, breathe, and compress.*

Holly wheezed a strangled cough and took a shallow breath on her own. Exhaled, and then drew another.

"There. Good. Keep breathing. Slow and easy, Holly, I love you. You're going to be okay."

A phone. I needed a phone and help, now. I jumped to my feet, slapping my back pockets for my cell. The sooner the paramedics got here, the better chance Holly might have. It didn't matter that I had no idea where "here" was. They could track 911 calls, right? But I had no phone, I'd lost it in the fall.

Holly's eyelids fluttered. Her breaths were slow, shallow and irregular, but better this than the stillness of death just a moment ago.

I slid my boot backward across the ground, and then forced myself to turn away. But after only one step, I stopped. If I kept watching her, Holly would keep breathing and if she didn't, I'd make her. But I had to go for help, had to find a phone. Forcing myself to back away, not willing to take my eyes off my sister, I called, "Hang on Hol. I'll be right back."

The sun climbed higher in the sky and pink light melded to a pale winter-yellow--an omen things would be okay I thought. With that faint solace, I finally turned my back on Holly and dashed across the yard to the house.

I raced up the four wooden steps leading to the small back door, ignoring the relentless feeling that tugged at my mind insisting I'd been here before. There was no time for anything except finding help for Holly. I pounded on the window panes, not caring if I broke one. Maybe the noise of shattered glass would summon someone. I shouted, "Help! Help! Anyone home?"

No answer. I beat harder, using both hands, then tried twisting the handle, but the door refused to open so I kicked it. Inside, ominous silence hunkered beyond the blockaded entrance.

I shot a glance over my shoulder at Holly's still form. I wanted only to run back to my sister, but instead forced myself to jump from the landing. Legs pumping, I ran around the side of the house and jumped the wooden steps to the front porch. I pounded my fists on the engraved oak door. "Help! Help!" I kicked at the wooden barrier. "Open up, I need help!"

No one answered.

I'd go in and find a phone on my own then. I reached for the handle and pushed the heavy door with my shoulder. It swung open with a low-pitched sigh.

A sweet smell floated toward me, and though I couldn't identify the aroma right then, it carried a nagging insistence, like a long forgotten memory tugging at my mind, coaxing me to another time. An overwhelming feeling of déjà-vu settled over me. But I'd never been here. Hell, I didn't know where I was. I needed a phone, paramedics, doctors, and an ambulance.

I peered into the shadowy interior of the house, and called, "Is anyone home? Help, I need a phone. Hello?"

No answer, so I burst across the threshold. Inside, the air had an even heavier, thick, saccharine smell. Furniture oil and vanilla. Sweet, and so familiar. I glanced to my right. A living room, everything in it turned over. Papers from drawers were thrown in haphazard piles. Gold framed oil paintings on the walls hung askew. Pristine antique furniture--a settee, a drop-leaf table--lay overturned.

Goose bumps marched up the staircase of my spine, wrapped around my neck and crawled down my arms and for a moment, time stopped.

I knew this room. This house. Turning left, I ran toward the parlor. Even before I turned the corner, I expected to see the large, ornately carved mahogany piano. Still, the sight of it stopped me cold. My breath whooshed from my lungs as if I'd been gut-punched. I stared at the instrument.

In my head, the vexing almost-memory nagged louder, pulling at me. The same buzzing noise from before beat at my ears--silent moths against glass. A low fluttering whisper without definition before it changed to a higher pitched vibrating hum that filled my body until I felt it everywhere at once. My hands, toes, backbone, even my hair resounded with the whirring purr.

Something was oddly comforting about this place, as if I'd come home. Home. Holly. Holly! I was fairly certain I'd only been standing here a few seconds, but seconds counted. A quick glance around the room confirmed what I already knew. There was no phone. I had to hurry. Had to get...

I shook my head violently. Crossing over the hardwood floor in the hallway, my leather boots whispered, *shush, shush*. At the threshold of the living room, I paused. A wool carpet in deep maroon and midnight blue tones filled the room. I didn't want to go any further, knew I shouldn't. Moving forward was a bad thing.

"Walk on rug, bad." The voice was jilted and had a guttural, low-pitched articulation, feminine, but deep. English this time.

My voice. Or was it?

I forced my feet onto the carpet and ignored the words batting at my ears. I jogged around an overturned table and down a short hallway to a narrow staircase. Pausing at the bottom, the roar of a thousand angry bees buzzed in my ears.

At the top, was a bedroom, and I *knew* a brass bed sat on polished hardwood floors, *knew* the exact shade of robin's egg blue the walls were painted, *knew* the west-facing window had a view of a mountain range. I knew these things, all right.

But mostly, I knew the place was a sad room.

With one sweaty palm, I grasped the handrail and forced my feet up the stairs. I didn't want to go. Didn't want to see that room. But I had to, I had no choice. As if I had no self-will, I took one more step and then another, until I was at the top. I didn't pause, just turned left, the way I *knew* I was supposed to, and entered the blue bedroom.

The brass bed sat on shiny hardwood floors, the window faced west, and had a spectacular view of the mountains. Everything just as I'd known, except for one thing. Instead of the room being neat and tidy, it looked as though some sick and perverse giant had stirred it with a big stick. The bed was rumpled, sheets and blankets tumbling to the floor. Broken pieces of pottery and clothes littered the room.

My head pounded with droning moth-winged memories that weren't mine. I raised my palms to my ears and shut my eyes. Maybe when I opened them, I'd be somewhere else. Home would be nice.. .

I opened my eyes to the same dismal mess. There would be no phone, I knew that, but searched the room for one anyway.

The best thing to do was get a blanket, go to Holly and try my damnedest to keep her alive. I grabbed a heavy quilt from the foot of the bed and turned to leave. A porcelain pitcher and bowl sitting on the bedside table caught my attention.

I stopped, and clutched the quilt even tighter to my heaving chest. I stared at the English Blue-Transfer pottery. Couldn't be. No way. But there it sat, the engraved handle facing to the right.

My Christmas gift to Holly four years ago.

~7

Tahcitan greeted the warmth from the sun. She threw her head back and her arms wide to give thanks to the Great Spirit for such a day and such a horse. Yet, the joy that would usually fill her when she prayed to *Heammawihio*, The Wise One Above, would not come on this day. Her heart weighed heavy in her chest, but the reason for her feeling was not clear.

Tall brown grass whispered against her buckskin leggings as she urged the *hemotsehno'ha*, the stallion, into a lope. The horse's easy, rolling gait combined with the gentle morning helped chase away some of her feelings of unease.

At the top of a small rise, she slowed the animal to a walk. She was not quite there. Being close to El's house made her remember the Iron Horse and brought back her night feelings of dread. To calm herself, she patted the bay's brown neck, then ran her fingers through her own tangled black hair. The motion did not settle her quivering nerves.

Ahead, the yellow house trimmed in white sat snug in a draw of rolling grassland. For a moment, she paused to look at Ella Mitchell's home. Behind the house, toward the range the white man called the Rocky Mountains, the tallest point they named Long's Peak, stood guard.

From nowhere, a gust of wind blew at the stallion and he snorted and held his head high. A chill crept down Tahcitan's back and she laid her palm against the bay's neck to calm him. In the language of the *Tsitsistas,* the People, she spoke so she might vanquish her fears and calm the horse. She also talked to him because he was the only other being, aside from El she could trust.

She was afraid. And though his moods often followed hers, her fears usually followed his.

This time, though, she had been spooked by what she could not see and what she did not know. The spirits and their strange message sent fear into her and so she spoke in the language of The People. She told the stallion about her dream--the vision of the Iron Horse and the death smoke that poured from its head. She asked the horse to help her understand the meaning of her dream.

At last, the huge horse stood still, and she knew he would help her.

From the top of the small knoll, she watched the quiet picture before her: El's house, with the hitching post in front of the wrap-around porch. And behind the building, the blackened square where the old barn had been before the fire took it. To the north, near the creek, stood the new barn.

The place was quiet, but the knowing of El in danger writhed as a snake would in Tahcitan's gut. She looked toward the pregnant mares grazing in their pasture. They seemed at ease, their heads bent to crop the dried grass.

Bright sunlight bounced off the windows of the house. Tahcitan squinted. Long morning shadows stretched behind the building, reaching for the mountains. Her heart beat a warning in her chest and her mouth tasted bitter. Something was wrong.

And then she knew what was missing.

Ella Mitchell could not bear to be chilled. The white woman kept a fire burning even in the heat of the summer. Yet three moons had passed since the warm times. Now, even the daylight hours were cold and El burned the wood from a pile in the yard.

On this cold morning, no smoke rose from the chimney of El's home.

Tahcitan hugged the stallion's massive neck, drummed his sides with her heels, and raced to the home of her only friend.

* * *

Wary. So cautious he was practically jumpy and that's never a trait a lawman should strive for, Sheriff Taylor sat stiffly in the saddle, his shoulders squared, and tried to look nonchalant. He glanced sideways at Frank Mitchell.

Frank sat so his hips followed his horse's motions in a relaxed, serene manner. Except for the white around his knuckles where his hand fisted around the reins, and the twitching muscle in his jaw, he didn't seem angry. Nor did he resemble a man ready to shoot his childhood friend for past liberties taken.

Frank cleared his throat and swung his head towards Taylor. "How far is it?"

Taylor couldn't help but wonder why he was still alive and if Frank would shoot him once they reached their destination. He ran his fingers over his coarse mustache, surveying the landscape. His nerves twitched involuntarily, like a sleeping dog's muscles. Maybe he could get away from Frank and Saul, just spur his horse and high-tail it over the next hill. Yet even as the idea flitted through his mind, he knew he wouldn't do anything of the sort. He drew in a deep breath. "Twenty minute ride west," he said.

"Good," he smiled, and to Taylor, Frank's toothy grin exactly matched a wolf guarding a hard-won carcass. He continued, "It's been a long journey, and I can't wait to see the look on my sister's face when we arrive."

His words were appropriate, nothing out of order to set off any sort of alarm. Yet Taylor found it difficult to ignore how his own nerves twitched at the sound of Frank's voice. Funny how guilt can turn a man's stomach to clenching, he thought. Frank's booming laughter shattered his musings. "It ought to be a hoot, seeing my sister's reaction. Don't you agree, Sheriff?"

Taylor nodded, wondering if "hoot" was the word he'd have chosen. Laughter would be the last response he expected from Ella. She and her older brother had never been close. As children, Frank had bullied all of them, and Taylor anticipated Ella Mitchell's response to waver somewhere between wariness and anger.

Although Frank grinned, his jaw muscle twitched and his hips locked so he sat his horse in a stiff manner. Taylor listened to what the man's body telegraphed, rather than what his mouth spoke. He watched the way his eyes flitted from the horizon to his saddle horn to a hawk soaring overhead. Frank was tense, all right. Maybe his nerves about seeing his only living relative after twelve years were the cause. But why? Because he planned on killing him when they arrived at Ella's so she could bear witness? The notion made no sense. He would have pulled the trigger already, if killing him had been his intention. Much as he mulled it over, Sheriff Thomas Taylor could not fathom why Frank Mitchell was here, now or what he might want.

Still, the most disturbing fact was how Frank's words clearly contrasted his emotions, and could only mean trouble. How much and how bad that trouble might be, Taylor could only guess.

* * *

Tahcitan believed El had built the hitching post out front just for her. The place to tie the stallion was hers, just as the back door was hers. The door gave her a place to enter the house so no dirt would fall onto the floor. If El's rugs were to ever have any moccasins with horse manure step to them, the white woman's anger would be as vicious as the badger. Though El did not often let her voice rise, Tahcitan did not enjoy the way El's face creased in disgust or how her thin lips pressed together when dirt fell into her house. Thinking of these things brought a heavy feeling to Tahcitan's heart, though she was not sure why this would be so.

She tied the bay, and ran her palm over his neck. Looking into his eyes, she sent him the mental thought to be still. Her strides were long as she went around the side of the building to her door. She ran up the back stairs, but the tiny hairs at the back of her neck stood on end like the quills of the porcupine. She listened and waited before entering.

Something was wrong, but not in the house. She knew this the same way she *knew* other things before they happened. She could tell what day a mare would allow the stallion to get her pregnant, or where to find a certain herb, and that her father would die on that horrible November day, exactly seven years ago, at the Sand Creek battle.

No, whatever the trouble was, it was outside. Behind her.

She spun on her heel until she faced the charred remains of the old barn. The barn had burned, or had been set on fire less than two moons ago. The heavy, sour smell of smoke and ash still drifted on the calm morning air, and she could still see, in the eye of her mind, the death. Horses screamed their fear, and their hooves kicked at the walls of the stable. The heat, the black smoke, and the hot flames were too much for El and for her. No water in the creek. No way to get the horses out. The bitter smell of burning hair and flesh.

She blinked to erase the memory and her eyes stung with tears. She drew the backs of her hands across her lids, wiping away the tears shed for the horses who had died that night. She would cry for the animals and the earth, but would not, *could* not cry for any of the people. Not since the death of her father, White Antelope, had she shed a tear for any other person.

She looked past the charred barn. There was a lump of golden-brown, darker than the grass and did not look as though it belonged. She looked at it for a long moment. , until almost as if it were a broken-winged bird, it fluttered.

She knew, and did not want to know. There, in the grass, El's favorite calico dress.

The air moved silently, an invisible hand pulling at the fabric until the hem of the dress rose, then settled on the still body.

No!

Panic raced on icy sweat on her skin. Her muscles quivered. "El," she screamed, but her voice was only in her head.

She jumped down the steps and ran across the yard.

Ella Mitchell lay on her side in the grass, eyes closed. Her right arm reached for something over her head. Her favorite dress bunched up around her hips and one leg was bent, graceful, even in death. *A leaping deer*, Tahcitan thought, *killed.*

She dropped to her knees. "El?" She whispered.

No answer. El did not move.

She knelt closer to her friend, the only woman, the only *vo'estan,* person, who had been kind to her since the loss of her people. It had not mattered to El that she, Tahcitan, was a half-breed. "El, it is me, Tat." She spoke the words and even remembered to use English. She did not know if El could hear them.

El remained quiet and still.

It was always the same. Everyone she loved died. Now, even El. Tahcitan did not understand how this could be--El was a White woman. Not *Tsitsistas*, Cheyenne.

Part of her vision, her dream, her spirit-story had come true. As it did at all times.

She reached to stroke her dead friend's dark hair, then did not. She leaned backwards and lifted her face and arms to the heavens. Drawing a deep breath, she prepared to wail the death chant of her people.

El stirred, barely rustling the grass around her, and moaned so softly, Tahcitan was sure that only her mind's eye had made the dead woman move.

El's finger twitched.

Tahcitan, her heart pounding hope through her veins, rolled El onto her back.

The wounded woman's eyelids fluttered. "Tat," she breathed. "Where did you go?"

Tahcitan's chest closed in on itself until she felt she could not draw another breath.

The English words never came first. She had lived near El for the past seven years, and always, she thought first in the language of *Tsitsistas*, the Cheyenne. Only then, did the white man's words come to her. With the meaning of El's words, came the bad truth of this being her fault. If only she had stayed here last night.

She stared at her only friend. So many wounds. So much blood. She must stop the bleeding and give El the herbs to heal so that she may live. She saw how much blood and knew El would find the Hanging Road soon.

Tahcitan felt the heavy with sadness. It was as if the robe of a buffalo covered her and she could not move. Could not breathe.

Ella Mitchell moaned, her eyes searching for something behind her closed lids. Her blue-tipped fingers opened, then closed into a fist.

The movement shook the guilt-hide of the buffalo from Tahcitan's shoulders. "Shh, El, be still. I will take you to your bed."

El's eyes opened. She tried to speak, but only coughed. A dismal sound that reminded her of a dying calf.

Tahcitan, for once glad to be so tall and strong, gathered her friend's broken body in her arms.

El's cool limp form seemed to have no weight.

* * *

I knew only seconds had passed. Yet, in that small amount of time, my heart pumped my blood through my body with enough force to make my head spun with vertigo.

Maybe I was hallucinating, imagining the whole thing.

The pitcher couldn't be Holly's.

I glanced around the landing. Why did this place seem so familiar? An emotion I couldn't identify settled around me. That feeling of reverence when inside an old church or maybe a museum, as if I should be quiet and careful not to disturb the ghosts of a time long-past.

Ghosts.

The word seemed most appropriate.

I hugged the blue and white quilt, then trotted down the steep staircase. I ran through the rubble in the kitchen, stopping at the back door. My hand resting on the glass doorknob, I tried to see through the sheer curtain covering the window.

I had to be either hallucinating or dreaming. Morning sunlight brightened the yard and bathed everything in yellow-gold light, so it was easy to see things. Holly still lay where I'd left her, out in the middle of the meadow between the house and the barn. Crouched over her, was a man wearing tan buckskins. Yes, buckskins, complete with fringed tassels at the sleeves and some kind of decorative hoo-haws embroidered at the cuffs and along the hem. Long, shiny black hair hung loose about his shoulders, covering his face.

An Indian. A real one. Straight out of the old west.

No way some Indian guy was going to take my sister anywhere. I needed to get Holly from him and the hell with anything else. I gripped the chiseled glass doorknob and turned it. I started to say something, though the words hung in my throat. I pulled the door toward me just as the man picked up Holly.

Looking down at Holly's face so his hair covered his features, he walked towards the house.

And again, I stood still. A coward. What the hell was wrong with me anyway? Because I couldn't move. My insides froze and at the same time, my muscles turned liquid, unable to respond. My pulse raced through my ears. I clutched the quilt to my chest with one hand and I still gripped the crystal doorknob in the other, but my feet stayed cemented where I stood.

He was nearly to the steps, but with his head bent, his face wasn't visible. He was about six-feet tall, thin and wiry. Graceful and sleek, he moved cat-silent and sure. His muscles worked beneath soft leather that moved softly and sinuously with each stride. At the bottom of the stairs, he paused, ready to step onto the first tread.

I glanced around the kitchen. I needed a weapon, either a knife, scissors, or maybe a cast-iron frying pan, something. My gaze flicked across piles of utensils, pots, pans, dishes, a hand-crank butter churn in perfect condition, a dish towel. There were things in the piles I didn't recognize--metal objects with wooden handles. Odd utensils that wouldn't make a good weapon.

Footsteps sounded heavy on the stairs outside. He was close.

~8

Sheriff Thomas Taylor, Frank Mitchell and Saul O'Greary stopped at the rise above the Mitchell Ranch to look over the valley below them. Still shrouded in shadow, the ranch appeared to still be sleeping. A new day, and the early morning sun lit Long's Peak so the snow covering the high mountains glowed a deep golden-rose.

The cheery mountain seemed to stand guard over the ranch. The sight boosted Sheriff Taylor's spirits and made him more hopeful than he'd dared allow himself to be all day. For a moment, he forgot about Frank Mitchell. He forgot about everything, and did what he always did from this knoll. He scanned the ranch looking for any sign of Tahcitan.

The bay stallion stood tied to the hitching post in front of the house. And even while Taylor tried to ignore the swell of emotion that sent his heart dancing, last night's dream crept into his mind--the silkiness of her hair, her touch, her voice. Maybe today she'd finally do more than glance at him from behind a curtain of shiny black hair before fleeing as though from a ghost. Maybe today she could look him in the eye and see his true feelings. Beneath him, his horse stamped a hind leg in impatience, jarring him back to the present.

Taylor cleared his throat and pointed at the white-trimmed yellow farmhouse. "Here we are. Your sister's ranch."

"Ella has set the place up quite nicely," Frank grinned.

Taylor nodded.

"Whose horse is tied out front? I thought we might be Ella's first callers of the day." The cadence of his words increased with each syllable until the last three words slurred together and became one.

Taylor wondered at the lilting inflections and simultaneously considered what Frank's reaction toward Tahcitan might be and how that reaction could be changed. Taylor didn't want the man anywhere near Tat. He could guess at what Frank might think, and what he'd say. Best to keep things simple until brother and sister had a chance to reunite. Avoiding the question was not an option, but he didn't want to witness Frank Mitchell's response toward the Indian woman, or toward his sister having a half-breed as a best friend. "That's Ella's helper. Takes care of the horses."

Frank nodded, then aimed his horse down the slope. "Shall we?"

There was something in the way Frank's mouth curved itself into a sneer instead of a smile, something about the way his knuckles whitened around the reins. He sat astride his horse grinning. The proverbial cat who's eaten the canary. Watching the man, Sheriff Taylor realized he needed to be focused and clear for whatever lay ahead.

They started down the hill, Taylor's mood sinking with each step.

* * *

I threw the quilt into a crumpled heap behind the piano and sank my knees into the soft mat. I strained to hear any sound, but could only hear my own blood rushing through my ears. What I couldn't tell, what scared me worse than anything, was what the Indian was doing with Holly.

The man dressed in buckskins had barely made any noise as he carried Holly upstairs. Only the light shushing sound of his moccasins skimming across the wooden stairs told his whereabouts until he'd reached the blue bedroom. Then, everything got quiet.

An Indian for God's sake!

The only thing that mattered was Holly. I'd wanted someone to help and now an Indian shows up. Nothing made sense. Had he helped her or hurt her?

Holly made no sound at all, and she might already be dead. I had to go to her now.

Oh God, I'd left my sister to die in the arms of a stranger.

I began to rise, my left knee protesting the movement. I stopped. Not because my knee hurt, but because I was afraid--afraid I'd be killed too. I wondered why my own life should even matter. With Holly dead, what was the point? But I didn't know if Holly had died. She could still be alive and that remote possibility was enough to spur me into action.

Leaving the quilt on the floor, I crawled from behind the piano and stood. I didn't want to go upstairs. Forcing my foot forward and ignoring the hot sweat prickling my spine, I headed toward the staircase.

A wail from the blue bedroom stopped me mid-step. It wasn't Holly's voice that had cried out, but rather the mournful, anguished cry of someone else. A woman's scream. High-pitched and tortured it was the sound of a deer being tortured by a pack of coyotes. The cry lasted so long, I thought it would never end.

I had to get to Holly. My legs were already running. Across the parlor, toward the stairs.

* * *

Tahcitan heard the breath leave her own chest as the sigh of a gentle breeze whispers through the branches of a tree.

She felt the last bit of warmth leave El's already cold hand. She did not want to think about what the death of her friend meant for her. She did not want to remember that once again, she was alone. The loss of El made her own heart heavy in her chest. Still, she did not cry.

First she must prepare El's body in the manner of the Cheyenne People. Her body should be dressed in her finest gown, and wrapped in a robe. A resting place needed to be chosen. Tahcitan closed her eyes and saw the cottonwood trees near the creek behind the barn. The way of the *Tsitsistas* required that a woman be buried with her tools, her digging stick, or her hide-fleshing tool. But El did not own such things. Her most prized possession was her piano. Or perhaps her precious rugs.

Tahcitan knew she could wrap El in one of the wool rugs for her journey, but how could she raise the piano into a tree? She could simply lay El's body on the ground and cover it with rocks. The piano could be covered as well.

She had not cut her own hair since her last time of mourning, seven years ago. Now, she would cut it once more.

Her mind settled, she released El's cold hand. She stood, but her legs could barely hold her. Wobbling, she shuffled to the corner of the room and leaned against the wall. With her eyes soft so all she could see became blurry, she studied the body of her friend. She imagined El's *tasoom,* her soul, riding the wind. Up, drifting, floating, until it reached the beginning of The Hanging Road--the great place in the night-sky where the stars made a clear path to the place where each *tasoom* must travel.

Smiling, she prayed to *Heammawihio*, asking the Wise One Above to receive El, a white woman. She asked that El be allowed to live forever among her long lost loved ones. El would know only love and happiness forever. In the language of the *Tsitsistas,* she asked, "El, go to my people, tell them I will see them soon."

Tahcitan stood in a trance of seeing her friend's spirit rising. Happy for El's journey up The Hanging Road, at the same time, sadness filled her. She knew it was the wish of The Great Spirit that she lose all those she loved. She did not know why this should be the way.

After the sadness, another emotion came to her. Loneliness. It stabbed into her heart, into her soul. The rest of her visions would come true also. Soon, the bay stallion would leave her and she would be truly alone once again.

Her throat swelled close with her grief. The palms of her hands slicked with sweat and a river ran down her spine. A burning feeling scraped her eyes. She lowered her chin so it rested on her chest. Her knees bent and her back slid down the blue plaster wall. She was breaking, falling, drowning. She was dying, and still, she did not cry.

Bravery, courage. She must be strong. She would fight this evil spirit who wanted only to bend her spirit and crush her. She must fight and win. It was the way of The *Tsitsistas*. Bravery was valued over all else and she would not shame herself or her people.

She asked how she could she be brave and fearless when she was so alone, but no answer came.

She hugged her knees and tried to breathe. Her throat fisted around itself and allowed no air to pass into her lungs. A pounding drum beat a tattoo against her temples and into her eyes.

Red. Black. Red. The colors pulsed before her, around her, within her.

She sobbed once, twice, then hot, burning tears flowed down her cheeks. Her nose filled, and her throat loosened and at last, she drew a deep breath.

* * *

Outside, a horse whinnied.

Across the kitchen and not quite to the stairs, I skidded to a standstill, head cocked.

Frisco. The same low nicker he voiced whenever a mare was nearby and he wanted her attention. He was here, he had to be okay. I pictured my horse, his neck arched, his nostrils flared, his muscles flexed. The memory of him brought images of home, and I wished we both were there, with Holly. I wished for phones and trucks, and even for Steve, who was the only potentially bad guy I knew. Without thinking, I started for the front door and as if he sensed I was on my way to him, he whinnied again. He was just outside the parlor window. I sprinted towards the door, towards Frisco.

A knock. Sharp and racking.

I slid to a stop on the polished hardwood, between the front door and the piano. A memory that was mine, but somehow not mine, pulled at my mind and erased all thoughts of Frisco and home. My knees went soft, rubbery-weak while my heart slammed against my ribs hard enough to make my vision pulsate.

I'd done this before--heard that knock.

Thoughts that weren't mine flew through my head as though I had someone sharing my mind.

A stranger's voice, deep baritone, called, "Anyone home?"

Shaking now, my blood turned cold, and every hair on my body stood at attention. I stood, but my legs quivered. My blood pounded icy through my veins. My mouth tasted as though I'd been sucking on pennies. The almost-memory prodded at my numb mind. *Oh God, what happens next?*

I spun to my left and bolted forward two steps.

Outside the massive oak door, a deeper voice rumbled and the sound stirred my thoughts into an even faster frenzy. I couldn't think and I didn't know what to do.

Again, the man shouted, but his words were disjointed. Something about the tone of his voice was familiar.

The deep timbre resonated in my mind--rocks rolling around the inside of my skull as if in a tumbler. I recognized his voice.

The killer. The man who stabbed Holly.

I had to do something. My legs pumped, but I didn't move.

I took a step towards the door. Stopped. My thoughts fired rapid-fast, so fast I had no time to question anything. On a hundred levels simultaneously, I puzzled over what to do. I concentrated on whether Holly might live, who the Indian upstairs was, who the men outside were, how to get to Frisco and get away from here before they caught me. It was too much to think about. A lump in my chest grew to a large suffocating mass and settled in my throat. An Indian held Holly upstairs. More men were at the front door. Frisco was outside and I might be able to escape this nightmare by getting on him and riding away. If I could just get to him.

I would not stand here in the middle of a stranger's living room waiting to die. I slowed my mind, forced myself to take a deep breath. Logically, why would the killers return? They'd gain nothing. Plus, if they were the killers, they certainly wouldn't bother with the nicety of knocking on the front door after stabbing a woman to death. No, the men at the door could not be the murdering thugs of this morning.

Maybe they could help Holly. My right foot sank into the plush maroon carpet and the buzzing noise from earlier returned. Humming a drone similar to a distant tractor plowing frozen ground, the sound grew louder, more insistent.

My knees buckled , and I felt about as able to walk as a baby. The comparison did not please me. I'd never viewed myself as helpless or hysterical until today. Until now.

Still, my pulse thrummed through my arteries in perfect sync with the droning hum in my ears. Fear. Mine, but not mine, snaked from deep in my chest and raced along every nerve in my body.

"Move. Run." No time to think. Irrational terror I couldn't ignore.

"GET OUT! NOW." As though God Himself had issued the command.

I had to obey. I didn't ask why, just spun around fast-- practically as though *someone had forced* me around--so I faced the kitchen. The sound of angry bees filled the house.

The men were after *me.* I had to get away. Had to save myself.

Down the hall, the kitchen door stood open, beckoning me.

* * *

The *hemotséhno'ha,* the stallion, whinnied.

The sound of the horse's call meant only one thing. Tahcitan sent him a silent message, *"Quiet, my friend."*

The voice of one man, a *Ve'ho'e,* drifted to her. Then the sound of another. She stole a glance out the bedroom window, afraid the men below might look up and see her watching them. The tops of two black hats and a head covered in red hair the color of a sorrel horse walked around the side of the house.

She ducked down, letting her breath out fast. Her buckskin shirt rose and fell with her rapid breathing. Although her body tensed, ready for flight, her feet remained still.

Seven years ago: *Blood. Everyone dead.*
Running, hiding. Gagged and tied.
Shiny gold buttons. The flash of a knife's silver blade.
Fear, followed by pain.
Then. A different pain between her legs. Sharp. Jagged.
Her hand fluttered to her left cheek. Traced the scar. Never would she allow it to happen again.

A ray of sunlight glanced off the star-shaped badge on one of the white men's chest. The *Ve'ho'e* law. Her distrust of men, especially white men who have been granted power over others, made her clench her teeth and grind her jaw.

* * *

"*Ve'ho'e!* Run!"

I felt the voice, as much as heard it. The sound had come from inside my head, yet it wasn't English. The accent was foreign, yet familiar, as was the strange guttural inflection. But I recognized the voice as my own. And I also knew it was not mine. "*Ve'ho'e*, white man". I understood the meaning of the word, and more importantly, understood the fear it evoked.

Not questioning myself, I ran down the hall, through the kitchen, and out the back door. I wanted to go to Frisco who was tied at the front of the house, but I couldn't. Instead, I raced down the four wooden stairs and across the yard, pausing only long enough to swing the barn door open and slip inside. The last lingering shadows of night filled the interior of the barn, leaving the air heavy with the odor of horses. Four stalls lined the wall along the right side of the room, and a window set in the back wall let in the most meager of gray light. In the center, a pile of hay was heaped.

I stood with my shoulder pressed against the rough wood of the door, panting and shaking. The familiar smell of horse manure and hay filled my nostrils and I inhaled deeply, but the normally comforting odor failed to provide its usual calming effect. From the gloom deep within the building came the rhythmic grinding of a horse chewing its breakfast. Between the horse and my own ragged breaths, I couldn't hear anything, and I needed to know where the men were.

Men. God, I was losing my mind. I should greet them, run to them, and beg for their help. Lead the way upstairs to the blue bedroom, to Holly. But I couldn't do any such thing.

The men are not here to help me or anyone else. They will only blame me for Holly's death, then hang me for murder.

I didn't bother to question how I knew this.

Turning slowly, I faced the door. With my cheek pressed against the freshly cut wood, I peered through a crack between two boards.

Three men rounded the corner of the house: a redhead who looked much younger than the black-haired killer, and the newest member of the group who wore a cowboy hat. He glanced in each window as he passed by, keeping his head turned so I was unable to get a clear look at his face. He was maybe six feet tall, and built more like a Thoroughbred than a Quarter Horse--lean and angular. He walked with the confidence of a man used to commanding respect, but then, so did the black-haired man who was Holly's killer.

I should run to them and claw their eyes out. I could do it using no tool other than my bare hands. But instead of anger, all I felt was terror. And I was positively certain, and *knew without a question* the men were after me.

They had come to kill me.

This insistent panic made no sense. I told myself so, and then tried to make the feeling go away. Tried to be Paizely--that's how I thought of it--independent, self-assured and confident. But the problem was, the feelings I had *were* mine, no one else's.

I was going to die at the hands of these men. I couldn't move.

I needed to get a grip and snap out of this stupor, so I raised my hand and slapped myself hard across the cheek. Stinging pain slashed through the numb fear in my mind. At last, I felt as though my thoughts were my own again. And since there were no accompanying uninvited voices, I concentrated on what I needed to do.

Getting home and away from all the cowboys and Indians would be the first step. Then, I'd somehow get Holly and Steve to agree to walk away from one another.

The question of how to get home mixed with the knowing Steve was very likely sharpening his knife right now made my skin crawl. Stuck here, saving Holly or myself was not going to be easy. With the right plan, I'd have a chance. Half a chance anyway and right now, half looked pretty good.

I watched the men through the crack and thought hard about how I was going to get home in one piece and save Holly's life.

~9

Tahcitan hid behind a flimsy window curtain and watched the *Ve'ho'e*, the white men, in the yard below her.

They would come into the house.

They would find her.

They would kill her.

She looked at El. El had saved her life and then become her only human friend. It was not right of her to wish for a dead woman to come back to life, but she could not keep the thought from her mind. Since the time of Sand Creek, when the *Ve'ho'e* killed her people, she had not been this scared or alone.

El had always spoken to the white men when they came to the ranch. But El was dead. And now Tahcitan did not know if she could make her mouth form all of the English words she would need. The *Ve'ho'e* would kill her before she could talk since this was their way.

Her eyes searched the room. El's white under-garments covered the floor. Every one of her favorite ivory and china statues--little children and small animals--had been thrown with force against the blue plaster wall. All were broken. Between piles of clothes and broken glass, El's blood marked the hardwood floor with dark purple spots. Proof of the hatred of all *Ve'ho'e*.

Tahcitan glanced one last time at El, and in the language of the *Tsitsistas*, she whispered, "I go now, my friend. Rest at the end of your journey. I will find the key."

If only she could take on the spirit of the eagle. With his wings, she could fly from this room. Instead, she ran down the staircase, her moccasins not touching any one step for long. At the bottom, she turned left, then spun right, away from the kitchen door, into the parlor.

El's room. The piano room. Where the key was hidden. Here, bookshelves laid flat on the floor. The books themselves were thrown to each of the four directions. In the morning light, ceramic and glass shards glistened where the sun caught their ragged edges. Tahcitan gasped at the savage way the white man had gouged through El's house.

From the kitchen, heavy men's boots echoed.

* * *

Sheriff Thomas Taylor figured since Frank Mitchell hadn't shot him yet, he probably wasn't going to. Maybe Frank had somehow seen fit to forgive him for the liberties he'd helped himself to way back then, and what was in the past might best stay there after all. And though his musings should have made him feel better, Thomas Taylor still couldn't shake the feeling of impending doom.

At the back door, he climbed the four wooden steps, leading the way into Ella Mitchell's kitchen. Instead of the neat and orderly room he was so familiar with, the place looked as if it had been pulled apart by angry wolves. His pace quickened and he called out, "Ella? Ella, you here?"

Ella didn't answer. Taylor's stomach churned, sending a vile taste to the back of his throat. Whatever happened here, it was clear Ella was in serious trouble. The house had the silence of a tomb, and the image did nothing to comfort him. He paused, motioning the others to be quiet.

Frank nodded, his face held in a rigid mask. Saul O'Greary stared at the floor, a blank and distant look on his face, though his eyes were focused on something. Taylor's eyes followed the red-haired boy's gaze to dark purple-brown drops marking a clear path toward the shadowed staircase.

Without a word, Taylor reached across his waist and drew the pistol from its holster. He glanced at Frank and raised his left hand signaling them to stay where they were. He spun away from them.

He let his pistol lead the way along the blood trail toward the staircase. At the first step, he heard the distinct shuffle-drag of Frank's bad leg. The men were following him. Damn it, he wished they'd do as he asked. He shot a quick glaring glance over his shoulder, but Frank ignored him. He didn't have time to turn them back, he needed to find Ella. Besides, if the intruder were still here, having her brother behind him might be a good thing. Quiet as he could, he went up the stairs with both men in tow. His heart twanged with the knowing that something bad was up the stairs and he couldn't help but feel pity for Frank.

At the top landing, Taylor held his gun so it rounded the corner of the hallway landing before he did. His ears strained to hear any sound, but only silence beckoned him forward. Behind him, the drag-clomp of Frank's heavy boots echoed in the narrow staircase. At the doorway, Sheriff Taylor stopped.

On the bed, Ella Mitchell lay on her back dressed in a ripped gown, still as stone. Her skin had the dull blue tinge of a dead body. Her chest did not rise and fall and her eyes stared at nothing. The blood-soaked bed sheets beneath her confirmed what he suspected but didn't want to admit.

* * *

Tahcitan felt her stomach become a knot against her ribs. She ran across the parlor to El's beloved piano.

Dark shadows filled the corner where the piano sat, and she threw herself into the space between it and the wall. Here, someone had tossed the quilt from El's bed. She found it strange, but her thoughts stayed on the piano. Even in the shadows, she could see the instrument was the only thing in the house untouched by whoever had done this. On the tray, papers with the small black marks still stood on the front, above the keys. A sigh escaped her lips before she could quiet herself. The evil *Ve'ho'e* had not touched the part of El that mattered most.

Tahcitan knew where El had hidden the key. In the front of the piano, near knee-level, and behind the wooden panel on the left. She had only to lift the lid, twist the tiny wooden rod and reach back into the darkness, and she would have it.

Boot heels clopped loudly across the kitchen floor. The sound echoed through her head, her heart, and into her soul. Blood pounded a drum beat through her temples.

She could tell they were trying to be quiet, but the rumble of their footsteps on the stairs shook the walls.

Trembling and afraid as a rabbit, she forced herself to sit down and be still. She breathed as the sleeping dog does. Slow and deep. She tried to hear where they stepped on the wooden floors. Above, the scuff of boots scraped across the landing.

She could get the key, and run out the back door. But the noise of her flipping the latch and then pulling the wooden piece out would tell the men she was near. Even above their loud walking noises, the men would hear the loud screech.

Outside, the stallion's hooves struck the hard ground as he pawed his impatience. He whinnied once before the men's horses answered.

At the sound of her horse, Tahcitan opened her mouth to call a soothing word to him.

* * *

Frisco whinnied and I ran to the barn door and opened the door. His name rose in my throat and my mouth opened to shout before I stopped myself and backed into the barn. I'd heard Frisco, all right. I'd know his nicker anywhere. His call tugged at me just as strongly as if the horse had been my own child crying to be fed. My chest ached at the sound of his whinny. My eyes burned with wanting to see him. And if I'd been certain I'd survive and not be gunned down, I would have been out the front door, where I *knew* he waited for me. It took every bit of will-power to stay put. I wanted to go to Frisco more than just about anything I'd wanted since this nightmare began.

Instead, I forced myself to stay still, but I was ready to bolt, listening to a palpable silence. But there was no more sound of the dreaded men, or of Frisco. Squinting, I put my eye to the crack between the door and the jamb, but could see only the back of the silent house. The same pull of emotion I'd felt earlier, and tried so hard to disregard, tugged harder, drawing me outside, toward where Frisco's gentle nicker had come from.

With my shoulder against the door, I leaned into it slowly, until it swung open. My feet shuffled in place and every nerve in my body twitched with anticipation. Tentatively, I took a step outside. I stopped, standing solid as a cement pillar.

The dense silence was even heavier out here. My throat closed around itself until my vision was clouded gray and I was convinced I'd simply die of suffocation. The cords in my neck creaked as if I had held the same position for so long they had locked in position. And still, I didn't move. I *couldn't* move.

A thump from somewhere near the front of the house broke whatever spell I was under. I sucked in a lungful of air, then spun around until my arms windmilled awkwardly and reeled myself back into the safety of the barn. I needed protection and wished I'd kept my pistol with me instead of in the holster clipped to Frisco's saddle. Yes, a gun would be good, a cannon, even better. Since neither of those choices were available, I hoped to find a pitchfork or a shovel. I ignored the voice in my head asking if I honestly thought some antique garden tool was a fair match to a man with a gun.

Within the barn, shadows clung to the interior barn walls. I wouldn't have been surprised if bats had swooped, screeching and diving for my head. Aside from a weapon, I needed light. Back at the doorway, I ran my palm over the rough wood hoping to find a light switch. My finger succeeded in snagging nothing more than a splinter.

Turning around, I peered through the shadowy interior of the barn. To my right, there was a stall with both the top and bottom doors shut. At the next stall, a gray horse intently watched me with the eyes of a curious ghost.

I jumped at the sight of the animal's huge eyes in the darkness, my heart knocking against my ribs. My fear of a horse only proved how abnormal my mind was at this moment. I took a deep breath and whispered, "Hey buddy, you know where someone may have stashed a gun?"

The horse stared at me placidly, but gave no indication of pointing out where any artillery might be found.

I opened the wooden latch of the first stall and entered. Since the barn was new, this stall was being used for something other than housing livestock. Deep shadows hunkered in the corners and climbed the walls, but I recognized this room by the smell: clean leather, horse sweat, and dust. Memories flooded through me of cold wintry days spent before a warm fire, soaping and oiling tack, while Holly half-heartedly complained about the leather straps and metal bits that were strewn about the furniture to dry. But there was no time for daydreaming.

Every tack room is equipped with certain things--bridles, saddles, brushes, hoof picks, clippers, combs. Some barns even have telephones, and though I seriously doubted this one did, Lacking any optimistic enthusiasm, I scoured the walls. My eyes dropped to the racks of saddles. Antiques all, no doubt about it. Each western saddle had a high rounded cantle and bulbous pommel beneath a tiny brass-colored horn. Although ancient, the saddles looked brand new. These must be the replacements from when the old barn burned. The bridles were just as antique and also brand new. Intricately carved wide leather straps made up the headstalls, while each bit showed the uneven over-lapping of metal proving they had been forged by hand. The joints where the shank met the mouthpieces had lumpy and rough appearances, rather than the flawlessly smooth metal of modern-day bits. Examining a carriage harness, I saw that it too, was new. There were no cracks in the leather, no dust hiding in tiny crevices of the tooled strap. Obviously the tack in this room was cleaned on a regular basis, as it should be.

New antique tack. No phone. Quickly, I scanned the shelves for anything modern. Clippers, medications, a nylon halter or surcingle, a red plastic-handled hoof pick, heck, a plastic *anything*. But there were no modern conveniences in this place.

A chilling thread of fear snaked tighter around my chest.

I couldn't be here, yet I was. An actor in some horrific Western from Hell. A sick movie script shown at three in the morning, on channel two. The little voice inside my head, the one that usually warned me of danger and questioned my integrity, asked, "*Where are the phones? Why did the men ride off on horseback? What day is it? Phones, trucks, planes--*"

I slammed my palms to my ears, recognizing the gesture as that of someone off-their-rocker, flat-out bonk-shit-crazy. I ran from the tack room into the center of the barn. The pile of hay was still heaped in the middle of the room and I wanted only to crawl under it. Instead I ran to the door. The Hell with all of this, I'd find Frisco and go home.

Home. Phones, trucks, and the internet.

I reached for the door and as blackness crowded my vision and my hearing went quiet, I was going to sit down, whether I wanted to or not. Rather than doing so gracefully, I slipped down, folding over myself and landed in a crumpled heap. With my shoulder against the wall, I rested my cheek against the cold, rough wood and breathed in the smell of fresh hewn logs.

* * *

Tahcitan clamped her mouth shut. She could not call to the stallion or the men upstairs might hear her. She stayed hidden in the shadows behind the piano.

The sun called to her and promised her safety. She wished to be outside and on the bay horse and away from this place.

She reached out to the piano. With her palm, she stroked the dark wood. Cold and flat, the instrument was as dead as El. As dead as everyone else she had ever loved.

She laid her hand on the quilt that someone had left behind the piano. Silently, she pushed herself up into a crouching run. She bolted across the room, turned left toward the kitchen. It was not out of habit that caused her to choose that exit. The brass hinges on the heavy front door groaned, and she did not want the door to speak of her leaving.

In the kitchen, the back door stood open just as she had left it and just as the men had left it. She ran out into the morning, blinking her eyes against the brightness.

She jumped down the four steps and raced around the house to where the stallion waited at the hitching post.

He nickered to her and she calmed him by laying her palm against his neck. With her other hand, she worked at the rope to untie him. She swung into the saddle in one motion and a moment later, she and the Thoroughbred were doing what the horse was bred to do.

Running.

~10

She looked as if she were simply napping. But he knew better. He'd seen enough dead to recognize the stillness, the silence.

"Oh Ella," he whispered.

A quick sweep of the small unhappy room and Taylor knew that no one besides Ella was there. He holstered his gun and rushed toward his friend. Beside the bed, his knees folded on their own accord until he kneeled on the floor next to her.

Ella's face was still as bread dough, and more or less, the same color. The blue tinge to her skin might simply be a reflection of the walls. "Ella," Taylor whispered. And though he already knew the answer, he couldn't help himself. He asked, "Ella? You all right?"

He needed to be one hundred percent sure. He had to put his ear to her chest and listen for a heartbeat, but he couldn't bear the thought of laying his head to her bloody dress. Instead, he took her arm and felt for a pulse. His hand was shaking so badly he wasn't aware of anything except for the chill in Ella's wrist. He laid his hand tenderly on her throat where he'd feel the life of her if there was any to be felt. Although his still shaking hand sensed a small amount of heat, the stillness of her vein told him she was dead.

He stifled a sob and pulled indifference over himself as though he were climbing into a suit of metal armor. He pulled away from his emotions, sent his mind to dwelling on which course of action to follow. Gradually, the body on the bed became no one he knew--it was just a corpse. At one time the corpse had been a person. Someone had killed that person. He must find the killer. These ritualistic commands to himself calmed him.

Pleased to have finally succeeded at shoving his emotions back and down, yet knowing he'd face the demons later, he set to work. First, he began his inventory of what must have happened.

It was clear that Ella had not walked up the stairs herself. She was too badly injured and no blood smeared the walls. No footprints smeared the floor indicating she'd dragged herself to the bed. Ella Mitchell had been carried upstairs after she'd been killed. The trail of tidy droplets declared the truth of what had happened.

His thoughts churned with questions. What makes a killer move the person he'd murdered? Why put her in bed? Who had done this? Why?

The killer had to have been a man, and a strong man at that. He had stabbed the woman many times with a long, sharp knife. The wounds were gaping holes that pooled dark blood.

Taylor made a mental note to himself to find the actual murder site. Again, the question of why the killer brought Ella to the bedroom pulled at his mind, and led to his pondering what other evil act the man might have performed. No, he didn't want to think about that.

But there was that group of men that came through these parts a few days ago. They'd attacked the Simm's girl, and though they didn't kill her, they had done things to her that she'd likely never recover from. And though he'd tracked them out of town until he lost their footprints at the river, he knew they could have come back here.

The shuffle-drag of Frank's leg betrayed his slow progress up the stairs, but he'd arrive soon enough.

Grimacing, Sheriff Thomas Taylor used his thumb and first finger to carefully lift the hem of Ella's bloody dress. Thankfully, her undergarments were intact. . Hopefully , the killer hadn't touched her in that way. As if it burned him, he dropped the dress and scrubbed his hands on his trousers. He tried to forget the image of her pale, bare legs.

He clenched his jaw, furious that he'd had to dishonor her by looking up her dress. His anger built until it was the "I'll-kill-whoever-did-this" kind of fury. He wanted to smash the murderer's head and make him suffer the way Ella had.

Although his wrath comforted him, he knew that until he smothered his rage, he couldn't think straight. He stepped back and took a shallow breath. He had to be calm, and think, not react as a madman.. He swallowed and sucked in the air in huge gulps, telling himself to settle down. Finally, his mind began working again.

Ella must have either let the killer into the house, or he had broken in. Although it had been early, she was already up and dressed. It was possible that Ella had been expecting someone, and that meant she knew her killer. If that were true and he then stabbed her to death, maybe shame had caught up with him and in his remorse he'd tried to comfort her in death by putting her to bed.

Didn't seem probable.

A scraping sound on the floor of the landing told Taylor they were close. He needed to think quicker, figure it out, stop Frank from seeing his sister lying on the bed, dead.

Then, Taylor knew. Tahcitan's horse, the Thoroughbred stallion Ella had given her, had been tied to the hitching post out front when Frank, Saul and he had reached the knoll just after sunrise. Yet he'd seen no sign of the Indian woman. She must have found Ella where she'd been murdered and had carried her into her room. She could do it, she was plenty strong enough. He wondered if perhaps Ella had still been alive. He peered closer at the body, searching for signs that Tahcitan had treated her friend's wounds but there was no indication of any such thing having happened.

Tahcitan. He needed to talk to her, to see what she knew.

His heart raced at the thought. Every time he'd tried to talk to her before, she had run, clearly terrified of him. First, he had to find her, and then he'd worry about getting her to talk to him.

His gaze drifted over the room. The place was a shambles. All of the drawers had been emptied, their contents of female undergarments strewn about the floor. The killer must have been searching for items of value and Ella had died for it. But a garnet ring still adorned Ella's lifeless hand. On the floor near the cherry-wood vanity, a silver-handled comb and brush set. If a burglar was to blame, he'd sure done a sorry job of relieving Ella Mitchell of her valuables.

Someone had searched the house looking for something precious enough to take a life over. Finding out what that item was might lead to the killer.

Maybe Tahcitan knew something. Maybe she could talk to him just this once.

Frank's foot dragging across the hardwood floor announced his arrival.

Taylor knew Frank had already seen Ella, he'd taken too long with his thoughts and ponderings.

He took his time to stand, his sadness weighing him down as if someone were holding his head under water. The words were chunks of glass in his throat, Taylor choked, "Frank, I regret to tell you that your sister is dead. I'm sorry."

Frank limped across the room, the boot of his bad leg dragging through his sister's drying blood, and smearing red-purple smudges across the floor. His face collapsed into the anguished semblance of someone in extreme agony. His teeth bared into a feral grin and his fists clenched in anger. "Ella!" He wailed, "Ella!"

From the doorway, Saul O'Greary bounded toward Frank like the proverbial faithful hound. "Frank, Frank, ye be all right, man." he called, his words ringing out in the lilting melody of an Irish dirge.

Taylor asked, "Frank? You all right?"

The man resembled a drunk trying to find words--his face contorted in an exaggerated way and shifted fast enough that each emotion lasted no more than a fraction of a second. Ever so slowly, as though donning yet another disguise, Frank's features rearranged themselves into one of bereavement. Frank could have been a stage actor, he demonstrated all of the appropriate emotions that a grieving brother might display and yet, they all looked *wrong*. Perhaps his reactions were simply the result of finding his sister dead after all these years of being apart. But in the back of his mind, the sheriff portion of

Taylor made note that although the man had reacted with the words and actions of being shocked by finding his sister murdered, somehow it seemed as though he'd carefully planned and rehearsed the entire scene. Taylor made note to himself to ponder this question later and said, "Why don't you go downstairs, Frank? Get some air. I'll be right along."

Frank shook his head from side to side, then shuffled backwards to lean against the wall, but he didn't leave. Saul, of course, stuck to his companion just as a pup waiting to be petted would.

Taylor turned back toward the body of his dead friend. He'd had supper with Ella just two nights before and following their meal, she had played sweet melodies on the piano. He had happily sung along, mindless of the fact that he couldn't carry a tune. Ella, bless her heart, played long into the night, smiling and nodding and even joining him in song more than once--perhaps in an effort to help drown out the bad notes Taylor bellowed. Of course when he asked her, she'd laughed and told him she just loved that he'd attempt to sing at all.

And now she was dead. It didn't seem real.

He stole a sideways glance at Frank Mitchell and Saul. Each leaned against the wall beside the doorway, their stances now relaxed. They were silent, their faces blank. Taylor was anything but calm and couldn't help noticing that their relaxed poses, though convincing, looked forced and he wondered what they were hiding.

Tension sang through every nerve of his body and underlying that was urgency. If he didn't solve this murder soon, things would only get worse, though he couldn't have said why or how that might happen.

Ella had been stabbed to death and he needed to find the killer before anyone else became a victim. As a rule, solving any kind of crime was an added benefit to being Sheriff. He found the work satisfying, the working of a puzzle until he found the answer in the whites of a guilty man's eyes. But this murder-puzzle was not fun. Taylor wished Frank Mitchell and Saul O'Greary were somewhere else, anywhere else. He found it bothersome to have relatives around a corpse. In particular, when the body was Ella and the relative was

Frank.

A trickle of nervous sweat slid down his neck to his spine. He needed to concentrate on the details of his job, which was exactly how he needed to view this. It was a job. Work.

His feelings were a matted mess: Anger at the killer, guilt for not keeping Ella safe, remorse over his own loss and pity for just about everyone from himself and Ella to Tahcitan and even Frank.

Frank hadn't seen his younger sister in twelve years and the exact day he arrives, Ella is murdered. The loss had to be devastating. Yet Frank stood leaning against the doorframe, a passive nonchalant look on his face. There was no sign of any inner turmoil or grief. No sign of anything the man might be feeling.

Taylor tried to mimic Frank's relaxed attitude, but he couldn't stop his mind from dwelling on his friend's death. His eyes kept returning to Ella's still body. In response, his pulse raced and his stomach writhed beneath his ribs. His nose filled with the iron smell of Ella's blood, and he opened his mouth to breathe, only that was worse, because now, he tasted the coppery odor. He had to get a hold of himself and control his emotions. Ella had practically been a sister to him, and her death struck sorrow and loss to the very center of his being. He looked again at her blood-drenched body, and his stomach clutched at itself.

The trickle of sweat became a river, and annoyed, he swatted at his neck. Hot bile stung the back of his throat and he swallowed hard, willing himself to have control. He wished Frank and Saul would leave before they noticed his condition.

He ran toward the door, his hand clamped over his mouth. Just as he was beside them, he lost all control and vomited, bitter liquid spewing to the hardwood floor. Collapsing to his knees, he hung his head and sucked in great gulps of the foul smelling air.

"Come on, Saul," Frank growled, pulling his companion by the arm. Their footsteps echoed on the narrow staircase as they made their way toward the front room.

Grateful to be alone, though embarrassed over his loss of dignity, Taylor struggled to his feet. He forced himself to swallow over and over, trying to get rid of the sharp acrid taste in his mouth. He leaned against the wall and waited for his mind to slip into the cold, analytical, detached area reserved for times such as this--times when he hated his job.

Finally he stood, trembling, and walked back to Ella's still form. His chest closed on itself. He laid his hand over Ella's cold fingers. "Good-bye dear friend," he choked. "I'll find whoever did this."

He took two pennies from his pocket. With his thumb, he kindly closed her eyelids and placed one coin over each eye. He pulled a sheet over her face, then turned away from her, his shield of protection having completely failed him.

* * *

The sheriff's boots scraped on the wooden stairs.

Frank stuffed an unopened box under a chair. "Put that down," he whispered. "He's coming. Get over here."

Saul's eyes widened. He dropped the papers he held, and rushed to where Frank stood. His arms were crossed loosely over his chest even before the pages across the room fluttered to the floor.

~11

Sheriff Thomas Taylor made his way down the stairs, still struggling to accept the truth that Ella Mitchell was dead.

He approached the man he'd known when they were boys together. He clapped his shoulder, hoping for the right words. Taylor cleared his throat. "We'll find who did this," he announced. His voice was low and thick, and his words had to swim around the huge lump in his throat, but he continued, "Must be hard for you, Frank. Twelve years is a long time." He paused, not knowing what else he could say, then, "Ella would've been happy to find you're alive. We, we all figured you were dead, you know, the war and all."

Frank Mitchell smiled thinly and nodded. He brushed his black hair from his face in a boyish manner that contrasted with the solid demeanor of the successful lawyer and Officer of the Army that he was. He stepped to the window and peered out. His back stiffened, then stood taller. "The killer!" He shouted, reaching for his gun. "It's a goddamned Indian."

His heart jumped into a gallop and Taylor reached across his belt buckle and pulled his own pistol from its holster. If the killer were within sight, he'd catch him. He shoved Saul away from the window and followed Frank's gaze.

Tahcitan.

On the bay, running full-out. The Indian woman and the stallion raced across the open grassland. The horse's hooves churned the ground in a blur, and Tahcitan leaned forward until she blended perfectly with the powerful stallion.

Taylor forgot the horror of Ella Mitchell's death for a moment, forgot the pain of losing such a good friend, and watched the pair glide across the prairie. He smiled sadly at the beauty of rider and horse, their black manes fanning out behind them in an invisible wind. He knew, without a doubt, that Tahcitan was not the killer. He also knew that convincing Frank of that would surely prove to be nothing short of a monumental challenge.

Frank's face loomed before his, "You going after him? It's the killer, don't just stand there."

How could he hope to persuade a former Confederate officer that Tahcitan, a half-breed Cheyenne woman was not the killer? He sighed. "Frank, that's Tahcitan, she is, uh, she *was* Ella's closest friend."

Frank planted his hands on his narrow hips and stood with his feet about a boot's length apart. Faint lines around his ice-cold eyes blazed white against his weathered skin. Waves of palpable hatred poured from his red-blotched face. "That's who killed Ella and now you need to kill that Injun warrior!"

Taylor smoothed his mustache. "Frank, calm down. I know how upset you must be, but that's no Indian warrior, it's a woman. Tahcitan. Ella's best friend and hired help. She takes care of the horses."

Frank's teeth ground together and his brow furrowed.

Taylor said, "Your sister loved her. Saved her life after the Sand Creek Massacre. Tahcitan is a kind person. Even the horses sense it. She quiets the wildest with no more than a touch. She'd never harm Ella, or anyone else for that matter."

Frank held his gun pointed toward the floor, but his finger glided smoothly to the trigger, floated over the curved metal, and rested there. "That Injun is a murderer," he shouted, raising the gun and waving it about. "And look at this house. Bitch robbed us blind, and you're standing there telling me she's innocent?"

"Easy Frank." Taylor looked around the room, remembering how fussy Ella had been about her home. His gaze went back to Frank. "I didn't see any other bodies upstairs, did you?"

The question unmistakably threw Frank off balance. He glared at Taylor and sputtered, "The hell you talking about?"

Taylor answered in a calm voice, "We ought to check around for other bodies."

"Why?"

"Because, Frank," Taylor said. "Tahcitan was here. We saw her horse tied out front. If she arrived in time to see the killer, I will guarantee you that we'll find the evidence."

"That heathen-whore IS the killer," Frank yelled. He aimed his gun to the rider in the distance, then spun to face Saul. "Let's go," he ordered.

Taylor stepped in front of Frank, and stared directly and deeply into his eyes. He kept his voice low and steady. "Tahcitan did not kill your sister. I will bet my life on it. So if you want to go after her, shoot me first, right here, right now."

Frank aimed his gun at Taylor's chest. He glared at the sheriff, his nostrils flared. He did not speak. Saul silently leaned away and studied the ceiling and then the floor.

Taylor recalled his reaction at the first sight of Frank. So here it is at last, he thought. "Go ahead, man, shoot me."

The gun wavered.

Taylor felt the muscles of his jaw relax, and said a silent thanks to God. Aloud, he said, "Frank, let's go find the real killer." He walked toward the unsteady gun, and past Frank's shoulder. He led the way through Ella's house, surveying the damage as he went. Tables were overturned, papers were thrown everywhere, and pictures had been ripped from their frames. He checked once to be sure Frank had holstered his gun, which he had.

Back in the parlor, Taylor paused before the piano. Everything else in the house had been rummaged through, then tossed into piles on the floor. Even kitchen items. Yet the piano hadn't so much as a smudged spot on its shiny finish. Even the music sheets stood neatly stacked where Ella had left them.

Taylor thought back to where the instrument had come from-- Kentucky, and Mrs. Irma Mitchell. Because it had been her mother's, it was Ella's favorite possession.

He lifted the lid that covered the ivory and black keys. A low groan escaped the wood at being disturbed, but there was nothing to raise any suspicion in Taylor's mind. He grasped the sheet music from the small holding tray above the keys and rifled through them. Nothing strange about the pages of music either. He put the papers back and walked around the room, examining every corner and paused to wonder aloud at the crumpled quilt behind the piano before continuing his search. He didn't offer any explanation to the men in the room, he just looked and probed. He finally grunted, "Tahcitan must have gotten here too late. No body."

Frank's face darkened. He crumpled the sheaf of papers he held. He scowled, his mouth turning down at the corners. "That filthy animal killed Ella! Now, Sheriff, are you going to go after her or shall I ride into that piss-poor town of yours and round up my own posse?"

Taylor's said nothing. Ella was dead, and the only woman he'd ever felt anything for was being called a filthy animal and a murderer. He fought the desire to ball his fist and smash it into Frank's face. He fingered the trigger of his gun. He wouldn't actually shoot Frank for angering him, but the motion settled his taut nerves. "Calm down, Frank. I don't think you realize how things work out here. You think you can round up a posse? Try. Your sister was, shall we say, not a well-liked woman. She was too independent, too all-fired sure of herself, too rich and too successful. She was a better rancher than any man in these parts."

He paused, surprised at the amount and the speed at which the words spilled from his mouth. He rarely spoke this much, but then, he'd rarely been so provoked. When and if a posse was formed, it was the sheriff's job to declare so. The mere thought of anyone overstepping onto his territory brought his blood to a boil. Add to that the detail that Frank was attacking Tahcitan, and Taylor couldn't keep his reserve from slipping.

He ground his molars until his jaw ached. "The other thing Ella was friend to an Indian and that didn't help her popularity any either. Actually, when you think about it, the only thing she had going for her was that she didn't raise sheep. So fine, you want a posse, go ahead and round one up. I'm sure the men in these parts will be more than happy to leave their families to go in search of a woman they can shoot in the back."

Frank straightened his shoulders, squaring them and pushing out his chest. He said, "They'll damn sure help me find a murdering savage, which is more than I can say for you."

Beneath Taylor's finger, the trigger of his pistol felt hot. His finger trembled but he didn't fire. Instead, his eyes locked onto Frank's while he deliberately shoved the gun into its holster.

The expression on Frank's face did nothing to hide the truth that he hated the Sheriff. Taylor wondered why Frank hadn't killed him yet. After all, their dispute went back many years. Back to Kentucky.

Taylor had been in the wrong, that much was true. He'd taken up with the woman Frank had been courting while Frank traipsed across the country for the Confederate Army. Taylor wanted to marry her and would have done so, if she hadn't died of a fever. Since Frank had obviously not perished in the war and had indeed returned home, he must have known about Sara and him from the gossiping biddies in town. Yes, Frank had plenty to be angry about.

Frank's face shaded pink to purple, before he spun on his heel and with Saul in tow, stomped through the parlor and down the short hallway to the kitchen. At the landing on the back porch, he spat. In a booming voice, he said, "Come on Saul, let's go do the lawman's job. We'll find that lice-infested squaw ourselves."

* * *

I sat with my back leaning against the rough wood of the barn door and hated myself for not being able to do anything. I was not a weak or fearful person. I was used to standing up to and for myself. But here, wherever here was, here, things were different. *I* was different. I held my breath and peered through the space where two boards met. I didn't move, just stared at the rear of the strange house where things seemed familiar, though I'd never been here. I silently told myself to get over acting the weak victim. I needed to save Holly, and prayed she wasn't already dead. I needed a plan. I took a deep breath and replayed in my mind's eye what had just happened so that I could understand what was going on.

The Indian man had come running out of the house, only it hadn't been a man at all. The Indian was a woman dressed in buckskins. Her hair, shiny and black, flew around her shoulders like a flock of ravens. She had jumped from the stoop without using the stairs and in her eyes, terror, drove her.

I trembled just thinking about her and my body felt *loose*, as though every bone had turned to liquid. I had to go into the house and save Holly and then somehow get us both home. I had to face the men. But the thought of doing so sent my nerves into frenzied twitches, and I knew I'd never go into the house while the killers were inside. They'd kill me too. I knew the truth of it in the same way I knew the sun rose each morning. I was in trouble.

My mind chanted one word, "Men, men, men," and with the word came images I didn't understand. Men chasing me, running with their mouths gaping open and their eyes alternately wide with rage, then veiled in lust. I was very aware that going crazy isn't any fun at all, it's sheer horror.

Although the memory was clear and felt real, it wasn't *mine*. No such thing had ever happened to me, and although I'd never been entirely comfortable around men, I wasn't terrified of them either.

I blinked hard, trying to make sense of what was happening to me. Outside, a gentle breeze waved the heads of the tall, brown grass between where I sat and the house. A bird screeched in the distance.

Behind me, in the dark of the barn, a voice said, *"Ve'ho'e!"*

My head snapped left, then right, but I couldn't see anyone, couldn't feel anyone's presence other than the grey horse in the stall. I pulled my heels back toward the wall where I leaned, and sat in a crouch, ready to jump up and run. My head pounded so loud I couldn't hear much else, until finally the distant twitter of the damn bird came to me. A happy and distorted song.

From nowhere, anger flashed lightning-fast through me. I didn't know where I was or what was going on, but worse, I didn't know if Holly was all right and hiding in a barn terrified of imaginary things and hearing voices was simply unacceptable. Standing, I said aloud, "I am sick and tired of being afraid."

Boldly, as though I had my pistol loaded and aimed, I raised the wooden latch and poked my head around the door.

There was no sign of the men, no sound from their horses. Maybe they'd left, gone out the front. I moved forward.

A man's deep baritone words stopped me. "...Kill...squaw..."

It was a real voice, connected to a real man. I quickly pulled the door shut then let the wooden latch settle into its nest, hoping they hadn't heard anything.

The men were going to kill the Indian woman and she was innocent. And beneath the desire to save the woman was another emotion that I didn't have time to dwell upon. Something about the Indian and the memories of fear tugged at my mind. Something I needed to know, but didn't.

"Stop it!" I whispered.

The men I was watching were the killers and if I could only find a cop, a sheriff, someone with some power to help, I could tell them. I needed to *do* something and I needed to do it now, before the Indian woman was... What?

Reality warped again, doing a slow belly-roll until up was sideways and down pointed north. I still couldn't help feeling they were coming after *me* and if I was right, I had to stay out of sight and out of their way. The only way to help the Indian was to find help.

Why was I so scared? I had always taken care of myself in any situation and done just fine. So what if I was somewhere I didn't know and killers were after some Indian woman I didn't know? Holly was in that house and I needed to go to her. And if she were dead, I needed to see that for myself. I stomped a small circle, kicking hay and clenching my fists at my sides until I couldn't stand not watching the house another minute. I returned to my post near the door and once again I squinted through the space between the boards. The two killers--the one with curly red hair and the other in a black duster--the same coat as in my visions--trudged down the back steps and rounded the corner of the house.

He has the same limp as Steve...

I held my breath, afraid of the men hearing either the voices in my head or my rapid, shallow breathing.

That made two of the men accounted for, but where was the third? As if in answer, hoof-beats thrummed the still morning air. Horses running, and then the sound receded. They were leaving. At least two of them were. And the third man, was he still in the house, or had he gone too? I tried to count the fall of hoof beats, to tell if there were two or three horses running. I couldn't tell, and finally, the sound faded until I couldn't hear them anymore.

Again, I held my breath and listened until only the silence of the morning and my own pulse boomed in my ears. Except for the occasional twittering bird and the metronomic *whoosh-thub* of my own blood rushing through my temples, it was quiet.

In the stillness, a realization came over me that I didn't want to face, but that I couldn't deny either.

Holly was dead.

How I knew this, I couldn't say. But I was certain that I only had to go into the house to see the truth of it.

~12

The *Ve'ho'e*, the white men, followed her. She worried they might see her soon. She knew they would kill her since it is their way.

Tahcitan asked *Ma'heo'o*, God, for the wings and the speed of the Eagle. She prayed the legs of the *mo'ehno'ha*, the horse, could soar as the wings of a bird. He heard her wish and she flew across the prairie. Afraid, she clung to the horse as if holding on for her life.

Already, one hour had passed since she had left El. And still, she rode hard across Mitchell land. Low hills in each of the four directions, and one bluff overlooking the farm. The land reached forever to the sky, rolling in waving grass the color of a yellow haired white man. The *Ve'ho'e* believed they owned all the directions now and the strange barriers they put across the land scarred it in a vicious way. She did not think she could ever know how land could belong to a man. She did not like the need to watch for the sharp wire that cut a horse's legs in the way of the mountain lion claws.

The stallion slowed to a trot and his breath came in hard bursts and made her afraid for him. She looked to the four points. No men. She slowed the *hemotséhno'ha*, the stallion, to a walk so that he could breathe with ease.

The sun was high in the sky and should have warmed her, but did not. Her body was cold as a stream after the winter and she wondered if perhaps the *Ve'ho'e* owned the sun along with the land. Neither the heat of the horse's body, nor the golden sun could penetrate her freezing muscles. Her teeth chattered and her skin pebbled in gooseflesh.

She had run away from the men not caring which course she followed. The stallion, however, had headed straight for home. She turned him south, the opposite way of her sod house. The men knew to look for her there. The bay did not want to follow that path and told her so by tossing his head. But then he did as she wished.

Tahcitan did not question if the *Ve'ho'e* would kill her. She knew their way was to place blame on others. She could not let them catch her. They would not hurt her ever again.

Except for the bay, she was alone once more. An aching hole opened in her chest. Her heart hurt with the loneliness. She tried to think of the good things El could see and do once she reached the end of her journey up The Hanging Road. The afterworld was a place much better than this world, full of happiness.

She recalled how she had not agreed with El about the horses last night. It was not a bad thing, she and El often did not see the same answers when it came to the horses. She remembered how she worried for El because of all the recent bad happenings. The barn burning down, the cattle acting unsettled, and El's feeling someone had been watching her. She wished she had not listened when El had sent her away. She remembered her friend's words, "I'll be fine Tat, no need to worry. Now take your crazy horse and go home. Nothing will happen to me."

She remembered El's wringing hands and darting eyes. El had been afraid, and she had said, "I see your fear."

El had laughed, "I'm not afraid, now go."

Only later, when the night was the darkest, and sleep left her fast as a cat darting up a tree, had she packed her bedroll and bear skin. She went to the stallion and saddled him. She had gone back to her friend, but the ride was long and she had not hurried enough. Because of this, she had gotten to El's house too late.

Now, her only human friend was dead, and the *Ve'ho'e* blamed her. She rolled her hand into a fist and slammed it into the bone over her heart. To be weak carried no honor, yet she *was* weak. She never stood up for her beliefs. Instead, she ran. She was running now.

Recognizing her own lack of courage, she made up her mind to change. She would go after the white men. She would find the one who killed El and take his life.

Her resolve was powerful and strong, and lasted for the time it took her heart to beat twice. Then, she accepted the desire to kill the White man was poison for her soul. She knew the poison might eat away at her just as maggots eat a carcass. If she killed for revenge, it meant she was the same as the *Ve'ho'e*. To become as the white man, would be worse than all the losses she knew.

She recalled her father, *Vo'kaa'e Ohvo'komaeste*, White Antelope, speaking of the need for peace with the *Ve'ho'e* as he stood in front of his lodge at Sand Creek. His arms folded across his chest and he stood tall and proud. His eyes held the longing of an eagle's hunger. He had chanted his death prayer: "Nothing lives long. Only the earth and the mountains." His voice echoed across the land, deep and sure, until the bullets of the *Ve'ho'e* cut him to the ground.

The death chant had been a good one. Her father had lived over seventy passing's of the four seasons. He had lived a long life, a full life. And El? How much had she lived in her twenty-four years? Or herself--what had she known in twenty-two years besides pain and loneliness? Even now, she faced only more pain, more loneliness, and more loss. Again, she thumped her fist into her chest, over her heart. She gazed up, toward the heavens.

Heammawihio, Wise One Above, show me the way.

Warmth spread through her limbs, and she knew the Great Spirit had heard her. She would begin now to change from her rabbit-timid ways by becoming the Wolf--strong and sure. No more could she stagger in self-pity.

She made a list of what she had: her small medicine bag, good for all but the most serious injuries or illnesses. Her winter buckskins and the bearskin she had tied to the saddle behind her, and she carried some jerky, corn bread, and dried fruit. The bladder was full of fresh water and she had the knife tied to her ankle.

Most important, she had the horse and for this, her heart felt light. He was her partner, her friend. They trusted each other and this would keep them together and safe.

After the death of her people, she had promised herself not to ever love again. But then, El had saved her life, and the bay stallion had needed her help.

That day in Denver, at the rail yard, the white men had pulled on the bay stallion's head to make him walk down a plank to get off of a boxcar. But their tugging did not allow the horse to look where his feet might step, and he had been frightened. He reared and struck at the air, shrieking in a voice matching the scream of the hawk. His eyes showed white and his nostrils flared red. Afraid, he fought their ropes and kicked at their whips. The *Ve'ho'e* responded in anger, and whipped the horse harder. Welts, the width of a finger crossed the stallion's hindquarters. Frothy sweat clung to his wet hide and dripped between his legs. Still the men beat him, and still, the horse fought.

Each time the whip lashed, she felt the hot sting. She did not think about what she was doing, but ran forward, not afraid of the men, not afraid of their whips. She tore the rope from the man nearest her and loosened the tension on the line so it sagged. El shouted for everyone to step aside, then nodded at her.

To help the stallion, Tahcitan first had to gain his trust. She knew the only way to do this was to open her heart, let him see inside to where her own pain hid. She stood before him, her shoulder turned toward his nose, her eyes aimed to the ground. In her mind, she sent him images of her own suffering, and waited.

Behind her, the big horse snorted, then snaked his head. His ears flattened against his head in rage. She faced him, her eyes on his, and not speaking words, told him he was safe and if needed to kill her, he could. Because of this, he could understand her heart was true and honest.

Above her, the tall horse raised his head high and blew the sound of alarm, a one-note tone echoed with the force of the Iron Horse. She stood very still, then once more, turned her back to him. She took a step, and felt the rope tighten. She straightened her arm to remove the tension, but did not look back at him.

The stallion stomped his front foot and She sent the horse a silent message telling him, "Good."

He trembled and lowered his nose to the wooden plank. Each time she took a step so did the horse, until they were on solid ground. Finally, she turned and faced him, laying her palm against his quivering muscles. In the language of the *Tsitsistas,* she whispered, "Thank you. Your trust is a gift I honor. You are very brave."

The men came to take the rope, and the stallion reared and screamed. Once more, she calmed him in the words of The People, then walked beside him to El.

El smiled, her eyes dancing. "Tat, the horse is quite wild, and it's clear he doesn't care for men. We'll use him for breeding the mares, but he is to be your responsibility."

A gladness the same as the morning sun warmed her, and she nodded. She could have the stallion as part of her and take him into her heart. And though she felt afraid, she knew she could love him. She already did love him.

The warmth of the day paled, drifted toward winter, toward now, and she let the memory of the horse's arrival from the place called Kentucky fade to the past. She reached down and laid her palm on his brown neck, in hopes that the motion of doing so might calm her. Tears burned her eyes and her throat tightened.

For now, she had the stallion.

* * *

In Ella's parlor, Sheriff Thomas Taylor leaned against the piano, staring out the window. Idly, he lifted his hat and shoved a few stray blond hairs under the rim, then settled it back atop his head.

At the window, he watched Frank and Saul O'Greary gallop their horses away, and head toward the road. When they were no longer in sight, Taylor could still hear the pounding of their hooves, a steady pulse drummed within his head. In time with the hoof beats, anger and worry intertwined and writhed through his brain. His fingers touched his temples and rubbed small circles in an effort to find relief.

Truth was, Frank would have no problem rounding up enough men to hunt Tahcitan to kill her, and Taylor regretted taunting him to try.

He went out the heavy oak door, slamming it behind him. Mounted, he pushed his buckskin gelding into a gallop and caught up to Frank and Saul at the spot in the road where it seemed there could be no other humans on the plains. Ella's house was out of sight behind them and town was still too far ahead to catch a glimpse of even the blacksmith's smoke. The two men walked as though on a leisurely stroll on a Sunday, and Taylor slowed his horse's pace to match theirs. "Thought I'd ride into town with you," he offered.

Frank stared ahead. Saul examined the dirt under his thumbnail. Neither spoke.

Taylor said, "We ought to get Doc Perry and his wagon out to fetch Ella's body. Take care of her."

Frank spun around in his saddle, throwing his horse a step off balance. His face contorted and bunched before turning red. "Are you going to help us find the filthy half-breed?"

Taylor nearly gave in to the urge to knock him off of his horse. Checking his temper, he said, "Just thought it'd be a good idea to make some arrangements for your sister."

"The hell you say," he shouted. "My sister is dead. Her killer is off running somewhere across the prairie. What exactly seems to be the problem, Sheriff?"

There had to be a way to change Frank's mind, but whatever the answer might be, it sure wasn't clear. "What can I say to convince you that someone else killed Ella? Ella and Tahcitan were best friends and they cared for each other deeply. She did not kill your sister, but there are plenty of other people who might have wanted to harm her."

"What other people?" Frank hauled on the reins, spinning his gray mare around to a lurching halt. "Are you saying you know who did this? Speak up, man!"

Truth was, he had no idea who might have killed Ella. If someone had asked him yesterday if he thought Ella Mitchell might ever be murdered, he would have laughed aloud. Yet, the impossible had happened, and Tahcitan was being blamed. And the fact remained that plenty of men around these parts would be more than happy to kill an Indian. Those same men could have killed Ella for being an Indian-lover. Telling Frank this would only encourage his desire to kill her.

He said, "Your sister was one of the most outspoken, hard-headed women I've ever known and some men, uh, most men even, did not appreciate her quick mind and sharp tongue. Any one of them could have decided a single woman who had money, land, and half a brain was just too much to handle."

Frank grunted, but didn't say anything, so Taylor continued. "Add to everything, the truth remains that Ella was a capable shot. She was independent enough to live alone and, well, any number of people felt threatened by her. You know Ella, she was a forceful woman and her ways didn't sit right all the time with folks."

Frank's eyes all but disappeared into his scowling face. "Do you know who killed her? Or are you just trying to save the heathen you care so much about?"

Taylor shook his head. There had to be a reasonable explanation for Ella's murder. Something he hadn't thought of that would lead to the killer.

He led the way to a trail following the creek away from the Mitchell house--a short cut, and it would shave twenty minutes off the trip. He studied the thin layers of ice frozen to the banks of the small stream. Another couple of weeks and the running water would be nothing more than ice. He pointed toward the canal. "What you aren't aware of is water--or rather the lack thereof. Water is scarce and is a precious thing around these parts. Your sister owns...uh, owned a great deal of land, and it has a lot of water running through it. Some people aren't so lucky. They don't have enough to keep their wells going all year and they think it's unfair."

Frank tipped his head in interest. "Now you think someone killed my baby sister for water?"

"It's possible. Point is, we don't know who to blame."

Frank grunted, his interest of a moment before, apparently gone.

At a fork in the creek, Taylor led the way up a cow-trail that angled away from the water. They topped a small rise, and then followed the narrow path through tall, dry grass. Below them, a man on a palomino horse whistled a happy tune.

Taylor recognized Jed, the man in charge of the cattle side of the Mitchell Ranch. He turned to the man riding beside him. "That's Jed. Ella put him in charge of the cattle. Your sister thought kindly of him, and respected his cow-sense. He's usually near the house in the early morning, maybe he knows something."

Even at this distance, Taylor couldn't help but notice how much the man and his horse resembled one another.

Up close, the resemblance was even more pronounced. Jed and his mount had much the same build, both were short and stocky. The horse was a palomino, a creamy-yellow color that perfectly matched Jed's white-blond hair and pale skin. Both the horse and Jed had deep brown eyes, the exact shade of black coffee. But while the horse's expression was one of intelligence, his rider's was just shy of vacant.

Taylor introduced Jed to his companions.

Frank dismissed Jed's "Nice to meetcha," with a quick nod. He leaned toward Jed, and all but spit his words into the cowboy's face. "Do you have any idea who could have done this? Have you seen anyone around giving my sister trouble?"

Jed carefully side-passed the palomino two steps away from Frank. He pointed his forefinger to the sky and shoved at the brim of his sweat-stained tan hat. He sucked on his teeth, then asked, "Your sister? Uh, who done what, sir?"

The skin around Frank's ears glowed ember-red. His jaw twitched, and he swallowed two times. "My dear sister, Miss Ella Mitchell, has been murdered. I am asking you to try and remember any information you think might be of help to us in finding her killer. I will, therefore, repeat the question. Do you know of anyone who would want to harm my sister?"

Jed stroked mustache hairs that were the same shade of blond as the palomino's mane. He pulled the brim of his hat down, looked up and over his left shoulder. He cleared his throat, spat a wad of saliva. The gooey mass landed somewhere in the vicinity of the creek.

Finally, he drawled, "Well, sir, I, uh, last night, I, uh, I stopped by house to tell Miss Ella about the cattle in the lower meadow. You know the one where Miner's Creek splits? Well, anyway, the cows, they been a wanderin' further and further away. I'm guessin' they're just lookin fer more grass, but yesterday, when I counted 'em, they was four short. They don't usually go too far so I'm thinkin' maybe somebody's been a stealin' 'em. They generally stay near the creek. I just can't figger on where them four cows got off to. That's what I'm doin' now, just tryin' to find 'em and bring 'em on back home where they belong." He looked down at his horse's neck and began plucking at the animal's yellow-white mane.

Taylor asked, "Jed, did you see anyone around the house this morning? Any strangers?"

"Oh," Jed grinned a lopsided smile showing more gaps than teeth. "I git off the trail now and again, don't I Sheriff? I just can't figger about them cows. Ain't like 'em to go wanderin' off like 'at."

"Jed?" Taylor prodded.

Jed snapped his chin up and looked at the three men. "Yeah," he said. "I did see somebody at the house, Sheriff, but it weren't no-one but the Injun lady, Tat. She and the Missus was havin' a argument. Yellin' and a squawkin' at each other loud as two hens."

Frank slapped his thigh, and his horse jumped ahead a step. He hauled on the reins, bringing the gray's chin to its chest. "That's it, I tell you! I'm going after the half-breed animal myself, Sheriff. You do as you please, and I'll ride into town and gather some men. Ought to be out of there by two this afternoon."

Jed pushed his tan hat up high on his forehead. "Sir?" He said, "I don't mean Tat *kilt* Miss Ella. They was just havin' a argument is all. They argue all the time. About them fancy horses, mostly, but sometimes about the barn and where the mares should be birthin' their young. But Tat, she wouldn't hurt no-one. She's too scairt."

Frank scowled. "What do you mean, too scared?"

Jed swallowed hard, his Adam's-apple bobbing up and down. "Uh..."

Taylor stood in one stirrup and leaned sideways on his horse, so he was closer to Jed. "Jed, you did fine. Now, you'd better go find out about those cows you're missing, but if you remember anything else, you come and find me, okay?"

Jed grinned and nodded, "Yes sir!" He turned the palomino back toward the creek.

* * *

Did the men have Frisco? I strained to hear any sound of my horse. There was no whinny or nicker, from the stallion. The silence was so complete, it was heavy, weighted. Especially after the last of the three men galloped away.

The light in the barn changed--it had started dull and shadowy pewter and brightened to bright and shiny silver. Outside, the day was nothing short of pure platinum--bright and iridescent, with an eerie quality and made the barn feel grand and majestic.

I stood an extra two inches taller, sure God, Himself, would appear any moment.

Of course, He didn't show Himself.

Another forever- minute passed, and the world took on a more mundane appearance. The light sank back into the same blandness it has on any average day. Overhead, out of sight, the downslurred screaming *kee-ahrrr* of a hawk sounded hopeful and sad at the same time.

There still was no sound out of Frisco. He hadn't called out, it couldn't have been him. Frisco was gone, but Holly must still be in the house. The men were gone, the place *felt* empty. Dead quiet and still.

I ignored the implications of the observation and lifted the wooden latch of the barn door, barely cringing at the squeak of the new pine bar leaving its snug cradle. I crouched and ran, bent over as though being led by a dog who had my wrist in its mouth, to the house. At the bottom of the four steps, I hesitated, listening, looking, but mostly *feeling* for any change in my opinion the house was not occupied.

"Good to go." I marched up the stairs, and into the kitchen.

In the house, I flattened my back against the nearest wall. If I didn't at least try to hide, I'd regret it too late as bullets from some antique pistol ripped through my body. No sound in the next room, or upstairs. I tip-toed down the hallway just in case. At the bottom of the stairs, I stopped to listen-look-feel for anything bad. The house still had the same empty, tomb-quiet feeling.

I was alone.

I started up the narrow staircase, my leather boot soles whispering on the hardwood steps. Maybe someone was waiting at the top of the stairs. If anyone wanted to ambush me, they certainly knew where I was. I stopped, my right foot poised above the next riser, and listened. My ears pulsated and vibrated as if I was inside a sound-proof room, but I heard nothing more.

I stomped my foot, both in determination and defiance as I went up the steps. And then did the same at the next, and the one after that. The hell with them. The hell with all of this. If anyone was waiting to kill me, fine. I'd rip them apart using my bare hands, gash open their throats and shove their hearts into their bowels. No problem. And if they killed me? So what? What difference could it possibly make? This was some perverted nightmare, anyway. Holly was dead, I was sure, and Frisco was gone. What the hell difference would my own death matter?

At the top, I crossed the landing, and turned left, into the blue bedroom. Only it wasn't the robin's egg blue I noticed. Because everything was purple-red. A sheet covered something on the bed and I knew it was my sister's body.

My resolve to rip the S.O.B.'s heart out faded to sorrow. My heart quit racing. I stood, not breathing, watching the shrouded form. I had to accept it was my sister lying there. My only living relative. My best friend.

"Holly's dead," I said to no one.

I walked to the bed. Using one finger and my thumb, I picked up the corner of the sheet, and pulled it off of Holly's face.

Amid model-perfect features, my sister's brown eyes gazed back at me only they weren't her eyes, they were pennies on top of her eyelids. Her eyes would never again sparkle and shine as she told a joke, or laughed, or petted a puppy. Holly would never again paint, or draw, or take lousy pictures with her Minolta camera. She would never come home, breathless and excited about a really good deal she'd gotten at some estate sale. She would never again harp at me to get a life.

The skin on her cheeks was the color of tallow paste--yellow-white. The muscles in her face fell slack, toward the pillow., and her face had no depth. No dimension. No life. The reality of Holly's death eluded me as efficiently as my understanding of quantum physics. Neither subject appealed to me.

My disbelief worked as a protective wall, and let me feel nothing. Even the initial sadness was gone. My mind clicked off commands and phrases--*you're sad, cry. Holly's dead, you'll never see her again, never talk to her,* but still, I couldn't feel. No anger, no sadness, nothing. I was a vessel, empty. Void of all emotion.

So I stood there. Blank and empty. Waiting.

The first emotion to return was desire. Desire, because I *wanted* to feel sad. I *wanted* to face the awful truth and cry in anguish over sister's death. I *wanted* to embrace my own anger and lash out at the men who'd done this--make them suffer.

But I couldn't.

I couldn't feel anything. Maybe if I said it out loud again. "Holly's dead."

Nothing.

My mind picked up the phrase and recited it as a mantra, *Holly's dead, Holly's dead, Holly's dead.* Maybe the truth would sink in and I could do whatever it is you do when your sister dies.

I had no idea what might that be. Holly would know, but I couldn't ask her and get an answer. I stood staring at Holly's face, and then stroked a strand of damp hair across her forehead.

I leaned over Holly and wanted to scream at her to stop this right now. Take the damn coins off of her eyelids and wake up. Wet drops fell onto Holly's waxen face and I realized I was crying. And it hurt the same way it would if someone were stabbing me--ripping through my heart, tearing at my flesh. The feelings I had asked for earlier, were here. I welcomed the pain and embraced it, sobbing without making a sound. My breath came in great heaving gulps, but I didn't care if I breathed. If I could die too, it would be best.

My vision fogged until all I saw was the blue coverlet transposed over the white sheet blooming red flowers.

Flowers of Holly's blood.

Oh God, flowers and blood and Holly is dead. The room began to tilt. My knees buckled and I fell to the floor next to Holly. The room spun, and the blood reds and blue wall pulsated and blurred together. I'd never fainted in my life, had never been so weak or frail, I looked forward to the event now. Blissful, cool and dark. Anything to stop this pain, this torture.

The darkness never came. Instead, the room settled.

My heart jitter-jumped, and my gasping sobs now echoed in the small room. I was being ripped apart and hurt as if my insides were being yanked and torn out of my body. It wasn't fair.

I hauled myself up to my knees and threw my arms around the cool body. "I should have been here, Holly. I should have been here. I'm so sorry, I'm so so sorry."

* * *

Sheriff Taylor followed the loitering thought circling his mind in the same way a lazy dog's eyes follow a buzzing fly on a hot day. It was practically inconceivable, this idea, but with merit as well.

Frank rode his gray mare holding his spine rod-straight and set. His hips stayed locked in tension instead of following the horse's easy rolling gait. Stark white creases lined his darkly tanned skin, and his jaw muscles pulsed. He noticed Taylor's gaze and grinned. "What did the thick-headed cowhand mean, 'The Indian woman is too scared?' What might be the exact source of her fear?"

Yes, well. Where to begin? Perhaps even more important, *should* he begin? Somehow, telling Tahcitan's story seemed wrong. Then again, maybe the telling would help Frank see her as a real person, someone who would never harm another human. He ran his hand over his chin, carefully measuring the weight of his words. "It was

November, 1864, and Tahcitan's entire family had been killed at Sand Creek. Ella found her lying naked, cold and bloody under a scrappy bush. She was barely alive, almost frozen to death and terrified."

Taylor's stomach lurched when he spoke and a bitter taste rose to his lips. He swallowed, "Even though she is nearly six feet tall, your sister somehow managed to hoist her into the back of the wagon. She, Tahcitan, was no more than fifteen or sixteen at the time, but many men had...well, let's just say they were men lacking in moral fortitude." Taylor lowered his voice, looking straight into Frank's face. "If that isn't enough to put a scare into a person, then I don't know what is."

"Hhummph," Frank grunted. "Put the scare into a *person,* yes, but this heathen is not a person. Nothing human about it. I'd be happy to partake in the spoils, myself, mind you, but that's for another time, isn't it, my friend?" He shifted his weight back and gave his pelvis a little thrust. He grinned, licking his lips. "Seems to me, Sheriff, the heathen animal is seeking revenge on the white man and it is purely our civic duty to stop her from killing any more of our folk. It is quite clear to me this stinking creature has waged war against us, and it is equally clear we must stand up to the challenge and kill her. Save the women and children of our town."

Save the women and children? By killing Tahcitan? Save *our* town, did that mean Frank planned on staying? Taylor concentrated on staying in his saddle. He did not pounce on the irritating man and rip his throat open. Instead, he shook his head. "You don't understand, do you? White men attacked Tahcitan. They raped her and left her for dead and your sister rescued her. Ella and she grew to be best friends, and blood-sisters couldn't have been any closer. There is no reason for her to harm Ella. I'll find whoever did this, you can count on it, but I am not going after her and neither are you."

Such a long-winded dissertation was out of character for him, he seldom spoke so much or for so long. But then, he hardly ever had to convince someone the woman he loved was not a killer. He would never admit out loud he loved her, no, that wasn't in his nature. Besides, saying so aloud would make it real. Love from a distance suited him just fine. He asked, "Have you thought about the funeral arrangements? There's a burial plot out back of the barn."

"You leave my family matters to me." He smiled cordially. "Are you going after the pagan or am I?"

His teeth set, Taylor said, "I *will* find the man who did this, so to answer your question yet again, no, I will not chase her and I won't allow you to do so either."

Frank's spurs dug into the gray mare's sides and the horse sprang forward, her eyes rolling white. Over his shoulder, he called, "We'll see about that, *Sheriff.*"

Saul gouged his pinto's sides and he followed Frank at a gallop.

* * *

Low hills covered in brittle winter grass stretched around Tahcitan. Riding at a walk, she looked to the four directions. Patches of snow dotted the mountains, reflecting the puffy white clouds in the sky.

She had traveled in her life, back in the time of her people. They had followed the hunters and the buffalo herds, left their summer camps to the winter camps. She could still hear the children running among the teepee lodge-poles squealing laughter, excited to be moving. The songs of the women packing their belongings sounded clear and sweet in the bright sunshine.

Such a short time ago--only six winters past, she had been a daughter, a sister and for a short time, a wife. She knew family and love and belonging.

Perhaps she had been the cause of all the problems of the *Tsitsistas.* Perhaps her being a half-breed brought evil and bad into the lives of the tribe. Only after her marriage to *Ma'eno*, Turtle, did the trouble with the *Ve'ho'e* begin.

Even though her mother was a white woman, Tahcitan had never seen her or any other white person. Her mother's life ended the day she gave birth and she had been raised by another of White Antelope's wives and by the entire tribe.

The first time she had seen a *Ve'ho'e,* she had been a small child. The pale man had wandered near the camp, bleeding and limping. His mind was broken, his words jumbled and foreign, and Tahcitan had been filled with fear at the sight of him. Yet she could not help wanting to touch his yellow hair to see if it was real. His eyes were the color of the blue ice in the creek in the early fall, crisp and clear and deep. At first, she thought he was blind. How could anyone see through eyes the color of the sky and the water?

The yellow-haired man stayed long enough for the moon to grow fat, then fade to nothing. When his wounds had healed and his mind mended, he prepared to leave. He gave her father, White Antelope, a silver ring that had a glittering red stone set among smaller blue ones.

The pale-skinned man was of good heart and full of courage. Not like the savages who eventually came to slaughter her people. Most *Ve'ho'e* had no honor. Instead, they held onto their hate and the desire to destroy and bring dark sadness to the world. These men, these *Ve'ho'e*, all had the same black hearts. No sense of respect and no tribal laws guided them. They did not plan for future generations.

So many white men, so much death. The buffalo, the deer and the elk. And now, they were after her. Always, they chased her. Hunting her as if she were a rabbit.

Shame filled her to know her mother had been one of them--she herself, was half *Ve'ho'e*. She looked into her heart and saw the smoldering hatred that lingered there so dark and black as the men she despised. If she could, she would happily kill them all, remove them from the earth.

But this is not how it would happen. She knew her fate was to die at the hands of the *Ve'ho'e,* just as her people had died at their hands.

~13

The hardwood floor made my butt cold enough it was going numb. Too bad the same couldn't be said for my mind, but no, my thoughts zipped along at Mach 9, thank you very much. I forced my head to raise up and I looked into Holly's face.

Now what?

What I wouldn't give for three or four Advil. Yeah, Advil and a shot--or twelve--of vodka. I wasn't much of a drinker, but being hammered couldn't possibly skew things any more strange than they already were. If only it were that simple. I just wanted to escape. Since I couldn't, I let my brain have free rein. Nothing to lose.

I was Alice, all right. Fallen right down the damn rabbit-hole and not a single talking Queen of Hearts in sight. I was on my own. I needed help in a big way, but would settle for a plan. First, I needed to know where I was. My knees didn't want to straighten, but I made them move, and stood. By the time I'd walked across the room to the west-facing window, both feet had a tingly ants-crawling-across-your-skin sensation when a limb goes to sleep. I pulled aside the curtain and looked out the window. A mountain gazed back at me. Not just any mountain, but Long's Peak, as familiar to me as Pike's Peak or Mt. Evans, or Lion's Head.

Which told me pretty much where I was.

Which wasn't anywhere near where I ought to be.

The crawling ants in my leg settled into some sort of slumber and left me alone.

I opened the sheer curtains all the way and studied the yard below me. The barn stood to the right of where Holly had been killed. I shuddered, and let my eyes drift upward, toward the mountain range. No mistaking it--Long's Peak, all right. Jutting into the crystalline blue sky as clear a beacon to me as a lighthouse would be to a wayward sailor lost in a storm.

I should be happy. At least I knew where I was. Only about two hours drive north-east of the ranch.

But how had I gotten here?

More important, was the question of getting back.

I gnawed at a ragged thumbnail and stared at Holly.

Two hours from home. No phones. No truck in the yard. No stallion by the name of Frisco in the barn. A nagging unsettled thought lingered, asking not *where* I was, but *when*.

I tipped my head back and searched the ceiling for one of those square opaque glass light fixtures that cover bare light bulbs. They were usually engraved with images of oats or wheat or some kind of grain waving in an invisible wind. I could see it so clearly in my mind; there, in the center, the gold button that had to be unscrewed in order to change a bulb.

On this ceiling, however, there was nothing but blue paint.

My eyes darted around the room. There had to be an electrical outlet, a heater vent, or an alarm clock--something electric.

Instead of a lamp on the bedside table, there was a kerosene lantern, and on the bureau, a half-burned candle rested in a pewter holder. No nightlight, no electrical outlet, no digital clock.

A sheriff on horseback. An Indian woman in buckskins.

I turned toward the door. Glanced back once, then walked out into the hallway.

The pitcher and bowl I'd given my sister four years ago still sat on the table. It wasn't Holly's pitcher. It couldn't be. Still, I stared at it a long time, my mind silenced at last.

Goosebumps sprang up on my flesh and ran up my arms, down my spine, across my stomach. I tried to erase them by rubbing my sweaty palms up and down my thighs.

I went to the bowl and pitcher, and gazed at my image in the mirror behind them.

My mirror image wavered and became more of a super-imposed photograph of a stranger. Coarse features, and a nose larger than my own. High cheekbones framed by long, black hair. Brown eyes.

The picture convulsed and flickered, transposed by my own green eyes, my own small nose, and my own mousy-brown hair. My face was pale, as though the sun-tanned skin had been stripped away, and there was something else.

I angled my head left, then right. There, on my jaw, a line. A scar.

Frowning, I leaned toward the mirror for a closer look. I tilted my head, pointing my chin to my right shoulder. Even stretching her skin taut, the mark remained. Using my left index finger, I traced it. Long and smooth, a lazy S drifting from ear to chin.

I stepped back, and from a distance, examined the strange formation.

As a child, I'd fallen from a teeter-totter once, but that scar--I tipped my head back to look now--was on the under-side of my chin. Tiny and white, barely visible.

I inched forward and crowded the table until my face was inches from the mirror. The pathway was thin and white and looked as though it had been etched into my face for many years. The only other addition to my face was the scuffed abrasion under my right eye where Frisco's head had hit me. I must have a concussion which explained a lot.

Only one thing to do--get Holly's body home.

Down the narrow staircase, my footfalls echoed off the wooden treads, hollow yet absurdly loud. I didn't have a particular destination in mind, but just walked through the house thinking. I had to get us both home and it was a two-hour drive. A two-hour drive if I had a truck, which I did not. I looked out each window, searching once again for a vehicle. And once again, there were none to be seen. Back and forth through each room, until I found myself in the parlor standing before the piano. This room made me think of happy times. Even the air in the room was sweet--a combination of lavender and vanilla. I could hear the classical music, could see Holly's fingers flying over the ivory keys.

But Holly didn't play the piano.

I shook my head, chasing the false memories away. I raised the piano's lid, and it let out a plaintive moan, upset it had been disturbed.

I stared at the ivory and black keyboard, and then pressed the key closest to me. A low-pitched note filled the room and perfectly matched my own mood. I shut the lid and turned around, letting my feet resume their aimless tour, trying to decide how to get Holly home.

I stopped in the front room, near an overturned table, numb. Not sure where to go, what to do. On the floor, a calendar lay. There were only two sheets of paper left—the others had already been torn off.

November.

Large X's had been drawn through the numerals, as though someone had been counting the days to some upcoming event. The last X was through November 28.

I picked up the calendar, my blood pulsing through my temples as I tried to grasp the meaning of those X's. How did it get to be November when I'd gone riding to the landslide in May?

I looked at the top picture--an illustration of horses racing. Across the center, the year.

1871.

Yeah, right. I looked again, squinting so the numbers were clear.

My feet were stuck to the floor and wouldn't budge even when in my imagination, I saw myself twisting away and bolting from this place.

In some deep corner of my mind, I admitted I'd already known I was in a different century. But to make the admission aloud, to *say* it, well, that was too spooky.

1871.

Back in time. Accepting the truth gave the world a warped sort of logic. The lack of electricity or phones or trucks. It fit. It worked.

I tried to wrap my wits around the idea of time-travel.

Couldn't.

Had to.

I walked down the hallway and into the kitchen, then into the living room, the parlor, back into the kitchen. Finally, I leaned against the counter and let my eyes roam the pile of utensils, dishes and pans in the middle of the floor. Everything I recognized was an antique. I even owned some of them: a wooden-handled potato masher, a wooden-handled egg-beater, a glass butter churn. Holly had collected old things for years--it's how she made her own money and how she spent her days--shopping estate sales and selling things on eBay.

I opened a cupboard, searching for an electric mixer or a food processor. I found neither.

Okay. "1871," I said it aloud. Felt the numbers tickle my tongue the same way champagne bubbles did, only this was no celebration. *Or if it is 1871, then maybe Holly is still alive at home, in the 21st century.* If I wasn't dreaming--and the searing pain in my head told me I wasn't--there could be only one other possibility: I had lost touch with reality somehow and had crossed over into the minority of the mentally ill. A picture of myself curled into a fetal position, leaning against a white padded wall, holding my temples and rocking. Maybe throw in a straight jacket with colored ties binding my arms and a mean nurse glaring at me through a small rectangular barred window. The image seemed both prophetic and fair.

My fingers knotted into tight fists and my short, ragged nails dug into my palms. The sharp pain brought me back to myself.

I laughed out loud, it was so ludicrous. My laughter was the weird cackle of a deranged woman and I was certain I'd gone over the edge. Which was a good thing actually, because it relieved me of so much responsibility. It didn't matter if I went to the sheriff for help, or if I went to sleep and forgot about the whole bloody episode. Holly couldn't be dead, because I wasn't even born yet.

Or maybe both I and Holly were dead, only I hadn't yet realized that truth. I was now one of those lost spirits haunting places for years because they just couldn't bring themselves to cross over.

I dismissed the thought. Somehow, I was in 1871. It made sense if Holly and I had been here before, together. What if I was here because I could make a difference this time?

But Holly was dead.

"Ah," the voice in my head said, *"But she wasn't when you got here."*

* * *

Tahcitan pointed the stallion to follow small deer paths. The brown grass would hide their foot prints. At each fork along the trails, she paused. She could not know which of the narrow paths would end suddenly in thick brambles and twigs, or which would go on for a longer way. A part of her mind listened to the common sounds of the day; the steady clop-clop of the bay's hooves on the hard ground, the breeze waving the tall grasses, the distant screeching *ker-aw* of the birds in the sky.

The day warmed and brightened, giving the world a joyful look. But for Tahcitan, this only darkened her mood. Her outer leather shirt was tanned the medium brown of the tree bark and blended well with the stallion's mahogany coat. Both reflected the red of the coppery dirt. The leather shirt weighed heavy on her shoulders, smothering and hot. She unlaced her top and pulled it over her head. Her undershirt was tanned a yellow-brown and better matched the color of the earth and grass.

She tried not to think of El lying in her own blood, but the image shimmered red before her. She wandered without focus, following winding trails that in the end faded into the ground and disappeared. South-east seemed the general course of her bearing, as though she were somehow being pulled toward her past. Toward Sand Creek, and strangely, the notion both saddened and comforted her.

Sand Creek was the last place she and her family had been together. The *Ve'ho'e,* the white man, called her people "Southern Cheyenne" even when they were told the word *"Tsitsistas".* For this, she hated them.

The *Tsitsistas* did not desire the habits of the *Ve'ho'e,* and tried to cling to the old ways. they wanted to preserve the customs of their grandfathers before them. They wished for the peace and calm of their lives before the white man had come to the world. They wanted to continue the life they knew, and chose to avoid contact with the *Ve'ho'e.* But after enough time, the white men were everywhere and although they tried, the *Tsitsistas* were unable to get away from them or their ways.

The Great Father of the white men, Governor Evans, believed the Indians were in the way of what he called progress. His course included the killing of the buffalo for their tongues and hides, leaving the bloodied carcasses to rot until only mountains of bones remained. When the *Tsitsistas* fought the *Ve'ho'e,* the Great Father, Governor Evans, sent even more of his white men to do battle.

Colonel John Chivington, the leader of the killing men, told the People, the Cheyenne, the Arapaho, the Sioux, to go south to Fort Lyon, where they would be safe from the "Indian Wars" raging across the lands. And the People, led by Black Kettle, trusted the white leader and went.

While the *Tsitsistas* camped at Sand Creek, Colonel Chivington was ordered by his Great Father to fight the Dog Soldiers north of Denver. Instead, the white man and his army attacked the small Indian band. Her own father died there. So had her brothers, her sisters and their babies. The white men killed most of the women and children. But she had survived, and only later did she come to realize that sometimes, death is better than living.

Her hand fluttered to her cheek. She traced the scar along her jaw where the soldiers had cut her with a knife. She could not recall if the cut had come after, or before they had hurt her in another way. A worse way.

The *Ve'ho'e* was death to all the four-leggeds and two-leggeds who walked the earth, and she had no doubt her days would end before the next moon. But she did not want to die and would not make the killing easy for the *Ve'ho'e.*

A small thread of hope burned in her mind. The bay stallion was fast, able to outrun any other, and for this, she was glad. It was good to be on such a strong animal and she thanked him for his courage. But her hope was small, not enough for her to truly feel safe, and so she urged the stallion into a gallop.

She could not see the men, but she knew they were coming, and her fear held her the way the steep banks hold a raging river. Hope and the desire to go back to El's tugged at her, but she kept running. Faster. Harder. She ran fast as the water of a mountain stream. She was the river. Channeled. Controlled. White water rapids. Mindless. Cold. Rushing.

Under the fear, in the deepest hole of the river, dormant as a lazy catfish, was anger.

She was alone, again.

Her anger swam from its dark recess, struggled to find the light above, and then reluctantly sank again. She would be alone from this day until she too, made the journey up The Hanging Road.

She had been alone before.

She sat deep into the saddle and slowed the bay to a walk.

The lazy anger-catfish rolled, breaking the surface, his eyes black with hatred.

For an instant, she desired nothing more than to feed the poison in her soul, to do what she had wanted since Sand Creek and to seek revenge on the white man. All white men.

Her emotions, the froth and foam of the rushing river, swirled. Anger, hate, sadness and hope. Each one a shade darker or lighter than the next. Each one the strongest for only a moment before diving to the depths of her soul only to rise again. Thrashing turmoil within her only confused her more.

Far ahead, a small bobbing dot along the valley's rim caught her attention. She stopped the stallion, and squinted to make the shape more distinct.

A man on a horse.

* * *

The sun had climbed higher in the sky and warmed the level land north of Denver where the three men rode. On a gentle late morning breeze, dry winter prairie grass moved in undulating waves.

Sheriff Thomas Taylor kept the two men ahead of him in sight, but hung back so he could better think of a way to stop Frank from chasing and killing Tahcitan.

Just outside of Longmont, nearly to the Harris Ranch, he loped his buckskin up to the two men. He ignored Saul and rode next to Frank. "What do you say we go to Johnston's and have a bite to eat? Best food around."

Frank shook his head, his face conforming into the now-familiar scowl of hatred. "The last thing on my mind is eating. I've got business to attend, a posse to form and a half-breed to hunt down. I've no time to waste."

Taylor gathered his reins, not so much to slow his horse down as to gain a hold of his anger. His hand fisted around the thin leather until he felt his nails biting into his palm through his gloves. Slamming his fist into Frank's face would have given him far more pleasure than he cared to admit. Instead of acting on the desire, he said, "Must be hard for you. Losing your sister on the exact day you finally find her."

Frank jerked back on the reins hard enough to pull the mare's front feet off the ground. He glared, his teeth clenched. "Yes, it is difficult, *Sheriff*. However, I am convinced this heathen is the killer and I am going to make certain justice is served."

Taylor locked his eyes on Frank's. "I believe you ought to be thinking about Ella's funeral arrangements," he suggested. "Forget about Tahcitan, you're wasting your time."

"I told you to leave my affairs to me, Sheriff. *If* you did your job, I would be able to tend to such matters as what to do with my sister's remains. However, since you deem it proper to allow the heathen-bitch to run free, I must consider the situation the best way I am able. We must hunt down and kill an animal that deserves to be punished. Once it is taken care of, I assure you, my concerns will turn to my sister's funeral."

"Tahcitan did not kill Ella," Taylor said in a low voice.

"So you say."

"There's no convincing you, is there Frank? Your mind is made up and you are never wrong."

"Apparently not." Frank's brow raised, and his head tipped to the left. "I have a question for you. The bay horse the Indian is riding? How is it such a fine animal came to belong to a savage?"

The question raised the hair at the back of his neck. What the horse had to do with a manhunt, he couldn't guess. "The stallion is the grandson of Stockwell. Said to be the fastest horse in the country."

"You haven't answered my inquiry, so I will repeat the question. How did this heathen come to own such a fine horse?"

Taylor cleared his throat, hating the words he had to speak. "Ella's dream was to breed the fastest horses. But when the stallion arrived by train, no one could handle him. Not even Ella. Tahcitan calmed him. Ella gave her the horse right then and there."

His face darkened, and he smiled. "You're telling me the horse is Ella's? Mine?"

"Your sister gave the stud to Tahcitan. He is hers now."

"Come now, Sheriff. Surely you are able to comprehend the legality of the circumstances surrounding this issue. The horse was the property of my sister and now she is deceased. What was her property becomes mine, as I am the sole living heir. The heathen has the horse without my having given her permission. I want the animal back and yet, where is he? As I understand the law, having graduated from Harvard Law School, as you know, the situation is a clear example of horse-theft. A hanging offense in these parts, if I am not mistaken."

Taylor's hand drifted across his stomach to his pistol. To hell with slamming his fist through Frank's teeth, he'd shoot him now and be finished with the whole matter. No one around except Saul to witness, and he'd shoot him just for spite. Through his glove, the grip felt warm. Comfortable. Just pull it, point it, and squeeze the trigger. Problem solved.

He pulled the gun half-way out of the holster before he regained his wits and shoved it back. He searched Frank's face and saw only contempt and satisfaction. *One bullet and this would be over.*

He spoke in a tone just loud enough to hear. "You have got to be joking."

Frank laughed, his teeth white as bones in a desert. "'Fraid not, my friend. I want my horse and I want the bitch hung."

~14

On this November day in the Colorado Territory, the sun promised a bright and warm future for Frank. The morning was more comparable to a day in spring than winter, and Frank held the reins in his teeth as he peeled off the heavy black duster. His horse matched its pace with the sheriff's while Saul and his piebald gelding, brought up the rear.

It pleased Frank to know that ever since his insistent and persuasive request for the sheriff to chase the heathen for horse-thievery, the three men had ridden in silence. They headed west, toward the new town of Longmont, following the long morning shadows stretching out before them.

Although he tried to appear calm, a mixture of emotions whipped through Frank until he was certain he'd burst. It was his opinion that the sheriff was a complete idiot, and this detail along with the pestering notion Thomas Taylor might somehow realize the killer rode next to him mingled amid an unexplained, but quite real, joyful exuberance. The very notion Sheriff Taylor would figure out what had happened was preposterous. The man was a fool. Obviously, the sheriff was in love with the Indian woman and not able to manage a coherent thought due to this reality. Frank knew the love the good sheriff felt would help, not hinder his own cause. The more Thomas

Taylor worried over his squaw, the less time he'd spend trying to solve Ella's murder.

To Frank, the whole episode was a joke. The excitement tickling his belly made it almost too much to keep up the somber, heartbroken appearance. He bit the inside of his cheek to keep from laughing out loud. He hadn't felt this good since he was a boy hiding some terrific secret, only this time, his private knowledge would make him wealthy once more. He gnawed at the tender flesh inside his mouth, savoring the tangy blood he drew. His smile broke anyway, and he glanced at the sheriff to make sure he hadn't noticed. Taylor seemed wrapped in some inner turmoil and Frank was quite certain the troubled man wouldn't have paid heed should a naked woman suddenly jumped from behind the next shrub.

Frank wanted to hurry this journey along, close the distance between here and Longmont so he could get a posse rounded up. His skin flushed in a happy wave that started in the center of his groin and spread outward. Nothing in the world compared to the exhilaration of a good hunt, except for maybe a fine Kentucky bourbon and an experienced whore.

Blaming the Indian hadn't been part of his original plan, but since she'd shown up so conveniently, he took her presence to be an omen, a true sign he was right. The fault was not his, but hers for being in the area. She'd brought the consequences upon herself, and the prize was his.

He watched Taylor from the corner of his eye, but the lovesick fool still lingered in some shadowy place inside his own mind, undoubtedly trying to find a way to save his beloved. The squaw would die and her death would be sweet, just as they all were. The killings before Ella had been nice in a different sort of way from his sister's. A little girl and her mother, alone on the prairie, happy to have some company, thankful he'd chopped the wood, then horrified when he'd raised the ax above...

In the saddle, his crotch seemed too large for his pants and he squirmed to relieve the pressure. No time for such pleasures now. His thoughts flashed through his mind very fast, no single topic capable of holding his attention. More images than ideas--women mostly, but knives and blood as well. Lately, he'd have a thought, crystal clear, and before he could examine it, foggy mist shrouded all but a hazy image. Unable to recall where his contemplations had been, fear would writhe in his gut until he felt compelled to either drink bourbon or vomit.

None of this was his fault.

His stomach quivered now and he reminded himself to play the part of the brother distraught over the death of his only sister, but damn, the task was difficult. He didn't feel any sadness, he was giddy with excitement and happy to be a rich man, free of any familial restrictions. On top of it all, thanks to the stupid Indian, he was going to hunt his favorite prey, an almost-human animal who possessed the ability to reason. He could only hope the varmint held sufficient intelligence and brains to understand she was being hunted.

The fun was in the chase, even more so than in the kill. There was nothing better than striking terror into the animal he sought--whether it had two legs or four. He relished the way the air thickened in a distinct sour, rank smell. The odor of the panic he induced. The terror as it rolled off their bodies...

His groin tingled.

Yes, hunting and killing were better than whoring. He shifted in the saddle, anxious to feel the power, the dominating strength he'd possess when he held her life in his hands. He could nearly taste the sweet and tender victory that was surely his. He'd scare the heathen so deeply she'd shudder and tremble, begging for her life, admitting his power in her frantic eyes. He could already hear her pathetic moans and pitiful cries.

He almost laughed aloud again, but caution set his features back to poignant broodiness just in time. Both of his palms were slick and sweaty in anticipation, and he wiped them, one at a time on his saddle blanket. His breaths were ragged and short. Too excited. His lips pulled into a grin and he smothered the expression behind the palm of his hand. He must act sad. His sister was dead. Murdered. It was a tragedy.

Again, his emotions flipped from ecstatically happy to angry, his mood shifting so fast, he knew he was losing control. He would discipline his thoughts and his feelings. He could do so, easily. He was smarter than any three men in the Territory. Especially the slow-minded Sheriff Thomas Taylor.

There. The cold water thought of Taylor drowned his euphoric mood. The whole thing should have been so easy, so simple. Just kill Ella and take the ranch. Easy. Straightforward. But here he was, saddled with Taylor. The fool was kinking the whole affair into a knotted, tangled mess by wanting to find Ella's murderer as well as protect the Indian.

Too many complications. He was rich, Ella was dead, and all he wanted to do was have some fun. Celebrate. To top it all off, there was the unexpected bonus of the Indian. Hunt, chase and kill. He slid his tongue over his lips, his mind leaping to his sister.

Only he knew her death had been her own fault.

She had always been a strong-willed child, spoiled by Father, and she hadn't changed much once grown into a woman. Hell, she hadn't even married. Of course, neither had he, but then, he was a man.

Father. That's where all the trouble had started. If the old man had only looked at the world properly, none of this would have been necessary. Father had chosen the wrong Army and the wrong child to pay homage to. He had betrayed not only his country, but his family as well. Father had caused all this by choosing to pledge his allegiance to the liberal North Army, while his only son had fought for the South.

When Father had died, Ella had inherited thousands of acres here in Colorado Territory, while he'd been treated no better than a homeless mongrel thrown a bone. Ashes is what he'd inherited; three hundred acres of war-scarred Kentucky farmland and not a shack left standing on it. He hadn't even bothered taking control of the place. Let it rot and damn it to Hell.

He looked down at his arm, as though he could see through the fabric of his shirt that covered his skin. He envisioned the long white scar roping its way from elbow to wrist, a jagged reminder of the war. This disfigurement was much smaller and of less significance than the one on his leg, but it was more ugly and more apparent, and therefore made him more self-conscious.

No one could blame him. He only did what he had to do. What he'd been forced to do by other people. He reminded himself that guilt was not the emotion inducing these thoughts. No, no remorse was required for doing a job that needed to be done.

The thought humored him. At first, when he'd come up with the plan to kill Ella, he'd dreaded the chore. He'd never killed a family member and he didn't want to admit a part of him was fond of her and perhaps even loved her. He had worried about looking into her eyes, and not being able to do what needed to be done. But then, she'd run screaming into the yard and he'd had to chase her down. Yes, then, he'd felt the icy tendrils of excitement as her death became a game he knew well. A game he loved. He paused for a moment and gave a silent thanks to her for turning his task into such an agreeable adventure.

No time now to dwell on past pleasantries.

He eased into the authoritative Esquire-Army-Officer role, slipping it on as smoothly as a well-loved coat. At long last, he felt his face settle into the facade of a grieving brother attempting to hide his pain. He wondered if he could pin the murder on the half-breed and get a posse rounded up for more than horse theft. He might be able to set up some sort of false clue pointing the sheriff in her direction. Too much to worry about though. Things were okay as they were, and besides, his head was pounding in familiar dread of what was coming. Too many things to think about. He needed a glass of good Kentucky bourbon and a place to rest.

Inside his skull, his mind once again, stumbled toward the dark place, where he would have no control over himself, his actions, his thoughts. From here, he'd awaken from in a few minutes or many hours, it was never in his control. Luckily, he recognized what was happening, and because he was a smart man, he knew what to do. He forced his thoughts to slow, willed his heart to pump at an even pace.

Concentrate. On the bitch. Her fault. Kill soon. Please the demons.
Yes. *Please the demons.*

He would hunt down the Indian-animal *and* get the papers. The goddamned papers.

Under his breath, he grunted.

He was all right now.

* * *

Taylor puzzled a moment over Frank's scowl and grunt, then went back to weighing the pros and cons of chasing after Tahcitan for horse-theft. On the one hand, if he found her before Frank did, he could keep her safe. On the other, he knew she was no horse thief, and he would play no part in lynching her. Still, his job was that of Lawman, and in the legal sense, she was riding a horse that wasn't hers, except he knew Ella had given Tahcitan the animal. Without a piece of paper documenting the piece of evidence though, his hands were tied. Later, at a hearing, the Circuit Judge could decide how to untangle the mess, but until then, it was his job to keep her out of harm's way. Finding her would be his highest priority.

"Frank, Tahcitan is no more a horse thief than a killer. You and I both know it. But I will oblige your wishes and focus my efforts on finding her."

Frank grinned a wicked smile and slapped his thigh. "Well Sheriff, it's about time you recognize your duty. I am pleased the see you know your job and are willing to perform it, regardless of any personal notions you may have concerning the outlaw involved. I shall look forward to the hanging."

Taylor clenched his jaw and said nothing.

* * *

I found myself back in the parlor, inexplicably drawn to this room as though Holly had beckoned me. My fingers tingled in anticipation as I reached out to stroke the piano. As though it were alive, a soft hum purred within the dark wood. Above the piano's lulling murmur, a false memory of Holly playing filled my ears. I closed my eyes, remembering and swaying to the phantom music. The melody carried me along until I drifted like a sailboat bobbing along in a flat, sun drenched bay. I was floating, dipping, rolling on a gentle sea. I tasted the music in the salt air, heard the ocean swell with each stroke of the key. The melody, the boat, the warmth of the sun. It all felt so serene, so peaceful. Holly's fingers danced over the keys and--

Holly was dead.

I yanked my hand from the warm wood of the piano. Red blackness clouded my vision. As though I'd been looking at the sun through closed lids. I blinked and strained to make out my sister's form in the dark parlor, afraid and hopeful at the same time.

The piano bench was empty.

"Holly," I moaned, then ran around the piano and swiped my hands above the empty bench as if tearing sheets from a clothes line. "Oh my God, oh my God, oh my God…Oh no, no, no. Hol-leee," I wailed. I ran through the room, snatching up stray papers from the floor and ripping them, kicking at wooden furniture, crying all the while. "What do I do? Where do I go? Oh God, how could you do this? Is Holly alive at home? Frisco, I need Frisco. Stupid horse got me here, he can damn sure get me back. God, just tell me where Frisco is, Okay? You took my sister, do you have to take my horse, too? Can't you let me have him back? Please. Please?"

I paused, expecting God's answer, but I knew the futility of my request and it flat out pissed me off. I raised my fist and yelled at the ceiling. "I can't even bury my sister here in the middle of winter in this Hell-hole you dropped me into. The ground is frozen, I'm lost and nothing is right!"

I picked up an overturned drawer, threw it against the wall, and snarled when it splintered, but didn't break.

"God, damn you! Damn you all to Hell! Give me my horse, give me my sister, give me my goddamned life!" I threw another drawer, this time harder and at a window. The glass resounded in a satisfying crash.

My chest rose and fell, rose and fell, the air rushing from my lungs, a rasping sound that made me wish I was dying. Tears rivered down my cheeks, and still I ranted. "I'll find the Indian, I'll get my horse. You hear me? I will. And then I'll go home, and if Holly is still there, if YOU haven't taken her yet, I'll stop You. There's nothing You can do, no way You can stop me."

A swift boot to a toppled chair sent it careening across the floor. "I'll get help. So what if it's the middle of the freakin' eighteen-hundred's? So what if 911 doesn't work. I'll go to town. I'll find a sheriff, a man of the law, a flippin' Texas Ranger. You hear me, God? I'm not done here."

With each step, my shouts decreased in volume until my words became more or less incoherent mutterings.

Once in the backyard, I raised my hand to my eyes in a salute to ward off the bright light. It had to be around ten, and I checked my watch. Mickey Mouse gazed skyward to where his yellow hands still pointed at two-oh-seven. Hastily, I set the time for ten, wound the watch and raised it to my ear. The steady tick-tick gave me no satisfaction. That task finished, I marched toward the barn.

Inside the new building, I chose a perfectly new antique bridle from the tack room and carried it to the pasture, intent on picking out the best horse to steal. Even from a distance, I could tell the horses were different from the animals in my world. These were coarser and smaller, but they had more bone and it made them appear sturdier. I walked toward a group of three, and clucked to them. A dappled gray mare raised her head and nickered softly, then trotted over.

I looked at the mare closely, judging the horse's conformation as if for a halter class. The mare's legs were straight and she appeared to be sound. Her eye was large and kind and she had a look of intelligence about her. Concentrating on the horse, I realized my pulse had slowed and my breaths had deepened.

A horse makes everything better, even an unfamiliar horse. I, brushed the mare's face using my hand and raised the bridle to her head. She dipped her muzzle and opened her mouth and I slipped the metal bit between her teeth. The horse stood calmly, rolling the cold metal between her lips, but not chewing at it as an unbroke horse would. Standing at the mare's withers, I tugged softly on the left rein, and was pleased when the horse turned her head in response to the pressure. I repeated the command to the right and the mare turned in that direction.

The horse reined--as good a sign as could be hoped for. Standing next to her withers, I jumped up and down twice. The grey stood calmly, turning her head as if to ask what all the fuss was about.

Leading my new mount to the barn, I paused only long enough to saddle her using a borrowed antique brand-new high-cantled, heavy western saddle. Thing was in better condition than most of my tack at home.

There was nothing left to do, except get on and ride. "God," I said, "If you want to stop me, it's best to just have this horse throw me quick. No need to draw this out any longer than necessary. You want me dead, just do it, okay?"

I led the mare out into the yard and put my left foot in the stirrup. She stood quietly, not moving, so I mounted.

No explosive bucking from her, even when I walked forward. At a trot, I was happy to find the mare's gait easy and free and smooth enough to promise an enjoyable ride.

Although the sun was higher in the sky and the day was warm, I knew that in November, Colorado could turn cold without any notice. Sunny one minute, snowing the next. But there was no time to look for a jacket back at the house. I'd have to find a town, locate the sheriff, and then try to find Frisco and get home to see if Holly was alive.

Holly.

I turned the gray mare around and stopped her to gaze at the house. Leaving my sister's body behind, and all alone seemed wrong in more ways than I could count. Holly was dead though. "Hol-lee," I shouted, "I'll be back." Leaning forward, I drummed my heels on the horse's sides, sending the gray mare into a gallop.

Long's Peak was the only landmark I had, and keeping it to my right, I turned south. Racing down the hard-packed and frozen road, I could only hope I'd find a town. The terrain was desolate, populated by small sage bushes that reminded me of Wyoming or Nevada, and tall winter grass that made me think of Nebraska. Above, the sky had the brilliance of a blue gas flame, sharp and crisp, but there was a strangeness about it I couldn't define.

If only I had the Ford, I could be home in two hours and I could check on Holly. I kept the mare on the high spot in the middle of the road, between the deep wagon-wheel ruts and tried not to think about home.

I heard the sounds of a town before I saw any sign of people or buildings, though had I looked up, I'd have seen a pillar of smoke that came from somewhere man-made. A steady *clang, clang* that sounded as if someone was pounding a huge metal drum, and the high-pitched squeal of children playing, told me people were close. At the top of a small rise, I paused and stared.

Gawked, might be a better description.

Wooden buildings, none taller than two stories lined a hard-packed dirt road. In front of the rows of structures, wooden planks reached to the street and formed a sidewalk. Hitching posts, some had horses tethered to them, were conveniently located near every door. There were no cars or trucks or tarmac avenues. No blaring horns or sirens, no telephone poles or wires, no neon signs. No fuzzy contrails hanging in the sky. Nothing familiar, and when I acknowledged that simple truth, I realized the reality. I *was* here. In 1871. Alone.

My heart changed places with my stomach, a flip-flop sensation that sent a buzz racing through me because there was something uncannily familiar about the place. Something solid and real and made me keenly aware I was supposed to be here.

I rode into town, a half-grin on my face and butterflies in my stomach. The settlement was straight out of Hollywood--a John Wayne movie complete with cowboys, horses and women in long gowns with heavy shawls. The strangest thing about this little town was the way each building appeared to be brand new. Construction was everywhere with new buildings looking as though they'd be finished any day. Even the boardwalks looked as though the wood was freshly cut.

In the company of both trepidation and exhilaration, I nudged the mare forward and read the hand-carved and painted signs that hung from the fronts of the buildings. There was a feed and grain store,

Johnston's Restaurant, and Mallory's Opera House. Along the west side of the street, saloons, gambling houses and bordellos claimed this part of town as being for men. No woman of any social standing would care to be here.

I knew the area was called 'the line' and didn't ask myself how I could possibly know such a thing. The line emitted a garish flavor all its own that was separate and apart from the rest of the town . In contrast with this part of the town's gaudy appearance, was a sense of sadness that didn't match the bright Colorado day.

~15

The deeper into the main street I rode, the louder the clanging became until I realized I recognized the sound. It came from the shop at the edge of town and filled the morning with the stench of burning hair. When hot metal is pressed to the bottom of a hoof, it has an awful smell that is similar to scorched flesh. This odor plus the tang of hot coal made it clear the building belonged to the blacksmith.

A blacksmith would know everyone who lived in the area, because without his expertise and knowledge, the town couldn't survive. He was the Kahuna of all repairmen able to fix wheels, wagons, and equipment, as well as shoe horses and sharpen blades. If it was metal, he'd know how to meld, mold and cut it, and therefore everyone would eventually have some sort of dealing with him.

At first, he didn't notice me, or at least he didn't acknowledge me. Big as a refrigerator, and just about as squarely built, he bent over a piece of metal on an anvil, hammering, changing the long pipe into a curved and flattened shape that might later become a horse's shoe.

He had shoulder-length hair that made me think of a horse's tail. His greasy hair was thick and scraggly and showed signs of age in the roan streaks of white hairs sprinkled in with the red. His wrists were thick as the fetlocks of a Clydesdale, and his hands were the size of a draft horse's hooves. His shirt cuffs were singed black and small charred holes dotted the bodice. Over tan pants, he wore natty, worn-out leather chaps that looked at least forty years past their prime.

Finally, the man glanced up, stopping his iron-work. He stared at me for a moment, then turned away. Holding a pair of long tongs dwarfed by his huge hands, he carried the curved metal to the flame. He rotated the object over the heat until it glowed white, then, carrying the hot metal, stepped toward me.

His pneumatic blue eyes locked onto mine, and he drawled, "Who're you?" His distrust and suspicion of anyone unknown was clearly apparent in the low timbre of his voice and the narrowness of his eyes.

The man's teeth, what few he had, were stained a deep brown-black, as though he'd been sucking on Oreo cookies and hadn't bothered to clear the crumbs from his mouth.

I had never seen teeth this badly rotted, never dreamed teeth *could* rot to this extent. He wasn't even an old man. He appeared to be maybe forty. The overwhelming smell of body odor and dirt wafting off of him gave me the distinct impression of a decomposing corpse. The image of the walking dead man and zombies stilled my thoughts and completely removed any chance of speech. I stared at him dumbly.

He said, "Hey there. I asked who you are."

My mouth opened, I tried to talk, but my tongue stayed still as a sleeping sloth. I cleared my throat, and the sound that came out was the squeak of a scared mouse. A trickle of sweat crept down my spine. My palms were slick and the reins slipped through my fingers a couple of inches. I couldn't speak, couldn't think of anything except getting away. I spun the mare around and jogged down the dirt street, heading deeper into town.

Behind me, the blacksmith called, "Hey you! Breed, c'mon back here. Y'wanna say sumpin' to me?"

I stole a glance over my shoulder. The filthy man scratched his head, and I imagined his fingers raking across and stirring up hundreds of head lice.

I'd never given much thought to the personal hygiene of the people in the 1800's. But seeing and smelling the obvious lack of cleanliness sent a shiver of disgust through me. It was difficult to remember that here, dental work consisted of nothing more than the town's barber yanking any bad teeth. And folks who chose to bathe, only did so once a week.

My excitement at being in 1871 dwindled until only a tiny thread of wonder remained, and even that was fading fast. I kept the horse at a trot until I was thirty yards from the blacksmith, then slowed to a walk.

Small groups of men and women lined the boardwalks. The people of the town stood as though watching a parade, gaping at me. Every hair on my body stood on end and my heart thumped hard enough against my ribs, the rhythm echoed in my ears. Beneath me, the horse picked up on my fear and pranced. I tried to calm myself in order to calm her, but her head kept getting higher and higher and her feet moved faster and faster. I agreed whole heartedly with her idea of running the hell out of here, but made her stay at a jog.

A woman dressed in a beige frock with a matching shawl and hat hid her mouth behind her hand and whispered something to her friend standing next to her. Above the beige woman's hand, her eyes flashed disapproval and her head nodded in quick little jerks so she exactly mimicked a hen pecking at corn.

I looked away from them and studied the ground as I rode past. I remembered watching criminals being handcuffed and thrown into a squad car while the watchful eyes of a news crew and their cameras recorded the event for the six o'clock news. I could relate to how they must have felt. The distrust and fear on the people's faces made me want to turn and bolt from this place, but I needed to find the sheriff..

A group of men stood in a tight knot in front of the feed store and reminded me of a gaggle of junior high girls whispering about someone they habitually picked on in school. Their faces held the same look of suspicion as everyone else along the boulevard and I forced myself to sit up taller and face them. I cleared my throat and hoped my voice would work. "Excuse me," I looked the tallest man in the eye. "Do you know where I might find the sheriff?"

The man, who looked as though he could eat an entire steer for breakfast and still have room for a stack of pancakes, stepped to the front of the group of men. "Who's askin'?" He demanded.

Oh God, who's askin'? The question sent panic racing through my veins. But my name wouldn't tell anyone anything about who I was, where I'd come from, so what was the harm? My pulse tempered itself, slowed so it wasn't booming in my ears. "My name is Paizely Dunn. I have some information for the sheriff, do you know where I might find him?"

Although the man's dark eyes held my riveted in a stare that never wavered, and even though he was roughly the size of Paul Bunyan, I wasn't afraid of him. I held his gaze and flinched only a little when his eyes dropped to my tight jeans and knee-high riding boots. He must have decided I was harmless, because he answered, "Hadn't come in yet."

The good sheriff was probably still with the killers. I shouldn't have come here. My information about the killers wouldn't change anything. The two men I'd seen would get away with murder. The sooner I realized nothing I did would save the Indian woman, the sooner I could get away. I asked, "When does the sheriff usually arrive?"

The big man stepped off the wooden porch toward me and tipped his sweat-stained cowboy hat off his forehead. "Just whose horse you ridin', Miss?"

Afraid the man would grab the reins, I backed the mare a few steps. *Whose horse, indeed?* Of course people would know their neighbor's animals by sight, just as I knew my neighbor's vehicles. I should have thought about that. I stammered, "I, uh, I borrowed her from a friend." Half-truth, anyway.

The man grunted. "Looks like Ella Mitchell's mare. She your friend?"

Sure, yeah. Ella Mitchell. "Yes, yes, she is. I'm here for a visit."

The man sucked on tobacco-stained teeth, considering my answer. "You take after that half-breed squaw she keeps over at her place. You related?"

Half-breed squaw? That couldn't be good."Uh no, no, I'm not."

"What business you got with the sheriff then?"

Behind the man, a knot of unhappy, suspicious folks gathered and looked as if they'd happily stone me for no reason other than a little noon-time workout to muster up an appetite before lunch. Then again, they looked more prone to lynching me right on the spot which would be cleaner, quicker and less trouble for them. Every one of my muscles twitched and inadvertently, I signaled the mare to move sideways. Since she was moving anyway, I spun the horse around and said over my shoulder, "Oh, I just, well, I'll come back later and see him. Thanks for your trouble."

I pushed the mare into a fast trot, wanting only to gallop full-speed away from the people and their mistrusting stares.

Ella Mitchell?

I decided to go back to the house for no other reason than to be near my sister's body and to try and figure out what my next move should be. Fresh tears burned my raw eyes and I blotted them with the back of my hand.

Who was Ella Mitchell? The name had no meaning to me. No subconscious effect, not even a tingle. Ella. Holly. The mares feet tramped out the names as she trotted down the road.

At the top of a knoll, I stopped, the chanting voice in my head ranting full-tilt now. Maybe Ella's name did have some meaning to me after all. I was an hour from the farmhouse-and although I couldn't see any portion of the dwelling, I knew without a doubt, its exact location, as if I had a sort of GPS system hard-wired into my consciousness. As if I'd been blessed with the homing instinct of a pigeon, I knew if I cut across the open fields, I'd stay off the main road, shave some time and come up on the back of the house. I could spot any sign of trouble and avoid walking blindly into it.

Mickey Mouse's hands pointed straight up noon and the day was warmer than most in spring. I cut over to the creek to get myself and the mare a drink. With my hand cupped, I dipped it into the ice-cold water and marveled I was able to drink and not worry about pollutants.

What disease lived in water anyway? Did it exist in 1871? To heck with it. The water was clean and sweet.

My belly full, I closed my eyes and tipped my face to the warmth of the sun. A low rumble of far-away thunder drifted across the vast open prairie, and it was a moment before the sound's identity registered in my mind. Men's voices.

The sound sent chills down my arms and froze the water in my gut so it hurt.

I was in an open meadow, in full view, with nothing more to hide behind than a few scraggly bushes.

The mare nickered.

If they hear the horse, they will come. And though the thought wasn't mine, it *was.* I couldn't let them see me, couldn't let them catch me.

They would kill me. I knew this to be true and wanted to fight the urge to run. I wanted to go to the men and tell them I knew who the killer was and ask them to help me get home. I wanted these things and thought I go to them, but at the same time, I didn't question my mind's insistence that I run.

I jumped onto the horse's back and looked for the men. They were not in sight. I kicked the mare's sides.

The horse reared.

~16

Ve'ho'e.

For the time it took her to breathe in three times, Tahcitan stared at the man on the ridge. Already they had found her. They would chase her. Kill her.

She watched the *Ve'ho'e* for a breath more, then looked for a place to hide. Farther down the draw, bare cottonwood trees lined the dry creek bed, the only haven she could see anywhere. She bumped her heels into the bay's sides, and guided him at a gallop toward the trees hoping for cover. Leaning forward, the pommel of the saddle dug into her ribs, making it hard to breathe, but she stayed low, ducking the stinging branches. She prayed to the spirit of the rabbit the scout on the ridge would not see her.

She raced along the trail beneath the trees. The stallion jumped a log and ran down the narrow creek bed. She prayed to the eagle spirit, asking for wings for the horse, her fear driving them both.

The narrow creek bed opened into a wide, sandy river-bottom and the stallion ran even faster. They were in the open now, away from anything larger than a small stone. No cover. Tears whipped from her eyes and the stallion raced fast as a moving river between the dry shallow banks. His legs churned, and still, she pushed him.

At last he could run no more. His breaths became wheezing whistles and his legs wobbled beneath him until he stumbled, practically falling to the ground.

Tahcitan gasped and pulled him to a stop. How could she have run him so hard and far without a care for his well-being? Jumping from his back, she stood near him and cried, sobbing her apologies for bringing harm to him. She hugged his head and wept into his sweat-soaked hair, then led him forward at a walk. She said, "You must walk and get your breath. Then we will rest."

The horse snorted and paused to rub his muzzle on the inside of his foreleg. He was the only friend she had now, the only someone to talk to, and she hugged him again.

She walked with him up and over the brim of the shallow riverbed, and into a large meadow. The yellow grass waved in a silent breeze. Overhead, the sky was blue and clear. With her hand on the stallion's neck, she let him guide her while she closed her eyes.

The place came into her mind quickly. A river, wild and fast, coursing down a mountainside to a cliff, where the water fell over the edge in sheets. Beneath the fall, a still pond floated ducks and an occasional beaver. It was a good place, her place, where no bad thing could happen.

With eyes closed, she breathed in the peaceful smell of pine and water and wet rocks, and felt the warmth of the sun on her cheeks.

Ve'ho'e, white men, appeared at the far shore. They raised big rifles and shot the ducks in the pond. Feathers puffed and drifted on the wind before settling onto the rippling water. The smell of gunpowder filled the air. The *Ve'ho'e* laughed.

Her heart drumming against her sides, she opened her eyes and dropped into a crouch. The horse glanced back at her, then lowered his head to eat.

There were no men, no pond, no mountain, no water fall. Only tall grass reaching to the heavens. She stood, and turned to her left.

Father.

He said no words, but he gazed into her eyes and she felt his love.

Her fists opened and her hand fluttered to her breast.

White Antelope smiled his sad smile. He spoke to her, "My daughter, you have endured many losses in your life. For that, I am sorry. But you have also gained much. You are a strong warrior. Brave." He crossed his arms over his chest and smiled. "You know what to do. Listen with your heart."

"Father!" She ran to him, threw herself into him, wrapped her arms around--

--*air.*

She fell to the ground, her sudden motion spooking the stallion so he shied to the left of where she had landed in a heap.

The horse lowered his head to her, his eyes wide, his ears pricked forward.

Frantic, she whipped her head side to side, searching for him. "Father?" But he was gone.

She sat looking up at the stallion and whispered, "Did you see him? Did you see?"

The horse stared at her, his nostrils flared wide. He snorted, then backed a step.

She pulled herself up. Shaking in fear and hope, scanned the prairie for any sign of her father. The same tall grass and in the distance to the west, the same mountains. There was no sign of him and she wondered if he had really been there at all. But she knew he had come to tell her an important message.

Her hand cupped around the stallion's ear, she walked beside him. In the language of The People, she asked, "I am a strong warrior? Brave?"

The bay reached for a clump of grass.

His breath came quieter now, and the sweat along his flanks had dried to a white crust. He was tired though, and she knew they both needed to rest. She searched the horizon to the west. No men chased her. Maybe the scout had not seen her. She took the bridle from the bay's head and told him to eat.

She cleared her mind, and listened to the day, the earth. A breeze moved around her and the grass rustled. A quiet sound the same as when she brushed her hand along the bark of a ponderosa.

The horse grazed, happy to eat as always. She laid down near his head and closed her eyes. In moments, she drifted on the gauzy edge between awake and asleep, foggy images before her eyes.

A horse running, frightened and alone, no herd for protection.

A golden eagle flying, black against a yellow sun.

Her father leading braves into battle.

The bay stallion, running with a herd of white horses until he glowed with light. White.

Tahcitan opened her eyes and yawned. The sun had edged around in the sky so even the smallest stone cast long shadows. Her left arm tingled when she moved it. Dry grass stuck to her clothes and hair.

The images from her dream told her many things, both good and bad. The colors in her vision held different meanings and some conflicted directly with another. White and yellow were new life and beauty, but the black eagle was death. If death were coming for her, maybe a new life awaited at the end of The Hanging Road.

Her mind was quiet, settled.

At her whistle, the horse trotted to where she stood waiting. She pointed the horse east, toward the big water the *Ve'ho'e* called the Platte River.

She would be a strong warrior. Brave.

* * *

I held the reins tightly, inadvertently pulling back on them even as the mare's front feet left the ground. The horse reared, then lowered her head and tapped the ground with her front hooves before standing on her hind legs again.

Time stopped, but my mind whirled fast as a tornado. I'd landed here when Frisco had reared, hitting my head with his. Now, the grey mare was doing the same thing. Maybe I'd land another century earlier, or maybe jump ahead to the year 2525, It surprised me to find I didn't care one way or the other.

Still, the will to live is amazingly powerful because I automatically loosened my death-grip on the reins and leaned forward, wrapping my arms around the foolish mare's neck. The horse stopped bouncing on her front end and stood calmly.

From somewhere behind me, a man hollered. Another answered.

The mare whinnied.

"Oh God, they're coming." I drove my heels into the mare's sides and the little grey mare launched into a gallop. Through a thicket of willows, alongside a half-frozen creek, we ran. The ground was rocky, but there was no time to worry about slipping and falling. If the mare couldn't handle the terrain, I'd know soon enough. Recklessly, we tore through the willows. The mare's hooves slid on the rocks, nearly sending us tumbling, but somehow, together, we caught our balance.

The men yelled something I couldn't understand, and I pummeled the mare's sides with my heels. Faster, we had to go faster.

I glanced over my shoulder, but couldn't see anyone. Leaning over the horse's neck so my face was close to the mare's ears, I said, "C'mon girl, go. Get us to a safe place."

As though she understood, the mare's legs churned quicker.

* * *

She was a warrior. Brave.

Calling the spirit of the fox, the Master of Trickery, she asked him to help her evade the men. She guided the horse into the frigid cold of the big water, and turned him north, upstream. The swirling current erased the hoof prints made by the stallion's feet. She did not believe the *Ve'ho'e* could follow any hoof marks, but if they stumbled upon her trail this would confuse them.

Upstream, about three hundred paces, she left the half-frozen water for the sandy bank. Behind her, obvious tracks on the soft bank showed she had gone east, away from the Mitchell Ranch.

When the sand turned to gravel and rock, she turned back into the river, and followed it downstream, back the way she had come. When the watercourse narrowed and the sandy bottom once again turned to round stones, she climbed the bank. She rode into the grassy flood plain and headed south-west, back along the banks of the Platte River.

She was careful to leave no footprints the *Ve'ho'e* might see, and when the grass became sparse, she turned the horse into the heavier forage or back into the river itself.

The *Ve'ho'e* could not track well and this gave her hope she could get to a safe place. Then she would plan how to get the key from the piano for El.

* * *

I raced the mare through the willows and across the open meadow until the horse was huffing and sweating. I'd never pushed an animal that hard, and I cried for doing so, but then, I'd never been running for my life. Even as I galloped, I looked over my shoulder for the men.

Behind me, only clumps of sagebrush and sparse grasses waved at me. I slowed the mare to a walk and scanned the horizon. Ahead, a herd of antelope grazed, and in a blue acrylic sky dotted with soft cottony clouds, red-tailed hawks wheeled and screeched. The afternoon air felt brand-new, fresh and undisturbed, so clear and clean it even *tasted* differently than it did at home. I stared south, to where Denver was most likely still just a one-horse town instead of a thriving large metropolis. I didn't fail to notice the brown cloud that perpetually hung over the city was also missing.

No smell of exhaust. No pollution to sting my eyes. Ironically, I missed it. Even with all the problems in my world, the smog, the crime, the traffic, all I wanted was to go home. The isolation of my existence *then*--the future--the choice to be alone except for Holly, had been mine. Here, the decision to be alone was forced upon me and the subsequent loneliness was far more cutting.

The mare's rhythmic four-beat cadence as we walked along lulled me until a feeling of depression settled around me. I pictured myself as a cartoon character with a black cloud hanging over my head and couldn't help but question if maybe I were a fictitious person, in a place of no reality. I pictured Dorothy, lost in the land of Oz. "There's no place like home," I muttered and seriously considered jumping off the mare to try clicking my heels together.

I brought my hand to my nose and inhaled the smell of horse sweat. In my dreams I possessed no sense of smell that I remembered. I looked up, straight into the sun and squinted at the sharp stab of light. I slapped my thigh and the mare jumped sideways at the unexpected sound. If this were a dream, it was the most precise I'd ever had.

Acceptance. That's what I needed.

Okay then.

1871, somewhere north of Denver, east of Long's Peak, and my sister was dead.

I hung my head and closed my eyes. I just wanted to sleep. Sleep, and then wake up at home. Or not bother waking up at all.

The mare stopped walking. She raised her head and pointed her ears, and I followed her gaze.

Ahead, a man rode behind four head of cattle. He seemed unaware of me and I watched him for a moment, adrenaline thrumming through my veins.

He was a pale man with a face the exact shade of uncooked pasta. Wisps of platinum-yellow hair peeked from beneath a soiled tan cowboy hat. Everything he wore was either brown or tan and the muted colors, the yellow grass, and his palomino horse, all melded together. The resulting illusion was that the horse was an extension of the man's torso so together, they could be a centaur.

The pastel man sang in a deep baritone voice to the four cattle he pushed ahead of him. His song had a dark, melancholy feel to it-- something about a river and a love lost, and it matched my mood completely. I let the melody of the song carry my thoughts away from me and I absentmindedly stared at the man and his cows.

The cattle were small scrawny animals with long, curving horns and hides the muddy red color of a silty river after a summer squall. The whole scene had a Remington-aura about it--the Old West in paragon perfection. I forgot about being terrified and alone, forgot about home and for a moment enjoyed the faultless image before me. The song, the cows, the plains and the pallid man on the yellow horse all fit together to form the ideal picture.

I sat entranced, staring and realized I was smiling. The thought that he might be a threat never entered my mind. I waited for him to notice me, but he didn't. His cattle, however, saw me and took off as fast as a flock of frightened pigeons. He paused to see what had spooked his tiny herd and finally caught sight of me.

He opened his mouth as if in surprise, then raised his hand to the hat's rim and tipped it. He approached me in a casual "howdy-stranger-what-brings-you-to-these-parts" manner. He stopped his horse a few feet from me. His expression was sedate and serene as a Jersey cow, as if nothing in the world was worth getting too worked up over. Again, he tipped his hat. "Howdy, ma'am," he drawled.

His voice reflected the same timbre as a cow lowing in the night, and I liked him unquestionably. I smiled. "Hello," I answered.

A brief look of puzzlement shadowed his features. His eyes traveled from my face, downward, past my flannel shirt, to the tight denim jeans and my knee-high black riding boots. Finally, he removed his sweat and weather-stained hat to scratch his head. "Name's Jed," he offered.

"I'm Paizely Dunn, nice to meet you." Something was familiar about him--as though he were an old friend. I was certain he was good and kind. "Do you know Holly Dunn? She's my sister."

"Nope," he said simply.

"How about Ella Mitchell?"

His brow furrowed and a moment stretched past. "Well now, I shore do, ma'am." He spoke slowly, as if first searching for each word in some vast room. A look of suspicion darkened his face. "Er, least I used to know her. Seems she got herself kilt, so I guess I dunno her no more."

I felt the blood drain from my face. How could this man, in the middle of nowhere, know that Holly or rather Ella was dead? "Do you know how she got herself killed?"

"Sheriff and two men stopped me awhile ago an ast me the same thing. I'as out lookin for these fine ladies...they just up an left the herd, dunno why, and I finely tracked 'em over to the bog an now I'm takin 'em home."

"Two men and the sheriff?"

"Why yes'm, they stopped an ast if I saw anyone around Miss Ella's last night.'

"Did you?"

Jed's brows knitted together and his face turned pink, then darkened to red. He looked as though the strain was too much. Finally, he pointed with his chin, "Ain't that Miss Ella's horse? I know that mare--ain't nobody rides her but Miss Ella herself. Whatcha doin with Miss Ella's mare, ma'am?"

No doubt if I answered this query incorrectly, he'd clam up on me and I would lose whatever chance I had of getting information from him. I looked him square in the eye, deciding to tell him the truth, at least a round-about version of the truth. I smiled and tried to appear demure. "Jed, I'm sure you'll understand my embarrassment. I was riding my horse and I got thrown. Knocked out cold."

I paused, measuring his reaction. He leaned toward me and nodded in commiseration. "When I came to, my horse was gone so I went to Miss Ella's for help. I saw two men. One of them stabbed her and--"

"You saw two men?" Jed rubbed his chin thoughtfully.

"Yes."

"You know 'em?"

"No, I don't think so. They ran away."

"Sheriff had two men with him," Jed said. "One of 'em said Miss Ella was his sister. But Miss Ella, she was all alone, had no kin."

I gasped. "His sister?"

"Yep, that's what he told me."

"Big guy, wearing a black duster? Or the smaller guy, the one with no hat and orange hair?"

The same pink-to-red spots blotched his face again. "Uh...duster?" The word seemed foreign to him.

What would they have called them? "You know, a long, black coat? A dust jacket? Kind of a frock coat?"

He stared at me.

Oh for crying out loud. "A coat, reaches down below the knees, split up the back so you can wear it when you ride."

Jed had no idea what I was talking about, that much was clear. I asked, "Was one of the men wearing a long black coat?"

"Yep," he looked stricken.

"Was the man wearing the coat the one that said Ella was his sister?"

"Yep." His face took on a guarded expression. He shook his head slowly side to side. "They kilt Miss Ella? Then why didn't Sheriff Taylor lock 'em up?"

The image of Holly being stabbed in the early morning gloom brought the sting of hot tears to my eyes. I opened my mouth to answer Jed, but the lump in my throat swelled and I couldn't speak. With tears running down my cheeks, I nodded, confirming the first of his questions.

Jed swung off the palomino, dragging one rein with him so the horse followed. He walked to me and reached up to place his hand my arm.

At the touch, I felt my resolve to be strong slip away. I wanted someone to help me, wanted to share the burden of my plight. And here was this man, a stranger, willing to comfort me. I sobbed, not trying to hide my grief. I leaned forward until my head rested on the mare's mane.

Jed didn't speak, but softly hummed a tune, his hand moving up to my shoulder.

Ignoring the saddle's horn gouging my ribs I wept into the mare's neck. I grieved for losing Holly and I cried for Ella, and eventually for myself. I mourned my own life and the choices I'd made--the people I'd loved and lost. I bemoaned the mistakes I'd made in my life and the futility of my being thrown into this century. I cried because a stranger was reaching out to help me, humming a song for me. It seemed that once I started feeling sorry for myself, I'd never be able to stop.

Beside me, Jed kept humming the melancholy tune and rubbing feather-light circles into my shoulder, but he did not speak.

Finally, I sniffled and raised my head from the mare's wet mane. Turning to Jed, I said, "I'm sorry, I don't usually fall apart, but--"

He pulled his hand away and muttered, "S'all right ma'am."

I sniffled, "Do you know the men who were with the sheriff?"

"Nope."

I gazed at the fair man a long moment, measuring his integrity based on his humming abilities. Finally, I asked, "Is the sheriff a good man or is he in on the murder of my friend?"

The question seemed to confuse Jed and he was long in answering. "Sheriff Taylor reminds me of a horse I once knew. Kinda quiet and shy, but honest in his eyes."

I had known a few horses like that myself. I nodded. "Then why would the sheriff be with the killers? Did he arrest them, were they going to jail?"

"They was headin to town all right," he said. He tilted his head and looked up, over his left shoulder as if looking for the answer to my question. "That big feller, he said he's gone get hisself a posse."

"A posse? He's the one who killed Holly, I mean Ella. What's he want with a posse?"

"They's a goin after Tahcitan."

Tahcitan.

The word Holly had uttered before she died.

My stomach turned into itself, knotting into a cold wad. My knees trembled and my head reeled. Light-headed and dizzy, my temples throbbed with a headache so intense, I was sure I'd pass out and land in a heap on the ground.

I could have been made of warm, melting wax--none of my muscles had any strength. I slipped from the mare's back and slumped to the cold ground at Jed's feet. Looking up at him, I whispered, "Who is Tahcitan?"

~17

I sat on the ground, staring up at Jed. He shuffled from one foot to the other, his hands worrying over the rim of his worn and dirty hat. He stared at me, but didn't answer.

I tried to still my shaking hands by knotting them together in my lap. I repeated my question."Jed, who is Tahcitan?"

Jed sucked on his front teeth creating a high-pitched whistling sound that cut through my headache as effectively as a dentist's drill. His face took on a hard, blank look and he stared through me as much as at me. "Thought you was Miss Ella's friend. How come you dunno Tahcitan? They 'as like kin."

My mind raced, echoing his words. *They was like kin.* "We, we hadn't seen each other in a long time."

Jed sucked his teeth harder.

I went on, "Ella and I were once very close. We went to school together when we were girls."

He mulled the possibility over. Finally, he grunted, nodding his head. "Uh, Tahcitan is Miss Ella's friend. Almost sisters, they was, even though Tahcitan is half Cheyenne. They take care of the horses on the ranch. I'm the cattle boss." He straightened his shoulders and his voice deepened with obvious pride.

I pushed myself up from the ground. "Well, where is this Tahcitan?"

Jed held his hand out for me to grasp. "She lives over yonder," he gestured south-east with his chin. "In a soddie."

I brushed the dirt and dry grass from my jeans and straightened into an upright position. "Soddie? What is that?"

Jed jumped back a step, his eyes wide. His jaw hung open.

What was wrong with him? How was I supposed to know what a soddie was or that asking would cause such a reaction? "Jed, you all right?"

His jaw dropped even lower, and his face paled to a lighter shade of cream. He asked, "Where you from?"

The future. Mars. What difference did it make? I glanced down at myself. What had tipped him off? My clothes? I decided to answer truthfully. Sort of. "San Francisco, why?"

He slid his left boot back a step. "Miss Ella, she's from Kintuck."

What was Kintuck? Ah, Kentucky. I figured acknowledging what he said might be the best way to keep out of the deep end. "Yes?"

"And yer from San Francisco?"

"Yes."

"Then how come you take after her? I didn't see at first, you on the horse, cryin an all. But now yer off, a standin an sure 'nuff, you do."

What in the world was he yammering about? "I don't look anything at all like Ella. I'm much bigger than she is, was. What do you mean, I resemble her?"

Jed shook his head furiously. "Not Miss Ella."

"Not Miss Ella? Who then? Jed what are you talking about?"

"Tat. You take after Tat."

"Who is Tat?"

He sucked on his teeth. Narrowing his eyes, he said, "Tahcitan."

* * *

Already--though it was only two-thirty, barely afternoon--lanterns burned in most of Longmont's windows. Long shadows spread out across the buildings throwing an early twilight over the small town. The gloom perfectly matched Sheriff Thomas Taylor's somber frame of mind. A few people wandered the wooden boardwalks, carrying purchases to their wagons, and they nodded to him as he passed, but neither the recognition he received nor the two stray dogs chasing a group of boys down the street could lighten his mood.

In front of his office, Taylor nodded to Mrs. Andrews across the street, then dismounted. He glanced over the town looking for any problems, and was thankful all was quiet. The gray horse Frank rode and Saul's pinto were already tied in front of the saloon, and Taylor groaned. Getting Frank to be reasonable when he was sober was bad enough, but Frank drunk ought to prove to be downright unpleasant.

He needed to find Doc Perry, maybe *he* could talk some sense into Frank, make him understand that Tahcitan had nothing to do with Ella's murder.

The oily smell of chicken roasting and beef grilling sent Taylor's stomach to growling, but his hunger would have to wait. From the saloon, loud laughter was followed by a thud. He ignored both and set off in search of the good Doctor Perry.

* * *

I looked like Tahcitan? How could I possibly resemble a half-breed Cheyenne woman? I was Irish and Italian for crying out loud. Sure, my hair was long and dark, but in a mousy-brown shade. And my eyes a green so deep they looked more grey-black, but my nose was small and my lips full. No one had ever asked if I were Cheyenne, or any other Native American tribe for that matter.

My pulse quickened.

To everyone here, Holly had been Ella Mitchell.

At first, the stabbed woman hadn't resembled Holly, but then the pink light, the shimmering waves, the way her face changed.

The blacksmith had called me "half-breed." Even Holly had called me Tahcitan. Tat.

My mind spun, whirled, and boiled. The possibilities were better left to fiction. *What if...*

"Oh my God," I whispered.

No. The whole notion was too hard to grasp, too weird.

Time-travel, then this. Was it possible Holly had been Ella and I'd been Tahcitan? Was it even possible to see yourself in the past, and not die right there on the spot because of some great cosmic screw-up? I couldn't remember if in *Back to the Future*, McFly seeing himself was okay or if something terrible happened to him.

My own fear was reflected back to me on Jed's face. The guy was absolutely white, as if he'd seen a live ghost. Which, maybe he had. I wanted to calm him, to reassure him I was a good person, as scared, no, make that more scared, than him. But what could I say?

Bottom line, Tahcitan was in danger. More than just danger. Men were intent on killing her. I, Paizely Dunn, could save the Indian woman's life. Besides, it might be my life as well. I realized the idea was crazy, and I smiled.

Jed's eyes flickered with what I thought was fear, and he back-stepped another three feet.

Perhaps my own fate, or karma or whatever voodoo it might be, could be redeemed. All I had to do was go to the law and explain what I'd seen. I was, after all, a witness to murder.

"Jed," I said, "I need your help. This morning, the two men and the sheriff were talking about going after Tahcitan, and I know she didn't do anything wrong. I was there. I saw the whole thing. She didn't kill Ella, the man in the long, black coat did. We need to find Tahcitan. We need to help her. Do you know where she lives?"

Jed slid his foot back another step, and settled his hat back on top of his head. "Why don't you know where she lives? Yer her, ain'tcha?"

"No. No, I'm Paizely Dunn."

"You resemble her, all right. 'Ceptin you kin talk right good. Tahcitan, she don't never say nothin."

I waited.

Jed examined the sky. "Well," he drawled, "it's a gettin mighty late. I gotta get these here cows back over t'the ranch. They run off last night, all by their selves, I dunno what come over them to do such a thing."

Talking about the cattle seemed to calm him. He wasn't retreating from me anymore.

"Jed." I took a step toward him, "Jed, Tahcitan is your friend, isn't she? We've got to help her. If we don't, they'll kill her. You don't want to see her hang for something she didn't do, do you?"

He stared off into the distance, then kicked a rock. "Well now, I shore don't think that'd be right," he agreed.

"So you'll help me? You'll take me to her house?"

"Tahcitan, she lives in a soddie."

Remembering what had happened the last time I asked what a soddie was, I didn't pursue the matter. Instead, I asked, "Where is it Jed? Where does Tahcitan live? Do you think she's there? Can you take me to her home?"

Jed took his time checking the sky again, as if he thought something awful would fall from the blue air and kill him. He sucked his front teeth and rearranged his sweat-stained hat atop his head. Finally, he put his foot in the stirrup and swung into the saddle. "Yep, I guess I kin take you there, it ain't much outa my way. I gotta git these four ladies home though...They been traipsin' the country-side entirely long enough, and don't need to spend another night out here."

He aimed the palomino toward the cows and began whistling the same sorrowful tune he had been singing when I'd found him.

I stepped into the stirrup of the grey and turned to follow him.

* * *

Sheriff Thomas Taylor stood just inside the saloon's door, Doc Perry at his side. The sweet smell of tobacco and liquor hung in stale air and mixed unpleasantly with the odor of sweaty men and horse manure.

At the bar, Frank Mitchell threw back his head, downing what had to be the most recent of many shots of bourbon, then laughed and said, "Hell yes, we'll find her. Bitch killed my sister and now I'm going to kill her. So, who's willing to accompany me on this hunt?"

About a dozen men, none of whom Sheriff Taylor would have labeled 'upstanding citizens' stepped forward. Although different ages and from varying backgrounds, they all wore the same expression of blood-lust. Each of the men before him held a gun of some sort, rifles to pistols, some with more than one weapon. The men were obviously willing to kill, they were just unsure of how to proceed.

Taylor threw his shoulders back and stretched himself to his full six-foot, four-inch height. Leaving the good doctor standing at the door, he walked purposefully to where Frank stood.

Sheriff Taylor glanced at the crowd, meeting each vigilante's bleary eye."Tahcitan was employed by, and was friends with Ella Mitchell. She did not kill her. I don't know who committed the murder, but I promise you, I will find out. Now, each of you just holster your weapons and have another drink."

A low murmur passed through the half-drunk crowd. And Taylor caught the phrase, 'a hundred dollars' floating from more than one set of lips. Frank Mitchell shouted, "That's right, one hundred dollars to the first man who finds her."

He turned to Taylor and said, "In case you have forgotten, Sheriff, the heathen has also absconded with my horse, and I want her hung for horse theft along with murder. Too bad you can't hang the bitch twice."

Taylor kept his voice low. "Frank, your sister gave her that horse. I will be leaving first thing in the morning to find Tahcitan. Not to kill her, not to hang her, but to take *her* horse away from her. If you care to ride along with me, fine." He spun around, covering the distance to the door in only four strides.

At the door, he paused. "Oh, by the way, Frank, Doc Perry is here to help you with the arrangements for your sister's funeral."

* * *

Together, Jed and I pushed the four cows ahead of us. The pace was slow and in perfect time with Jed's ceaseless humming, singing and whistling.

Although the sun was bright, the afternoon had already grown chilly and I shivered, hugging myself. More clouds were drifting across the endless lake-blue sky, but not enough to block the bright, albeit weak sun. A slight breeze rustled the bushes and stroked my hair soothingly.

I sat slumped in the saddle, my hips rolling with the gray mare's lolling four-beat walk. I listened to Jed's songs and felt sad when the tunes slowed, and hopeful when the music clipped along, light and fast. The guy was better than any radio station because there were no obnoxious commercials about diamonds or mufflers. I was grateful for his companionship and for the way he'd taken my appearance in his world in stride, even when he'd been convinced I was some sort of possessed witch in Tahcitan's body. Obviously spooked by my manner of dress and my way of speaking, he had still been open-minded--or simple-minded--enough to accept me as I was. You had to admire someone who could do that, and I wished I could learn the trick from him. Maybe someday, I too, would be able to accept things for what they were and not try to control the outcome of every situation.

Yeah, sure.

The sun was sinking and the day was turning cold when finally, we reached the sod house. Two small scrub-oak-looking trees crowded the south--and-front side--of the low-slung building. Dried mud-bricks, each with wisps of brown grass sprouting from each in sharp quills somehow gave the place an air of lonely sadness. Only one small window, not big enough to crawl through, squinted dismally toward the front yard. On the South-east corner of the building, a small corral had been built complete with a narrow overhang to give the horse who lived there some shelter.

Staring, I forgot when I was, who I was, and how I'd arrived here.

My stomach jittered and fluttered, and sent a feeling that was nothing shy of elation singing through my veins. I grinned until my teeth hurt from the cold, then pulled my lips into a closed smile.

This was a real sod house...not old and dilapidated, not crumbling or deserted. A real, honest, down-home sort of place. New, with a fresh thatch roof.

The place made me happy, as though I was finally home after a long and tiring journey. And then slowly, the feeling *shifted* like when a cloud passes in front of the sun bringing with it a cold dread.

My mood sank just that fast, my elation and joy fading to black as quickly as a television screen ready to roll credits at the end of a movie. An overwhelming sadness, strong enough that I thought I might cry, seeped into me from all sides and invaded my very soul.

Did the place have the same kind of effect on Jed? He looked as impassive as a Jersey cow. "Kind of depressing, isn't it?" I ventured.

He shrugged.

But I couldn't shake the sad feeling that settled around me. The eerie dread was at once clammy, musty and suffocating.

At the rough hewn door, I raised my fist and knocked. In the distance, a red-tailed hawk screeched in answer, but from within, only silence greeted me. I gnawed at a tattered thumbnail. "Do you think she's home?"

Jed sucked his teeth and the sound annoyed me. He finally worked out whatever it was that was lodged between his incisors and spit unceremoniously. He looked at the empty corral next to the hut, and drawled, "That killer horse a hers ain't here. I'm guessin she ain't either."

A sudden gust of wind cut through my flannel shirt, causing goose-bumps to pebble my skin. I hugged myself for warmth but it didn't help much.

I faced Jed. Jed, my only friend, my only source of comfort. "Now what, Jed? We need to find Tahcitan and warn her about the posse. We need to ask her if she knows the man in the black coat. We have to do something to save her."

He hemmed and hawed and eventually spat a healthy wad at the ground. He spoke slowly, in a typical, if not irritating Jed manner. "Now, Tahcitan, she might could be back at the ranch checkin them mares. She shore does have a soft spot fer them horses."

Go all the way back to the Mitchell Ranch? Well, sure, why not? I'd been running in circles all day anyway, what difference did it make to chase four stupid cows and a man the color of pasta all over hell and gone? I pulled back my sleeve to check the time. 3:50. The sun had already dipped behind the mountains throwing long, cold shadows over the prairie. It'd be dark soon. The wind sliced through my shirt again and I shivered.

Jed's eyes locked onto my wrist. He stepped sideways. "Whatsat?" He pointed to my watch.

Now what? The guy was afraid of my Mickey Mouse watch? I pulled my sleeve back, laughing. "It's okay, it's just my watch."

He stood his ground. "Watches hang on a chain. Go in a pocket."

"True enough, my friend," I said, trying not to laugh. "But this one has a picture of a cartoon mouse on it, Mickey Mouse, see? Pretty cute, 'eh?"

Jed examined the watch, and looked a little embarrassed. He shook his head. "Just ain't right, is all."

The wind blew harder and colder. I held my hands to my mouth and blew on my fingers to warm them. "Sure wish I had a coat," I said.

Jed's hand snaked toward the wooden latch on the door. He spoke softly, barely above a whisper. "You and Tahcitan are the same size. Maybe she has somethin you kin use."

He opened the door.

~18

White curtains bordered in lace and tied with blue ribbons decorated the windows of the small Inn. Nine tables, each with three or four wooden chairs and a blue gingham tablecloth, sat arranged in precise order in the dining area. The door to the kitchen gaped open and from the room beyond, came the usual noise of clanging dishes, people talking and the delicious smells of roasting chicken, cinnamon baked apples and beef gravy.

Taylor sat alone, chewing his fried chicken and mashed potatoes. He chewed is food, ruminating. The day had been a long and a most unpleasant one to boot. Not only was his friend dead, and Tahcitan in danger, but also Frank Mitchell somehow seemed to be connected to both. He was certain if he could find the link between the two would solve Ella's murder.

Doc Perry was tending to Ella's body, though Frank hadn't been concerned about that aspect of the day's events. Rather, Frank had been hell-bent on chasing Tahcitan down to kill her. Last Taylor had seen of him, the angry man had been sitting at a table in the Lucky Gambler, drinking whiskey, and trying to stoke the furor of blood-lust in the men of his posse. The same posse who would hunt and kill Tahcitan like a pack of wolves.

Tahcitan.

Taylor recognized his own foolishness in his being smitten by her, knew that loving--dare he even think the word?--her made no sense. In reality, he didn't even know her and in actuality, he'd never spoken more than a few words to her before she ran away, furtive and darting as a frightened child. Nonetheless, and logic aside, no woman had captured his attention the way she had.

There was something truly wild about her, not something bad-wild like an unpredictable tornado, but good-wild, like the patterns and colors of a sunrise; purple-red smearing to pink and blue. He didn't want to tame her, either. Rather, she should be enjoyed for the natural loveliness that was hers alone. Sometimes, he wished the beauty of a sunrise would envelope him and hold him for hours instead of just moments. He thought of Tahcitan with a longing that held much the same sentiment.

Thomas Taylor had never wanted to settle down, get married, or have a family, but he knew that if she'd have him, he'd do so in a minute. Deep down, he recognized that part of his longing for her was due to the truth he could never have her. Something about wanting what he couldn't have made the desire safe somehow.

Ella was clear on her hope the two would somehow overcome their differenced and get together. She said it wasn't right to be alone and he had known it was her own loneliness that prompted the sentiment. She'd never gotten over the death of her beloved husband, Jeremiah, and she'd never gotten over feeling it was her fault he'd died on that snowy evening two years ago. He'd gone to town to get supplies when an unexpected blizzard hit early in October. Icy roads and a toppled wagon were all that were found once the weather had cleared. Taylor knew that deep down, Ella hoped he'd miraculously show up on her doorstep.

Just yesterday, Ella had spoken the obvious truth of his own cowardice concerning the feelings he had for Tahcitan, then had invited both Tahcitan and him to dinner. He had gone along with those plans Ella had so thoughtfully laid, even though all Tahcitan did was sit, not speaking and avoiding his eyes throughout the meal. Twice, he'd caught her stealing a sideways glance, but when he spoke to her, she acted as though she hadn't understood a single word he'd uttered.

He smiled at the memory while at the same time, a deep sadness crept over him. Ella was dead and Tahcitan was gone, and if he didn't find her, Frank would no doubt hunt her down and kill her as promised.

The mashed potatoes in his mouth tasted raw and flavorless, with the consistency of dough, but he swallowed them anyway. He would order some food for the road and leave tonight. No sense in waiting.

* * *

I ducked my head and followed Jed through the doorway of Tahcitan's soddie. Inside the dark, cool building, I stood bent at the waist, unsure of the ceiling's height. The smell of darkness, dank and moist, almost oily, licked at my nostrils, tickling my nose until I sneezed.

In my ears, the familiar low buzzing drone I'd heard this morning drowned out any other sound. I stayed bent over at the waist, and closed my eyes willing the racket to stop.

The noise faded and I opened my eyes. In the gloominess of the small house, I made out the lumpy shape of a grass bed in the far corner, and Jed standing off to my right, his hat in his hand. He cleared his throat and the sound was gravel rolling around in the back of a cement truck.

If only there were a cement truck here.

I stood and the low ceiling kissed the stray hairs at the top of my head. Cream-colored candles and kerosene lamps on tables made from wooden crates sat around the small room giving the place a homey-lived-in feeling. Hanging on the far wall, an elk skin stretched taut, but I didn't know enough about working leather to be sure at what stage the tanning process might be in.

Against the wall to my right, an oak sideboard, smooth, with a polished finish, glowed soft and golden even in this shadowed room. A flash of light drew my eye to the topmost shelf where a small glass figurine echoed the meager sunlight that fell through the open door. Drawn toward the tiny reflection like a moth to a porch bulb's gentle radiance, I picked up the figure. The glass cooled my hand, and was surprisingly heavy.

Four legs were frozen in the bent positions of a horse at a full gallop, its mane and tail flowing behind it in some imperceptible wind. The face, although the clear glass had been etched by the artist to show the features of any horse, seemed to perfectly reveal Frisco's personality.

Without warning, the world shifted, as though someone had tossed a rock into the fabric of the world, causing a ripple to skitter across a pond. I was tossed, bobbing and swaying and ducking to the floor. The hum in my ears rumbled deep. Instinctively, I hugged the glass horse to my chest, bent my knees, and tried to not to fall. The floor buckled, or at least felt as if it had, and I fell.

The pungent odor of oily dirt filled my nostrils, made my queasy, and I rolled onto my side. I clutched the small horse to my breast. I took a deep breath of the foul-smelling air. Gagged. Coughed. Closed my eyes.

From a great distance, Jed asked, "Ma'am, you all right?"

But I couldn't answer. I didn't know what to say anyway. And then, a feeling of happiness and love came over me. Sweet and warm. And I *knew.*

I knew this place and everything in it.

The floor evened out, then rested. The annoying jet engine in my ears faded to the whining buzz of a fat bumble bee. I stood, though my knees threatened to give way. I raised the glass horse to my face. I knew beyond a doubt, El had given it to Tahcitan and I knew El had loved her--me--like a sister. I placed the figurine back on the top shelf, careful not to break it. The little glass horse seemed to glow with an inner light of its own.

I knew that in the top drawer of the hutch, was an envelope, sweetened with the smell of vanilla and wrapped in a blue ribbon. It too, had been a gift from El. And somehow, the knowing feeling gave me peace. I opened the drawer and withdrew the envelope. Pressed to the front, a tiny dried blue flower had curled its petals around the ribbon.

I turned the envelope over in my hand. The paper had an aged look of crispness, with brown edges. How long had it been hidden in the drawer? My finger traced the blue ribbon. Faded not quite to light gray, the flower had turned the color of a late-afternoon sky in December. Still blue, though barely.

I turned to Jed. "Did Miss Ella give this to Tahcitan?"

He shrugged, then said simply, "Dunno."

"So you don't know what it is?"

He shook his head. "Nope."

I held the parcel to my nose and inhaled the soft, sweet smell of vanilla. It had to mean something--this unopened package. Maybe the contents would give me a hint as to where Tahcitan might be. Maybe it was a clue.

I turned it over again and studied the impression pressed into the dried wax that sealed the envelope. An image of mountains, two of them, perfectly matched in height. I stared at the peaks for a moment, then realized they weren't mountains at all, but rather, the letter M in fancy script. M for Mitchell.

I tickled the edge of the crisp paper, ran the pad of my finger along the hardened and cracked wax seal. It had never been opened.

Jed cleared his throat, and I jumped, startled. He said, "I, uh, Ma'am? I gotta git these cows on home now."

I shoved the envelope back into the drawer, and slid it shut. "Yeah Jed, let's go. Do you see a coat hanging anywhere? I thought maybe I could borrow one, you don't think she'd mind, do you?"

He fingered the leather shirts hanging on pegs behind the door. "These here might do," he said.

I hesitated a moment, then reached for the soft yellow-tan buckskin shirt with the fringe. It had taken hours to make the shirt. First, the leather had been tanned, softened. Then slicing the fringe, stringing the beads...

Her favorite.

How did I know that?

Half of me wanted to sit in this house for a long time and think--no, *feel* was a better word. Just sit and let the essence of Tahcitan sink into me. Maybe then I'd have some answers.

Jed interrupted me reverie by saying, "Ya gonna put it on?"

I brought the soft garment to my face and inhaled the clean smell of leather. Familiar and comforting, the feel of the soft garment buoyed my spirits. Happily, as though I hadn't a care in the world, I exaggerated the lilt in my step and walked from the sod house, lacing the front of the shirt as I went. Stooping to go through the front door, I grinned up at Jed, and drawled, "Let's git a move-on, Pardner."

Jed grinned with half of his mouth, worry furrowing his brow, and mounted the palomino.

My barrette fell from my hair and I shoved the shiny metal piece into my back pocket, then swung into the saddle. I glanced toward Jed.

Internal shadows skittered across his face and darkened his features, then vanished, leaving his face a ghostly white. His jaw hung slack, and his eyes had the distant look of a dying fish. "Jed? Are you all right?"

He nodded, not really seeing me. When he did speak, his voice barely carried enough force to reach me. "Who are you?"

What the heck did he mean? He seemed to be a simple man, true, but he couldn't have forgotten who I was. Instead of answering, I repeated, "Jed, are you okay?"

"You, uh, you a ghost?" He ventured.

The feeling of my knowing the Indian woman's things came back to me. I smiled. "No, Jed, I'm not a ghost."

He saw what I felt, I recognized the fear in his eyes--the recognition. I laughed, and even to myself, the sound rang false and shrill. "I'm Paizely Dunn, remember?"

His body stiffened, and his eyes narrowed. "You a witch?"

Yeah, that was it. I was a witch. All I had to do now was wriggle my nose like Elizabeth Montgomery and I'd be home. Or maybe I could laugh the same cackling laugh as the Wicked Witch of the West and some flying monkeys would come to my rescue.

The wind gusted and my loose hair flew around my face. Beneath me, the gray mare pranced. "No, Jed. I am not a witch."

His gaze was intent on my cheek, and he raised his hand to his face, then traced his own jaw-line. "You have her scar. Her hair." He turned the palomino away from me and spoke over his shoulder. "You're her, else you're a ghost." He spurred his horse into a gallop and raced toward the mountains in the west, his herd of four, forgotten.

I nudged the mare into a slow jog, and followed the only person I knew, the words to George Strait's, *The Cowboy Rides Away"* echoing in my ears.

What did Jed mean by, 'You have her scar'?

What scar? And then I remembered the line on my face I'd seen in Ella's mirror and wondered what that line, that scar could possibly mean.

~19

The farther ahead Jed got, the more nervous and excited the gray mare I rode became. Obviously, she didn't care to be left behind, alone. Still, I held her back, puzzling over the scar, the words to the George Strait song still tumbling through my mind, while the mare tugged at the reins and snorted. I raised my hand to my cheek, tracing my own jaw-line. There, on the left side of my face, a thin cord ran from ear to chin.

This morning, in the mirror, there had been a lazy S that was nothing more than a faint line. It hadn't looked or felt like a raised scar.

Tahcitan's scar.

Maybe the mark was a clue in this puzzle. Maybe if I figured it out, I'd know what I was supposed to do. I tried to remember how Tahcitan had acquired the scar, as if the memory was mine. But nothing came to me.

Jed would know what had happened to Tahcitan.

I leaned forward and kissed the air beside the mare's ear. The horse responded by leaping into a gallop, happy to race after the gelding.

By the time I'd caught up to him, Jed had slowed to a walk. Riding beside him, I remained silent. A thousand questions burned to be asked, but watching him from the corner of my eye, I knew not to utter even one. When he was ready, Jed would talk.

We rode in silence. I didn't look straight at him, but watched him as I would have observed a scared horse. I mulled my questions and his last words around in my mind.

I turned to him. Stared at him a full minute. Maybe more. He didn't return my gaze or seem to notice I was there.

Quite an aggravating man and juvenile to boot with his silent treatment and shunning. I couldn't stand it any longer. "Jed, how did Tahcitan get her scar?"

He rode on, silent. Finally, he began humming the same sad song about the river.

I wanted to slap him, but cleared my throat instead.

He remained aloof and oblivious.

Fury clenched my hands until they shook, and my teeth ground against one another so hard I was afraid I'd crack one. I needed his help, and he'd rather croon some stupid cow-poke song. Well, he'd forgotten all about his "ladies", as he referred to the four dumb cows, maybe that'd get him talking. I smiled, and my words dripping with the sweetness of syrup from a maple tree, asked, "Jed, what about your cows?"

He shot me a look of contempt, his anger obvious over my remembering his mission while he'd forgotten it. He glanced over his shoulder and I followed his gaze back to the cattle in the distance. In silence, and in unison, we turned their horses back.

I cleared my throat again, louder this time, and stared at the sallow man.

He didn't even blink.

I didn't want to beg and forced myself to stay calm. "Jed, please talk to me. I need your help. Where did Tahcitan get the scar? How did she and El, Miss Ella, become friends? Where did she come from?"

He hauled back on the reins, spinning the palomino around before stopping. His eyes were narrow slits in his pale face. "Where'd *you* come from?"

Yes, where indeed? I never had been any good at lying and besides, this sudden anger from him threw me completely off-balance. I opened my mouth, but couldn't speak.

Jed's dark eyes widened, then narrowed, his gaze drilling into me as though he thought he could extract the information he wanted by sheer will power.

I wasn't so sure his plan to bore into my soul would fail. I glanced away from him, then back into his intense stare. "I, I was riding, and my horse reared. I saw two men, I was--"

"Don't give me no story, ma'am, jus tell the truth." He'd spoken in a low-timbered whisper. His words drifted my way; butterflies on a soft summer breeze.

"It's no story, Jed. It's the truth."

"Why you ridin Miss Ella's horse? Where's yours?"

There was the sixty-four thousand dollar question. "I don't know where my horse is. I came to and he was gone.'

"He?" Jed's brows met in the middle of his face, and he leaned toward me. "He happen to be a bay stallion? Big?"

He'd seen Frisco? Fear crept over my skin as cold as a million snowflakes settling over me. I shivered. "How do you know what my horse looks like, have you seen him?"

"I can't rightly say, ma'am." He removed his hat and scratched his head. "I've seen Tahcitan's horse though."

What did Tahcitan's horse have to do with Frisco? The answer came to me as a loud smack, as if someone had clapped their hands over my ears. "Her horse," I said, and my voice sounded strained, false, as though someone else had spoken the words. "He's a bay stallion?"

Jed sneered. "Well now, how'd you know that?" He sat back and sucked his teeth, his satisfaction clear.

How? Lucky guess was all. Puzzle pieces, pure and simple.

Jed said, "Your horse, this bay stud, he run fast?"

I nodded.

"He got a star and one sock behind?"

Another nod, smaller this time.

"An' he don't favor nobody but you?"

A flash of anger cut through I and I snapped, "Are you saying Tahcitan's horse is my horse?"

Jed sucked on his front teeth, long and loud, then turned the palomino back toward the cows. Over his shoulder he said, "No ma'am, I was just thinkin it. Yer the one said it."

My horse is Tahcitan's horse. Frisco. The low nicker at Ella's house. I'd known then, hadn't I?

* * *

The sun hung in the sky, waiting. In a short while, it would hide behind the mountains, and take with it the warmth of this day. Tahcitan did not feel warm. Once the shadows grew longer, she would be even more cold.

Steep slopes dotted with scrub pines and boulders reached skyward, pointing to a few wispy clouds drifting in a sea of blue. Green winter bushes fought with icy patches of snow, struggling to bathe in the sun's rays. Beneath the scattered trees and shrubs, the earth was tan and brown and gold.

Only the stark white snow seemed out of place.

The colors matched Tahcitan's mood. Dull and sad.

She rode the stallion along winding deer paths, scanning the hillside ahead. At the base of the mountain, she angled toward the place where the skull of the bear rested, then cut back toward the southwest. She followed an ancient trail to the mouth of the cave where she tied the bay to a scruffy tree that was no taller than the horse's chest. Her open hand followed the smooth contour of his neck. "Wait here, my friend, I will see if it is safe."

The horse lowered his head to the ground and rifled the dirt in search of food.

Treading with light steps on the soles of her moccasins, she crept toward the black opening of the cave. She picked up a handful of rock and fired them one at a time into the darkness. With her head cocked sideways, she listened, but only the sound of stone hitting stone ricocheted back to her. She crept closer, her knees bent, ready to run if needed.

But no animal came to attack her and there was no sound in the cave. She stepped into the darkness and stood to her full height. Her eyes could not see and she blinked. She reached into her buckskin shirt for a wooden match.

A close smell, wild and oily filled her nostrils. She struck the match. The cave was as she remembered it, empty except for the bats hanging upside-down along the ceiling. The room was large enough for both her and the horse. Inside, it was dry, except for the spring that gurgled at the back of the cavern and drained along one wall. Although the summer moons had passed and it was the time of the winter moons, the cave was warm and comfortable.

She turned to the sun-filled opening and went to the stallion.

* * *

By the time Jed and I topped the last rise before Ella's ranch house, the afternoon sun reached toward evening. Long shadows stretched toward the east, away from the mountain peaks.

From the knoll, I searched for Frisco. I couldn't help myself. If he was here, I would find him. The house looked deserted, cloaked in an eerie silence. No sign of the sheriff, any of the other men, or Tahcitan.

In the yard, I dismounted and untacked the mare, then turned her loose in the pasture. "Jed, do you think they've taken Hol, Ella's body yet?"

"I reckon so, Ma'am."

"I'm going to check, okay?" I walked toward the back door.

Jed sat on his horse, staring first at me, then the cattle. When I reached the landing at the top of the four wooden stairs, he said, "That's the door Tahcitan uses."

Of course she does. I shot Jed a look I hoped he would interpret as shock on my part.

He turned the palomino toward the cows.

I entered the house. I pushed my way through the mess in the kitchen, pausing at the bottom of the narrow staircase. I didn't want to go up there and I didn't want to see Holly's cold body. But I needed to know if someone had taken care of her. I should have seen to that, and the fact I hadn't embarrassed me, yet still, I stood. I tried to think of anything else but the blue room and what it held. I still needed to find help--talk to the sheriff, assuming he wasn't part of the murdering mob, and I needed to look for Tahcitan and Frisco.

I placed the toe of my boot on the first tread. Took another step, then forced my feet to run the rest of the way to the top. I kept running and skidded across the landing. I turned left into the bedroom. My heart thudding, I glanced at the bed. Holly was gone, thank God. Only dried blood remained, staining everything.

I spun on my heel and dashed down the dark stairs, raced through the kitchen and burst through the back door and out into the yard. Jumping the four steps, I landed in a crouch. Evening shadows filled the yard with catacomb quiet and draped me in fear.

"Jed?" I yelled, snapping my head left and right. "Jed, where are you?"

There was no sign of him, no sound from him. Not even the cows made a noise. They'd all disappeared. Gone, vanished. It surprised me to note not only my dependence on Jed, but the degree. I wasn't used to needing anyone.

I heard him before I saw him. A man with a knife, riding a horse, running straight toward me, coming to slash me.

The killer.

Still crouched on bent knees, I willed my legs to move, run. But instead, something made me stand and I stood, waiting to die. The lingering question asked why wasn't I running and would death be painful? I wondered if I'd see Holly...

Slow motion. Time stopped. He wore a hat and I couldn't see his face. He was closer. The horse's pounding hooves beat in time with my heart. *Lub-dub, Dub. Lub-dub, Dub.* The perfect three-beat cadence of a loping horse coming closer and closer.

* * *

Tahcitan took the saddle from the horse's back and set it inside the cave entrance. "The night is near, my friend," she said to the stallion.

His muscles quivered beneath his hide. He raised his head to the heavens and snorted loud and long. "Be easy," she told him, but he did not listen.

She led him closer to the dark opening, speaking in a whisper to reassure him. He stopped, unwilling to enter such a place. She whispered a chant in the language of the *Tsitsistas,* from when she was a child and safe. Finally, he nuzzled her side and followed.

She showed him the water bubbling from the spring and he lowered his head to drink. She crouched beside him, cupping her hand into the cold, clear water, then raising her palm to her mouth.

Outside, the shadows cast by the mountain deepened and the afternoon turned purple and cold.

* * *

Sheriff Thomas Taylor paid for both of his meals; the one he'd eaten there and the one in the saddle bag swinging on his shoulder. On his way out, the bell above the door jangled a happy melody, but the sound didn't cheer him. He walked down the gravel street toward his office and as he neared the saloon, he slowed his pace, listening for Frank's deep timbered voice. The only sounds he heard included the usual raucous yelling and swearing that filled the tavern on any Saturday night. That today was Wednesday did not escape his attention, and he wondered at the strangeness of the day.

The heavy laughter of drunken men mingled with their loud swearing and harsh threats. Although he didn't hear Frank Mitchell's authoritative voice, the vigilante group boasted of how they planned on killing the squaw. However, with the men in their current condition, it seemed a safe assumption that Tahcitan would be safe for the night.

Taylor shook his head, pulling his time-piece from his pocket. Four o'clock, and already nearly dark. He opened the door, his mind tallying the things he needed. Leaving the door open, he tossed his saddlebags onto the desk.

A board creaked behind him and in one fluid motion, Taylor sung around, drew his pistol, cocked and aimed at the shadowy figure in the doorway. His finger rested on the trigger, ready.

The man laughed a hollow sound that rang with a tinny falseness, and Taylor recognized Frank Mitchell.

"Just about got yourself shot," Taylor said, holstering his gun. "You ought never sneak up on a man like you just did."

Frank crossed the small office in two stride, laughing. "Scared you, good friend? My deepest apologies. My inquiry pertains to the hour we shall be heading out tomorrow. Shall we say five?"

His breath stank with the pungently sweet odor of alcohol and the heavy rankness of cigars. That Frank would wait until morning and announce this statement puzzled Taylor for a moment. He'd been so all-fired to go after the woman immediately. Perhaps the lure of liquor was sufficient cause to make him forget about Tahcitan. Taylor smiled a genuinely happy grin. "Sure, Frank. We'll meet at the hotel."

Frank said, "I'll stay at my house tonight, it's closer to yours. We can leave from there, find the heathen killer and return to town before noon tomorrow."

Frank declaring Ella's house as his own grated against Taylor, but instead of saying such, he repeated his earlier convictions. "Going after Tahcitan is wrong, Frank."

"Oh yes, I had almost forgotten. However, we shall be hanging her for horse-theft if I am not mistaken."

"She didn't steal the stallion."

"So you say, my friend, so you say. However, it is now my horse and I want it back." He made his way to the door. Over his shoulder he said, "I'll look forward to seeing you at five."

Taylor stood at the doorsill and called after Frank. "By the way, Doc Perry went and picked up Ella's body. Talk to him to make arrangements for your sister's burial."

Frank waved over his shoulder as if swatting a pesky mosquito and shuffled, his bad leg dragging, back toward the saloon.

* * *

The ground shook. The man on the horse galloped nearer.

The man had no face, only a black shadow beneath his hat. The horse slid to a stop and the familiar musk of horse-sweat enveloped me.

I didn't want the killer's face to be the last image I ever saw. Squeezing my eyes tight, I pictured Frisco cantering, Holly laughing, the mountains in autumn, and the ocean at sunset.

I pulled my elbows to my ears and hunched my shoulders, curling myself into a fetal position.

The man's horse blew from his nose as if sneezing.

A fine mist of spray showered down on my head and I waited to die but no knife plunged into my back or slid between my ribs.

I peeked from between my laced fingers and saw a horse's nostril.

Jed's horse. Lowering my arms, I looked at the rider. Jed. His eyes were bottomless cups of rich black coffee. "Ma'am? You okay?"

I opened my mouth to speak, but no words came. My throat tightened around my heart and hot perspiration pricked at my armpits. I gulped cool air; a welcomed salve to my rattled nerves. "Jed, where were you?"

"Jus puttin' them cows in the pasture."

"Oh," I said, standing. "I thought you'd gone and left me here all alone."

He took off his hat. "I can't figger why you'd care. Tahcitan prefers to be alone. I reckon you must not be a ghost if'n you're scairt to be alone." He scratched his head. "I jes can't figger what you are Miss Paizely. Or what's got you spooked so."

Trembling, I bit my lower lip and said silent plea that I not let Jed see me cry again. I'd never been so weak or felt so helpless in my life. I hated to admit, even to myself, my fear of being here, especially now that night had fallen. I took an inventory of myself: Afraid of being alone, afraid of the dark, afraid of dying.

Having Jed near made being here easier, not quite so frightening. The idea I wanted him around both surprised and made me angry. My self-image consisted of independence, self-reliance and courage. I ought to be able to handle anything that came my way. I expected nothing less from myself.

But I needed Jed. Needed him not only as a source of comfort and security, but as a guide in this strange place. Admitting the truth made me feel better though I'd never say aloud I needed him and wanted him to stay with me. I threw my shoulders back. "What do you say we go to town and find that sheriff of yours? Maybe we can get something to eat, too. I'm starving."

Jed's brows crawled together. He frowned, studying the ground. "Uh, I can't go into town. I have a wife 'n family waitin' for me. Little bride's due to birth any day now, an she's pro'ly a wonderin' where I been off to all this time."

That he had an existence away from the cattle he so loved seemed unthinkable. Guilt warmed my cheeks and made my skin flush. I hadn't given a thought to what his life might be or the possibility of his having a family, especially a wife. "Why Jed, you never mentioned anything about them, I just assumed you lived alone."

His smile was instant and warm. "Shore do, Ma'am. Two boys and a girl, and a new baby on the way." He paused, took off his hat, scratched his head, and frowned, before settling the hat back atop his blond hair. "Uh, if'n you'd want, uh, you could come on home with me. The missus'd be more'n pleased to fix you supper."

In that instant, I felt more alone than I ever had. Here was a man who obviously had everything important the world had to offer.

Either world.

He was a man who loved and was loved in return. A wife, kids, and a job he enjoyed. What did I have? I had a ranch. I had enough money to be comfortable. I had education and privilege. Yet compared to simple Jed, I had nothing. I didn't have a husband or even a prospect for one--which was okay, I reminded myself, I didn't want to be married. Holly had most likely been murdered by now, and my horse was gone. I was trapped in the past, had a splitting headache and no Advil, and if I cared to admit the truth, men were chasing after the person I used to be in this life, which meant the possibility of being killed soon myself was to be expected. The idea of dying soon made me want to throw up so I laughed instead, and even to myself, I sounded hollow and weak. "Thanks Jed, but I think I'll just ride along with you part way, then I'll go back into town alone."

"Back?" He asked. "You already been to town?"

I told a brief, albeit colorful story of my excursion into town earlier in the day. When I finished, Jed said, "The smith, that's Junior. He and Tahcitan, they had a feud. Seems he wanted somethin' she didn't wanna give." He sucked his teeth.

"What was it, what did she have?"

Jed squirmed, casting his eyes about as though following an errant fly. "Well, lemme tell it this way. I believe when she cut his leg, she meant for the knife to go a little higher and a little deeper. Ol' Junior, he limped for a solid year followin' that incident, and he hates Tahcitan sumthin 'fierce. Far as I kin tell, though, he plum deserved what she gave to him." He studied the darkening sky. "We best be getting' along. Sheriff oughta be headin' home here 'fore too long."

I nodded. "I need a horse. The gray mare's tired. I've been riding her all day. Any suggestions?"

Jed sucked his teeth and surveyed the herd. "See the bay over there, four white socks?" he pointed with the ends of his reins. "She's a good ol' gal. Take her."

I climbed through the fence and went to the bay mare, carrying the bridle I'd hung on the fence when I turned the grey loose. Once I had the bridle adjusted, I led the horse through the gate to the barn.

Jed said, "I kin gitcher saddle."

But I declined his offer and swung the heavy thing onto the mare myself. I tightened the cinch and eased onto the horse. "Let's hit it, Hombre," I said, hoping my tone masked my apprehension and fear.

We rode in silence, my thoughts preoccupied with what kind of woman Jed might be married to--was she kind, smart, and funny? I wanted to ask him, but kept quiet and found myself musing over Jed's life. A life full of love and caring, while my own existence paled in comparison. I didn't want to talk..

An hour away from the ranch, Jed reined in the palomino. "This here is where I turn to git on home."

I was surprised at the lump in my throat. "Thank you for all you've done for me. I appreciate your kindness more than you'll ever know."

"Well," he drawled, "'Twas nothin'. Just bein' neighborly is all. You goin' be okay? You kin come on home with me for a bite of supper if'n you'd want."

The temptation to stay with him was overwhelming, the thought of a hot meal so alluring, I almost said yes. But I couldn't shake the feeling of doom-around-the-corner and responsibility. I needed to explain to the sheriff what had happened that morning. To top it off, I had to find Tahcitan. My hand drifted to my face and traced the corded scar along my jaw. "I'll be fine, but thanks anyway."

Jed must have seen my finger trace Tahcitan's scar, my scar, because he said, "That mark you carry? Tahcitan came here with the same scar. Happened at the massacre. Sand Creek. Jus' thought y'ought t'know."

"Thank you, Jed. I appreciate knowing. And Jed? You tell your wife I think she's one lucky woman, okay?"

Even in the gathering darkness, the deep crimson of Jed's face was obvious before he turned away. Glancing back, he tipped his hat with his finger. "Happy to oblige Ma'am, good luck to you."

I turned the bay mare toward Longmont and nudged her into a trot. The sky had darkened to the black-gray of thunderheads, though only a few sparse clouds clotted the horizon. Far to the south, a sliver of a moon hung like a stage-prop.

Sand Creek. Tahcitan was Cheyenne and had most likely lost her entire family there since I remembered reading about the anniversary date. Seven years ago today, Tahcitan would have lost her family and once more, on this day, she has lost her second family.

The worm in my brain stirred, mumbling about revenge and fear and somehow, it made a little more sense to me--why I might also be afraid of both loving and losing. Why killing Steve before he could kill Holly had been such an easy leap. I am not a killer, but I've also lost family and people I loved. Holly being the last person in the world I care about, it made sense I'd do whatever I could to save her.

I followed the winding gravel road toward nightfall, the mare's hooves a metronome beating the night closer. If only I could turn around, run after Jed, have supper with his family. But town was near, and already, a faint cast of light glowed and reflected off the clouds.

I glanced over my shoulder, but Jed was probably home by now, wrestling with his boys or cuddling his daughter. Or maybe his wife's time had come and a new life would enter the their lives tonight.

I was on my own.

~20

Frank Mitchell hunkered down behind a water trough near the livery stable at the edge of town. He gripped the glass tumbler hard enough to cause his hand to shake. The amber liquid spilled over the rim and ran down his cuff.

He watched Sheriff Taylor ride along the dirt road on his way to the Mitchell ranch. His ranch.

Still, Frank sat, not bothering to follow the man. He gripped his glass but did not sip the fine bourbon. He watched the good sheriff until the evening swallowed the man's form. In celebration of the sheriff leaving, he tossed his drink down his throat, savoring the warmth of the liquid. If they left now and cut across the fields, they would reach Ella's, no, *his* house before Taylor.

He'd spent all afternoon thinking about where she might have hidden the letters and he thought he'd figured out where to look. With any luck, he'd be able to locate them and burn them before anyone even knew they existed.

* * *

Thomas Taylor relaxed into the easy rhythm of his gelding's lumbering gait, his feet swinging in the stirrups. The first few stars sprinkled the purple-grey sky like mischievous eyes. To the south, the moon smiled sideways, jeering as though in complete agreement, and though he searched the heavens for an answer to where Tahcitan might be, the sky stayed quiet, laughing at him from behind a curtain of wispy clouds.

Ella had shared details about Tahcitan's life with him so he knew about the death of her mother when she was born, the loss of her family at Sand Creek, her capture and consequent torture by the Confederate soldiers, and her distrust of people, white men in particular. She could track better than anyone and could vanish without difficulty if she didn't want to be found. Ella taught her to read and to write, but Tahcitan refused to learn to play the piano. Not because she couldn't understand the concept, but because the instrument was too big to carry on a horse or drag behind on a travois, and consequently, no more discussion was necessary.

So where would she go? Without Ella, she would feel alone and vulnerable. Frightened. He tried to put himself in her place. Keeping himself and the stallion safe would determine his actions, and he believed the same would guide Tahcitan. Of course, he would look to the law for help, but the chances of her coming to him were slim since she couldn't, or wouldn't look him in the eye. He had no way of knowing where she'd go, or where to start looking for her.

The purple sky turned dusky-black, and the darkness hung about the prairie like a shawl draped over an old woman's shoulders. The glitter in the stars seemed dimmer, their laughter silent. Even the moon's sideways grin hid behind the clouds.

* * *

My back ached and my butt felt like compressed and hardened clay.

Something ahead sounded like a machine or maybe a drum. A steady noise, and coming closer. The mare I rode raised her head high and flared her nostrils, then stopped, planting all four feet in the universal equine stance of fear and concentration.

I patted the grey mare's neck--a nervous habit I always did with Frisco to calm him as well as myself. This time, it failed to settle either of us. The mare's back raised and her muscles tensed, while my palms slickened with sweat. Both the animal and I strained to listen.

Ahead, the steady fall of hoof beats echoed across the pastures, filling the night.

* * *

Sheriff Thomas Taylor stopped his horse and listened. A humming crackling noise, like the swarm of a thousand flitting grasshoppers came to him from up ahead. The sound reminded him of summer insects and this late in the fall, that could not be the case. He turned his head, listening with his left ear. The sound dropped a little in volume, but nothing else changed.

The gelding pranced, straining at the bit as if the strange noise beckoned him, but Taylor held him back, commanding him to walk.

The moon cast a faint silver light upon the road and ahead, he could just make out a horse and rider. A woman, her hair streaming about her shoulders, riding as though atop a ghost animal. Tahcitan? But the horse was not the bay stallion; it was not big enough, nor fast enough. This horse had a more feminine appearance, with mincing steps and a high head.

The crackling noise steadied.

Taylor halted, waiting for her to see him, to say something.

Horse and rider were close enough he could clearly see plumes of breath spewing from the animal's nostrils. With all the strange events of the day, this woman riding on the edge of night spooked him. Sweat pricked his neck and slid down his spine. His hand reached across his belt buckle to his pistol, stopping to rest on the butt of the gun. "Hey!" He called out, "Who goes there?"

The woman pulled back on the reins so hard, the horse's mouth gaped open as it slid to a stop. The woman's teeth were bright white and reflected moonbeams as if made of metal.

The buzzing deepened a shade sounding more like bees than grasshoppers.

Tahcitan.

She stood right in front of him. He had to stay calm or he'd spook her. His pulse quickened and his hand flitted from the gun to settle on his thigh. He smiled and dismounted, holding one rein. "Tahcitan, it's me, Sheriff Taylor. Don't be afraid, I've come to help you."

* * *

The man claiming to be Sheriff Taylor stood before me and he was tall. About six-four in height and in perfect proportion with his weight. Not too heavy or too thin. He had removed his hat and was fingering the rim. His blond hair was neither long or short, groomed or messy. His long mustache sculpted around his mouth so the ends crawled down either side of his lips and stretched toward his chin. His eyes flashed silver in the fading light and his smile showed even, white teeth.

He made me think of the Marlborough Man cowboy. Holly had posters from the 1970's with his picture and I'd always found the cardboard man to be good-looking in macho guy kind of way. Here, this live one was gazing steadily at me, causing my heart to flip-flop in my chest and my breath to catch in my throat.

My first conscious thought was a vain one; my clothes were filthy, my hair was a fright and I smelled like a horse. I brushed my unruly bangs from my forehead, and glanced at the road. In search of any sense of balance within myself, I wrapped a mental fist around my turbulent and unexpected emotions. He was the sheriff, but he had also been with the killers earlier. For all I knew he led the marauding bunch of murderers and played at being a cop as a disguise.

I turned to him and looked straight into his eyes. I searched for any sign of malevolence or violence.

A feeling of sadness emanated from him, at odds with his shining eyes, making him appear tough and vulnerable at the same time. He cocked his head sideways, listening, but for what, I couldn't tell. I held my breath and tried to hear the sound he sought.

Finally, he said, "Pardon me?"

I hadn't spoken. Couldn't have, even if I'd wanted to, which I did not. Maybe he was missing a couple of marbles. Figured. Here he was the embodiment of my vision of the perfect man, and he had the wits of a moth.

Disgusted with myself, I decided to find out exactly who he was. He seemed harmless enough, but I stayed sitting astride the horse in case I needed a quick get-away in a hurry. Clearing my throat, I said, "I'm not Tahcitan, though it seems I must look an awful lot like her. My name is Paizely Dunn."

Sheriff Taylor gazed at me, a dumbfounded expression creasing his features and dulling his silver eyes to pewter.

"Who?" He asked.

He truly *was* slow.

* * *

Afraid his jaw was hanging open and he looked like the village idiot, Taylor snapped his mouth shut. His teeth slammed together with an audible *click.*

The idea of this woman not being Tahcitan, was a hard thing to understand. She wore the familiar fringed leather shirt, and had the same practiced way of sitting on a horse. Yet, she looked different enough; like they were twins, but not identical. He opened his mouth to ask, when the woman spoke.

"Paizely Dunn, sir, nice to meet you."

She spoke effortlessly without the halting accent of the Cheyenne woman. Her words had a sweet lilt to them, like birds singing in the summer and was higher pitched than Tahcitan's.

He couldn't help staring at her, his face frozen in the huge toothy grin of an awestruck adolescent. In the moonlight, her brown hair shimmered and her eyes were huge and mysterious. On closer inspection, her features were a mix of Tahcitan and some other woman. The resulting blend was attractive and he felt an inexplicable pull toward her he neither understood or liked. Even with Tahcitan, he'd never felt as off-balance as he did right now. "Are you in some sort of trouble, miss? Do you need help?"

She met his eyes squarely, in the same forthright manner a man would. Nothing coy and demure about her. She seemed fearless, as though nothing could stop her. Her self-confidence radiated from her like heat rolling off a fire. Her hands quivered though, and a mild tremor shook her whole body. She was afraid, but of what? Him? An amusing thought. Smiling, he asked, "Are you all right?"

Fear and bewilderment raced across her face, and then disappeared. She straightened her spine and looked into his eyes. "I know about the murder. I know who killed...her."

Her words whipped the smile from his face. His knees went soft and he reached to steady himself on the buckskin's saddle horn.

* * *

He was a big man, this handsome sheriff, yet he'd grabbed at the saddle horn like a drowning person reaching for a lifeline.

Great. Not only slow, but likely to pass out at the least provocation. What caused his reaction, I couldn't guess. Probably a man of no fortitude. Wouldn't it figure? Good men everywhere were either married or damaged emotionally--must've always been so. But maybe he was scared. Maybe he *did* belong to the murdering crew.

I couldn't see any fear in his eyes. If anything, he looked relieved. I needed help and I'd gone looking for this lawman. Trusting him was my only choice. "I was there, this morning," I paused. "When she was killed, I mean. I saw the men."

His head snapped up, an expression of intelligent curiosity on his face. "Men? There was more than one?"

"Yes." I exhaled, "One man stabbed her."

His whole demeanor changed and he looked more like *Walker, Texas Ranger* than some backwoods bumbling fool. A smoky curtain fell over his eyes and I figured he'd be able to karate-kick any bad guy to Hell and Gone with ease.

"These men," he said, his voice the deep timbre of crushed velvet. "What did they look like?"

I tried to focus on his question, wanted to, so the killers would be caught, but the cadence of his words, the tone of his voice--everything about him muddled my thoughts. It was so unlike me on a good day, let alone this day. I reminded myself Holly was dead and to straighten up and think.

There.

I said, "The big one wore a long black coat, the small one had red hair. They rode a gray and a pinto."

"Frank!" The word exploded from him. He swung onto his horse with practiced ease. "Let's go. We can be in town in less than an hour."

He spun his horse around and took off at a gallop.

The sheriff was already fifty yards ahead of me and the distance between us was steadily increasing. The little bay mare I rode could not keep up with his horse, but I hugged her withers and urged her on anyway. "Wait up," I called to the man's back.

Sheriff Taylor must have heard me, because he did slow to a lope. I pulled my wheezing mount up alongside the buckskin gelding. "Good grief, Walker, are you trying to kill us all? It's so dark I can't even see where we're going."

He glanced at me, befuddled grief masking his face. "Who's Walker?"

"He's, he's...Do you know where Tahcitan is?"

He yanked back on the reins and the horse's front feet stopped before his hind ones could. It looked like the gelding would topple right over into a somersault. Halting my mare, I asked, "What's wrong?"

He sat as rigid as an IRS agent during an audit. "Who are you, Miss?"

"I told you. I'm Paizely Dunn."

"You know Tahcitan? Ella?"

Oh God, here it comes. How could I explain who I was? I nodded an affirmation to his question, but didn't speak.

"Where do you live?" His voice loomed deeper than the dark of the night.

"Um." What could I say, that I was from the future? "San Francisco."

He stepped his horse closer to hers. "Where'd you get this mare?"

"I, um, I borrowed her from El."

"Before or after she died?"

What was he getting at? "After."

"Where'd you get the buckskin shirt?"

"Borrowed it." My voice rose an octave with each syllable.

"From who?"

I looked straight into his silver-blue eyes. "Tahcitan."

"When did you see her?"

I said, "I didn't. I took it from her house, her soddie."

"Why were you there?"

"I went looking for her to warn her about the men on their way to kill her."

His brows furrowed. "Why would you think such a thing?"

My turn to scowl. "I heard them say they would."

He glared at me, but didn't say anything. He nudged his horse into a walk, watching me with suspicion. Finally he asked, "Where are you from again? How do you know Tahcitan?"

I wanted to tell him but I didn't trust myself at the moment. Hell, I didn't trust many people, ever, but most especially, men. I told myself he was different. His mannerisms, his way of speaking, his hands, his eyes. He was honest and full of integrity, to the point I swear, I could feel goodness emanating from him. It sounded crazy even to me, but I did trust him. It was that simple.

He had to believe me, to understand my fear and mostly, he had to trust me. I coughed. Cleared my throat. Looked into his face and held his gaze. "I was riding along a ridge. A gust of cold wind blew gravel into my horse's face and he reared. Must've knocked me out, because I woke up and saw a man stabbing--"

He spurred his horse ahead, then cut right in front of me, blocking me. "What ridge?" He demanded. "There's no ridge near Ella's. And why did you call her El? Tahcitan calls her El and you seem so much like her in so many ways. Now, tell me, on what ridge were you riding?"

My throat clamped shut. Tears spilled over my lashes and pooled under the lower lids. I bit my lip, trying for control, but it was hopeless. "Forget it." My voice sounded thick in my own ears.

He sidestepped the gelding toward my horse and wrapped his hand around the mare's headstall, holding the horse so she couldn't move. His steel eyes bored into my soul. "Tell me one thing," he said, "You show up out of nowhere, watch while a woman is murdered, and then tell me you know who did it. Seems a bit--what's the word? Convenient, wouldn't you agree? You didn't just happen to be there when we arrived this morning, did you? Didn't happen to get a good look at Frank and Saul and decide to blame them for what you'd done? Is that how it happened?"

He was blaming me.

Perfect.

I narrowed my eyes. "Listen, the other two, Frank and Saul is it? They came to El's early--before the sun was up. Frank stabbed her and left her in the yard for dead. I tried to save her life, couldn't, went into the house looking for a pho-- For help. Then, Tahcitan came and she carried El upstairs. When you showed up, Tahcitan ran out the back door. End of story. You think what you want."

* * *

El. Tahcitan always called her El. Sheriff Taylor studied the strange woman's face. Her clothes were strange too. Tahcitan's fringed buckskin shirt hung over denim pants that fit the woman's legs like tight stockings. Her riding boots came up to her knees but still, he could tell her legs were strong and lithe. No woman in these parts dare dress in this manner, including Ella Mitchell. "You a friend of Ella's?" He asked. "I don't recall her mentioning you."

She smiled. "I told you, we grew up together, went to the same school."

An outright lie. "I've known Ella Mitchell all my life," he said, his voice stern. "We came here together from Kentucky, back even before Longmont became a township."

She gnawed on a ragged thumbnail. Noticing his stare, she dropped her hand and studied the top of the saddle horn as though it was the most interesting piece of brass she'd ever seen. One moment dragged on and became two, then three, and still, she remained quiet. Finally, she said, "The point is, I saw the killers. Jed, he works, um, worked for El, told me Tahcitan is being blamed. Is that true? Are you going to arrest her?"

Although fully aware of the woman's tactics to turn the subject away from herself, Taylor followed where she led. Saving Tahcitan from Frank and the posse he'd gathered was the most important thing. "Frank is intent on hanging her for horse theft."

"Horse theft?" Paizely's expressions of consternation and defiance struggled with one another. "She steal a horse?"

He mused for a moment over the cast of her face, wondering why she stiffened at his words. "No, she is not a horse thief. Ella gave her a bay stallion, the grandson of the great Stockwell. Worth a fortune and Frank wants him."

She stared at him, into his soul, her eyes willing him to listen. "Sheriff, we have to find her. If we fail, Frank will kill her. You know it's true."

He broke free of her gaze and let loose of the mare's bridle. His thoughts skittered across his mind like tumbleweeds blown by the wind. So many questions, yet her story made sense. He knew Ella had been carried into the house and up the stairs because of the blood trail on the hardwood floors. But this woman, this stranger, could have done those things herself. Where had she really come from and who was she?

He glanced at her. Her face was practically Tahcitan's, and so was her body. Both women were tall and well-muscled, with long legs and shiny hair. Both rode with an ease that few people--men or women possessed. Looking at her, his heart ached with an emotion he didn't recognize and didn't dare acknowledge.

He *wanted* to believe her.

~21

Tahcitan waited inside the cave. The bay stood next to her and for this, she was glad. Together they watched the moon creep across the sky until it was high in the night. Many stars blinked behind the drifting clouds and they laughed at her.

She sat wrapped in the skin of the bear, leaning against the cold stone walls of the cave, thinking of the horse. She knew she would die soon. This, she accepted. But losing the stallion she loved so much burdened her with great sadness. He was strong and brave and this helped her know he would find many mares on the prairie and he would have a new life. To know he would be with others of his kind made her happy.

In the dim moonlight, she saw the horse stood with one leg cocked, dozing. He did not mind if they did not sleep in their own home on this night. His deep and steady breathing calmed her, and she too fell into sleep. Dreams of the *Ve'ho'e* brought the bad spirits to visit. They chewed at her like mice gnawing through burlap feed sacks. Their squeals as they feasted on the bay's body ripped her from her tortured nightmares. She woke shaking and sweating, the bearskin tossed to the side in a tangled heap.

The sounds of the mice echoed through the dark cave. Were they chewing on the stallion? She screamed. The horse jumped, sliding on the stone floor so his metal shoes flashed blue and yellow sparks before he stopped, quivering.

The screeching of the mice came from high in the cave and then she could see they were not mice, but bats. They welcomed their new day with high squeaks and chirps, and flitted together near the ceiling.

She stood, calling to the horse in the language of the *Tsitsistas*. As she saddled him, she explained what they would do, where they would go. She told him this may be their last ride together and to be ready for whatever was ahead of them. She told him she loved him as she loved El and she would go to El, but not take him. He should find mares and have many foals living free. That no white man should touch him did not need to be said.

Out of the cave, the silver light of the moon lit the way and for this she was glad. She rode the stallion to the top of the ridge, then followed a narrow deer trail until she came to a fork in the path and followed it down the mountainside. Both Longmont and the Mitchell Ranch were far below her. The sky above the town glowed with the faint light of the *Ve'ho'e* and she could make out the lighted building at the Mitchell Ranch.

Someone was there.

* * *

Sheriff Thomas Taylor had been silent since quizzing me about my relationship with Ella Mitchell. That he might be taking me to jail crossed my mind, but the idea seemed absurd. Clearly something bothered him so waiting to find out was the best solution.

While he pondered whatever occupied his mind, I turned my attention to the possibility I'd been here before, in a time I'd forgotten. The idea was too abstract for me to wrap my mind around so I thought about how best to save Tahcitan.

His voice cut the night like a knife through a wedding cake. Slow and precise. He asked, "Why are you so worried about Tahcitan? You and she are good friends?"

Such quietly spoken words. I didn't know how to answer him and I didn't want to lie to him. "She just looked so terrified when she ran from the house, I wanted to help her. I know she didn't kill Hol--Ella. I want to help her because I'm worried and it's not right to stand by when I know something."

"Um," he grunted, nodding. "Some of what you say makes sense. When did you borrow the shirt?"

"I told you, I rode with Jed to her sod house. He said I could borrow it." To myself, I sounded ten years-old attempting to explain myself to adult, knowing they'd scold me anyway.

Taylor ran a large hand through his mustache. With his horse right next to mine, and looking into my eyes, he asked, "Do you know her? Do you know Tahcitan?"

Back to that. "No. And I'd rather not discuss it right now."

Maybe he'd let it slide.

Of course he didn't. He said, "Paizely, I want to believe all you've told me, but it doesn't fit. What ridge had you been riding on before you got thrown? How do you know Ella? What happened to your horse? Where do you live? Talk to me and maybe I can help."

He was right, none of what I said made any sense. If I were him, I'd buy none of it. But if he knew the truth, he'd likely run for the hills pulling hands-full of hair from his scalp while screaming at a decibel he didn't know he could reach.

A deep tiredness fell over me and I sagged into the saddle wondering why any of this mattered. My sister was dead, and I was stuck in a different century. I hung my head and picked at a stray piece of rawhide on the shirt I wore; a shirt Tahcitan had made. The leather was supple and warm, almost alive.

Smooth and honeyed as the scent of flowers on a summer's eve, his voice wafted toward me. "Paizely, you all right?"

I looked into his eyes and the concern in his eyes startled me. I trusted this man, but the theory I had on where I was and who I was would make him look at me as a seriously deranged human in need of hospitalization. I sucked in a deep breath, my gaze shifting from him to the stars to the ground. "I, I want to talk to you, to tell you everything. I need to tell someone, but I don't think you can possibly understand."

"You think I'm too ignorant?" His words were gruff, deep.

"No, no, it's not that. It's just too, too strange. I don't understand and I'm the one it's happened to."

"Try me," he coaxed.

* * *

Weak, yellow lantern light flickered across the shallow creases lining Frank Mitchell's hands. The color gave him the sallow skin of a sick old man. He shifted his attention to the amber whiskey swirling in the tumbler he held and relaxed his eyes making them unfocused and soft. Mesmerized, he watched the liquid catch golden rays reflected in the dark brown and golden-red hues.

He sat with his feet propped on the large mahogany dining table, droplets of glistening bourbon decorating the front of his shirt. Around him, Ella's belongings were strewn and heaped into huge piles. He took a sip, letting the whiskey warm his lips and tried not to feel anything but justification for what he'd done. He hadn't seen her in so many years and it would have been nice to have been welcomed by her. That was her first offense. All he'd ever wanted was to be recognized and valued. All he'd ever gotten was looked over, passed by, and then given the leftovers. He set his back teeth together and ground them before tossing back the rest of the drink.

From the kitchen, the clatter of drawers being pulled out and dumped onto the floor mingled with an Irish tune Saul whistled while destroying the once impeccably kept house.

The racket ceased. Footsteps approached.

Beneath his orange-red hair, Saul's freckles danced across pink sun-kissed cheeks. He frowned, making him appear slightly older than his twenty years. "Nothing here, Frank," he said.

They were here, all right. He knew his sister too well. Knew she'd never dispose of anything so important. He let loose a long-winded belch. "If we don't locate those papers and that moron of a sheriff does, we'll both hang. Keep looking."

"Aw, Frank, they not be 'ere." Saul sang his words--a sing-songy Irish lilt that grated on Frank's nerves. Lately, everything vexed his nerves. It all should have been so simple. Easy as pie. He tossed back the rest of his drink. Ella, the bitch, wouldn't tell him where she'd hidden the papers. No, instead, she had the gall to offer him half the ranch. Half! As if that small pittance would be fair.

He slammed the fisted tumbler to the table and the whiskey bottle teetered and wobbled. He stood, grabbing Saul by the throat lifting the small man off the floor. "Do as I say, and you may live to see your next birthday. Now, find them!"

The Irish lad fell in a heap sputtering and choking. "I'll do it now, me friend," he sobbed. "Ye jus' be calmin' ye'self."

But calming himself was the last thing on Frank's mind.

* * *

Tahcitan crouched near a bare willow bush watching the icy water below her. The stream was a shiny snake in the silvery moonlight. From the pond to the pasture holding the mares, the water still ran, but soon, would freeze and need to be broken for the horses to drink. Behind her, the stallion grazed on the dry winter grass, happy to be eating with the moon to light his way.

Lights flickered in the windows of the house. Tahcitan's hands balled against her gut at the thought of the men sitting in the parlor. With the *Ve'ho'e'* there, she did not know if she would be able to get the key. Maybe she would go without the key. Go from this bad place and head to the lands of the *Tsitsistas*. Other People had escaped from Sand Creek. She would ride the bay, find the People, live with them.

But El had told her to get the key from the piano and so she would.

The moon slid across the sky until her shadow lay before her. And finally, the lights went off in the house. She waited, crouching.

When the moon was above her, she stood and went to the horse. While he grazed, she ran her hand along his neck and whispered, "I go now, my friend. You wait here and I will return."

When the moon slid behind a cloud, she jogged to El's house.

* * *

I hoped my intuition, most times as reliable as any compass, was still intact.

He had to believe me and he had to trust me. I coughed. Cleared my throat. Looked into his eyes. *Here goes.* "Okay Walker, you asked, but I'm warning you, you won't believe it.

Taylor grinned a small lopsided grin, his teeth flashing white in the night air and waited without saying a word.

Drawing a deep breath, I began. "I'm from a small town, just outside of Denver."

His expression encouraged me.

"I was born in San Francisco," I paused, gauging his reaction. He showed no sign of disbelief, so I plunged ahead. "I am the firstborn daughter of two full-fledged Nam-protesting hippies who believed in the good life which included Drugs, Sex and Rock 'n Roll. Once I came along, they quit and became yuppies and were quite successful in their business. They were program developers for Microsoft and made a ton of money. I have a sister, Holly who's three years younger than I am."

No questions from Taylor. No wonderment or emotion on his face. Impassive and patient, his features were stone. His silver eyes clouded to the dark gray of billowing thunderheads, but he didn't speak.

"Yesterday, Holly and I got into an argument, which is rare for us because usually, she yells, I wait, she screams, and after awhile it's over. I don't like to fight with her. But I've been having nightmares lately. I tried so hard to get her to listen, to pay attention and do what she needed in order to protect herself so she wouldn't be killed."

Still no outward reaction from the Marlborough man.

I said, "In my visions, I kept seeing her fiancé, Steve, stabbing her and it scared the hell out of me, the thought of losing her. Whenever I see someone I love die, it happens within twenty-four hours. I tried to warn her, to stop it from happening. But she wouldn't listen. She started screaming at me and told me to get out and stay out of her life." My voice cracked. I glanced at the sheriff. He remained rigid and pulled his horse to a halt, then nodded politely for me to continue.

I decided the next part of the story needed a little white-washing since admitting to a man of the law that I was going to meet Steve with the intention of putting one, maybe two bullets into his chest would end any kind of trust-inducing attempts. "I went to the barn and got Frisco, he's my horse, and I went for a ride to clear my head and give Holly and me a break from each other. I rode up the ridge trail, across the road from our ranch. The path leads to the top of an old landslide, and then it winds around and back down to the Purple Meadow, which is where I was going. Lots of purple thistles, beautiful really, and peaceful, and I needed that, man, I needed some peace and quiet to think."

I paused for a moment, and thought the story was unfolding quite nicely. More importantly, I figured he had no idea of my real intent of murdering Steve. I tried to gauge his reaction, but couldn't see any emotion at all, and so I said, "Anyhow, at the top, a weird wind, icy cold and really strong, blew gravel right into Frisco's face and he reared. I fell off. I guess I got knocked out and when I woke up, I was here. At Ella's I mean. And, I saw her being stabbed."

He simply nodded.

I continued, "I tried to help her, tried to get to her and stop the man, but it was like someone was holding me down. The ground heaved and rolled and I couldn't get up. Finally the men left, the one in the duster and the red-headed one, too. I got up and ran to the woman. At first, she didn't look like Holly, no, she didn't, but then something happened, and she *was* Holly. Everyone here knows her as Ella, but it's Holly, all right."

I paused, waiting for his reaction.

He sat stolidly.

I cleared my throat hoping to get him to talk. His silence made me jittery and nervous. I needed to hear his thoughts and since I had nothing more to add, I said, "If you were the real Walker, Texas Ranger, you'd understand. He'd understand. He's a sensitive man. Open to the notion that the universe is a complex thing. He'd be interested in time travel and reincarnation. Yes, Walker would."

Sheriff Taylor blinked and just sat there.

"One more thing. My best guess is that I must have really screwed up in a past life or I wouldn't be here now, explaining all this to you."

His eyes narrowed and his head moved slowly, left to right. "What are you saying?"

"I'm not done yet, wait."

"There's more?" His words were a just a tad louder than a whisper.

"Yes, if you'd watched more television and seen *Back To The Future*, we wouldn't be having this problem. It's like Michael J. Fox, when he went back and saw not only his father as a teenager, but also himself. You see, I think, I'm not positively sure, but I *think* I might have been Tahcitan. And she is me. I'm afraid if she dies, I will too." Speaking the elusive and, up until now, unspoken thoughts made them real, and my own words made me want to cry.

I either had to keep talking or turn and bolt from him. Like an idiot, I kept talking and thoughts I hadn't completely formed into coherent ideas came out in a tumble. "I think Frank is Steve because they both limp. and I'm afraid that he kills Holly in every life they go through together. I think he's already killed her at home. You know, my home. But what if he hasn't? What if there is a chance I can save her? If I can get back and tell her what happened here, she'd have to believe me, don't you see? He's already done it here and he'll do it again. Right?"

Taylor's head pivoted left and right, and his eyes glowed mercury-silver. He raised his chin and eyebrows, then tilted his head. All in slow motion. "You think you're Tahcitan?"

He didn't understand. I didn't know if I was right about any of it, and since I'd told him so much, and obviously, he thought I was a nutcase anyway, what difference did it make if I kept talking? "No," I said, "I don't think I am Tahcitan *now*. I'm Paizely. Paizely Marie Dunn. But I think I *was* Tahcitan. In a previous life. In *this* life. And I'm pretty sure I must know you too. Even though I was afraid of you at first, it was someone else's fear. *Her* fear." I chewed my thumbnail. "You like Tahcitan, don't you?"

For an instant, he looked puzzled. He leaned back in the saddle and sat up straight before he grinned the smile of a patronizing father placating a three-year-old. "You live more than once?"

"I know it sounds crazy."

"You don't believe in Heaven? God?" He asked, his concern for my eternal soul quite apparent.

What the hell was he talking about? I'd spoken of reincarnation, time travel, television and hippies, and he comes up with, 'you don't believe in God?'

"I don't see what God has to do with this."

His eyes darkened to slate-gray. "You were right," he said. "I don't believe you or this story you've told."

* * *

Silent as a fish gliding through water, Tahcitan tip-toed to the rear of El's house. Her moccasins whispered in the dry brush, and a rabbit scurried away. Closer to the building, she crouched and ran to the north window of the downstairs bedroom. This had been her room when she had stayed nights at her friend's house. Peering through the bare branches of a dormant lilac bush, she saw the man with the sorrel-colored hair sleeping on top of the bed. With one hand over his head and the other fisted at his mouth, he sucked on his thumb like a baby. She watched, and he snuffled and rooted at his hand.

The piano sat two rooms from this one, and she could get into the house and to that room. The groaning of the piano lid when she raised it would wake him. Still, she knew her way through the dark house and she might get the key and be gone before he awoke. She folded her hand into a fist, then gnawed at her knuckle. A habit that nearly drove El wild. She would say, "Tat, don't chew on yourself like an animal."

The words echoed around her now and she pulled her fist from her mouth.

The risk of sneaking into the piano room was great, but she would go in through the woodbin, get the key, then leave. Quietly, she crept from the window and the sleeping man.

From the porch at the front of the house, a man coughed.

* * *

I trailed behind the sheriff cursing my own stupidity. Why I thought he'd believe my story was beyond the scope of anyone's imagination. If I ended up in jail or dead because of the decision to trust him, it served me right.

He was a man of strict morals, tenacious in his opinion of how the world worked. There was a God, who, when you died, decided if you got into Heaven or went to Hell. Period. No reason to question any other possibilities because none existed. Everything in life followed explicit patterns and truths and that system could not be wrong or fail. Nor should it be examined, because there simply was no need. It just was.

More I thought about it, the more nervous I became. I fiddled with the reins, chewed my fingernails and shifted endlessly in the saddle.

The good sheriff rode along in broody silence which only increased my feeling of paranoia. I wondered what he was thinking about, dismissing one idea after the next until I realized he was probably contemplating whether or not to arrest me for Ella Mitchell's murder. After all, here I was, a stranger who dropped out of the sky, didn't believe in God, and had supposedly witnessed a murder and yet had nothing to do with it. Made sense that I was the killer.

Well, so be it then. If he was dragging me into town to throw me into a jail cell, he was in for a rude surprise. I'd be gone so fast, he'd never catch me.

The fact his gelding could run circles around the little mare I rode did nag at the back of my mind, but I'd figure a way around that tiny detail when the time came. If it came. There was no reason not to believe him when he'd said he was going after Frank. And the pace he'd set for us matched that of a Domino's Pizza delivery guy racing to beat the thirty-minute deadline.

Truth was, if Sheriff Taylor really did lock Frank in jail, Tahcitan would be safe.

I'd be safe.

But was he going to lock Frank up, or me?

My thoughts ricocheted around my head like jagged rocks in a tumbler. I wondered what was going on at home. When Ella had been killed here, had Holly also been murdered? I pondered the idea of Tahcitan and I both living in the same time and same place together. Was it even possible or would some hiccup in the time-continuum lash out and take both our lives? If I came face to face with Tahcitan here, now, would we both simply vanish?

It was like being thrown into *The Wizard of Oz,* where everyone was really someone else; Holly and Ella, Frank and Steve, and Tahcitan and myself. But how Sheriff Thomas Taylor or Jed played into the whole story was beyond me. The whole topic was enough to drive a person nuts.

I grumbled aloud, the vocal groan matching the one in my belly. I was hungry. And thirsty. And tired. And no doubt totally insane, off my rocker, bonk-shit crackers.

For some unknown reason, I'd ended up alone here, stuck seemingly forever. Unless Tahcitan could help me return. Indians were surely more mystical, spiritual and open-minded than some hick cowboy-sheriff; that much was certain. Tahcitan would happily send me back to my own time and my own world. No sense both of us being here.

I urged the mare into a trot, slowing only when I was next to the big man on the buckskin. "Look, Walker, it's been real and it's been fun and all, but I gotta go. You know, places to go, things to do, people to see." I tried to keep my voice light and spoke in clichés on purpose. Chances were, he'd never heard them anyway.

His face darkened. Storm clouds in tornado country looked friendlier. "Where Paizely?" He snapped. "Where are you going? Who do you have to see? Tahcitan? You said you didn't know where she was, now you're going off alone in the dark to look for her? In a place you say you've never been? Just how do you suppose you'll find her?"

How would I find her? A ludicrous question if you thought about it, because it seemed pretty certain to me that I *was* her. I said, "How hard can it be to find one's self?"

And then I thought of all the New Age ideas and theories on finding yourself, learning the lessons, progressing forward in your life and those thoughts made me giggle. The sound rang in my own ears like a completely unhinged and demented woman. The idea of being crazy sent me to the brink of hysteria and the giggles rose from my chest like waves racing to the shore. Through misted eyes, I glanced at the sheriff.

He stared at me blankly.

Obviously, he didn't get it. Best joke in two centuries and he was missing it.

"Yeah, you'd think--" I tried to explain but laughed harder. "You'd think--" Too much, the irony was too much. I was cracking myself up, and that sent me right over the edge. I couldn't stop laughing, but knew I had to or risk losing my mind completely.

I thought of Holly. Dead.

Sobered, I looked into Sheriff Taylor's face. "You would think I'd know where to find myself, wouldn't you?"

The blank look of incomprehension on his features erupted into a wide grin, and he laughed too. From his belly, deep and honest.

The sound rippled across the night, filling the black corners with light. Unable to keep a straight face, I joined him and for the first time all day, I felt good. Like sweet water on a dry, parched throat, laughing with him felt like when the sun peeks from behind a cloud on a wintry day. I had no idea hysterical laughter could induce this emotion, yet here it was--the warm bond of close friends.

Self-conscious and unsure of myself all of a sudden, I said, "Let's go, Walker, you've got some sheriffing to do."

~22

This new emotion of camaraderie and peacefulness might not be the best thing for me right now. Wrong time, wrong place for me to find comfortable friendship with a man. My nerves rang raw and my brain's neurons had stopped firing in any kind of correct sequence.

The temperature seemed to drop a degree a minute and I hugged myself to stay warm. The air smelled like winter, cold and fresh. Beneath the horse's hooves, the ground crunched as though frozen, though it wasn't icy. Plumes of steamy breaths blew from each of the horse's nostrils so they resembled magical dragons.

Maybe if they were dragons instead of horses, I'd be able to fly fast enough to return home. Perhaps I could convince Thomas Taylor to come along and like a storybook tale, we'd live happily ever after. Why I thought such a thing, I can't say; something about the man made me feel like I'd known him forever. Sounded crazy to me, but being here was even crazier.

If Tahcitan was hung for horse theft, then so be it. I'd likely die at the moment the rope tightened around her neck. And if Holly had already been killed by Steve, then the reason to go home vanished. Staying here with Walker until I died kind of seemed all right in a warped sort of way. Living in 1871 with a Mickey Mouse watch strapped on my wrist and full knowledge of what the future held in a historical sense might even be a good thing.

Right.

I squirmed in the saddle and turned to look at him. He rode with the quiet assurance of a man who knows what life is about and what he can expect. My being here surely threw a monkey-wrench into things for him, but he seemed to take it all in stride. I wished he'd talk to me about his immediate plans. Since he was absorbed in himself and his private thoughts, I didn't ask him to share. Instead, I let my mind drift to Holly and what might be happening at home. I tried to do the math of the time change; I'd landed here at daybreak, but at home it was just after two in the afternoon, so what would the time difference be? Maybe a six hours? What if the only thing that mattered was the time of day and was I six hours behind here, or eighteen hours ahead? I had no way of knowing. May to November, two in the afternoon to daybreak. How did it work?

If my vision were correct, Holly would die in the morning. Or maybe she'd already been murdered since time had warped. I decided to go with the belief of Holly alive at home. This made sense to me because if I was Tahcitan in 1871, yet I was here as Paizely, then Holly was separate from Ella as well.

The conviction of this truth brought back my resolve to get home. If Holly was still alive and if there was any small chance I could somehow get to her, I had to get back. Not knowing the sheriff's plans gave me a headache. I glared at Thomas Taylor. "Walker, are you planning to lock Frank or me in jail once we get to town?"

He stopped his horse and leaned toward me to look into my eyes. "You need to be thrown in jail? I thought you were just a witness. Have you done something against the law?"

I could tell by the tone of his voice his true intention, which was to stop Frank from killing Tahcitan. I answered him with a smile, "I haven't done anything wrong, Walker. You can rest easy. I just want to help Tahcitan and get the killer behind bars. Where do you think Frank is now?"

Taylor laughed and said, "I'm glad to hear you're not a criminal. My best guess, Frank is either passed out drunk somewhere or still drinking at the saloon."

"Good. I hope you're right."

The sheriff shrugged. "He's a dangerous man, for sure. Unpredictable and dishonest as they come. I'm sad to see him settle in these parts, tell you the truth."

He must not believe Frank would pay for murdering his sister if he believed Frank would settle down here.

We rode on, each of us wrapped in our own thoughts. We aimed toward the town of Longmont, the night dark and quiet around them. I had ridden at night before, but always in the warm summer months and for pleasure, not as a means of primary transportation. We were almost to the fork in the road where we could turn east toward the Mitchell Ranch or go on into town. Above the settlement, a faint light glowed.

With no warning, a gunshot split the silent night and echoed across the prairie sounding as though it came from the Mitchell Ranch.

"Damn it!" Sheriff Taylor cursed and turned his horse east. "Frank. He told me he planned on staying at Ella's tonight but I didn't think he'd be there already. Let's go."

I nudged the mare to move faster and hoped Tahcitan wasn't Frank's target.

* * *

Frank wondered if he'd hit her. He was a good shot, but he'd had much to drink tonight, and his vision blurred and wavered. Under his breath, he cursed the whiskey.

Indians deserved nothing more than slow, painful death. Damn heathens. He'd kill her in the proper manner if he hadn't spared her by hitting her square.

He'd missed and squinting through the gun's sights, he followed the fuzzy image of the Indian. With the rifle butt tight against his shoulder, he walked across the porch with a slow, shuffling gait. He didn't watch where he was going, and when his foot stepped forward and then landed on nothing, he pitched forward, falling onto the steps.

The gunfire crashed in his ears and he cursed.

* * *

Taylor's horse was faster and he was far ahead of me. I drummed my heels on the little mare's sides to get her to run faster and wished I'd taken a bigger horse instead of this one.

Another shot cut through the still night.

Faster still, Taylor pushed his buckskin gelding, leaving me in the dust.

Galloping in strange terrain and in the dark made me wonder if I'd die when the horse beneath me fell headlong into a ditch, breaking her leg. Whatever or whomever Frank fired at, likely needed help and I had no choice but to push the bay to her limits. I concentrated on Sheriff Taylor's back and urged my horse into an even faster speed.

* * *

Frank hauled himself up and fired the rifle into the sky before limping into the house. He shouted, "Get up, let's go! She's not far ahead!"

From each of the rooms, men grunted and coughed and one by one emerged with guns ready and a lust for killing clearly etched on their faces. Nine men headed to the barn to saddle their horses. Within minutes, they ran across the yard, toward where Frank pointed them.

"She's not far, and no one shoot her until I give the command." He spurred his horse forward and the chase began.

* * *

Finally, I saw Taylor pull his horse to stop and I pulled up beside him.

"We need to see what the idiot is shooting at is anyone's guess. Lights are lit in the house, but it's quiet." He nodded and said, "Be careful."

We rode at a trot the rest of the way in to the ranch; me afraid of what we'd find there, and next to me, the sheriff all business.

* * *

Frank led the men at a gallop, staying on his horse with the luck he knew he deserved. The death of the heathen Indian whore was his right and he was glad he'd missed hitting her back at the ranch house. He'd find her and gun her down after he'd done some other things to her. Things his mind dwelled on even now as he clutched at the saddle horn to stay on his horse.

The men whooped and hollered their glee at chasing the Indian and the dogs bayed in excitement. He needed all of them to be quiet. He held one hand up, signaling the men to halt. As they all gathered near him, he said, "Hush! All of you. Fan out and don't lose her. Catch her, but don't shoot her. I will do the killing. Now move!"

As the men spread out and loped behind Frank Mitchell, only the sound of horse's hooves drumming the cold, hard earth was heard.

* * *

No sound from the Mitchell Ranch, though lights shone from every window. We rode to within a hundred yards from the ranch, then dismounted. Leading our horses to the back of the house, we tied them to a tree and crouched low to peer into the lower level windows.

The place appeared to be empty. No Frank, no Saul. No one. They'd all gone chasing whoever the shot had been fired at and I had a sinking feeling that someone was Tahcitan. Why she'd come back to the ranch, I couldn't imagine. I wanted to ask Taylor what he thought, but we were already tying our horses to the trees out back of the house.

We ran, crouching low beneath the windows to the front porch and I led the way through the open oak door. Behind me, Sheriff Taylor followed with his gun held in front of him.

* * *

Saul whacked her hard across the temple before he had time to think about what he was doing. The woman fell into a crumpled heap just inside the front door. Bright red streams of blood oozed from the wound near her eye. She laid still, so still he wasn't sure if she was alive.

Oh God, if he'd killed her, Frank would be fuming mad.

He'd never killed anyone, no man and certainly no woman. His stomach clenched, but there was no time. He had to stop the man who came in behind the woman.

Afraid he'd lose his nerve, Saul O'Greary faced the stranger's chest. He did not look into the tall man's face. Instead, he thrust the gun at the intruder's midsection.

In a fist the size of a bear's paw, the stranger's gun was dwarfed and though small, it was aimed straight at him.

"Don't show fear," Saul remembered Frank's words clearly. He barked, "Drop your gun," and to his dismay, his voice cracked. He sounded more like a frightened woman than a man in control.

The man's shiny pistol tipped toward his left eye.

Saul tried not to blink and failed. He cleared his throat, waved his own gun and didn't look into the large man's face. "Drop it, I said."

"Saul?"

He tilted his chin enough to look up into the man's face. Christ Almighty, it was Sheriff Taylor. Frank hadn't told him what to do if the sheriff showed up. And he'd knocked the lawman's lady-friend out cold. Maybe even killed her. Frank had told him time and again the law was a bad thing and to always walk easy around any sheriff, most especially this one. Fear rippled through him so his teeth chattered and his eyes watered.

With the woman lying on the floor between them, Taylor's gaze darted down to her, then up to him.

Saul tightened his hand and squeezed the gun harder. The weapon wavered, snaking back and forth in little jerking motions. He raised his left hand to steady it. "Sheriff," he said, his voice quivering. "Drop your gun."

The sheriff stared at him, "You don't want to do this."

Saul's neck burned. Sweat flowed down his face. His mouth went dry and his breaths became more shallow. "Drop it."

The sheriff glanced at the woman again.

The sheriff was more concerned about the woman than with him. Saul dropped to his knees and held the gun to her head. Craning his neck, he looked up and said, "Drop it, or I'll shoot her."

Taylor's Colt fell to the floor with a loud *Clunk.*

Saul licked his cracked lips. With the muzzle at her temple, he commanded, "Kick it away."

The sheriff complied, sending the gun skittering across the floor. "What are you doing, Saul? Where's Frank?"

"Don't you be worrying about him," Saul said, hating the sing-song lilting of his words. He deepened his voice, "Who is the lady?"

"Nobody. She's got nothing to do with any of this."

Saul stood and nudged the woman's side with the toe of his boot. She didn't move, so he poked her harder. He could see no sign of her breathing. Her buckskins laid against her back like a cloth on a table. Her clothes. Was she the Indian? "Who is she? Roll her over, let me see her face."

Taylor kneeled next to Paizely's shoulder and eased her onto her back. Long strands of hair covered her cheek and the sheriff tenderly brushed it away. His fingers paused at the gash on her temple.

"That's enough," Saul barked, but even he heard the hesitancy in his voice.

The woman looked like the Indian, but he couldn't be sure. He'd only seen her from a distance, watching her and Ella for the past six weeks. She was the right size, but when she and the sheriff had been talking on their way to the house, there had been no trace of the Cheyenne accent. This woman's voice was soft, not harsh as the half-breed's had been when the barn had burned and she'd screamed for the horses to escape.

He couldn't be certain and his uncertainty made him weak. He had to hide those feelings from the sheriff. He cleared his throat and said, "Is this the half-breed?"

Taylor's stare bore through him and inside, he cringed. "No."

God, Lord above. Frank hadn't given instructions on what to do in these circumstances. He wondered if he should kill them both and hide the bodies from everyone, including Frank. He'd already harmed the woman; for all he knew, she might even already be dead. His hands shook uncontrollably, waving the gun in wide sweeping arcs. He didn't know what to do so he bit his lip and said, "Bind her."

The sheriff stayed hunkered over the woman, his gaze focused on her.

Saul had never been in control before, that was Frank's job. And now, this sheriff wouldn't listen to, or obey any commands. This was too much, too much. He had to think. Had to decide if he should shoot them both. He'd never killed anyone. He was afraid of guns. He hated his own fear and weakness, and knew this is what drew him to Frank in the first place. Frank liked making decisions. Frank always decided when, how and why they did anything. The arrangement worked for each of them.

Saul didn't want to be responsible for this whole mess. If he bungled it, Frank would not show any mercy and all hell would break loose. Stupid sheriff. Stupid woman. He wished they'd never come here.

He swung the gun to Taylor's throat. Managed to hold it still. Said, "Tie her up, Sheriff. Now. If she gets free," his voice cracked. "I will kill her."

Taylor glanced at the woman, concern etching his face with deeper lines. He reached his hand to touch her, then stopped. "I don't have anything to tie her up with, Saul."

Clearly, the big man cared for her a great deal. For a reason he couldn't explain, realizing the sheriff had feelings for the woman angered him. He didn't question his anger, why it had come or from where. Instead, he drank it in--fed off of it until he felt its hot force begin to flow through his own pallid veins and he felt powerful. Like Frank must always feel.

His hand steadied. "Go into the kitchen and find some rope." His voice had lost its quaver as well, pleasing him. He barked, "Get moving, Sheriff, or I'll shoot her right now."

He crouched next the woman, holding the muzzle to her head. "Get what you need," he said, staring into the tall man's eyes. "You step wrong, I shoot."

* * *

In the kitchen, and out of Saul's sight, Taylor caressed the James Bowie knife that lay snug against his hip. Thankfully, it was hidden beneath his heavy coat and Saul hadn't bothered checking for any weapons other than the gun. He pulled the long blade from its scabbard and shoved it handle first, up his sleeve. Yanking the sheath from his belt, he threw it to the heap on the floor and held his belt in his hand.

He scanned the pile for anything else he might use as a weapon.

"Sheriff?" Saul's melodic voice sang. "You get out here where I can be keeping an eye on you, now."

With a final cursory look around the kitchen, Taylor grabbed a small paring knife from the floor. His thumb flicked across the dull blade. He shoved it into his back pocket, and called out, "I can't find anything in this rubble."

"Get out here where I can see you," Saul called.

Rounding the corner from the kitchen, Taylor searched for any sign that Paizely had awakened. Her chest rose and fell in the steady rhythm of someone sound asleep. "There's nothing to tie her with, besides, Saul, she's asleep. No threat to you. Let her be."

Saul's rheumy eyes dashed around the room. The gun he held aimed at the sheriff's chest bobbed like a bird on a branch in a high wind. Finally, he sang, "Use yore belt, Sheriff, and bind 'er tight."

Careful to keep his elbow bent so the knife wouldn't slip from his cuff, he rolled Paizely onto her side. He tied her hands behind her back loose enough that when and if she came to, she would be able to get a hand free. Never taking his eyes off the reckless Irishman, he stood.

Saul kept the gun at chest level, but changed it from his right hand to his left in short jerking motions. His feet ran in place as though he needed to relieve himself and his eyes watered and dripped as though he suffered a high fever. He looked like a bug on a hot griddle and in other circumstances Taylor would have laughed aloud.

Paizely moaned and her chin lolled to her shoulder.

Saul ran faster and still went nowhere, the gun bouncing from one side of the room to the other. Tears rolled down his sweat covered face and his lower lip quivered.

The red-faced boy was too foolish to know what to do and now was as good a time as any to get this nonsense over with. Taylor stepped closer to Saul.

"Sh, Sheriff," Saul sputtered. "You just stop right there."

Taylor took another step. "Let's talk about this." He gestured to the bottle of whiskey on the table. "Would you like something to drink? I'm happy to get it for you."

Saul's freckles disappeared beneath the rising red blush on his cheeks. The gun waved like a flag in a breeze.

Taylor took another step. "Sit down for a moment, let's talk this out, man to man."

Saul clutched the gun in both hands, hugging it to his chest. "Stop, stop ri--" His tinny voice cracked and he gulped air like a fish stranded on shore.

Taylor took one more step. "Easy, Saul."

"Stop, or I swear to the Lord above, I will shoot."

Fear glistened Saul's teary eyes and Taylor raised his arms, palms facing the trembling lad. "Let's talk. Have a drink."

"STOP!"

Taylor stared down the barrel of the gun.

Saul pulled the trigger.

The blast rattled the windows and black smoke rolled in great billowing clouds towards the corners of the room.

* * *

A loud crack, like an old Chevy backfiring ricocheted off the walls of my skull, hammering at my ears and I tried to clasp my hands to my head. But something bit at my wrists, holding them together.

I opened my eyes and knew I was dead.

My teeth chattered, filling my head with the incessant haunting rattle of chains in a ghost-infested attic. I was dead and I was in Hell.

The odor of Hell's heavy blackness scratched my throat, and my gasping and coughing made me realize I wasn't dead. Above me, a cloud of thin acrid smoke filled the room. Inside my mouth, bitterness gnawed and I coughed again, then blinked to clear my vision. Panic tugged at me, nipping like a small dog until I thought I'd scream. I had no idea where I was, why the place was filled with smoke, or how I could escape.

Lying on my side, the sweet smell of floor polish contrasted with another more sulfuric odor. I rolled onto my back and kicked my feet in an effort to stand, but the heels of my riding boots only slid across the slick hardwood.

Riding boots.

Frisco.

Holly.

Walker, Texas Ranger.

I called out, "Walker? Walker, you here?" But my shout was no louder than a coarse whisper. No longer shivering with chattering teeth, sweat streamed off me until my shirt stuck like Saran plastic-wrap to my back. My breathing sounded ragged, like a wheezing old man's. I had to calm down, think, and figure out what to do.

My gaze stuttered around the room, over the piles of papers and overturned furniture. I couldn't see anyone and I heard nothing. Maybe I was alone and could get free. I tugged and pulled at whatever held my wrists and called out, "Walker?"

But no one answered. Maybe he was somewhere behind me. I arched my neck, pressing the back of my head into the floor. It hurt like hell, but I kept at it, hoping to see what was behind me. Finally, I looked over the top of my own forehead.

And stared into the barrel of a smoking gun.

~23

Sheriff Thomas Taylor opened his eyes to smoke and the acrid odor of sulfur. He lay flat on his back feeling no pain, but he'd been shot before and knew that it sometimes took a few minutes before those particular fangs of misery took their bite.

Above him, in a swirling mist of sooty smoke, the Irish man stared vacantly into the middle distance seeing nothing. Sharp crimson freckles stood out in bright contrast against the pallid skin of Saul's face. His fingers opened and the Colt Navy .36 slipped to the floor. It landed with a loud clang near Paizley's temple, but Saul didn't notice her or the gun. He turned to Taylor. Blinked. "I said...I said, stop," he whispered.

The gun's crashing fall still jangled Taylor's nerves, yet he felt nothing that resembled pain. He lay still a moment longer, waiting for the sharp heat of the bullet to course through his shoulder, but the agony never came. With care, he sat up and starbursts of pain radiated from his right shoulder, a clear enough message that too much movement would be a poor idea indeed. Breathing shallow sips of air, he held himself rigid and still. "Saul," he whispered, locking his eyes with the Irish man's. "How bad is it?"

Saul's face paled until his skin was a whiter shade than boiled potatoes. His right foot scraped the floor as he slid his heel backwards.

Raising his hand and turning his face, he said, "I do not-- I don't want to see blood."

"Saul," Taylor said. "I need your help."

The lad quivered and his cheeks reddened until most of the freckles disappeared in the flush. "Saul, please. How bad am I hurt?"

Saul shook his head.

Paizely called to him, "Walker? Walker? You okay?" Her voice matched the screech of a hawk.

Taylor ignored her hoping Saul would too. His gaze steady on the young man's face, Taylor said, "Untie her, Saul. I need help."

Saul shifted his weight, staring ahead. "I, I...What do I do?" He asked no one in particular.

Paizely squirmed at Saul's feet, trying to simultaneously get away from Saul and get closer to Taylor. Her leather-soled riding boots slid across the polished hardwood and in no time, it was clear that she was winded. Droplets of sweat slid from her hairline toward her ears and her eyes filled with tears of frustration. Taylor hoped she was a strong as he thought she was and would be able to hold herself together to help him.

Taylor whispered encouragement, "Come on, Paizely."

Her hands still bound behind her, she worm-wriggled across the floor.

Taylor stole a glimpse at Saul. The man's hair stood in sharp spiking red curls against his white face. Oblivious to his surroundings, he stared at nothing, seemingly unaware of Paizely's slow progress.

Taylor willed her to hurry. He hoped she'd realize her hands could be freed. Saul might snap out of his stupor at any moment.

The blood at her temple had dried into a crusted mass and her hair hung in matted strands. Paizely sat up, feet in front of her, hands secured at her waist, heels gouging the floor. She alternately bent and straightened her legs, sliding her bottom across the slick hardwood. Her progress was slow.

The pain he'd been waiting for finally appeared. Biting and fierce, it stabbed at his shoulder. *Hurry, hurry, hurry. There's no time; he'll remember us any minute.*

As though she'd heard his thoughts, Paizely scooted faster.

Taylor kept his eyes on Saul and motioned to Paizely with his left hand. "Come here," he mouthed. "I'll untie you."

She leaned forward, closer to him.

Having her so near sent a shiver of relief through him. She was all right. They might get out of this yet. He bent his head, tipping his mouth to her ear. "Hurry," he whispered. "We've got to be ready. Do you hear me?"

She nodded. A slight motion of her head moved her hair and tickled his nose.

He continued, "In my sleeve, a knife. Take it. Get the gun."

She stiffened against him.

"Can you do that?"

Hesitation, then a tiny nod.

The belt came loose and he laid it in her lap. "Turn around," he breathed.

She did as he asked. Kneeling, she reached behind her to tug at the rope binding her ankles. Her eyes were wide with fear, but she was strong. Clearly, she'd be able to do whatever needed to be done, and the relief he felt was enough to forget the stabbing pain in his shoulder for just a moment.

A quick glance in Saul's direction confirmed the man's dazed state complete with a blank stare, a slackened jaw, and a drop of spittle that had gathered beneath his lip.

Ignoring the rat-teeth gnawing at his shoulder, Taylor lowered his right hand so the Bowie knife slid to the end of his cuff. He dropped his eyes to the shiny silver blade, motioning for her to take it.

In her deep brown eyes, he saw a faint flicker. Doubt. If she couldn't do it, if she didn't get the gun at Saul's feet, they were in trouble.

Once more, she seemed to read his mind and a look of defiance crossed her face. Solid determination replaced any lingering shadows of doubt as she snatched the knife from him and held it in front of her. In one swift motion she stood, turned toward Saul and tucked the knife behind her.

* * *

The knowing and the doing of a thing are often worlds apart, and even as I closed the distance between myself and Saul, I was painfully aware of how close the doing and the knowing had become in this instance. I had to get to Saul, bend over and grab the gun. If he moved, I had to stab him.

I'd always known that if I were ever in a situation where it was them or me, I wouldn't hesitate and my willingness to kill Steve was proof enough. At home, I slept with either my .380 or my .22 under my pillow just in case I needed it during the night. But knowing I'd be able to shoot an intruder from a distance, however short that distance might be, was much different than stabbing someone. Stabbing was so much more up close and personal. I tried not to think about what pushing an eight-inch blade into a man's flesh might feel like--even if the man was Holly's killer. But he wasn't. Holly's killer had been the other man, the bigger one. Where was he right now? With joy, I'd shove the knife through his ribs and into his blackened heart.

My grinding teeth made a squeaking sound in my head and I realized where my mind had wandered to in so short a time. I glanced at Saul and was happy to note he still wore the moronic face of a man in a trance.

One more step and I'd be there. I watched his unfocused ice-blue eyes, thrilled that they did not track my movement. Willing him to ignore me, I bent over quickly and swept the gun into my left hand.

Something heavy dropped over the back of my head and stayed there, holding me.

Saul's fist closed around the hair at the nape of my neck and jerked me up so I stood. My foot slipped on the hardwood just as my head was plunged down toward my knees. The same motion as dunking someone under water, he held me to the floor. He pulled my head up and back, then shoved me down so hard that the front of my skull cracked with a ping on my own bony knee. He hauled me back up to a standing position and I realized that although we both were the same height of five-nine, he was a heck of a lot stronger than me. Dangling from his fist, I hung like a ragdoll being shaken by a child. My feet slipped and churned, and I couldn't find purchase with anything that wasn't slippery. I didn't see stars exactly, but I heard bells, that's for sure.

I felt as though my head would be yanked from my neck and that my hair would be ripped from my scalp. If I pulled away, my entire head of hair would come off in his iron hand. Despite the tears stinging my eyes, I held my ground best I could and felt the knife slide down to my elbow.

Taylor called something to me, but I couldn't understand his words.

Saul yanked harder.

The scab at my temple broke and fresh blood clouded my vision. My hands clutched at the gun and the knife, but I couldn't bring either weapon into a position to use. Off-balance, I thought I'd fall, and my head would be split open.

The heavy pistol slipped from my grasp until I held only the slick barrel in my sweaty fist. Even if I couldn't fire the gun, the weight of it gave me a measure of comfort. I could club the asshole to death if I had to. Shoving my shoulders back and pushing up fast, I forced myself into a standing position. My hair fell across my eyes, blocking my view of him. Didn't matter, I knew where he was.

"You're the Indian. Frank said to kill you. You're the Indian. Frank said to kill you. You're the Indian...," he chanted.

He swung my head in rhythm to his song. I pulled to my right, stabbing at him with the long knife. The blade sliced cleanly through air.

He jerked my head harder and I heard a plucking sound as hair was ripped from my scalp.

My foot slid forward and I braced against it, twisting to face him. I brought my right hand up, pointing the knife at his chest. Tossing my head, I threw the hair from my eyes. My lips skinned over my teeth and I growled, "Let go of me." My voice was low, a feral menacing sound that made it clear I meant what I said.

He stared at me through red-rimmed pneumatic eyes. He blinked, but still held my hair in his fist.

I pushed the knife forward. Pressed the shiny tip against the plaid of his shirt, just under his sternum.

His eyelids dropped.

Progress, I thought, and pressed with more force. I kept my eyes on his and waited.

His stare went to some faraway place where he didn't have a knife pushing into his gut.

I drew a long breath and let loose with a high-pitched yell that sounded just like an Indian warrior's whoop. Loud and long, the sound reverberated off the walls and echoed throughout the house and even to me, seemed to last forever.

Saul's distant eyes widened in terror and focused. His mouth formed a large, silent "O". He released me and held his hands over his ears like a small boy might when a fire truck with its siren wailing passes by too close.

I scuttled backwards, flipping the gun around so I held it by the grip. I was right-handed and the heavy pistol wavered in my left. Even at this range, I wasn't sure I could actually hit him if the thing even fired. Did old pistols need special priming or did one just pull the trigger? I wanted to ask Taylor, but there wasn't time for that. I stepped back another step, forcing my grip on the gun to loosen a bit. Steady.

In my right hand, I twirled the long knife around so that the blade came out the bottom of my fist. In one arcing plunge, I could thrust the thing in to the hilt.

Saul raised his elbows to his ears and hugged his head, sobbing. He looked about twelve years old and if this had been any other situation, I would have pitied him. I could almost feel sorry for him now, he looked so pathetic.

Survival. That's all that mattered. This pitiable man was the enemy and this was war. I'd do whatever it took to win. I yelled, "Put your hands behind your head." The volume of my own voice scared me just a little.

He grabbed onto his ears and held them.

"Get on the floor," I ordered. "On your stomach. Now!" I sounded like a Drill Sergeant, the amplification of my voice hiding how frightened I felt. I didn't stop to question what might be the biggest source of my fear; him, or my own willingness to kill.

My finger traced the trigger, and with my thumb, I drew back the hammer. *Click.* "Get on the floor," I commanded.

Through watery, blood-shot vacant blue eyes, he peered at me. With a whimper, he dropped to one knee.

Holding the gun steady, I commanded, "On your stomach. Spread your legs. Keep your hands on your head." Part of my mind recognized that I'd seen cops do this on TV, but I had no time to think about that now.

He did as I said.

I stooped and jabbed the point of the knife into the soft flesh at the base of his skull just enough to dimple it. Holding the knife still, I set the muzzle of the pistol against his temple. "Breathe wrong, Scumbag, and I'll kill you so fast, you won't even know you're dead until tomorrow."

Like a baby, he sniffled.

Over my shoulder, I called, "Walker, can you get up yet?"

A shuffling scrape of fabric against wood told me he was on his way. I stayed bent over the Irish man, drops of my own blood falling onto his plaid shirt.

Taylor managed the weapons while I bound Saul's hands and feet. When he was tied and crying, I collapsed, my own acidic tears blinding me. I always reacted this way in a crisis. I would handle the situation with strength and determination, then disintegrate afterwards. I hated myself for acting so weak and swiped at my wet face before Taylor noticed my breakdown.

"It's all right, Paizely." Taylor's hand on my shoulder should have been comforting, but instead, only made me cry harder.

* * *

Sheriff Taylor didn't tell her, but he thought she'd done one hell of a job. Without her, he'd most likely be dead.

Still, it seemed a good idea to stay quiet and let her sob while he rubbed her taut muscles. There'd be time enough for talking later.

"Please, Sheriff," Saul whined. "Please shoot me before Frank returns. Make it quick, yes?"

Sitting with his knees bent, Taylor shoved the toe of his boot into Saul's flank. "Where is Frank?" he asked.

Saul turned his head so one bleary eye was visible. "He and nine other men are after that thieving bitch. Or, they be after who they think is her." He glanced at Paizely and smiled down at the floor. "They will get her, too, when they return. Now shoot me, please?"

Taylor wanted to bash the sniveling redheaded man's face until he looked like sausage gone through a grinder. He growled, "Do they know where Tahcitan is?"

A look of sheer confusion swept over Saul's features. "I'll be telling you so you can return the favor and shoot me, yes? How did the squaw get here with you? Right after she left here, Frank and the others went after her. Headed south-east." He tried to lift his head, but stopped when he felt the muzzle of the gun gouge his temple. "Did Frank follow you back?" Saul asked, trying to glare at Paizely. "Oh, he's going to be hoppin' mad when he finds out you here."

"Never mind that, you little runt." From his pocket, Taylor withdrew a bandana. Handing it to Paizely, he said, "Time for a nap. Blindfold him."

As the cloth covered his eyes, Saul grinned, "What are you doing with the filthy animal? Think you'll get lucky?"

Taylor raised the heavy gun and slammed it onto the back of Saul's head. The simple act of raising of his left arm, the one not shot, sent waves of nausea roiling through Taylor. Leaning back, he glanced at Saul who lay still as a corpse. The rise and fall of the still man's ribs proved he still breathed and that gave him no satisfaction.

Taylor sighed and looked to Paizely. "Help me to my feet, let's see how bad this is."

Paizely reached for him and he shook his head. "Just stand there. Bend your arm, yes. Thanks."

She reached for him, trying to wrap her arm around his midsection. She asked, "Do you want me to help lift you? I can put my arm around your waist and you can lean on me."

He smiled through the agony in his shoulder. "No, just wait." He turned his body away from Saul's still form and tucked his left leg under himself. Pulling his other knee up, he rocked forward until he was kneeling. The movement sent another wave of nausea coursing through him and he hissed. Grunting, he reached for her arm with his left hand. He pulled himself up, and then fell against her. "There," he huffed.

The room spun and whirled just about knocking him to the floor. Leaning on Paizely, Taylor stumbled toward a chair and sat. "How about you, are you okay?"

"I'm fine," she said. "Now hold still."

Her touch was feather-light as she unsnapped his shirt. But even as careful as she was, searing bolts of hot pain shot from his shoulder to his hand as she pulled blood-soaked fabric from the wound. A small raw-edged hole evidenced where the bullet had entered his shoulder. He bit the inside of his lip to keep from moaning. He bent forward, inhaling a hissing breath. "Find the exit."

She pulled the shirt over his shoulder and a chunk of metal fell to the floor. The size of a nickel, it was covered in blood and flesh. She looked at the backside of his shoulder and found a wound. "This one is bigger. Worse." Her voice sounded distant and frail.

"How much blood?" He wheezed.

"It's not bleeding now. But it's big, Walker, it needs stitches I think."

He sat up, pulling his shirt closed. "I'll be fine, just hurts a bit."

Paizely paced a small circle in front of him, wringing her hands and he wished she knew how much he appreciated her concern and her help. He stepped away, turning so she wouldn't see him wince. Over his shoulder, he said, "We've got to get moving. Tahcitan needs our help."

* * *

I couldn't believe that after being shot, Walker could hobble out, climb onto his horse, gallop into the night and single handedly stop ten or so gun-wielding drunks. But that was exactly what his plan entailed. I wondered how such a seemingly intelligent man could make such a moronic decision.

He led his buckskin to a log and told him to stand, then put his left foot in the stirrup to mount. When he realized that he needed his right hand to pull himself onto the horse, he turned the gelding around and mounted from the off-side. He sat swaying, barely able to stay in the saddle and I thought for sure he was going to fall off the horse before he got settled.

I hollered at him, "You okay, Walker?"

He grunted.

Shaking my head, I said, "Hang on there, Cowboy. You need a bandage before you go quantum-leaping across the prairie."

He hesitated, bewilderment and pain twisting his face into a grimace. "What?"

"Just wait a minute." I grabbed some cotton dish cloths from the pile in the kitchen and began tearing them into strips. "Since you can't move your arm, the least I can do is put it in a sling and keep it immobilized. Only thing I remember from First Aid anyway."

* * *

The dogs bayed their usual excitement at the prospect of hunting, but by the sound, the men hadn't yet caught up with their quarry. Frank slowed his horse to a cadenced lope. He didn't feel like being in the company of fools.

His mind toyed with the memory of stabbing his sister and he wondered at his own current lack of emotion over the event. He'd felt a little remorse earlier, but now, with a few shots under his belt, he felt nothing. He knew his apathy did not make him some sort of monster.

Ella had simply left him no choice. Knowing he was right should have made him happy. And damn it all, he was right. Had always been right. He was not to blame for the outcome.

Father. That was where the blame should lay. Father had always favored Ella over him. He, Frank Mitchell, had received a pittance of land; a lousy few-hundred burned and scorched acres that remained of the Kentucky plantation. Blackened and worthless. Ugly. Small. Anyone could see that the whole idea of giving a woman--*a woman* for Christ sake--thousands of acres in Colorado Territory was preposterous and asinine. Women couldn't own a ranch like that and he'd come to collect what was rightfully and lawfully his.

And Ella. Hell, if she'd only understood that the Mitchell Ranch was his, not hers, then things might have worked out differently. But she was spoiled and always had been. Daddy's little girl--so prized and loved. And that wasn't his fault either.

No, fighting him by offering him only half the land had been her choice and in the end, dying had been her choice, too.

The sound of the baying hounds and the raucous laughter of the posse in the distance beat at his ears. Each step his horse took pounded a concussive rhythm through his skull. He was tired.

He wondered where the harlot bitch was and how she'd enjoy her last few minutes on this earth.

* * *

It was late, past midnight, and the half-moon hung to the northwest like a pale sun, one with no warmth. The air had a shivery brittleness that cut through my skin and made me wish for the warmth of my Ford's heater. At the back of my head, a burning cold sunk into the bald patch where Saul had yanked my hair out. Gingerly, I patted the sticky soreness and discovered it was the size of a silver dollar.

We headed southeast, the way Saul had said the men had gone. Ahead of us, our shadows led the way, disappearing when a cloud coasted in front of the moon, and then reappearing to show the crisp silhouettes of us and our horses. We followed their wavering shadows like sheep in a storm.

Periodically, I glanced at Taylor's progress. He seemed to ride all right if you didn't count the short, rapid breaths he sucked through clenched teeth or the way his upper body listed to one side. My own pain pulsed through my skull in waves. My head pounded, my temple throbbed, my back ached and my butt was sore. For the hundredth time that day, I wished for painkillers in the traditional form of Advil. But this time I wished for them for him as well as for myself.

Catching Taylor's eye, I asked, "Hurt bad?"

"I'm fine," he mumbled. His right arm lay immobile across his belly. I wished he would have let me put it in a sling.

Changing the subject might help both of them forget their discomfort. "Where do you think Tahcitan might be?"

He shot me a sideways glance, raising one eyebrow.

I ignored the implications of his look and rode in silence. Finally, I said, "Tell me about her."

His brows furrowed. "Why?"

"I'm curious, that's all. You know her, I don't."

His smile was forced. "I thought you were her. Why do you need me to tell you anything?"

"Listen Walker. I told you. I *was* her. I think. I don't know for sure. Maybe if you tell me about her, it might trigger something and we can take a better guess at where she is. What do you say?"

He remained quiet for a long time, and then began, "She's a half-breed. Cheyenne. White Antelope was her father. A good man killed by the Army at Sand Creek. Seven years ago, November, 1864. Tahcitan escaped but was just about dead when Ella found her. They, the men, the Army, had done terrible things to her and she still hates men because of what happened. She loves horses though and has a way with them. That's all I know."

At a visceral level, I felt the words he spoke. I nearly remembered the fear that wasn't mine, but belonged instead to Tahcitan. I tried to think of what I might do in Tahcitan's place. For me, I knew my feelings of loneliness and desperation would drive me to something familiar, something comforting. For Tahcitan though, I had no clue where that place of comfort might be.

I sank into a sort of fugue, dimly realizing that she was drifting, floating, seeking. No one left that could be trusted. Men were chasing her. An image, shimmering...her father...tee-pees and a river bank. *The Big Water.*

I shivered. What the big water was, I couldn't imagine, but it had to be important to Tahcitan and had to do with her family. Sand Creek. "Walker, I think she's going home. To where her family is, or was. Sand Creek."

"I never thought she'd want to go back to that place. Why would she?"

"It's familiar, it's comforting. It draws her, um, *home.*"

He didn't answer me right away, but after a moment, his eyes flashed hopeful in the silver moonlight. Nudging his horse into a lope, he smiled, "Let's go, that's a two or three day ride from here."

* * *

Tahcitan rode the stallion harder. She ignored the tears that streamed from her eyes that the wind had whipped. She ran south, until she came to a town of the *Ve'ho'e.* Not wanting the white man to know of her, she slowed the horse to a walk.

The stallion's breathing was hard and foamy lather ran down his neck and over his flanks. White steam rolled off of him in great billowing clouds. He could not go on much longer.

For the first time that day, she knew all would be right. This horse, her totem and guide had saved them both once again.

She stopped and listened for the men. She heard nothing and walked the stallion so they could avoid the small town. With the reins hanging loose, she let the stallion lower his head and stretch his long neck to the ground. She petted him and thanked him for his strength and for his heart. In the language of her people, she thanked him for her life and spoke of her love for him.

She got off the horse, crying at his condition. They would both die if they didn't rest. Leading him by cupping her hand around his ear, she said, 'I will walk with you, my friend, until we find a place to hide."

The bay snorted, and she smiled to think he agreed.

She walked with him awhile longer breathing in the cold night air. An owl cried out and she stopped.

Death.

A shiver shook her spine and she tried to shove away the feeling of doom. She walked faster.

Behind her and far away, the baying of hounds cut through her. She mounted quickly and told the stallion, "I am sorry, my friend. I must ride and we must run. The *Ve'ho'e'* still comes."

* * *

I slowed the mare to a trot, and then stopped. Ahead, the sound of dogs barking, braying like jackasses. Hounds. Hunting dogs happy to announce they were on the trail of the prey. I turned to Taylor. "You hear that?"

"Can't be that far ahead. It's got to be them and it sounds like they are on her trail. Let's go." His buckskin lunged beneath him, pausing mid-air before launching full speed into a gallop. Behind him again, I cursed Jed for having me take the slowest horse I'd ridden in two centuries.

I'd never be able to keep up with Taylor, and who knew what I'd find once I did catch up to him. I kicked my own horse with my heels and whooped once, hoping that would get the nag going faster.

~24

"It's about goddamned time," Frank muttered. He spurred his horse hard, gouging the metal across the animal's sides so the horse leapt into a gallop. He raced to where the posse of rowdy men laughed and hollered their way toward a rail yard.

A rush of excited anticipation rushed deliciously over him as he made his way to the group leading the pack. Once beside the leader, a brawny man on a big gray, Frank demanded, "Where is she?"

"Close," the huge man shouted. "You kin smell 'er."

Frank grinned and urged his horse in front of the gray. He held up his hand and the men halted their horses behind him. When some complained and wanted to continue the chase, Frank gave them with a look so commanding, it silenced each of them. He said, "We will split into two armies. You," he gestured to the giant leader. "Go around the rail yard. Take half of these men with you. Circle wide and keep your eyes open."

A blond man who looked small on the large bay he rode, meekly said, "We thought we saw her a ways back, Mr. Mitchell. We're just not sure which way she went. The dogs are on to some trail though." He paused and gazed at the ground, then cleared his throat. "I think your plan is a good one, Sir."

Frank ignored the urge to shoot the man square in the chest. He turned back to the man on the gray, "Go, and watch closely for her. Rest of you, come with me. Move out!"

The posse split up so each group consisted of five men and they rushed toward the bounty they hunted.

* * *

The bay put his nose on her arm and shoved.

Tahcitan winced.

Time seemed to not move. The night was dark and silent. She heard no sound of the men and even their dogs did not bark. The quiet did not calm her. Instead, she knew this was a sign of something bad to come soon. Already, the bay was injured and she could not help him. The needed to find a safe place to rest. She worried about where the *Ve'ho'e* were. And she wondered if the omen of death sent by the owl would now come true.

She tied the stallion to the water tower near the Iron Snake trail. Then she climbed to the top of the mound, where the round feet of the Iron Snake walked. Her moccasins slid on the small gravel and rocks fell down the hill behind her. They made a sound of *shush-shush* each time her foot hit the ground.

The *Ve'ho'e* were gone. She could hear no sound of them.

The horse was hurt and she was hurt. A place to hide until daylight would give them both time to rest. She looked across the rail yard. The train station, unlit and deserted stood among tall mounds of black coal. Beyond these black hills were buildings. She did not want to be trapped, but the horse needed rest. If one were empty, she and the bay could hide inside until the morning.

* * *

The hounds had been quiet for a time, but now they bayed without letting up even a little bit. The racket stirred Frank's mood into a frothy lust for blood. He wanted nothing more than to feel the immense release that always came with a kill. The men would get the money he'd promised, but the kill was his and his alone. He knew they were close. He sucked in his breath and felt the familiar tingle of excitement deep in his groin.

* * *

Tahcitan touched the stallion's nose and led him into the small shed. He limped but not as badly as he had. Once inside the dark room, she bent to feel his legs for wounds. A large gash bled at the knee and made his leg slick all the way to the hoof. On the other leg, she found the same kind of injury. She needed water to mix the poultice for his healing. It would also ease the pain and swelling. She did not want to leave the bay alone, but she had no choice.

At the water tower, she bent to fill the bladder she would use to mix the herbs.

A horse called out, a short whinny to ask if anyone was near. The voice was not the sound of the stallion.

Tahcitan's chest closed around her heart. She held her breath.

Silence. Then, the sound of dogs. Close.

She turned and ran toward the building where she had left the bay. On her toes she ran. But she was hurt too, and her legs did not move in the normal way. Her knees were raw and bruised and each step felt like fire. Hot.

The dogs howled. At the stallion's shed.

She stopped.

Sneaking around a mound of coal, she could see the men surrounding the small building and the dogs scratching at the door. The *Ve'ho'e* aimed guns, long smokepoles and shorter pistols at the door. A man shouted, "Come out!"

Tahcitan stood frozen as a rabbit does sometimes before the chase begins. She heard the low hum of the white man's voices and she felt her heart pound like a ceremonial drum. She heard the words of her father, "You are a brave warrior…" and she set her teeth together and clenched her jaw. *The time is here.*

She called on the spirit of the Eagle, the Bear, the Horse and the Fox. The strengths of her totems would help her conquer the *Ve'ho'e*. She would live.

Her lips skinned back over her gums and she narrowed her eyes. She pulled the knife from the sheath at her ankle and gripped the wooden handle.

A mare whinnied.

The stallion answered.

* * *

We galloped across the dark prairie toward the noise of the hunters as though on some eerie fox hunt in England or something; like it was natural and normal and expected. The smell of burning torches lit the air with an acrid smoky odor and the smell had to mean death and Hell both.

The men bellowed to one another: "Get around the side of the building!"

"Hold your fire!"

"Cover me!"

Dark mountains of coal hid the men and only their voices cut above the hills and into the night. But so far, they weren't firing their guns. That particular detail lacking, I held onto a sliver of hope and pushed harder, demanding more speed from my tired and winded horse. I tried to catch up to Taylor, but couldn't and fear crept into my chest once again, obliterating the tiny bit of hope I had.

My heart raced and my body was sheathed in sweat. Hot, then icy cold, but I felt neither for long. I called to Taylor, "Wait up." But it was an exercise in futility and I knew it. Not only was my voice barely a whisper in my parched throat, but if he actually heard me and waited, it was likely Tahcitan would die.

* * *

The stallion smelled the heat of the mare, heard the stomping of hooves.

He nickered.

She answered.

He pushed at the wooden door with his nose, his injuries forgotten.

* * *

In the dark and the speed, I lost sight of the sheriff. He'd gone up and over the railroad bed before me and disappeared.

I kicked the mare's sides and followed him up the steep embankment, my horse's hooves slipping on the rock gravel until I was certain we'd fall before reaching the crest.

Mixed in with the sounds of men shouting and gravel sliding, the same humming buzz from this morning filled my head--the bumblebee droning that sounded like a thousand of the insects were flying around my ears. I ignored the irritating distraction and rode to the top of the rise. I stopped to see what was happening below me.

Torches lit the scene and sent shadows that wavered and crawled on the log walls. Men on horseback and men on the ground surrounded a low building. Dogs that looked other-worldly ran around the structure scratching at the ground, trying to get in.

Taylor raced toward them.

* * *

To my left, at the bottom of the tracks, something glinted in the moonlight. I turned to see Tahcitan crouched, a silver blade in her fist, a feral grimace on her face.

The humming in my head intensified. Louder, until I couldn't hear anything.

I nudged the mare down the slope, toward the Indian woman, keeping my eyes locked with hers. I called, "Tahcitan!"

The woman's lips pulled back to show large, white teeth. She raised the knife above her head and crouched.

I stopped, jumping from the horse in a single motion. I held my hands up, palms facing Tahcitan so the Indian would see I had no weapon and meant no harm. "Tahcitan, wait. I've come to help you."

* * *

Tahcitan watched the white woman coming toward her. She could not understand how the stranger could be wearing her own favorite buckskin shirt.

For a moment she worried about the stranger, then saw that she was looking at herself. She let the knife drop to her side, a sense of calm falling over her as the blade lowered. The calm came from her father's words, "Nothing lives forever."

She would die now, a brave and courageous death. This vision of herself disguised as a white woman was here to help her.

The vision-woman's mouth was moving, but Tahcitan heard no sound. She stared at the spirit. She raised her hand and made a sign to show that she gave her buckskin shirt as a gift.

The vision-woman pulled the leather shirt over her head and with her arm outstretched, held it toward her.

What was the meaning of this? Tahcitan did not know and she worried the spirit-woman's trying to return the shirt was a bad omen. She did not want to see such a sign. She spun away from the image.

The scene before her made her stomach feel afraid. She did not want to cause shame to her people. Only the words of the death chant of White Antelope, her father, speaking the words, "Nothing lives forever" met her ears. She knew the time to join her family and journey up The Hanging Road was near. The thought brought her happiness except for leaving the stallion. She looked to the building where she had left him.

The night was without color. Only gray shadows danced before her. Men creeping around the horse's hiding spot.

The closed door that hid the bay slid open.

The men shifted in their saddles, straightening their already stiff backs. Smokepoles spit fire and smoke hung over them.

The stallion's face, neck and one ear were shot apart. Blood and flesh fell to the ground. The horse's legs folded and he fell forward, then down, to the ground.

A long, high-pitched screech left her beloved horse as he fell and she heard this.

An anguished cry ripped from her body.

* * *

From the corner of his eye, Sheriff Taylor caught sight of Paizely with Tahcitan. He had to get between the women and the posse. He reined his horse hard to the left and raced between the piles of coal, toward the women.

He did not see Frank with the men, but assumed he was at the front of the pack.

To his right, the men yelled like bloodthirsty coyotes at a kill.

He raised his left hand, shoving the reins between his teeth and shot his gun into the sky.

The men kept shooting the dead horse, laughing.

Finally, they paused, reloaded, turned toward him, their rifles aimed.

The bullets punched his body, and he fell with his horse.

* * *

The *Ve'ho'e* would pay for killing the bay stallion.

Behind her, someone called her name, "Tahcitan!"

She turned and faced the vision of herself.

The stallion was dead. The *Ve'ho'e* would pay.

Tahcitan spun around, facing the men. She paused, looking over her shoulder at her vision-self. It too, was ready. Was already moving forward.

She shrieked the warrior call and raised the knife over her head. She and the vision-woman ran toward the men together.

The men turned, aimed at her chest.

She held the knife higher. She would kill them all.

She ran tall and proud, straight toward them.

The bullets hit her and still, she ran.

* * *

Lying on the ground, his dead buckskin gelding crushing him, the last thing Sheriff Taylor saw before he died had to be an hallucination. He knew it couldn't be true.

Tahcitan, her hand clutching a knife, ran straight into the army of men firing at her. Behind her, Paizely followed.

He yelled, "NO!" But his voice was silenced by his own blood rising into his throat.

The bullets tore into their bodies, and still, side by side, the two women ran.

Gunfire shredded the night, filled the air with smoke. And still, the women ran.

Taylor heard both of their trilling battle cries and saw their outstretched hands.

The men reloaded and kept firing.

Finally, both bullet–ridden women had fallen. Their bodies landed in the same position: arms reaching, legs bent. Paizely just behind Tahcitan.

And then, perhaps because he was dying, he watched the two women's bodies float up, and then toward one another.

When they melded together, Sheriff Thomas Taylor closed his eyes.

~25

I'd been shot!

I feel no pain. They say you don't know you've been hit sometimes for minutes. I keep my eyes squinched as tightly as my jaw and gingerly touch my chest where the bullets had slammed into me. Only the soft fabric of my flannel shirt meets my touch, there is no moist sticky blood. Beneath my shirt, my heart hammers against my ribs, proving I'm not dead. Or maybe I am, which would explain the lack of blood and pain.

I know I have to look to be sure, so I raise my hand to my face. I open my eyes and bright sunlight stabs my night-accustomed eyes. It hurts and I clench them shut again.

Oh God, now what? It had been nighttime, I'd been shot, they'd all been shot, and now it's day. If I'm all right, then maybe they are too. A tiny speck of hope spreads through me. I open my eyes again, ignoring the sting of sunlight. "Tahcitan? Walker?"

Holding my breath, not breathing, not thinking, I wait. There is no answer. There is no sound at all.

I squint up at the hard sun and take a deep breath, then raise my hands, palms toward me and examine them. They are my own familiar hands, covered in grime and horsehair, with dirt under every short, unmanicured nail. Not a drop of blood on either one. Looking down, I examine the front of my green plaid flannel shirt. Dirty, but no blood drenches the fabric. I have no gunshot wounds and this makes no sense to me. Maybe I'm hoping for proof of being shot to prove I'm not insane, which makes a good argument for the possibility of my being nuts.

I swallow hard. Above me, the sky is a brilliant crystalline blue, spotted with a few wispy white clouds. Pine trees sway in a kind breeze, their long needles whispering against one another. The green grass around me still has the look of fresh spring grass, bright and crisp and new, and the boulders and rocks are stacked just as they'd always been; just as the landslide had left them.

No snow.

No moonlit night. No men in a posse. No train station. No tracks. No coal. No Tahcitan or Taylor. No bay stallion shot and dying.

I'm home.

Home!

Somehow I had landed right back where Frisco had crashed his big, thick skull into my head when he reared. When he had lost his mind.

I raise my wrist, checking the time. Mickey's yellow hands point to two-ten, so three minutes later than when I checked in 1871.

Three minutes had passed since…when? Today? Last night? I shake my head. It should be after midnight. I hold my breath and press the watch to my ear. *Tick-tock, tick-tock*. The steady rhythm taunts me.

I'd fallen a little after two o'clock in the afternoon, but *there*, my watch had stopped working at two-oh-seven. I take a deep breath and go over what I remember. Riding Frisco, he'd reared and I'd awakened in 1871 where I found myself thrown into a world I didn't understand and where I'd been accused of murder. No, wait, not me, Tahcitan.

Tahcitan. I listen for the tracking dogs, the shouting men--but there is no sound.

Frisco. I listen for the sound of his teeth grinding against the fresh green grass, or the stomping of his foot at the flies, but I hear nothing.

I try to stand. Moving my legs for the first time, my muscles cry their protest, but they move. Nothing seems to be broken. I push my bangs from my forehead and my fingertips meet dried blood, matted hair.

Saul. He'd bashed me in the head with something.

Kneeling, I let my fingertips carefully resume their probing search. At the base of my skull, a large patch of hair is missing where Saul had yanked it out.

Under my right eye, the cut where Frisco had hit me with his head. Three minutes ago.

Here

I call out, "Frisco," and my voice cracks the sound of a dying person's last croak.

Hearing how weak I am scares me and my body tenses. I'm rigid and ready to bolt as a new rush of adrenaline slams through me. My muscles twitch and spasm. What the hell happened? I have to find Frisco, get home and check on Holly. Is she here, alive?

Today is still now and tomorrow isn't here yet. I can save her. I will save her.

Struggling to my feet, I stumble to lean against a tree, bracing myself against the warm trunk. My knees are spongy--more like overcooked macaroni than solid flesh, and they refuse to hold me upright without support. "Frisco," I call, clucking my tongue against the roof of my mouth. "Frisco? C'mon boy."

In the distance, a hawk screeches, a long and drawn out sound. Melancholy. But there is no sign of the bay stallion.

Damn horse most likely ran off and left me here when I'd fallen and now I have to walk home. Or, if it really is just after two, Steve should be driving up in Holly's Jeep so we can shoot pistols during our planned target practice.

What an idiot. Him or me, I'm not sure who the sentiment is aimed at.

My mind wheels like a small bird caught in a strong wind. Memories of 1871 swirl before me and it's hard to remember I'm home with a sister whose life needs saving. Still, lingering thoughts and images of Taylor, Tahcitan, and the men shooting.....I have to quit thinking about them, but I feel as if I'm standing in two places at once.

A sound of leaves skittering across concrete catches my attention and I stop breathing and hold still, listening. The noise is so out of place, a long moment passes before I realize it's not leaves, but gravel rolling downhill. I look over the edge of the landslide, and maybe fifteen feet below me, wedged between a huge boulder and a pathetically scrawny pine tree, is Frisco.

His neck is twisted so his head rests on his back, over the saddle.

My breath catches in my chest and I stand frozen for what feels to be about a month, then somehow, I get my body in motion, and suddenly I'm running, my feet sliding on the loose ground sending rocks careening ahead of me like missiles toward him. I try to stop and end up sliding on my butt down the steep hillside to my best friend, chanting, "Oh my God, Oh my God, Frisco, please be okay, don't be dead, don't die, hang on, I'm almost there."

When he sees me, he struggles to get up, thrashing himself against the boulder. The motion sends a spray of dark blood spurting in an arc at least a foot into the air and I see the artery on his back leg is severed. It's bad.

"Hang on, hang on, hang on." My words fly down the mountain with me, ahead of me, behind me. Finally, I reach him. So much blood, the ground is soaked and dark in a semi circle that creeps ever farther from him. I rip off my shirt and tear the sleeves from their seams, then tie the two pieces together. "Easy Bud. It's okay," I murmur to him, running my hand over his hip so he'll know I am with him.

At my touch, the big horse relaxes. I trail my hand along his thigh to his stifle, then his gaskin, down to his hock and just below it, to where the big vein is sliced. It's not a huge cut, but it doesn't take much to cause death when an artery is opened. I wrap the fabric around his leg and pull the cuffs together, then tighten the makeshift tourniquet around his leg once, then again. I snug it as tightly as I can before tying it so the knot is directly over the bleeding gash, hoping it will add some pressure and stop the bleeding.

It isn't enough. I know this.

Turning away from him, I put the remains of my shirt on. I'm shaking so badly I can only manage to fasten two buttons before I give up.

Frisco is hurt seriously enough that if he lives, it'll be nothing short of a miracle. I wish I could pray with conviction to ask God for His help. But I can no sooner pray than I can miraculously produce suture material and a needle to sew up my horse. I want to talk to Frisco, but no words will come. I can't reassure him. My breaths come in huge lunging gasps, ragged and torn as my shirt. Tears flood my vision, bath my face, and fall to my chest.

I need help and I hope Steve will show up soon.

Silently, I sooth Frisco with my touch, because words sure aren't going to come and I know I'm trying to both offer and receive strength from the familiar. He shouldn't have to die with a saddle on. I smooth my hand over his barrel and unbuckle the girth from the billets. I tug the saddle from his wedged body, surprised that I can, then fling it to the ground. Glancing at the tourniquet, I'm horrified to see the green plaid material is already soaked with his blood. Dark red, purple.

I wish my love was enough to save him.

At his head, I pull the headstall over his ears and the bit from his mouth. Holding the bridle and standing in the middle of nowhere with me dying horse, my sobs choked my words, "Frisco," I moan, "Frisco, don't die, please don't die. I love you and I need you. Don't die, Booger, please stay with me."

His eyes have a dull sheen to them, waxy and I know he is at the end. I can't stand watching the life leave him so I look at his leg. The ground beneath is saturated, a muddy black puddle in the brown-gray earth.

He will die soon and there is nothing I can do. I have no way of helping him.

Again, I beg him, "Don't die, Frisco, please don't die." I jump up, scaring him enough that he blinks, but not enough so he tries to lift his head. There has to be a way to help him, to save him, for Christ's sake! I run around him looking for an answer. But I can find no way to escape his death. I remind him, "You'll be okay, boy. Don't leave me alone. Hang on."

But he will never be okay again.

I hug his massive neck and try to pull his head around so he will be more comfortable. But it is both too heavy and lodged too tightly against the boulder. Impossible.

I can't help him. Can't save his life. Can't make him more comfortable. He is going to die and there isn't a damn thing I can do about it. The spiraling despair that engulfs me is more than I have strength for. My frozen insides shatter and fragment before settling into something safer, something I can handle: The detached place I retreat into when death shows up unwelcomed and uninvited.

Watching myself from the outside, I see my connection to the present, to reality—whatever that might be—break. Everything moves in slow motion, as if looking at photographs page by page, one by one. And since photos aren't really real, I don't have to feel. I can just watch and stay removed from the pain.

Imminent death muddles my horse's eyes, and they glaze over, oil on water, murky clouds replacing the clear brown intelligence that defines him.

I hold his head, kissing the soft spot between his nostrils, and feel myself come back to myself, to him, to the present. Tears burn rivers down my face, wrenched from the very depths of my soul--of his soul. My best friend is dying and I cannot stop this from happening. I try to grasp that concept and fail. My mind simply refuses to acknowledge that truth.

I stare at the pistol hanging from the saddle. If I had to, could I shoot him to put him out of his pain? Could I?

I don't know. How do you shoot your best friend?

Slowly, I remember I'm not in 1871 anymore and-- wait! Where is the damn cell phone? Still holding Frisco's head, I search the hillside looking for the brushed silver of the phone's cover. It has to be here somewhere. Frantic, I look around where Frisco lay, but see nothing silver or manmade. Finally, I realize the phone wouldn't be near Frisco; he'd fallen down this ravine. It would be at the crest of the cliff, near where I'd landed. I kiss his forehead, "I'll be right back, boy. Hang on."

Before going back up to call the vet, I take one last look at my horse. Memories of 1871 flood my mind, uncalled for, unbidden--El dead, Tahcitan dead, the bay stallion, dead. I whisper, "Frisco, you can't die. Everyone I love dies. You can't die. You'll be fine. You have to be."

My eyes burn.

As I had done in 1871, when I'd left Holly on the ground, I force my feet to take me away from him, and try not to feel like I am deserting him. I run up the steep incline as fast as I am able and reach the top of the ridge huffing to draw in air. I scan the ground and find the phone sitting nestled against a rock.

I run to it and flip the cover open. The glass front is shattered and a hundred spider web cracks obscure the screen. I run my finger over it and no pieces fall out. It still may work. Squinting, I look to see if there is a signal. Nothing. I walk too fast at first, then more slowly, making myself go one step at a time. The whole time, I want only to run back to Frisco. I'd go to him as soon as I could, but right now, I needed to get help here fast. I step to the left and stand, knowing that it sometimes took a moment for the signal to lock on. I wait. Still nothing. I walk another ten feet to the left, climbing to the highest point and hold the phone to the sky. I make myself be still and begin counting, "One, two, three, four, five, six,"

Beep!

I didn't dare move. "There is a god," I mumble and press the Favorites icon. First in the list is the veterinarian's office. They answer on the third ring and I explain what has happened and where I am. The receptionist tells me that Kyle, my regular vet is on vacation, but they'd hired a new guy, Andy Keifer. She asks me to hold while she called his truck. I want to pace while I wait for the man to pick up the phone, but if I move, I might lose the signal even though the icon now shows I have a full five bars. Standing on my tip- toes, I try to see Frisco, but can only make out the curve of his rump.

Finally, a voice on the phone, "Hold on please, and I'll patch you through to Dr. Andy Keifer."

There is a faint click and then dead silence.

Shit.

"Andy Keifer here," a deep voice says.

I let my breath out and tell him where I am and how badly Frisco's cut is bleeding. I tell him how my horse's breathing sounds like a huffing marathon runner at the end of a race and how his eyes keep going blank. I don't tell him that I'm on the verge of losing my best friend, along with my mind. My voice stays calm and even until I ask, "What can I do to save him, Doctor?"

"I'll be there in a few minutes. I'm just down the road, near Bradley Brother's."

Didn't he hear me when I told him we were on the top of a mountain, away from any road? One of us isn't thinking straight. "Um, I'm not sure you understand where we are…I mean, you do know we're on a mountainside in the middle of nowhere?"

"I'm on my way," the deep voice responded.

Idiot! "Do you know this trail, this mountain? You can't just drive up here."

"I grew up on the Rocking R Ranch, just down the road from where you are. My friends and I rode our dirt bikes all over that landslide. Miracle we didn't kill ourselves. Where are you, exactly?"

I tell him which ridge we're on and how far down Frisco lay wedged between boulders and trees.

"I know exactly where you are. What is your horse doing now, can you see him?"

He really *is* coming and he knows how to find us! "I can't see him very well from here and if I move, I'll lose you. Let me go check him and I'll call you back, okay?"

"Sure. But I'll be there in a few minutes. If you can, get me his vital signs, pulse, respiration, and check his gums for capillary refill time. Can you do those things?"

I can and I will. I hang up and shove the phone into my back pocket. I race in long lunging jumps down the hill, wishing I could fly. I call to him, "Frisco? Frisco, are you okay buddy?"

When I get to him, his tongue slips out the side of his mouth, from that place in his jaw where a horse has no teeth and the normally pink flesh is mottled gray and blue. His eyes look backwards, searching for something behind him and with his head flat in my lap, he whinnies once, then, is still.

I wait for him to inhale.

He does not.

I know he's gone and I know I can't bring him back, but I do not accept this detail. I scream at him, "No, Frisco! No! Goddamn it, don't you dare die! Stay here with me. I need you. Frisco!" I howl the words, screeching them so that he will hear. But still, his life drains from him in a long exhale that settles the matter once and for all.

I can't think, I forget everything and remember too many things all at the same time. All that happened in 1871 comes back to me, but doesn't touch me, or sadden me, or worry me. At the same time, the memories wrench the very life from me and rips me apart like a paper doll being torn and shredded. I remember all of it in no particular order from Ella, my parents, Sheriff Thomas Taylor, my father, my dog, White Antelope, my grandfather, Stands Under Trees, Sand Creek, the *Ve'ho'e* and the bay stallion when he was a colt.

And I forget everything in the next breath.

The tourniquet is a soggy mass of dark red-purple. Bloody. I needed to change it. Tighten it.

He is still. I have to hurry.

He is still.

My heart aches. And. I know. He is dead.

My mind goes blank, with no thoughts, no colors, no sounds. I don't think, don't remember, and don't cry. I just sit with him. Stroking his cinnamon-brown neck and running my fingers through the coarse black hair of his forelock.

He exhales slowly, then blinks. And at first, I think it is my imagination. He sighs once more--long and shallow. My heart throbs in my chest. "Frisco!"

He nuzzles my palm.

A breeze pushes my bangs into my eyes and I swat at the nuisance, then stand up. My legs tingle with the blood rushing back into my cramped muscles. I have to do something to help him, he's lost so much blood.

He lifts his head an inch and his ears point toward me. His eyelids are half closed, but he isn't dead. He is looking for me and when we see each other, my heart soars, lifting my soul until I feel light, like a bird in flight. Hope.

I glance at the makeshift bandage I'd wrapped around his leg and am happy to see that the blood soaked fabric is brown now, not bright red that would mean fresh blood was seeping to the surface. I kiss his ear and ignore the coolness of it against my lips. *Hurry, Keifer, hurry.*

I am not a veterinarian, but I've been around horses long enough to know the vital signs and the normal range of each. I memorize the numbers for his pulse and his respiration; both are higher than they should be, but at least he is alive. His gums are pale pinkish-yellow, which means the capillaries are contracted, exactly as they should be for a horse that is injured this badly. He is stressed and losing blood. The thing that worries me most is the just-shy of vacant look in his eyes like he is drifting away from me. From life. I tell myself he's in shock and that's all, that he'll be fine. That the vet will arrive any minute.

Tears blur my vision. I watch him lying there all broken and bleeding, and I lay my hands on him and will my own life force into him.

His mahogany coat glistens in the warm afternoon sun.

And though he isn't wet and the air temperature is well above fifty degrees. From his body, white steam rises into the air, hovering in a heavy mist. Preternaturally silent, it swells above him, hovering like it's alive.

I check his eyes and they are closed. Is he dead?

My blurry eyes are playing tricks on me and I wipe my face with the back of my hands ignoring the burning sting as my tears scrape the cut below my right eye. The steam, or whatever it is, bunches together and then smashes in on itself, until it is a dense white sphere. Near the top of the strange cloud, a single strand lifts, like a horse raising its head after a nice roll in the sand.

It *is* a horse's head! Two front legs unfurl and the horse shape lifts itself up onto its forequarters, then, in a smooth lunging motion, stands.

I sneak a glance at Frisco's eyes. Still closed.

The white horse looks directly at me, then tosses its head and rears. Turning on its haunches, the horse spins in a tight pirouette like a reining horse until it faces me again.

Frisco does the same thing whenever he's excited.

I don't breathe. I stare at the ghost horse with my mouth hanging open. Around the lump in my throat, I whisper, "Frisco?"

The white horse tips his nose toward the sun.

Happiness larger than I could ever have dreamed fills me, though I am not sure why. I watch the ghost of Frisco--that's exactly what this had to be, a ghost--and gratitude and love and joy flood through me. I know he really is okay. I *know* it.

Okay, so he has no body. He is still with me and that's what matters. I am not alone even if he dies right now. Or if he's already dead. For the first time, I know that death doesn't mean "The End." I can't explain how I know this and don't try. It's more like knowing that the sun comes up every single day and that night falls every night. I stretch my hand out in front of me and take a tentative baby step toward the gossamer horse and whisper, "Come here, boy."

The white horse rears, tapping the ground with his front feet.

I stumble backward, raising my arm to shield my face.

The horse's see-through colorless body solidifies and grows brighter, until he shimmers an iridescent blinding silver-white. The muscles in his body stand out, defined by faint shadows cast by the sun.

I have never seen such a magnificent image or a white as blindingly solid. His body shines with a smooth silkiness that makes him look as though he is created from satin or some liquid shiny metal. I want to touch him and lean forward to take a step.

The white horse strikes out with his front foot, the same action Frisco uses to tell another horse to back off.

I understand, and stop dead still.

His voice isn't a voice at all. Rather, it is water and fire and earth and sky. It is yellow and red and blue and white.

And it is nothing.

I hear him, but do not hear words. The message is clear and muddy, soft and loud. Cold and dark and light and hot.

It comes to me at once, this thing the white horse tells me, shows me, breathes into me. It is a truth, a knowledge, a consciousness, an understanding.

The white horse speaks, *"The end is only a door that you've already walked through. The answer, the question, the truth, is Love."*

And I *know* that this is everything I ever need or want.

The spirit horse wheels about, dancing in the air above Frisco's body. With a toss of his silvery mane, the white horse leaps into the air. He gallops into the wind, becomes the wind with his mane and tail streaming out behind him. He races toward a cloud that grows larger and larger, until I see that it isn't a cloud at all.

It is a herd of white horses, each as brilliant as he.

Frisco runs into that herd and like a flock of faultless white birds, they turn and fly into the sky. Their bodies disappear into the distant clouds, wispy and white.

~26

A ghost horse talked to me?

I feel my mind slide sideways, slippery along a horizontal wall and I know I'm going crazy. Not in a funny-ha-ha manner either, but genuinely insane. I shake my head, trying to balance myself and get rid of the memory of the white horse. What had just happened? If Frisco isn't dead, does that mean that he will die? And why in the world had I felt such happiness and joy at seeing the spirit horse or whatever it was?

I hurry to finish taking his vitals and chant the numbers so I can tell the vet when he arrives. *If* he arrives.

I hear the truck before Frisco does and that worries me. The horse always notices faraway sounds before I do and will alert me by lifting his head high into the air, snorting while pointing his ears in the direction of whatever danger awaits us. This time though, he doesn't hear the revving engine, or at least he doesn't respond to the noise. Either way, it isn't a good thing.

His chin rests on his back and his neck is still bent unnaturally, but he doesn't seem distressed about how he's lying there. His ears loll out to either side so they look like airplane wings. His eyes vacantly stare at nothing and his gums were white.

Bad signs, all.

At least help is almost here. My pulse races and my breathing is ragged, either in excitement or worry, I'm not sure. Andy Keifer, DVM just needs to hurry and get to us, and then he needs to save my horse.

A screeching sound of metal on stone.

At the bottom of the hillside, coming around a huge boulder is a red Ford Ranger. Every vet at the hospital in Lakewood drives a different color Ford pickup, from small Rangers all the way up to full-size F-250's. I'm not sure what or who decides which truck each doctor drives, but apparently a red Ranger is Andy Keifer's. And he knows how to four-wheel. He has the truck in low and shifts with a smooth, determined easiness that makes me hope he is as accomplished in veterinary medicine as he is at navigating the treacherous trail that leads to us.

The truck crawls up the steep rocky slope, tree branches scraping shiny red paint from its metal sides. The sound apparently is loud enough and strange enough to cause Frisco, even in his stupor, to finally notice. He raises his head a few inches and his ears point listlessly in the general direction of the commotion.

His feeble acknowledgement from him thrills me. I run half-way up the slide and wave at the vehicle, and then run back to my horse.

The engine cuts off and the silence that follows is filled with hopeful promise. The passenger door opens and a man wearing a blue medical smock and jeans gets out of the truck. He's big, maybe six - one, but the man who gets out of the driver's side is bigger. Obviously, the driver is the good doctor. Broad shoulders, about six-four, with short cropped blondish-graying hair and laugh lines at his temples, he looks about thirty-five years old. He walks towards me, his gaze fixed on Frisco. The vet's eyes are somber and chocolate brown and warm. First impression, he seems not only competent but capable and caring.

He looks at me for only an instant, and holding the stethoscope dangling around his neck, he begins charging down the slope to Frisco's side. His focus is tight on the blood-soaked bandage. His jaw twitches and he says, "Looks good. The bleeding has stopped."

"I thought so, too," I answer. I watch his face, looking for anything that will give me hope and I try not to choke on the lump that all but shuts off any air supply in my throat.

Andy Keifer slowly strokes my stallion's face from forehead to nostrils, a long comforting gesture that introduces himself to the horse. "Vital signs?" He asks, while gently prying Frisco's lips apart and pressing his thumb to the yellow gums as he checks the color and capillary refill time. He then pulls the lower eyelid down to check the color of those membranes as well.

I answer, reciting the numbers I'd memorized, but even before I finish, the doctor has moved to Frisco's side and has his stethoscope to Frisco's heart. He listens intently, pressing the scope to different places, moving back from the heart and lungs, towards his gut.

Finally the vet stands and says, "He's lost some blood and he is in shock. I think he's scared himself as much as hurt himself. His color is good enough, not perfect, but good for what he's been through. We need to be sure there aren't any other things going on with him, no head trauma or spinal injury. From what I can tell, so far, there doesn't appear to be anything more seriously wrong than the cut artery."

Nothing seriously wrong? *Is this guy for real?* I keep my voice from screeching and ask, "Um, the artery. That's serious, isn't it? I mean, it's an artery. Blood squirted from there to here." I walk to the dark spot in the gravel that was two feet away from where Frisco lay and point at the evidence.

"Yes, like I said, he's lost some blood. Quite a lot of blood, even, but he's healthy and young. We need to take him to the clinic overnight for observation and to be sure the bandage holds. Your tourniquet likely saved his life. Good job. Actually, I'm going to leave it on until we get to the hospital. I'll just add another layer of bandage on top of it to be sure it holds." He turned back to his assistant. "Josh, grab the bandage box and let's wrap this wound and get him onto his feet."

Wrapping the wound and getting Frisco up sounded like a good idea, but did this good doctor not notice that the horse is wedged between the boulder and the tree like a piece of driftwood in a fast moving river? Getting him up wouldn't be as easy as helping a cast horse in a stall. Besides, we were still down a ways from the top of the landslide. A trailer couldn't make it up this mountain, which meant Frisco would be walking out on his own. Still, any plan to get him down the hill and to the clinic was far better than the alternative of figuring out what to do with his body. The outcome looked optimistic and I clung to that prospect like a drowning person to a life raft.

The vet did not remove the bandage I'd put on Frisco's leg, and instead, wrapped over my makeshift tourniquet using cotton, then VetWrap and finally, Elasticon to hold the original dressing in place. "We'll get him to the clinic before we take a look at this cut. I'll feel better opening the bandage there in case I run into a problem. Until then, some pain killers will help him feel better for the hike out of here."

Josh went back to the truck and returned with two liquid-filled syringes, a halter, lead rope and a long, white cotton rope. With the halter on Frisco, the two men cranked Frisco's head around so he was able to right himself to a sternal position. He was still stuck, but at least his head now faced forward.

Josh hands the lead to me and says, "Here ya go. You hold his head up and we'll lift from behind." He speaks with authority and acts as if they do this very thing a hundred times a week and it's no big deal. He threads the rope behind Frisco's hindquarters, above his hocks and under his buttocks. They each stand with their feet planted wide apart and wrap their fists around the rope. Shoulder to shoulder with the horse between them, they face his tail. Leaning back and looking across Frisco's back at Josh, Dr. Keifer nods, "Ready?"

The two men hold the thick rope chest-high and pull hard enough they each almost sit on the mountainside to help the horse stand. I can't help thinking that right about now would be a great time for that loser, Steve, to show up and help us, but there is no sign of him.

I hold Frisco's head up and with the tip of my tongue held against the roof of my mouth, I give the clucking the command telling him to move his feet. Frisco rolls his eyes back toward the two men, and then struggles to get himself up. I pull on the rope by leaning backwards and encourage him. "C'mon boy, you can do it."

The men reorganize themselves and we all repeat the process. One more heave and Frisco lurches to his feet. He stands with his front legs spread apart like a newborn foal. His head hangs so his lips are only an inch from the ground, but his ears pivot backward, toward the men behind him, then forward to me.

"Good boy, Frisco, good boy," I murmur. I kiss his forehead and stroke his neck, and hope no one notices the tears I swat from my cheek with the back of my arm. "Good boy," I say again. I turn to look up at Andy Keifer. "Thank you," I try smiling but I'm crying instead. "Thank you so much."

"We're not done yet, Paizely." Keifer said, slipping a needle into the horse's neck. "Painkiller," is all he says in reference to the shot, then announces the next one into the muscle is an antibiotic. "We've got to get him off this mountain and to the clinic. You ok to lead him down the hill? You got banged up in the fall too, I see." He leans down and reaches for my chin. "Let me look at that cut."

"I'm fine," I tell him, turning away. "Let's get him out of here."

"We'll follow you," Andy Keifer answered and I notice Josh has dashed back down to gather my tack from the ground. Either he doesn't notice or chooses to say nothing about the pistol strapped to the pommel.

I lead my horse slowly and carefully the distance up the steep incline to the crest of the landfill. I can hear the men talking behind me, but can't make out their words. At the top, Dr. Keifer holds his position behind Frisco, while Josh throws my saddle and bridle into the back seat before getting into the Ranger to follow us. I glance back frequently to check Frisco's progress and even though I have a million questions, I don't talk to the vet walking behind my horse. The man is hard focused on Frisco's legs as we make our way down the hill and his intent concentration both worries and comforts me. Good to have the doctor here, but how much blood did a horse have to lose before he couldn't come back? Would he need a transfusion? Did they still have that horse at the clinic that donated blood if Frisco had lost too much?

To me, my horse looked depressed even now, with painkillers and antibiotics streaming through his veins.

Each step raises my hopes though, until I feel just about giddy when we finally reach the flat land at the bottom of the mountain. Andy Keifer, DVM, steps to my side and asks, "Do you have a trailer? I'll stay with Frisco and Josh will take you to get it."

Leave my horse? "Um, no. I mean yes. I have a trailer. It's at the ranch, but can Josh go get it without me? Or can you go? I don't want to leave Frisco."

Andy Keifer laughs, throwing his head back and guffawing as though he'd heard the greatest joke ever. "Paizely, I understand that you love your horse and are worried about him, but I promise I'll take good care of him while you're gone. Don't you live at the ranch with the white barn and the white fences? Used to be the old Sorensen Ranch? It won't take you long and like I said, I'll take good care of him. I promise."

I chew at my fingernail. "Okay, but it's a forty-five minute drive from here down to the hospital, Will he be able to stand that long?"

"Yes, he'll be fine. If you would like, I'll ride back there with him to be sure. I have a cell phone. It's legal as long as we have communication between the truck and trailer."

"You would do that?"

"Of course. Now go. Josh will drive you to the ranch to get your trailer."

I pet Frisco and tell him I'll be right back, then turn to leave.

"Oh, and Paizely," Andy called, "Don't forget the truck to pull it." He winks and his eyes smile all the way down to his mouth.

* * *

I ride with Josh to get my trailer, anxious to get Frisco down the hill and to the clinic. At home, I want to run into the cabin and tell Holly about Frisco. I want to ask her to come down with me to the hospital so she can keep me company and give me strength. Although the vision shows Holly being killed tomorrow, I try not to follow the snaking thought that Steve has moved his killing day up by one.

If she were with me, Steve can't kill her while I'm down the hill. But there is no time to get her. Besides, Holly's Jeep is gone and since Steve never showed at the landslide, she must not be home.

Just then, I hear him. The sound of the old Ranchero he drives consistently announces Steve's arrival well before we see him and this time is no exception. He pulls up beside us and says, "What's going on, Paize? I thought we were supposed to meet at the landslide?"

I don't even glare at him. Hell, I didn't even look at him. I say, "Frisco's hurt, I gotta go. Do you know where Holly is?"

"She said she'd be home by the time I needed the Jeep so she should be here any minute."

"Steve, I need her to meet me at the clinic. Will you tell her? "

I don't wait for his reply, I get into my truck and Josh guilds me back toward the tongue of the trailer. Still, hitching takes too long. We need to go and the more impatient I am, the more frustrated I get, the longer it takes. Once hooked, I gun the motor so the truck tires kick up a rooster-tail of gravel and the trailer fishtails out of the drive.

I speed to where the vet stands with my horse. Horse and vet look like they are deep in conversation and I watch Frisco dip his ear to the man. I wonder what Dr. Keifer is saying to him and I say a silent gratitude for Frisco's life and for the kindness of the vet that stands with him. Frisco looks better than when I'd left and I leap from the vehicle, calling, "You must be a good vet…he looks happy to have you with him. He's going to be okay, right?"

"He's doing fine for now, Paizely. Let's get him loaded and down to the clinic."

We lead Frisco to the back of the horse trailer and he loads into it the same way he always does. First, he touches the floor and the walls with his nose, and then he walks in and begins shuffling the hay in the feed manger with his lips. I watch him for a moment, hoping he'll take a bite, but he doesn't. Josh puts up the butt bar behind Frisco and closes both back doors and we're ready to go.

Dr. Keifer says, "Let's roll. Sooner we get him to the clinic and settled, we'll all feel better."

I thank him again and get into the driver's side of the truck. I roll down both windows so I can hear if Frisco falls and place my cell phone on the dash. I drive slowly, maneuvering the rig around and down the dirt road that leads to the highway. On the way, I call Holly, but she doesn't answer. I leave a message asking her to meet me in town and hope she comes soon.

I cringe with each bump and watch the road with an intensity that rivals any marksman shooter taking down his prey. Periodically, I glance at the quiet cell phone in case it should ring the alarm of a problem in the back. And I wonder why my sister doesn't call me, even though Steve may not have talked to her yet.

I need to see Frisco once more before heading onto the highway, so when I reach the highway junction, I pull to the shoulder and park, leaving the truck running. I open the front access door and look up at Frisco and the vet. Inside the trailer at the front, there is tack area big enough for Dr. Keifer to stand and still be separated from the horse. A door leading into the stall would allow him to help the stallion if needed. Both horse and human look fine; happy even. Darting a look toward the vet, I mumble, "I just wanted to see him for a minute. Is he okay?" I realize he might consider me rude and added, "Are you okay?"

Even to myself, I sound like a paranoid over-protective parent, but Dr. Keifer just smiles and pets Frisco's nose. "We're fine. Your driving is terrific. No sway back here and we hardly felt the ruts in the road, did we big guy?"

I reluctantly leave them and go back to the truck. I speed down the highway with two goals: get there fast and keep both passengers comfortable and safe. Still, it takes the usual forty-five minutes to pull into the Lakewood Equine Hospital. Never have I been happier to see the little tan building surrounded by the three-rail white fence. At the back of the facility, I park and notice the overhead door has been raised, in anticipation of Frisco's arrival. Two technicians are waiting to help unload my horse and already have the doors open and the butt bar down by the time I make it to the back of the trailer. Dr. Keifer gets out with Frisco and calmly gives his instructions as to which fluid the horse should receive and at what speed the drip should be set. Technicians take Frisco through the waiting area and into the stall that's been prepared for him and I follow.

Dr. Keifer takes the thermometer from his shirt pocket and shakes the mercury to the bottom. He checks his watch, takes Frisco's pulse, checks the color of the horse's gums and eyelids, and counts the rate of respiration. I stand outside the stall watching, wanting to be in with my horse, yet afraid of getting in the way. Although I'd been a vet tech for two years after high school, this is different. This is Frisco.

Finally, Dr. Keifer steps around the back of my horse and smiles. He says, "Big guy knows we're all here for him. His vitals look great and the bandage is holding just fine. We won't take it off today. I'd rather wait until tomorrow and let things settle down. Stopping the bleeding saved his life." He pauses, grinning, then adds, "Didn't do much for your wardrobe though."

I had forgotten about ripping the sleeves off my shirt. I attempt a laugh, but an exhaustion that feels like a heavy blanket settles around me and I only manage a weak smile. I look deeply into the doctor's eyes. "Thank you. Thank you so much for coming to help us, for knowing how to find us, and for riding in the back with Frisco." The image of the white horse flashes through my mind and I add, "He's a special horse. If I can ever repay you, tell me."

He looks at me for a long moment. "Well, I'll think on it and let you know, but I think when you get the bill, you won't feel the need to repay in any other way." He pauses, his eyes twinkling and he smiles. "Although, riding in a trailer with a client's horse counts in the same price range as say, an emergency call on Christmas Day."

Like money even mattered when it came to Frisco. "Add it to my bill," I grinned. "I'll pay whatever you want."

"Oh, and there's one more thing, Paizely."

"Yes?" I asked.

"You should call me Andy," he smiled. And once more, I notice his smile starts in his eyes and travels down to his mouth.

~27

Holly glanced in the Jeep's rearview mirror, checking to see if the car behind her, driven by the most handsome man in the world was still there. In reality, she didn't need to look; she could hear the rumbling of the vehicle just fine. The cracked exhaust pipe growled like an overburdened tugboat. It wasn't a tugboat though. It was 1957 Ford Ranchero, a prehistoric dinosaur of a thing that Steve loved. With round hooded headlights, and triangular fins, the red and white beast looked like a mutant cross between a Cadillac, a T-Bird and a pickup. Steve said he couldn't find the part he needed to fix the noise, but she thought it was one of those macho guy things that somehow made a loud engine equivalent to strength and power. Men. She grinned and tilted her head and Steve must have noticed because he laughed and honked. She answered by waving her hand out the window.

Her cell phone rang and she flicked it open to see who was calling. Paizely. Holly didn't want to answer and talk to her sister right now. It would be the same old story: "Steve is going to kill you...Get away...He's a murderer....I dreamed it so it's true...blah, blah, blah..."

Ever since Mom and Dad died, Paizely acted like she was her guardian, which she had been, but she took the job way too seriously. They were both adults now, not the kids they'd been three years ago. Holly knew she should have moved out before now. She should have gotten away from her older sister's clutch, but she felt obligated to stay. Paizely had given up her own social life in order to care for her, and Holly couldn't bring herself to leave her sister alone. Because even though Paize would never admit it, she hated being alone.

But Holly was tired of all the arguing and disagreements. And Paizely's latest conviction that Steve was out to kill her was nuts. Worse, Paizely wouldn't let it go. She wouldn't let up about the visions and premonitions and kept harping about how Holly needed to watch her back and how he was going to stab her to death and frankly, it was all just too much. She and Steve would be married in a month and Paizely damn well needed to get used to that fact starting now.

Adamant, Holly ignored the phone and pushed the Jeep's turn signal down to indicate a left turn.

Behind her, Steve did the same thing, and the ancient amber turn signal light blinked on and off.

* * *

For the third time, I wait for my sister's outgoing greeting message to end, and for the third time, I start with, "Holly, are you okay? We've been in an accident, Frisco and I. I am at the clinic with him now and I'm worried about you. Where are you? Where is Steve? Call and let me know you're all right. I'm staying down here for a bit longer, and then I'll be home. I, uh, can meet at home for dinner, say around six? It's four-thirty now. Call me and let me know you're all right. I have a lot to tell you, I love you, Hol."

I hang up the phone and stroke Frisco's neck, just behind the taped bandage that encircles his throat and holds the catheter securely so that fluids drain into his artery. His eyes are half closed and he looks exhausted. He chews his hay slowly, and that isn't like him, but at least he is eating. And, he's alive. I cough, squeezing tears from between my swollen lids, and hug Frisco, "I love you, Booger. Thank you for not dying."

My words echo in the cinderblock stall and seem too loud and I'm happy for the sound of the overhead fans. No one has heard my confession, not that it would have mattered if they had, I guess, but still, I'd rather keep my feelings private. I step away from my horse and for the tenth time in a half hour, check the I.V. tubing that hangs from the ceiling and trails into his neck. Everything looks good, no kinks in the line and the drip is steady. I sit down at Frisco's head, cross my legs and lean back against the loose hay that has fallen from the manger. My gaze follows the contour of the bay stallion's belly and I take in every gentle swell of muscle along his body. I can't help admiring the sleek shininess of his mahogany coat, and the way the brown hairs of his upper leg blend into the black of his lower leg.

I'm so tired. Actually, tired doesn't even come close to what I feel. A better description would be utter exhaustion. I lay my head back against the wall and close my eyes until Frisco is a brown blur in front of me. His teeth grinding steadily together as he chews his hay lulls my mind to quiet. I think back over the past day. The time spent in 1871: Sheriff Thomas Taylor chasing Tahcitan had seemed so real. Had I done that or just been knocked out cold so my mind dreamed up the entire thing? I read once that dreams happen in a manner of seconds, but when we wake up and recall them, we think they'd taken hours. Time has no meaning in sleep.

Sheriff Taylor was real enough though. As was Ella Mitchell's murder. And the knots on my own forehead are very real. My fingers gently probe the tender spot at the base of my skull where Saul had yanked out my hair.

Yep, all real.

* * *

Holly parked and got out of the Jeep, laughing at Steve's crazy curly blond hair and lopsided grin. The dimple on his chin gave him a little-boy look that she found adorable. "I love you, Steve," she said. "A month is a long time to wait, I can't wait to call you my husband."

"Call me anything you want, Darlin', I'll come runnin'." He bent his head to hers and kissed her.

Holly leaned into him, and then pulled away. "We've got to hurry. It's late."

He grinned again, looping his arm around her shoulders. "We have plenty of time. They don't close for another hour. You just want more diamonds on that pretty little finger of yours, I know how you are."

"Oh, it's not that, Steve. I just got a call from Paizely and she's been in some sort of accident. Frisco's at the horse hospital and you know how attached she is to him. She sounds worried and scared. I need to get back to her soon."

Steve bowed his head and Holly noticed the muscle in his jaw twitch once. Twice. "She'll be fine, Hol. Leave it." He practically dragged her across the parking lot toward the jewelry store where their wedding rings waited.

"Sweetie, I know she makes you nuts, but I, I can't just leave it. You know how upset she is lately. She's convinced you're going to stab me to death any minute." Holly stopped, hauling him to stop. Widening her eyes and trying to look scared, she tipped her head to the side. "Wait. You don't have a knife in your pocket, do you?"

He took off walking without her, calling over his shoulder, "Oh for God's sake, Holly. Stop it."

"Wait. Seriously," she called after him. She laughed and ran to his side. "Paizely is upset and she thinks she's my personal body guard since mom and dad died, you know that. She gave up everything for me. She took care of me and I owe her. I need to go to the vet's and help her if she needs me."

Steve's eyes narrowed. "You owe her nothing. She just wants to keep you under her wing and in her control for the rest of your lives. That girl is so scared to take chances she'll do everything in her power to keep things status-quo, including stopping you from having any kind of life away from her. Is that what you want? Is that what you're willing to do? Let her run your life forever?"

"No, of course not."

Steve cupped her chin in his hand and looked directly into her eyes. "You need to choose, Holly. Me or her."

Holly laughed, hoping to diffuse the seriousness of the moment. "Yeah, right. Like you'd ask me to do that for real."

Steve laid his hands on her shoulders. His blue eyes bore steel gray and his gaze did not waver. "I'm not asking, Holly. I'm telling you. Her or me. You need to decide what you want."

* * *

I'm falling. My balance is off and my muscles won't respond. I jerk my head back so quickly the back of my skull slam hard into the concrete wall. I wake up and realize I'd been asleep in Frisco's stall. He stands over me, his chin just above my shoulder, his eyes half closed, dozing, but he's keeping watch over me at the same time. The bag of fluids still drips steadily through the tubing and into his neck. I must have slept longer than a few minutes because enough time had passed that he's eaten about half the hay in the manger.

My Mickey Mouse watch shows that it's already after six. I told Holly I'd meet her at home at six and I'm still forty-five minutes from there. Getting up hurts more than I expect. Every muscle cries out in protest and my joints join in the chorus so I force myself to stretch for a count of ten even though I need to get going.

Frisco looks tired, but otherwise, all right, so I kiss his forehead and go to find Dr. Andy Keifer to tell him I'm leaving. He assures me that my horse will be monitored overnight and that if anything happens, they'll call me. So I say goodbye to him and tell Frisco I'll see him in the morning. I unhitch the trailer from my truck and leave it in the parking lot since there's no good reason to haul it up and then back down the hill.

Driving home I turn on the radio and focus on the words to the songs. The trip is over before I know it and recalling any single song I'd heard is impossible. I pull into the ranch and see Holly's jeep parked in its usual place outside the cabin. Why didn't she call? On the heels of my anger comes happiness. I'm happy and relieved that she's home. I'm even happier to not see the Ranchero. Stepping through side door that led into the kitchen, I call, "Holly? You here?"

Holly is sitting at the breakfast counter, her eyes red-rimmed and puffy. She's obviously been crying and my own problems are forgotten immediately. Holly must have felt something similar about me because at the same time, we ask one another, "Oh my God, are you all right?"

After a long embrace, I examine Holly's face, searching for the reason for her tears. Physically, my sister looks fine, and that is a relief beyond comparison, but her eyes are full of dark clouds and I know she is wounded from some kind of pain that I can't read in her expression.

Worse, Holly refuses to talk about what has caused her sadness. I force myself to turn away.

I go to the cupboard where the Advil lives and pour four little red pills into the palm of my hand, then dry swallow them before taking a cold can of Coke from the fridge. Exhaustion accompanies me to the bar stool next to my sister and I slump into the chair like a puppet whose strings have been released. I sigh and close my eyes, then turn toward Holly. I don't say anything, I just wait.

Finally, Holly says, "You know, Steve is a good man."

I don't think before answering. "Who are you trying to convince?"

"He is, Paizely. He is a good man." Holly rests her forehead in the palms of her hands and stares at the cobalt blue counter top.

Her voice is laced with a note of resignation that taints her proclamation of Steve's sainthood. My heart reacts first; an exuberantly happy dancing cadence, and I hope Holly's somber tone and red-rimmed swollen eyes mean she's broken up with Steve. To hide my joy at that possibility, I carefully examine the red aluminum can I'm holding.

Holly bites her lower lip. "I'm sure," she begins, then sniffles. Tears well in her eyes and she says, "I'm sure you'll be happy to know that Steve and I broke up."

My heart flies on delighted wings for a moment, but my exhilaration is short-lived. Taking a sip, I look impassively over the rim of my can of Coke. What if Steve is one of those men who believes that Holly belongs to him and if he can't have her, then no one can? Maybe the breakup is the reason he murders Holly. This theory rings with a possible truth I don't want to acknowledge. "Why, Holly? What happened?"

"Doesn't matter."

"Yes it does," I say, and I'm entirely sincere. Knowing what happened between them might indicate whether or not Steve would show up with a knife in the morning. "Of course it matters. Talk to me, sis."

"Let's just say that you were right. He's, he's irrational sometimes."

I don't like the sound of this at all. "What did he do that's irrational, Holly? Did he hurt you, or threaten you? Are you all right? Who broke up with who?"

Holly stands up and runs her hands through her hair. "Let's just drop it. Wedding's off and that should please you. I'm going to bed."

I stare at the empty doorway that Holly has gone through for a long time. I can't shake the feeling that Steve and Holly breaking off their wedding seems to be the perfect catalyst for a madman to go on a killing streak.

~28

My second shower in twelve hours felt good, but having my morning coffee is even better. Mostly though, I don't find myself feeling much anything other than scared. More like terrified, really. Today, if my talent-gift-curse shows itself as true, Steve will kill my only family, my only sister. The undeniable truth that this can, and likely will happen sends adrenaline humming through my veins and jangles my nerves so my muscles twitch uncontrollable.

My wet hair hangs in long ropes down my back, soaking through my blue terry-cloth robe, and I shiver. The combination of the cold wet robe and the possibility that I'll have to shoot my sister's fiancé before lunch sends me to my room to get dressed. It's only five-thirty in the morning and the sun is still sleeping behind dark storm clouds. My plan is to feed the horses, clean the stalls and be back in the house before Steve shows up--which I'm certain he will. He usually comes by just before seven on his way to work, his old Ranchero roaring through the yard, scaring the wildlife and inadvertently desensitizing the horses to loud vehicles.

Lightning pops like a strobe from God, and out of habit, I count to myself. *One my little pony, two my little pony, three my little...* Thunder booms. Three miles away then. The rain comes down like spray from a shotgun, fast and hard, pounding the cabin's roof. Ominous and foreboding.

I pull on a tee-shirt and grab the .22 from under my pillow. I wish I had the .380, but it is still in the truck with my saddle and with this weather, the idea of trekking through the rain to retrieve it is more than a little unappealing. The .22 will work just fine if needed. I'd never shot a man, but then, my sister had never been in danger of being stabbed to death either. Stuffing the pistol into the waistband of my Wranglers, I tiptoe out to the living room, wary, but certain in my ability to take his life to save hers.

Thunder rocks the cabin again and following it, the familiar roar of Steve's rickety truck bellows.

What the hell? He's here earlier than usual and that can't be a good thing. Holly is most likely still asleep, but to be sure, I go to my sister's room and peek in. Her blonde hair is fanned across her pillow and one leg sticks out from the covers. Beside her, Bugalone--so named when Holly had yelled at the tiny tabby kitten to leave that bug alone--is curled in tight ball next to her so it looks as though he's sleeping on his head. Neither move so I ease the door shut and pad quickly into the kitchen.

Six feet from the door, I take a shooter's stance, gun aimed at the glass window, and wait for Steve to enter. The roar of the Ranchero finally fades and along with the spattering rain drops, I hear the pulse of my heartbeat pounding in my head. My arms strain to hold the gun steady and I wonder what is taking him so long to come into the house. Maybe he's gone to the front door since that entrance was closer to Holly's bedroom. Keeping the gun raised and aimed, I step closer to the window to see where he is.

Catching sight of him limping towards the house isn't what turns the blood in my veins to ice.

What he is wearing does.

Fanning out from his knees, the hem of a long, black trench coat billows like the wings of a ravenous dragon swooping in for the kill. Steve has never worn such a coat. Ever. And sure, it's raining hard, but the coincidence of his wearing the same thing that Frank had. . .

My heart twists against my ribs, slamming itself into a frenzy and my teeth begin to chatter uncontrollably. My premonition, dream, whatever the hell it was will come true if I don't figure out some way to stop him.

There is no way he's getting past me to Holly. I'll die saving my sister, and I'll go to prison happily for that honor. I'll shoot him. I will.

The worm in my brain reminds me that if I don't kill him, things will get real ugly in court and so I better aim for his heart and nail him on the first shot.

I will wait until he is in the house, aim for his chest and then claim that I thought he was an intruder, I didn't know it was him, and the Colorado 'Make My Day' law will protect me. As long as he's dead anyway. And if not, well, at least my sister would be alive.

I clench my jaw to quiet the annoying rattle of my teeth.

The sound of his heavy boots echoes as he climbs the back stairs and with each step, my hand trembles a little less.

The outside door swings open and he pauses on the landing of the mudroom to take off the raincoat.

I clear my throat.

Steve glances up, then turns to hang the dripping slicker on a hook behind him. He must have noticed the gun aimed at his heart because he never finishes the task, spinning to face me instead. His eyes wide, he drops the garment to the floor and sticks both his hands high in the air, fingers clenching and releasing. He shouts in a voice as high-pitched and shrill as that of a schoolgirl, "Hey, put that thing down!"

I do not.

In a fraction of a second, I take inventory of him that includes his looks, his mood, his stress level. He doesn't exactly look like he's come to assassinate anybody. His curly blond hair hangs in loopy ringlets about his face. His cheeks are flushed pink by the cold so his eyes look like blue sapphires. He is scared, but of the gun, or his intent to kill, I'm unsure. He quivers all over, so he's not real calm, but again, I question from where his anxiety originates.

Slowly, in the time we each take three breaths, a calm change veils over him and surrounds him until he no longer shakes. His breathing is metered, even and yes, calm. He repeats his request that I lower the weapon--this time without the shrill pitch to his voice. His stare bores through me and he pushes his shoulders back and stands straighter and taller. His eyes narrow and I'm pretty sure the blue morphs into a shade of dark purple. As though he can make me do what wants by sheer willpower, he commands, "Paizely, put the gun down. Now."

From behind me, Holly screams, "Paizely! What the hell are you doing?"

I glance toward my sister and know immediately that I shouldn't have. In that instant, Steve bounds across the threshold into the kitchen and hits me with his shoulder, knocking me to the floor. The gun falls from my hand and skitters away, chattering and laughing at me. I crab-crawl after it, hollering, "Run, Holly! Get out of here, run!"

Steve grabs me by the leg.

I flip over so I can kick him. I draw up leg and aim my heel at his chest.

He throws himself onto me, straddling my pelvis and pinning my wrists to the floor. He looks down, his teeth grinding so the muscles at his jaws jump. He doesn't say anything.

I wish I could spit in his face.

To my left, Holly picks up the pistol and flicks the safety on before putting it into the pocket of her robe. I watch them both and say a silent "Bravo" for my sister having kept the gun with her. Too bad she's set the safety, but it wouldn't take but a fraction of a second to reverse that decision should she need to.

"Steve, are you okay?" Holly asks.

"Steve, are you okay?" The ape is sitting on me and she asks is he's okay? "What the hell, Holly? Get out of here, run!"

Steve ignores me and looks at her. "Yeah, I'm fine."

I'm pretty sure he was going to say more, but I didn't give him a chance. "You bastard," I say through gritted teeth. "You'll have to go through my dead body to kill her. It's not gonna happen so get off of me and get the hell out of my house. Now."

Steve laughs, hard enough that his grip on me loosens by a fraction. But it's enough. I twist away from him so he falls sideways to the floor, still laughing.

Wishing I was wearing my riding boots and knowing my next move would likely hurt me more than him, I go ahead and kicked him hard in the shin with my bare foot. It hurt me for sure, but the satisfaction of getting at least one good hit is worth it. I jump up wishing I could have landed a swift kick to his precious gonads instead.

Steve quits laughing. On his hands and knees, he crouches, then manages to stand. He looks bewildered though not injured. Holly runs to his side and asks, "Sweetie, are you all right?"

"Oh for God's sake, Holly. Give me the gun," I demand.

Holly ignores me. She looks up at Steve, her eyes soft and fluttery."Babe, I'm sorry. Paizely had a rough day yesterday." She stands on her tiptoes and kisses his cheek. "I tried calling you last night, but couldn't get a hold of you and I didn't want to leave a message after our argument."

I step toward them.

Holly snaps her head around and glares at me. Steve, the sorry jackass starts laughing again.

Something was wrong here. The two of them watch me, one angry, one grinning like a half-witted goon. I can't *feel* any anger or animosity from Steve. Nothing indicates that he is ready to murder Holly or anyone else for that matter. Maybe I'm wrong. Maybe the 'gift' is wrong.

Yeah, and maybe the sky had turned green overnight. I didn't check to be sure.

Holly's mood changes from anger to something that borders along the lines of a mother gently prodding a three-year-old to hurry to the bathroom and use the toilet. "Paizely, you need help. You're acting like an idiot. Now go sit down."

I stare into my sister's eyes, silently begging her to please be reasonable and get the killer out of the house.

Holly, of course, doesn't pay attention to my unvoiced pleas.

Steve stands leaning against the counter with that same stupid lopsided smile on his face. His eyes on Holly, he reaches into his front jean pocket.

I am across the small kitchen slamming into him sideways, shoving my shoulder into his ribs as hard as I can. I hear him gasp and pull my fist back so I can smash it into his stomach.

Before I can deliver the well-intentioned blow, Holly grabs my arm. "Damn it Paizely, stop it!"

Steve has a hold of my other arm and he doesn't hold it with much pressure, just has his big paw wrapped around my wrist and he holds me so I can't move. His eyes bore into mine and he speaks slowly and deliberately, "Paizely, I don't know what is going on with you, but all I'm trying to do is give Holly a present."

Give her a present, my ass. "Like what, an eight-inch blade, ya sonofabitch? I don't think so."

"Now, I'm going to let you go and you're going to stop attacking me, right?"

I stand very still and do not answer.

Steve takes my silence to be a sign of my consent and loosens his ape-grip on my wrist and once more, reaches toward his pocket.

I spin out and away from him and duck my head. Two steps backwards and I run forward ramming him like a linebacker. Steve *oomphs* a gasping breath and falls like a redwood, hitting the wooden kitchen floor with a satisfying thud. I grab Holly and drag her across the room, succeeding only because her slippers slide on the slick hardwood. The whole way, she tries to dig in and stop me, but she can't. At the doorway into the carpeted living room, I still tug on my sister, but Holly finally hits solid ground to stop her skidding feet.

"Paizely!" Holly screams, "Stop!"

Something in her tone makes me do exactly as ordered. I glance past Holly to the would-be assassin who was holding his stomach with one hand while pulling himself up the lower cupboard doors toward the sink with the other. He looks a little pale and grunts in pain which gives me an enormous amount of satisfaction.

I continue dragging my lovesick sister away from the killer and into the living room. I grope for the gun along the way and she swats at my hand. I whisper into her ear, "Holly, go to your room and shut the door until I get him the hell outa here."

She lifts her left foot and stomps on the top of mine as hard as she can. Sure, she has slippers on, but her bony heel digs in so hard it hurts enough for me to loosen my grip on her. She twists away from me and runs to Steve.

He doesn't pull a knife out and begin stabbing her, he just stands leaning against the counter holding his stomach with one hand and Holly with the other.

Since he didn't kill her with a magically produced knife and since he didn't reach for the gun in her robe pocket and since I was across the room from them, I realized that maybe, just maybe, he wasn't really here to murder anybody. The vision-dream always showed them outside, him wearing a duster when he killed her. Just like I'd seen in 1871. Here and now, neither of them seemed to fit the part. Right now wasn't the moment my sister would die at his hands and I needed to accept that.

Steve keeps his eyes locked on mine and doesn't speak. He reaches for the ceiling, his palms facing me, then slowly, slowly reaches into the front pocket of his Levi's. I don't rush him or throw anything at his head.

He pulls out a small box and shows it to me, then Holly. He opens it and faces her. "I love you so much Holly. If the only way you'll wear this engagement ring is for me to accept that crazy sister of yours," he glances sideways at me, "Then so be it. I'll take both of you. Anything to keep you in my life...because, without you, I'm nothing and I can't imagine living without you. Holly, you mean everything to me."

I succeed at not rolling my eyes toward the ceiling.

Steve kisses Holly, slips the ring on her extended finger and walks over to me. I try to step back, but he reaches out and holds me by the shoulders. "Paizely, I want you to know that you have nothing to worry about. I'd kill myself before I ever thought about hurting Holly. To prove it to you, I'm willing to stay completely away all day today and tomorrow too, if you want me to. I want to make sure I don't accidently stab Holly to death and if we can keep her alive until your vision is proved wrong, I'm happy to do that. Only stipulation is that you have to keep her safe from any other killer. You have to be the insurance policy, okay?"

I can't speak so I just nod.

"Holly," Steve said, "Bring me the gun, please."

Holly dumbly walks to where he still holds me by my shoulders and hands the pistol to him.

He says, "Here you go, Paizely, take this and keep it with you all day today. Stay with her and watch over her. Call me when I can come back over and until I hear from you, I won't bother you."

Holly said, "No, Steve--"

"No Holly, you stay with Paizely every single minute today. She has never been wrong and when you look at it that way, the fact is that someone--not me, but someone else, may want to harm you and we can't take that chance."

I can't believe my ears. I can tell he means every word though, so the only thing to do is keep Holly, my .45 and the .380 with me all day. No problem.

The two lovebirds kiss goodbye and with the engagement ring on Holly's finger, Steve leaves.

* * *

Holly and I don't say anything to each other for a few minutes. I know I have to break the silence since Steve obviously was taking the high road here, but I don't want to. No, I'd rather have told her what an ass he is for being willing to stay away for the next day if he thought a killer would suddenly surface. I wanted to tell her that if he really loved her, he's the one who would protect her. I wanted to point out what a pompous jerk he is, but face it, there is no way she'll believe or agree with anything I say. Instead of continuing the argument, I ask, "What do you want to do today, Holly?"

She glares at me. I try again, "Okay. You're right, he's a nice guy."

"Really, Paize? That's all you can say?"

I know she's right. I've been acting crazy and Steve proved his trustworthiness by leaving. I know these things and I hope that everything is as it appears, but I'm still scared for her. For me. I chew my thumbnail before saying, "Well, the day isn't done yet, but I seriously think that for the first time, I'm wrong--the visions are wrong I mean, and you're not going to be murdered by your fiancé. So what should we do today? I need to go see Frisco, want to come with me?"

Holly stands, shaking her head. She said, "Yeah, I'll go. When?"

"Soon as we're ready. I'll go out and feed and clean the barn while you shower. And Holly, I'll take you to breakfast if you want. That good place we both love in Golden?"

She nods as she leaves the room.

* * *

Holly and I went to breakfast, then back to the clinic to check on Frisco before heading back up the hill towards home. We don't speak much, Holly and I, but only because I'm so busy hoping my premonitions have stopped that I am afraid to say anything. I am so absorbed in the ramifications of this prediction being wrong--and the possibility my 'gift' is completely gone--that I spend the trip trying to define myself without the forewarnings being a part of me.

Sure, maybe the vision could still come true, but so far things look hopeful. My cell rings and I answer using my ear-bud Bluetooth. It's Steve, and he's called me, not Holly. He asks about Frisco first, then wants to know how Holly is holding up. I feel so awful for hating him for being exactly who Holly says he is, I hand her the phone. I'd leave so they could have privacy, but we're still in the truck.

I ignore her side of their conversation and tell myself Holly will be fine and Steve is not an assassin. Hard as it is to wrap my mind around, I need to accept she will marry him in a month and I'll be on my own. I question if my not wanting to be alone might be the real reason behind my distrust of Steve after all, just as they'd accused. I honestly don't believe this is the case. I'm simply not that weak, or needy. I can't be.

Thing is, I like being alone. It makes me feel safe and yet, I have always felt safer with Holly there with me. I want to let her go. I want to get on with living my own life as well. Maybe there is a Thomas Taylor for me here and now. Something about him made me hopeful and why that would be the case, I have no clue.

Which brings me right back to 1871. Had I actually gone there? I drive the truck without thinking about what I'm doing and instead envision the world I'd visited yesterday. I should have Holly drive, but I don't want to break my reverie or bother her talking with Steve.

Was it real, 1871? I'll Google the year and the place and see what comes up. If I find proof of anything--Ella's murder, a sheriff named Thomas Taylor, Frank Mitchell--anything at all, well, I'm not sure what that will mean. Other than perhaps I'm not truly off my rocker.

If I don't find any proof, then that will mean something too. And though I don't want to admit that I've imagined the whole ordeal, I need to get a grip on what happened.

What about the white horse over Frisco, the one that flew into the cloud herd? The voice, the *knowing*. That was not something I conjured up, it couldn't have been. I had felt that bright all-encompassing presence of love and purity the spirit horse had surrounded me with. I'd heard his words and knew the truth of them way down into my soul.

Something happened to me when I fell from Frisco. When he went crazy. What it all means and how it will affect the rest of my life, I can't guess. I don't believe my own imagination is good enough to have made up the trip to 1871, and if it is, I should write screenplays and become rich. Yeah, right.

No, I'd experienced something I didn't understand and now I needed to do two things: keep my sister from getting killed and figure out if I'd time-traveled or simply lost my mind.

We walk through the back door into the kitchen and I go straight to the study. I pull out the phone book and began leafing through the yellow pages under the heading "Psychiatrists".

Just in case.

~29

I know which one I'll go with soon as I read their names, but I go through a process of elimination in a logical way first. Yes, even as I go down the list, I know, I absolutely know I will choose the last one because making such a decision is exactly what a deranged human would do.

I find the listings of psychiatrists in the half-inch thick phone book and read each name twice, willing myself to ignore the last name. I look through the ads for the doctors who appeared to the most popular or at least made enough money to afford a half or full page of advertising. I disregard those.

This leaves the last name on the list along with three others, two of which are women. If I choose a woman, she'll either be more willing to listen to me with an open, imaginative mind or she'll be harsher with me. I'm not sure which would be the most helpful for me so I disregard the women as well.

Of the last two men, including the final name of all the listings, I dismiss the one named Paul, which was my father's name. The idea of talking to my dad about time travel and the voices in my head... well, I just can't imagine how disappointed he'd be with his daughter ending up in a mental ward.

If I truly am unstable, the voices in my head will drive me stark raving mad before I have the psychiatric appointment and I'll end up in the loony bin before I have a chance to foal out all the mares or see my sister marry Steve. But if I wait until after the wedding, it might be worse and I'll start chanting about green Volkswagens driven by giraffes wearing purple scarves.

Who knows, maybe seeing a shrink will be like going to the doctor for a stomach ache and he'll give me some medicine to make it go away. Was there a pill to chase away what I'd experienced? Probably. They had a pill for everything.

I call the Evergreen phone number and set up my free consultation appointment for the day after tomorrow. If Steve or someone else murders Holly before then, I'll need a shrink just as much as if everything turns out like some fairy tale starring Holly and Prince Charming himself, Steve. Accepting the idea of Steve as a good guy isn't easy and I remind myself how wrong the vision was this time and try to convince myself that everything will be fine.

Maybe I'd been changed somehow by being thrown and hitting my head hard enough to think I'd gone to 1871. Maybe the white ghost-horse was right and all I need to do is let go and accept the truth--just because I loved someone didn't mean they'd die. Maybe though, just maybe I really had gone off the edge and the reality is I am compromised mentally.

I still haven't told Holly the 1871 adventure details and I don't tell her about the psychiatrist, or what his name is, or why I chose him, either. If I do, she'll stress over the whole thing. I'm not ready to have her see me as a crazy person.

In every passing hour, Tahcitan haunts me. The fear that was hers is not with me here. I left it in the past where it belongs, but her? Oh, she is still with me, alright. She is in me, around me...*of me*. I can't shake her and I find myself saying her words over and over. Silently mouthing them, just so I can feel the substance and weight of them in my mouth. Words like *"Ve'ho'e"* and even her name, "Tahcitan".

I want to understand what happened and what might still happen and somehow, *I know* the two things are related. But how?

It's late in the afternoon, but I have time to do some research before feeding the horses. In the study, I boot up the computer and

Google *1871, Sheriff Thomas Taylor, Longmont, Colorado Territories.* Nothing comes up that helps me and there is no such person to be found. I try *Ella Mitchell, 1871,* then *Frank, Francis and Franklin Mitchell.* Again, nothing. I try *Tahcitan* and even tried to find the stallion she rode--the grandson of the great Stockwell, but which grandson, I have no way of knowing. I have no luck finding anything or any of them to prove yesterday's experience .

This can only mean one of two things and helps me not even a little bit. Either I went or I didn't. Either I'm crazy or I'm not. Nothing is proven or disproven and I'm right where I started.

I go into the kitchen and call Steve from the land line, not sure what I'll say to him or why I'm reaching out to him. Maybe it's just what crazy people do. They act irrationally and this is about as irrational as anything I'd ever done since I set out to shoot him on the ridge and bury him there. Or, perhaps it's his lack of self-grounding that allows me to see my own unsteady existence so clearly and so now we have a shared kinship.

Great.

He answers on the first ring. What, is he sitting watching the phone, waiting for someone to call? "Hi Steve, it's Paizely."

"Hey," he says. "Is everything all right?"

He probably thinks my call is bad news. Why else would I call him? The old saying about keeping your friends close and your enemies closer tumbles around in my head. Yes, better to know exactly where he is. I smile, hoping I'll sound sincere, happy, engaging. "Hey Steve, nothing's wrong. I'm just thinking maybe you'd want to come over. Grab a pizza and I'll make a salad. I mean, if you want to."

Silence on the line as he considers, then, "Are you sure?"

"Yeah, Steve. I'm sure. I think it would be a good idea. I didn't tell Holly I'm calling you so she'll be surprised and happy to see you."

"Um, okay."

"Steve, since you didn't kill Holly this morning, I'm guessing you aren't going to, right?" I laugh and ignore the hollow tone I hear in my own voice. "And if we're going to be family, I'd better get used to you being around all the time and I better get to feeling good about it, right?"

Right. That, and if he's here, sitting in front of me, I can keep an eye on him. Any sign of danger and I'll blow his happy butt to Kansas before he even sees me flinch.

"Okay, if you're sure. You like the same pizza as Holly or do you want something different?"

Like I cared about eating. "Sure, anything is fine, see you soon."

* * *

When he arrives, we each get a Coke and a piece of pizza and I tell the story of my fall, my journey to the past and conclude with the white horse. I watch Holly to gauge her reaction and I watch Steve for any sign of him being a killer--just in case I'm wrong about him. They both nod and asked a few questions but otherwise, they listen to my tale like two toddlers being read a good book by their feeble grandmother. Neither seem inclined to think I've time traveled or been privy to a view into a past life. Their complete lack of curiosity demonstrate how they view both me and their world and after an hour, I give up and go to bed.

I don't sleep though. I listen to the sounds of them cleaning the kitchen and then their murmurs as they watch some movie we'd ordered through Netflix. Every fifteen minutes, I tiptoe to the door and peer at them through the crack to be sure Steve isn't pulling a hidden knife from his pocket, though I know he is not going to. Finally, around eleven, Steve leaves and Holly goes to bed.

One more hour and my vision will officially be wrong.

* * *

What does a potentially crazy person wear to a psyche appointment anyway? I've changed shirts a good fifteen times already and finally, fed up with myself, I throw on an orange peasant blouse that has little blue and white flowers embroidered around the neckline. Clean pair of Wranglers over new never-been-to-the-barn boots, and I'm ready.

I drive past the lake, through Evergreen to Bergen Park, following the directions from my GPS I affectionately call Edith. Edith has one of those irritating screeching voices that reminded me of Archie Bunker's wife on the old television show, *All in the Family*. Funny, but I wouldn't even know about the sit-com or Edith, if it weren't for Steve. He loved Nick at Night TV, so when he was around, we watched his favorites. I didn't much care for most of his choices, though *MASH* was worth watching and *Bonanza* too, but when I thought about it, the old west sure wasn't portrayed in any way remotely close to what I'd seen on my little adventure. I guess actors with rotted teeth would discourage viewers though, so it made sense the producers would clean them up. I wouldn't have known about *Walker, Texas Ranger*, either, if it weren't for Steve and his love of Nick at Night.

Edith commanded me to make a safe U-turn soon as it was possible.

Back on track, I realize I am following a road through a neighborhood and wonder if I am lost after all. I slow the truck to look at the printed driving instructions I have on the seat next to me. I am exactly where I need to be and smile to myself at the irony of such a statement. I drive on, turn right for the last time and pull into a paved drive lined with pine trees and a split rail fence. I park next to a statue of a wolf, bronze, life-sized and so real looking I sit gazing at it for a moment before pulling the visor mirror down and checking my hair and face. Deep lines around my eyes make me look worried. Not how I viewed myself in general, but then again, I'd never truly doubted my own mental capacity. Disgusted, I slam the thing shut and got out of the truck, leaving the keys in the ignition and not bothering to lock up.

Just as I'm turning away from the driver's side door, something or someone rams me from behind, hitting me hard between my shoulder blades. For an instant, I imagine that the bronzed wolf has pounced and is lunging into me, ready for the kill. I swing around, ready to push away my attacker to find a huge Great Dane, white with black spots covering his face, grinning at me like a drooling child. I laugh and he sits, beaming at me, then jumps up, resting his paws on my arms and licking my face as though I were his long-lost best-ever friend. I laugh again and he pushes off of me, taking off with his butt tucked and back legs churning. He looks over his shoulder at me, then flattens his ears against his head and runs a small circle around the driveway, across the lawn, past the trees, past a huge lilac bush. With his tail tucked once again, and his ears flying and flapping behind him as if they were flags in a high wind, he comes back to me. He sits happily at my feet; tongue lolling, tail wagging and stares at me as if I ought to do something equal to either his display of incredible athletic ability or at least, his exuberance. I do neither.

He tips his head to the side so one of his uncropped ears stands up while the other falls to the side of his head. The pale underside makes it look like he's wearing a yellow-pink banana leaf.

"You're a goof ball," I tell him, laughing.

He smiles at me.

I grin and crouch down to fix his inside-out ear. He swipes his tongue across my cheek, and I mop the slick smear of dog drool from my face with the back of my hand. "C'mon big guy, let's go see the good doctor."

He leads the way to the front of the house--a two-story place painted grey with white trim that somehow manages somehow to look like a Victorian wanna-be log cabin. The color makes the house look like a pristine city dwelling, but the architecture is more rustic somehow. Set amongst huge Ponderosa pines, bordered by a garden of wildflowers and rocks, the house welcomes visitors in a way that makes me wonder if inside is a grandfather kneeling with open arms.

I follow the flagstone path past some enormous bush to a front porch where I see a man through a hanging planter filled with pink, yellow and purple flowers. He is holding his ears and shaking his head. He catches sight of me and says, "Hello, hang on, sorry about the dog." He shakes his head side to side and cups his hand over his left ear. "Ear's ringing, not sure why or how to stop it. Come on in."

My stomach rolls over once and my heart, my heart clenches itself into a knot then flutters. I look closer at Jeffery Walker, PhD. He is tall, taller than me by at least six inches, so he's maybe six-three. His light brown hair is cut to medium-smart length, but not perfectly. Stray hairs stick out over his denim shirt collar and others fall over his brow. He's young for a doctor, not much older than thirty by the looks of him. His eyes are squinted as he tries to stop the noise he hears, but I can see they are a blue the shade of a periwinkle flower. Violet. His nose is the perfect size for his face and he is, to me at least, quite handsome.

He says, "Paizely, right?"

I nod, feeling more like someone possessed than anyone who might resemble a normal person. I look for the dog. He's already in the house and tail wagging, looking over his shoulder and inviting me in.

I follow him and Doctor Jeffery Walker follows me.

Once inside, I stop, not knowing which way to go since in front of me is a hallway of sorts and on either side are two doors. I'm standing in a foyer about the size of my bathroom. It's not huge, but not small either. The floor is covered in warm chocolate colored tiles. The walls boast beetle-kill wainscoting--blues and grays streaking the light pine tongue and groove, and above, the walls are a friendly brown coffee with cream.

The dog waits at a wooden door, expecting me to open it for him. I do no such thing, but the doctor does and we all walk into another room the same warm brown color as the foyer.

He has the place decorated with nothing too personal or too opinionated on the walls, just some nondescript artwork that could hang anywhere anytime. The couches, there are two of them, one larger than the other, are a deep brown leather. Fluffy green pillows invite a visitor to sit comfortably or maybe to lie down during a session. The dog sits next to the smaller couch, his chin on the cushion as if asking if it's okay to get up onto the soft plush seat. As calming as the place is, my mind and my muscles are taut.

Walker. Was I nuts to have chosen this guy because of his name? And he's good-looking and kind, and he'd heard buzzing in his ears when I'd arrived. What was I thinking?

He stands before me, poised like a waiter or a concierge and said, "Have a seat. Would you like some coffee, or tea? Water? Juice?"

"No thank you," I pause. "What's your dog's name?"

He laughs in his eyes first, obviously quite attached to the big hound. "Winston. But I call him all sorts of other names and he seems not to care. I'm sorry he jumped on you out there. He never jumps on strangers. He likes people, but doesn't greet them as if he's known them forever. He hardly ever jumps on me, even after I've been gone awhile."

"It's okay, he's a sweet guy. I like him too."

He said, "My receptionist is out sick today or she'd have greeted you in a more customary manner." He laughed and I smile. He says, "Would you mind filling out some paperwork before we get started? And are you sure you wouldn't like something to drink? I just made fresh lemonade."

"Uh, sure, lemonade would be good. Thank you."

I begin working on the questionnaire. It asks all the usual things until I reached the third page and then I pause. *What is the reason for today's visit?* I'm guessing to write the truth, "I'm pretty sure something is seriously wrong with my mind" is not the best thing to say, but I write it down anyway.

By the time I'm finished with the paperwork, Winston is fast asleep on the small couch taking up the entire length of it and snoring the comfortable drone of an old man. I hand the clipboard to the doctor and wait for his verdict. Of course, he gives no indication about his feelings regarding anything I've written down, he just begins asking questions. Before he gets too far into the inquisition, I politely inform him that I'm not a prospective long-term client, I just want to run some ideas past him and see if maybe he thinks I can remain living in the real world alone without becoming a menace to myself or society. He laughs first in his eyes again, but his lips remain set in the same noncommittal straight line. I don't have to lie back in a reclining position and he doesn't take notes while wearing round rimmed spectacles. Instead, we sit talking like two old friends sharing lemonade and reminiscing about the past. The notion that the past is 1871 and I am convinced I've been there just yesterday seems not to matter one bit.

I tell him the entire saga complete with details of my journey. I show him the bald spot on the back of my head where Saul pulled my hair out by the roots. I show him my Mickey Mouse watch and hold it to my ear to verify it is indeed still working. I sound like a lunatic, completely bonk-shit mad. I know this, and yet, I keep on talking.

When I finish, he looks into my eyes staring, boring into my soul and I feel exposed, vulnerable and uncomfortable at first but then calm. He says, "You believe you were in 1871 and saw yourself as a half-breed Cheyenne woman whose father and entire family were killed at Sand Creek. You were still Paizely while you were there and you saw your sister being murdered, but she was someone else back then too. You and your other self, Tahcitan, were both shot by the same men who killed Holly, Ella. You think you were there for about eighteen hours or more before you woke up at the same place where you had been thrown by your horse. You found him injured and became a spirit or ghost horse and he spoke to you in your mind. Do I have the story correct?"

The story.

Indeed it did sound both correct and crazy. I should just write a book about it instead of thinking it's real. I stare at my white-knuckled hands willing my muscles to release and relax. Worst case, he'll call the little white van and they'll take me to quiet, wall-padded cell where the keepers offer room service complete with various drug cocktails to help me stay calm. Knowing this can happen I obediently say, "Yes. You have it right." I wait for him to pick up the phone and dial.

He does no such thing.

Instead, he says, "There are a couple of things we can do here. My first choice is to offer you a hypnosis session and regress you to what very well may be a past life. We could probe around and see if you were ever a Cheyenne woman in Colorado Territory in the 1800's or not." He pauses.

I assume to gauge my reaction.

My jaw drops, and I shut it. My mouth opens again and my lower jaw sags, but not a word do I utter. Attractive as that might have been, I next burst into tears and sob out loud. I sniffle as a final testament to my flagging mind. I choke, "You, uh, you believe me?"

He chuckles out loud this time, both eyes and mouth laughing together and says something, but I don't' understand or care what he's talking about. Winston raises his head looking around and blinking.

I take a deep breath, but I'm still a puddle on the floor, multiple pieces of myself trying to reconnect like mercury spilled on a table. I pull myself together. If he is willing to do a past life regression, then maybe I'm not going to be committed to a mental ward. I say, "Can we do it now?"

He looks sideways at a clock and then stands up. "Let me check. Most times I like to wait to schedule a session until after we've met a couple of times, but I think you're ready and I also believe you are my last patient of the day. I was going to go fishing this afternoon, take Winston the wonder dog and just sit. I'll go look at my schedule, be right back."

"No, I um, I don't want to keep you from fishing. I can come--"

"Paizely, do you know how often I've seen patients who are able to recount an experience as vividly as you can? That would be never. I know I shouldn't say this, but I am excited at what we may find if we do this. If I do have sessions on the book, I plan on cancelling them right now. Besides, I can go fishing anytime. And, look at the dog. He's happy right here."

Winston opens one eye at the word "dog," and then closes it, falling right back to sleep.

* * *

Either the good Doc Walker and I are about half nuts or both of us are perfectly sane and yes, there could be such a thing as reincarnation.

I'd never given the subject much thought. We die, it's over, the end. No Heaven, no Hell, no Afterlife, just a blank nothingness. The idea of being recycled and could revisit is something I've never believed in. The whole idea sure worked to my favor when I thought of the alternatives--living forever locked up in a hospital with my days spent in a drugged stupor. Alone. Let's not forget that part, so yeah, sure, reincarnation. Why not?

The regression began with Dr. Walker telling me I'm safe and can end the session anytime I wanted to by telling him. I laid back and sank into the overstuffed leather couch and Dr. Walker told me a story about my picturing myself on a hillside on a warm day, where, to my right, there was an escalator that led downhill. I almost laughed out loud at this image, but kept quiet and tried to see the electric staircase. I wanted to ask him if it was a silver metal escalator when he suggested I decide what the thing was made of. He said it could be anything I wanted, metal, brick, wood, clouds, feathers…anything. The image of it being built from colored crayons made me chuckle out loud so I went with that idea. When he asked me to walk down the stairs, I was so worried about slipping on the round risers, I conjured up traditional metal grated steps instead.

Secure now, he had me continue down to the first landing and he paused the escalator. He told me this would be my birth day and to look around and describe what I saw. I'm not clear on everything I said, but it must have been sufficient for him because he soon had me coasting down the staircase again, his soft voice soothing any worries I might have been hanging onto.

He had the escalator go down and then down some more, telling me the dates and stopping at November 14, 1871. I wanted to tell him I was there on November 29, but he told me I was just an observer, watching a movie, looking for anything that looked familiar.

I saw plenty I recognize. There was the yellow house with the white trim standing with Long's Peak in the back ground, the new barn being built and the pungent ashes from the barn that had burned. I watched Ella Mitchell playing the piano and then suddenly stop to stand up and pace a small circle on the fancy rug, wringing her hands as though strangling a bird. Her face was tight and she looked so worried and I loved her so much.

"Does Ella Mitchell look like Holly?"

"No, she is El."

"Can you tell what she is upset about?"

"No. She goes to the piano and walks away again. She does not show me what troubles her."

He asked, "Do you see Tahcitan?"

"I am Tahcitan. *Natsêhestahe.*"

"What does that mean?"

"I am Cheyenne."

"Very good, now, can you describe what Ella is doing? And you will speak only English from now on."

"Yes. El is bending over at her piano. She is reaching into the side under the white and black noise-making parts. She is pulling something out."

"Can you see what it is?"

"Papers bound with a blue ribbon."

"Do you know what the papers are?"

"Umm, no. I do not know."

"Are you in the room with El? Can you ask her about the papers?"

"No, I am not there. On that day. I only see her from here."

"Do you know where the papers are now?"

"El is putting them back into the piano."

"Do you know why she would do such a thing?"

"No, I do not. El told me there was a key in the piano. I do not see a key."

When he brought me out of the trance, we sat without speaking for a few minutes. He had filmed the session and we watched it together so I could see myself telling him what I'd seen and what I'd said. At the end of it, I told him I just remembered too much from when I'd fallen from Frisco and saw 1871. I told him I was just repeating the same images I'd carried with me since the fall. Couldn't my own vivid imagination conjure up those 'memories' on their own?

"Yes, you could imagine it all and it could all be hogwash. And there is a theory that the hypnotic state is nothing more than the sheer willingness of the subject to fulfill the suggestions of the hypnotist. But you watched the tape, do you think I influenced you or suggested anything to you?"

I had to admit, no, it didn't seem to be the case. Thing is, I didn't really feel the trip to 1871 was a problem as much as I felt Holly would be killed soon. We both decided that since she hadn't died on the day I knew she would, she most likely was going to live to be eighty-nine or so.

The agreement didn't let me relax any though.

I went back to see Dr. Walker often enough in the next month, we became friends. He asked me to call him Jeff on the first day we met and he stopped charging me his regular fee on the third visit. I admitted to picking him from the list of Psychiatrists based on his last name and my calling Sheriff Thomas Taylor "Walker". He laughed at me or with me, and I'm still not sure which--or if it even matters.

I asked him what the ringing in his ears may have been the day we met and he said he'd gone to his physician and found he had tinnitus caused by a sudden excess of wax in his ears. What had caused the sudden build up, the doctor couldn't guess at.

~30

Holly and Steve got married under the big Ponderosa pine on a day that threatened rain right up until it was time to say, "I do". At that very moment, the sky made a hole above them and poured sunshine down onto the entire gathering. As if God were saying, "Here you go, kids, an omen of light and goodness from Me to you. Happy Wedding day." Sounds hokey, I know, but that's exactly what it seemed like.

Holly had already cleaned out her room and moved it to Steve's house. They were planning on remodeling the bathroom upstairs and were talking about getting a dog. All they were missing was the traditional white picket fence and my sister would have been the poster child for the happiest woman on Earth. Everything she'd ever wanted, she had. Even I was following a path she approved of.

I'm guessing that Jeff wouldn't have wanted to be referred to as "a path", but I bet he'd be happy about the truth of it, if not the label. We had become such good friends that this ending was inevitable as I look at it in hindsight.

In those first few weeks of seeing him, Jeff Walker helped me by believing in me. He let me talk and yammer on and explained that I was mourning the loss of the vision of who I thought I was, nothing more. We didn't do any more regressions, I figured that one was plenty. Had I been Tahcitan? Was there such a thing as reincarnation? Or had my mind just manufactured the details and the story as some form of entertainment? Who knew? I decided I didn't need to know. What I really needed to do was live here and now, let Holly have her own life while I have mine. I needed to accept that everyone I love isn't going to die just because I love them.

I need to remember that the fear of that happening was Tahcitan's and not my own.

The white horse? The voice that filled me? Yeah, I have no explanation that I truly believe. A part of me is convinced that the spirit horse was real, that his message came straight from God or the

The Wise One Above. Part of me thinks Tahcitan sent him to me so that I'd know all would be all right.

I have no answers, but I do keep those words with me. I do remember the blinding silvery light that filled me and loved me.

Mostly, I remember the entire encounter with the white horse with a sort of reverence, like I'd been selected to experience something most people never do. I am grateful to know that the end, is not "The End".

Am I crazy then? Maybe, but Jeff gave me my graduation papers and assured me that I was fine in the head area, not crazy and that if I ever needed to see another psychiatrist, he'd let me know since he couldn't see me once we began dating. He told me that would be very soon if I'd have him.

The real truth for me is that I'd always wanted to love someone and to have him love me right back. Admitting such a thing was nothing short of impossible, though. Right up until I went to 1871, or didn't go, whatever the truth might be on that subject.

Maybe I'd needed to have that particular hallucination or head injury to be able to let go of the Talent, and the fear it had brought along with it. Maybe Jeff Walker and I had been meant for each other all these centuries, maybe it was just chemistry here and now, I didn't know. I find I don't much care either.

* * *

I sit on the white wooden fence watching Frisco run through the pasture. More like a vigilant guard than an observer, I want to be sure he doesn't kill himself with his craziness. He doesn't just run, he cuts zigzagging patterns that include fast starts and sliding stops. He leaps into the air twisting himself into horse cartwheels that make him fart with the effort. His joy at being outside again makes me smile and I swear he watches me from the corner of his eye and laughs with me.

I can't keep my gaze from the healed scar where he'd cut his leg and I hope the fool doesn't tear it open again with his flying, galloping, bucking and kicking. I probably should put him back into the barn, but

I can't. He's having too much fun. He launches himself over the creek like a kamikaze lunatic as the thought flits through my head, just to prove his point.

Sailing, graceful and sure of himself, he flies through the pasture, and for a moment, I am transported to that cloudy, misty memory of the white horse. The ghost horse I thought had talked to me. What was it he said?

"The loneliness you feel is yours to release. And the end is only a door that you've already walked through.

"The answer, the question, the truth, is Love."

Maybe it was all a dream, or maybe he was my totem, my spirit guide sent here to walk with me once more. I'll never know if the words were his or my own and I don't care either way.

Frisco runs to me and skids to a perfect stop, shaking his head before rearing and snorting. As if he knows what I was thinking, what I was remembering.

Stupid horse, I think. And I laugh out loud.

* * *

The End

Made in the USA
Monee, IL
15 December 2019